Large Print Rosenber

Revenge of innocents /

Nancy Taylor Rosenberg.

Jun 2007

REVENGE OF INNOCENTS

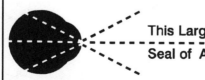

This Large Print Book carries the
Seal of Approval of N.A.V.H.

REVENGE OF INNOCENTS

NANCY TAYLOR ROSENBERG

WHEELER PUBLISHING
An imprint of Thomson Gale, a part of The Thomson Corporation

Detroit • New York • San Francisco • New Haven, Conn. • Waterville, Maine • London

THOMSON

GALE™

LIBRARY OF CONGRESS CATALOGING-IN-PUBLICATION DATA

Rosenberg, Nancy Taylor.
  Revenge of innocents / by Nancy Taylor Rosenberg.
    p. cm.
  ISBN-13: 978-1-59722-465-9 (alk. paper)
  ISBN-10: 1-59722-465-0 (alk. paper)
    1. Sullivan, Carolyn (Fictitious character) — Fiction. 2. Probation officers —
  Fiction. 3. Ventura County (Calif.) — Fiction. 4. Large type books. I. Title.
  PS3568.O7876R48 2007
  813'.54—dc22

                                                          2007001702

Published in 2007 in arrangement with Kensington Books,
an imprint of Kensington Publishing Corp.

Printed in the United States of America on permanent paper
10 9 8 7 6 5 4 3 2 1

To Michaela Hamilton,
and in memory of Hyman Rosenberg.

CHAPTER 1

Death showed up amidst the smoke and flying embers. She was sitting on the front steps of Ventura High when she saw his car. He would wait for her on a side street. If she made him wait too long, he would beat her. Today, he would wait.

"They announced on TV that the schools were going to be closed," Chloe said, a short girl with brown hair and freckled skin. "I can't believe my stupid mother didn't tell me. I could have slept late. Now that we're here, want to do something?"

"I can't," she said, raising her eyes and then lowering them. "I have an appointment." What would she look like in her coffin? Would they leave it open or closed? How many people would show up? The only thing that bothered her was not being able to control what they did to her after she died. It would be over, though, and over was enough.

"What kind of appointment?"

"I don't remember."

"What do you mean, you don't remember?" Chloe said. "Is it a doctor, a shrink, a dentist? Do you at least know when you're supposed to be there? If your appointment is this morning, we might still be able to do something this afternoon."

"I have an essay I have to finish."

"So what? Let's have some fun today. You're too uptight about everything."

"I should have graduated last year, Chloe. I'm eighteen and I'm still in high school. How do you think that makes me feel?"

Chloe reached over and touched her arm. "Hey, are you okay? You've been acting weird lately. Where were you last week? You and Reggie didn't run away and get married, did you?"

"No," she said. "I was sick."

Chloe persisted. "Did you have the flu?"

"I have to go," she told her, annoyed by the barrage of questions. She stood and made her way through a small throng of students.

"Maybe we'll get another day off tomorrow," Chloe yelled. "Who knows? We might get lucky and the school will burn down."

Her plan to hold him off wasn't working. She'd devised a new plan, but the timing had to be perfect. Weak and dizzy, she knew if she passed out in a public place, they would take her to the hospital and find out what was hidden underneath her clothes.

As she stared at the black clouds rising into the atmosphere, she noticed her sweatshirt was covered in ash. When she tried to brush some of it off, strands of hair became tangled in her fingers. She coughed from the smoke, causing her ribs to ache.

She entered the girls' bathroom and locked herself inside a stall. Maybe he didn't know school had been called off because of the fires. If she stayed in here long enough, he might leave. She wanted to put an end to it today, but she was afraid.

Facing death wasn't easy.

Thirty minutes passed. She left the stall, walked to the door, and peered out. The school appeared deserted. Her throat was sore from breathing in the smoke-filled air, so she got a drink from the water fountain, then returned to the bathroom and squatted down in a corner.

The door burst open. "You saw me out there," he shouted, his face flushed with rage. "You know how long I've been waiting?" He grabbed a handful of her hair and yanked her to her feet. "I'm parked in the regular spot. To make certain no one sees you, wait five minutes before you come out."

He stared at her, then added, "You look like shit. Comb your hair. And why are you wearing those heavy sweats on such a hot day?"

Once he left, she splashed water in her face and smoothed down her hair. She didn't have a brush with her. No wonder her hair kept falling out. It wasn't strictly poor nutrition. He kept pulling it. He even did it when other people were around, but he always laughed, making it seem like a game.

She walked to the street behind the school. He called it their special meeting place. To her, it represented the gate to hell. When she saw his car, she looked straight ahead and continued walking. He slammed on the brakes and leapt out, rushing over and seizing her by the arm. Her books tumbled to the ground. "Don't act like this," he said. "I have a surprise for you."

"Oh, yeah?" she said, glaring at him until he released her. "What kind of surprise?"

"Get in the car and you'll find out."

Fighting him was useless. She couldn't remember when she'd eaten. Was it last night or the night before? Every other day, she sliced an orange into three equal pieces and parceled them out over the course of the day. She was getting forgetful and suspected days passed when she didn't eat anything at all. Since she cleared the plates every night, no one knew what went down the disposal. She glanced at her books on the sidewalk, but made no attempt to retrieve them. If everything went the way she'd planned, she would no longer need them. "I don't care about your surprise."

"Get in the damn car!" he said, the words roaring from his mouth.

His mouth formed a perfect circle when he yelled at her. It was as if his lips became a megaphone. In the past, she'd cowered in fear. What frightened her now wasn't his voice or even the things he did to her.

He glanced up and down the street to see if anyone was around. "If you keep this up, you'll ruin everything. Are you going to get inside the car, or do I have to make you?"

She climbed inside, not bothering to buckle her seat belt.

"Are you still pissed off because I said something about your weight?" he asked. "I didn't mean anything, baby. Since you've slimmed down, you look great. Maybe you can be an actress."

She closed her eyes, trying to forget where she was and what was about to happen to her. When she opened them and realized they had traveled a long way, she asked him, "Where are you taking me?"

He placed his hand on her thigh. She was

wearing two pairs of sweatpants, so all she felt was a small amount of pressure. Even that repulsed her. She scooted closer to the door.

"The least you could do is smile," he said, placing his hand back on the steering wheel. "You look so pretty when you smile."

He turned into a parking lot and parked the car.

"Is this your surprise?" she asked, looking up and seeing a motel sign.

He pulled out a key and jangled it. "When we get to the room, I'm going to make you feel like you've never felt before."

She'd already accomplished that without him, although she knew he was referring to sex. Starvation was interesting. Something new happened every day. That is, as long as you didn't cheat. But she was long past cheating. She was tired of waiting, though, and fearful someone would find out and stop her. It wasn't herself she was concerned about. The previous week, she had seen him with her younger sister.

She followed him up the stairway to the second floor, holding on to the railing for support until they reached the room.

"We don't have to hurry," he said, once they were inside. "That's why I got the room. Take your clothes off. No one's going to bother us here." He turned on the air conditioner, an old floor unit. "Man, this thing really blasts, doesn't it? While everyone's sweltering out there, we can cuddle under the covers."

"I have to go to the bathroom," she said, placing her hand inside her sweatshirt and clasping her cell phone. She closed the door behind her and flushed the toilet so he couldn't hear.

When she came back, he shoved her sweatshirts up to her armpits.

"Jesus, you're skin and bones. Are you sick?"

"You told me to lose weight," she said, fixing him with a look of defiance. "Isn't this what you wanted? My breasts are gone. I look like a little girl again. That's what turns you on, isn't it?"

"I — I didn't mean you should . . ." He walked around in a circle, coming to terms with what he had seen. "It's okay. You just went overboard. Start eating again. You'll gain the weight back in no time." He came up behind her, and pulled her to his body. "I want you so bad," he said, moaning. "It's been too long."

"I'm going to tell the police."

"Don't talk, baby," he panted. "We've got all day."

"Didn't you hear me, asshole?" she shouted, twisting away from him. "I'm going to tell the police what you've been doing to me. They'll send you to prison."

His face became distorted with rage. He pulled back his arm and punched her hard in the abdomen. She doubled over in pain. "Look what you've done," he said, massaging his knuckles. "You know you can't threaten me like that."

"I can do anything I want," she snarled. "The only way you can stop me is to kill me."

He grabbed her arm and dragged her into the bathroom. After he kicked her several times, he fell on top of her and began pummeling her with his fists. The lower half of her body was sandwiched between the toilet and the bathtub. The sweat dripped down from his face and stung her eyes. She felt a blow to her chest, then her ribs, and another to her groin area. When she saw the next blow coming, she intentionally turned her face into his fist.

The beating stopped. His fury turned to fear. When he beat her, he never struck her in the face. He made certain all the blows landed on her torso, so she could cover them with her clothes. He moved her jaw from side to side. The pain was excruciating, but she forced herself not to cry out. She didn't want someone in the motel to hear and call the police. It wasn't time yet.

"Jesus, your jaw may be broken." He walked out of the bathroom, and then returned, standing in profile in the doorway. "We'll think of something. You could say you tripped and fell on the sidewalk. I'll go and get some ice to put on your jaw."

"If you leave," she said, pushing herself up on her elbows, "I'll call the police and tell them you raped me."

"Why are you doing this?" he said, placing his hand on his head. "If you wanted to hurt me, you have. You've lost too much weight. You don't know what you're saying. I didn't mean to hit you. You provoked me. Everything's fine now. I'm sorry. I'll find a way to make it up to you."

"How can you make it up to me?" she yelled, her pent-up emotions spewing out. "You're a filthy, disgusting pig. I hate you. I'm going to tell everyone. They'll put your name in the newspapers. They'll —"

"You ungrateful little bitch," he said, swiping at his mouth with the back of his hand. "This is all because of that guy." He grabbed her shoulders and shook her. "What did you do with him? I warned you not to get involved with gutter scum like that."

15

"You're a wimp," she yelled, her face twisted in contempt. "A third grader could hit harder than you. You don't scare me. I want a real man, not some stupid prick like you."

"Shut up," he said, his chest heaving.

"You can't get it up with a real woman," she pressed on. "Pretty soon, you won't even be able to get it up with a kid. Who do you think you're fooling? You're a perverted freak."

He hoisted her up in his arms and then dropped her into the bathtub.

Her back felt like it was broken. Blinding pain rushed through her body. She wasn't sure if he was going to wash the blood off or drown her. It had to end now. She'd rather die than have the same thing happen to her sister. And dying was the only way. Murderers went away forever. Everyone else got out.

His thumbs dug into her throat, his eyes bulging.

"Kill me!" she choked out. "Do it, bastard! Do it now or I'll tell."

CHAPTER 2

Carolyn Sullivan's eyes rested on a framed print to the right of her desk, a winding path through a lush, green forest. Only a year ago, the walls were covered with pictures of Brad Preston standing in front of high-powered race cars. When the director of the Ventura County Probation Department had retired, Preston had been promoted to chief deputy over probation services. Carolyn had been appointed to his position as division manager over the investigative unit.

She was finally earning a decent income. The only problem was it came with a heavy price. Her wedding was only two weeks away, and all she could think about were the horrible crimes human beings committed against each other. There was no way to stop them. The only thing she could do was punish them.

Carolyn spun her chair around to face Veronica Campbell. At forty, Veronica was an outspoken woman. She had a daughter almost the same age as Carolyn's son, John, as well as three other young children. She wore her curly blond hair short, and had a round, friendly face. She'd never lost the weight from her last pregnancy, and the extra twenty pounds had settled in her mid-section and thighs. The two women had known each other since grade school. They didn't always agree on everything, but they were best friends. "Brent Dover should spend the rest of his life in prison," Carolyn told her. "Unfortunately, we don't have that as an option. How could you not recommend a prison sentence? Dover sodomized Patricia Baxter. She has permanent brain damage. As far as I'm concerned, he killed her."

"For one thing," Veronica countered, "Patricia Baxter is a guy, not a girl. His real name is Patrick, but he went to court and changed it to Patricia. Cute, huh? Only a few letters difference, so he wouldn't forget it. Secondly, Brent Dover wasn't convicted of sodomy or attempted murder. This is a 245 violation, Carolyn. He didn't use a gun, a knife, or a baseball bat. I'm not sure how we even got him for assault with a deadly weapon."

"This whole thing is the DA's fault," Carolyn answered, shoving a thick mass of wavy brown hair behind her ear. The year before, she'd chopped her hair off during a midlife crises. It now brushed the top of her shoulders, and was far more flattering to her heart-shaped face. Like Veronica, she'd also turned forty the previous year. Now that she'd gotten over the hump, she realized that forty was young. People today were living longer. Since she'd never smoked, drunk heavily, or gorged herself on fatty foods, she might have another fifty years ahead of her. If she died prematurely, it would be from stress. "Dover would have been convicted of attempted murder if they hadn't tacked on the assault charge."

Prosecutors frequently filed a number of counts, all representative of the same crime, just with varying degrees of punishment. The reasoning was if the jury didn't find sufficient evidence to convict on one count, they might convict on the other. Anything was better than an acquittal. "Dover is a linebacker at Ventura High," Carolyn continued. "His body is a deadly weapon. He beat Baxter to a pulp. He bit off her nipples, for Christ's sake. He demolished her face. To look even halfway normal, she'll have to go through years of plastic surgery. The jury should have convicted on the GBI charge." GBI was great bodily injury, and served as an enhancement to extend the term of imprisonment.

"Don't you believe the victim carries some of the responsibility?" Veronica said, swinging her leg. "Maybe none of this would have happened if he hadn't tricked the defendant into believing he was a girl. I mean, it's not like I think Baxter deserved to get the shit kicked out of him. I just don't see how sending Dover to prison will accomplish anything. His grades are excellent. He goes to church every Sunday, even sings in the choir. You should read the stack of glowing letters people sent me about him. A year in custody at the local level and a ten-thousand-dollar fine isn't exactly a walk in the park, Carolyn. He's already lost his football scholarship. Send him to prison and he'll come out a hardened criminal. How's that going to benefit society?"

"It's called justice," Carolyn said. "Maybe in prison Mr. Dover will find out how it feels to be violently sodomized."

"Yeah, sure," Veronica said. "What was Baxter doing in an alley behind a bar in a ten-inch skirt? He was a prostitute, Carolyn. Isn't it obvious? It was to the jury."

Carolyn was inundated with the details of every crime that passed through the system. She had to know as much about the case as the investigating officer. That meant reviewing police reports, trial transcripts, evidence. After the probation officers conducted their investigations and made their recommendations as to an appropriate sentence, they then had to conference the case with Carolyn to get her approval. She felt like a computer about to run out of memory. She had to shove things to the back of her mind just so she could answer a question.

This particular case was controversial in a variety of ways. Brent Dover was white; the victim was black. Ten members of the jury had been not only men, but Caucasian. They probably perceived Baxter to be a twisted pervert who'd enticed a clean-cut young white boy into engaging in sex. The facts clearly refuted such an assumption. The case made Carolyn's blood boil.

She wouldn't be having this discussion with Veronica if the crime wasn't what they referred to as a wobbler. Section 245 of the California Penal Code allowed the court to sentence the defendant to serve a year in the local jail, or two, three, or four years in a state prison facility. The Judicial Council in San Francisco had developed specific rules that were to be applied to determine if the interest of justice would be best served by one sentence or the other.

"Don't you understand?" Carolyn argued, slapping back in her chair. "Whether the victim was male or female doesn't matter. Patricia Baxter is only a few months past her nineteenth birthday. When her sex organs didn't develop normally, her mother made the decision to raise her as a girl. Granted, this may have been a poor decision, but Patricia wasn't the one who made it. She'd never had sex with anyone, male or female. Her mother was saving money for a sex change. Regardless, the medical report showed significant injuries from a violent sexual assault. The jury simply chose to ignore it because of the circumstances." She paused and sucked in a breath. "So what if she was hanging around a nightclub in a short skirt? Would you feel the same if something like this happened to Jude?"

"Hey," Veronica said, pushing herself to her feet, "if you want to trump me on this one, go right ahead. You're the boss now. No one cares what I think."

"You know I respect your opinion," Carolyn told her. "I have to call the cases as I see them, Veronica. This was a brutal attack that resulted in great bodily injury. Circumstances in aggravation clearly exist and support the maximum term of four years in prison. I'm sorry, but I have to ask you to rewrite the report and submit it under those conditions."

"Can I go now?" Veronica said, her voice tinged with sarcasm. "I have to track down a probationer."

"Which one?"

"Phillip Bramson."

"Is he in violation?" Carolyn asked, hating it that her investigators had to supervise people because of the overflow in field services.

"I called the place where he works yesterday and they haven't seen him in over a week. My guess is he's using again. I left a message on his cell phone. He didn't check in, so I'm going to try to track him down today."

The details of Bramson's case were beginning to surface in Carolyn's mind. "Doesn't he have a suspended sentence?"

"Yep," Veronica said. "He doesn't get to pass go or collect his two hundred dollars. If he tests dirty, all I have to do is put him on the next bus to prison."

Because of the overcrowding in the state prisons, judges were utilizing suspended sentences more often. "I'm going to get these supervision cases off your back," she told her. "I'll dump them on one of the new people. It was a mistake to assign them to you in the first place."

"I could manage if I didn't have to rewrite reports."

Carolyn was upset that her friend was taking things personally. She could understand Veronica's jealousy over her promotion. They'd been on the job for almost the same amount of time. What Veronica didn't factor in was all the time she'd taken off on maternity leave, as well as management's belief that a woman with four children might not be able to meet the demands of the position.

Carolyn had also made a name for herself as an interrogator, and had years of experience assisting Brad Preston, the former supervisor of the unit. "Your dress is at my house. Are you still going to be my maid of honor?"

"I guess," Veronica said, shrugging.

"Please, sit back down," Carolyn said, gesturing toward the chair. When Veronica settled herself in the seat again, she noticed the dark circles under her eyes. She'd always been an earthy type, but lately she'd stopped wearing makeup. Something was bothering her. She should have noticed it before now. "I've been so busy, we haven't had much time to talk outside of work," she said. "Marcus and I should have got married by a justice of the peace. I never thought this wedding would turn into such a big production. How are things with Drew and the kids?"

"Fine," Veronica said, still miffed.

"Look," Carolyn said, folding her arms on top of her desk, "we promised we wouldn't let my promotion come between us. Let's go to lunch one day this week." She glanced at her calendar. "Friday works for me. How about you?"

Veronica stood, ignoring her question. "You're probably right about Brent Dover. After what happened last year, I've become more sympathetic toward people who make mistakes."

Carolyn knew what she was referring to, but she also knew this wasn't the time or place to discuss it. Both of her lines were ringing. Her assistant, Rachel Mitchell, would pick up one of them. She reached over and grabbed the other. "I'll be with you in a minute," she said, placing the caller on hold so they could firm up their lunch date. When she turned back around, though, Veronica had already slipped out of the office.

Driving dangerously fast over the narrow residential streets, Veronica kept her fingers locked on the steering wheel. She and Carolyn had grown apart recently. It was more than the promotion. While she was living a nightmare, her friend seemingly had everything. She was marrying a wealthy, handsome man who was madly in love with her. Her son was attending college at MIT, studying to become a physicist. Her daughter was one of the most popular girls at Ventura High.

Veronica had been assigned to handle the unit while Carolyn was in Europe on her honeymoon, with no compensation above her normal pay. She couldn't fault Carolyn for the supervision cases, however. She had asked for them so she could qualify for a county car.

Her husband no longer loved her. They hadn't had sex in four years, not since their last child was born. She was certain Drew was having an affair, but she had no way to prove it. In reality, the problems had been present from the onset of their marriage. Now they seldom spoke. They lived together like strangers.

Veronica's biggest problem was her eighteen-year-old daughter. Jude had become pregnant at thirteen, claiming she'd had sex with too many boys to identify the father. This had been the onset of a five-year period of promiscuity and delinquency. She got involved with drugs, served two terms in juvenile hall, and had undergone a number of abortions. Since Jude was now legally an adult, Veronica refused to continue supporting her. Although she had no means of support, she was going to demand that Jude move out by the end of the month. It was a hard decision for a parent to make, but she had no choice. She had to safeguard the well-being of her other children.

Veronica had distanced herself from her religion because of the way the church had sheltered priests who were known sex offenders. Her belief in God had fallen by the wayside as well. There was too much evil in the world. If the devil was responsible, then God was either indifferent or powerless. All the innocent children who died agonizing, violent deaths needed a God who would protect them. The promise of eternal life with Jesus and Mary meant nothing to a kid in the hands of a sadistic maniac.

During the past summer, Jude had slept all day and stayed out all night. When Veronica gave her a list of chores to do around the house, her father sometimes did them for her. Usurping her with her daughter was another way for Drew to express his contempt for their marriage.

Veronica slammed on the brakes at a stoplight, reaching in her purse for a bottle of pills. She popped one in her mouth and swallowed it without water. Her doctor had placed her on antidepressants, and given her a referral to see a psychiatrist. Her daughter was the one who needed counseling. She didn't have time for Jude's bullshit. She had five reports due next week, and she had to chase down a drug dealer who should already be in prison.

Hearing a horn honking, Veronica realized she'd dozed off waiting for the light to change. She stepped on the gas and took off. Everyone placed demands on her. The previous year, the agency had implemented a new program that allowed investigators to work from their home three days a week. She'd jumped on it, thinking she could save a fortune in day care. During the past six months, she'd desperately tried to keep up with her caseload, but concentrating with three kids under eight and a belligerent lazy teenager in the house was next to impossible.

When Veronica finally went to bed, sometimes as late as four in the morning, as soon as she drifted off she would jolt herself awake, as if there were something in her subconscious she couldn't bear to face. The problems with Jude weighed heavily on her mind, but what she sensed was more sinister. It was like glimpsing something just outside your range of vision, and then forgetting what it was you saw. Was it her guilt over her daughter's abortions, or was she having a legitimate breakdown?

She and Carolyn used to talk about people who caved in under pressure. They'd been certain it would never happen to them. They were rocks, machines. So what if they dealt with violence on a daily basis? They could handle it. They were seasoned officers. There wasn't anything they hadn't seen before.

Carolyn would find out the truth any day now — that Veronica's recommendations weren't appropriate because she didn't know half the facts of the case. She regularly fabricated the defendant and victim interviews. If you were going to make things up, she'd decided, it was better to err on the side of leniency. If a judge didn't think the sentence she proposed was severe enough, all he had to do was ignore it. Judges were esteemed members of the community, with a salary far above that of a probation officer. She was tired of doing their job for them.

Drew was a technician at Boeing, but even with both of their incomes, they couldn't make ends meet. The price of raising four children in today's world was insane, and the cost of living was still rising at an alarming rate.

In addition to everything else, Veronica had become Jude's chauffeur. Her daughter would disappear for days, and then place a frantic call for her mother to come and get her. The Ford Taurus they had bought for her sat in the driveway. She'd forbidden her to drive it until she began contributing to the insurance. Jude was supposed to graduate the year before, but she'd flunked several of her classes. She was a smart girl, so things didn't add up. Why did she stagger around with a blank look on her face? Why had she abruptly ended her relationship with Haley Snodgrass, a girl she'd been close to for most of her life?

Veronica's red-rimmed eyes scanned the buildings. She steered the car into a parking lot, getting out and hiking up the stairs to the second floor. As she was trying to focus on the arrows that showed where room 246 was located, she heard the sound of footsteps behind her. She managed to open her purse and pull out her gun, but before she could turn around, someone reached around her waist and wrenched it out of her hand.

CHAPTER 3

Tuesday, October 12 — 5:30 P.M.

The Ventura government center was similar to a small city. The courts, the district attorney's and public defender's offices, as well as the records division, were all housed on the right side of a large open space. A bubbling fountain stood in the center, surrounded by concrete benches and blooming flowers. To the left was the probation department, the sheriff's department, and the women's and men's jails. The general public assumed the two structures weren't connected, yet an underground tunnel was used to transport inmates back and forth.

Carolyn headed to her new red Infiniti M35 in the parking lot. The wildfires had been contained, but her car was covered with ash. The car was a wedding gift from her fiancé, Marcus Wright. Two weeks ago, the house she had raised her children in had sold and she'd no choice but to move into Marcus's home in Santa Rosa. She'd wanted to wait until after they were married. She was old-fashioned when it came to certain things. And why have a formal wedding if you were already living with the person?

Carolyn's old house would fit into Marcus's living room. Her son, John, was in his first year at MIT. Rebecca, her sixteen-year-old, adored Marcus and was elated they were getting married. Everything was finally coming together, and Carolyn couldn't be happier.

A forty-year-old wearing a wedding dress seemed absurd, but Marcus had insisted. Both of their first marriages had ended in failure, so he wanted to make it a special occasion. She had intended to exercise and lose five pounds. Any mention of the word *diet,* though, and she became ravenously hungry. With all the hassle of moving and planning the reception, she'd gained seven pounds. Yesterday, she'd gone to the tailor and had the seams let out on her dress. She wasn't heavy, just curvaceous. She didn't need to look like a waif.

Her cell phone rang and she fumbled around in her purse to retrieve it. "It's Hank," a gruff male voice said. "Where are you? Are you on the road?"

Hank Sawyer was a lieutenant in Ventura homicide, as well as a long-term friend. The tone of his voice was alarming. "What's going on?"

"Are you driving?"

"No," Carolyn said. "What difference does it make if I'm driving or not? I can listen and drive."

"I have some bad news," he said. "I don't want you to be behind the wheel when I tell you."

"I'm in the parking lot. Tell me, for Christ's sake."

"Veronica Campbell is dead."

Carolyn dropped her briefcase on the pavement. "God, no!" she exclaimed. "What happened? A traffic accident . . ."

"Charley Young thinks she was shot sometime this morning. The maid at the Motor Inn on East Thompson found her around three o'clock."

"I'm on my way." She swept up her briefcase and jogged toward her car.

"There's nothing for you to do here. Charley just gave the okay for us to transport the body. I'm sorry, Carolyn. I know how close you two were."

"It's a mistake," she said, panting. "It's someone who looks like her. You don't know Veronica that well, Hank. I'll come —"

The detective cut her off. "We have her badge, as well as the county vehicle she was driving. I thought you'd want to be the one to tell her husband. Can you handle it?"

"I can't . . . do anything right now." Carolyn leaned against the Infiniti, then slid to the ground on her knees. People were walking past her and staring. She covered her face with her free hand, then grabbed on to the door handle and pulled herself up, unlocking the door and ducking inside. "Tell me she didn't suffer, Hank."

"For what it's worth, she probably never knew what hit her." He stopped to bark orders to one of the officers at the scene. "Do you know what she was doing at a motel?"

"She mentioned trying to track down a probationer she thought was in violation. His name is . . . God, I can't think . . . Bramson, Phillip Bramson. He has a prison sentence hanging over his head. I'll go back to the office."

"Give me whatever you can remember," Hank told her. "Bramson is in the system, right?"

Carolyn pressed her fingers against her eyelids. This was the worst thing that had ever happened to her. Images from the past darted through her mind. Giggling when she'd told Veronica about her first kiss, their high school graduations, their weddings, the births of their children, all the years they'd worked together. It was the same as losing a sister. Worse, she decided. Most siblings didn't see each other every day.

"We're losing time."

"I know." She had to detach somehow, do whatever had to be done. "Bramson is a white male, mid-thirties, tall, slender. I think he has dark hair but I'm not certain. I've never seen him in person, only his mug shot."

"What's the underlying offense?"

The more she talked, the easier it was to remain in denial. It was work, she told herself, just work. Right now, that's the only way she could handle the situation. The words tumbled out. "The sheriff's office arrested Bramson with a large quantity of crystal meth. The DA originally charged him with possession for sale, but they pled it down to simple possession. The judge imposed a year in prison, then suspended it and placed him on three years of supervised probation. Veronica suspected he was using again."

"Do you know what kind of car he was driving?"

"No," Carolyn said. "Everything's in Veronica's file. I'll go back to the office and get it. You can't let this bastard get away, Hank."

"Someone tipped off the media. If you don't get to her husband and family fast, they're going to hear about it on the six o'-clock news. Oh, and we need the husband to identify her body. It'll be at the morgue within the hour. I'll broadcast what you gave me and whatever else I can pull up on the system regarding Phillip Bramson. Call someone in your agency and have them go through his file, then get the info to me ASAP. The most important thing is a vehicle description."

"Wait," Carolyn said. "Who rented the motel room?"

"A black male in his twenties," Hank said. "The owner of the credit card is white. We've already contacted him. He claims the card was stolen."

"But Bramson is white."

"Maybe the black guy was a drug buddy," Hank said, impatient. "We've barely scratched the surface, Carolyn. Let us do our jobs here. I'll need to talk to Veronica's husband sometime later tonight."

She disconnected and called Brad Preston. After she filled him on what had occurred, she cranked the engine on the Infiniti and sped out of the parking lot. "I assigned this case to Veronica, Brad. My investigators shouldn't be supervising people. They're not used to it. They might not take the necessary precautions."

"Get a hold of yourself, Carolyn," Brad told her. "You won't do anyone any good if you fall apart. I'll grab Bramson's file and relay the information to Hank and the PD, then meet you at Veronica's house. She still lives on Tremont, right?"

"We'll need someone to watch the kids," Carolyn said, her thoughts racing. "How can I tell them their mother's dead?"

"That's not your responsibility. Veronica's husband will tell them when he feels the time is right. Doesn't she have a teenage daughter?"

"Jude," she said, trying to navigate through rush-hour traffic. "I don't even know if she's still living at home. They've had all kinds of problems with her. Veronica was going to throw her out if she didn't get her act together."

"I need you," Brad said, talking to someone in the office. "Linda Cartwright is here. I'll bring her with me."

"It could be someone other than Bramson. I — I can't remember what cases I assigned her."

"I'll print out a list from your computer," Brad said. "We'll be there as fast as we can.

Whatever you do, don't talk to the press."

"Hurry," she said, hitting the wrong button to end the call and speed-dialing her brother, Neil's number. She flipped the phone closed and tossed it back into her purse. She hadn't called Marcus yet. She didn't have time to talk to Neil.

Fifteen minutes later, she pulled up in front of a modest stucco house. The exterior needed painting, and most of the flowers had died from lack of water. A bicycle was lying on its side near the sidewalk. When she reached the front door, she could hear the TV blasting inside. It sounded like cartoons or some other type of children's program. Thank God, she thought, it wasn't the news. She swallowed hard and rang the doorbell.

A tall, attractive man with prematurely gray hair and pale blue eyes answered the door. Drew Campbell was barefoot, wearing jeans and a green cotton T-shirt with some type of stain on the front. "Carolyn," he said. "Haven't seen your face in a month of Sundays. Veronica isn't home, but come in." He stepped aside and gestured toward the living room. Toys were scattered everywhere, along with juice cups and half-empty bowls of cereal. Stacy, their eight-year-old, was sprawled out on the sofa watching TV. She was tall for her age and reed thin. Her blond hair was tied back in a ponytail.

"Excuse the mess," Drew said. "We live in a perpetual state of chaos. You look like a wreck, Carolyn. Getting ready for the big day, I presume. I was planning to call Marcus and tell him I wouldn't be able to make his bachelor party. Nice of him to invite me, though. Seems like you're getting yourself a swell fellow there."

Michael, the couple's four-year-old, raced into the room screaming, "Petey took my truck and won't give it back."

"Gotta share, kiddo," Drew said, hoisting him up in his arms. "You know who this lady is, don't you? This is your godmother, Carolyn. She came to see you. Why don't you give her a hug?"

"No," he said, pouting. "I want my red truck."

When Carolyn gazed at the child's round face and wide-set eyes, she saw a miniature version of Veronica. "Is Jude here?" she asked.

"I'm not sure," Drew said. "I just picked the kids up from the babysitter. I think we found a live-in, but she hasn't started yet. What's going on? Jude's not in trouble again, I hope."

"No, no," Carolyn said. "Why don't we sit down? Something's happened. I thought

Jude could look after . . ." She waved her hand in front of her. "Never mind . . . it doesn't matter."

"Turn the TV off," Drew said to his daughter. "You're not supposed to watch TV until you finish your homework." When the girl ignored him, he barked, "Now, Stacy."

Once Stacy had left, Carolyn started to ask him to send Michael to the other room as well, but decided he needed something in his arms when she told him. He took a seat beside her on the sofa. "Veronica was shot, Drew."

Michael saw a toy on the cushion behind him, and tried to climb out of his father's arms to reach it. Stacy passed through the living room on the way to the kitchen, a spiral notebook in her hand. Carolyn's eyes darted around the room. Her head was spinning. There were too many things going on at the same time, and far too much clutter.

"I'm sorry," Drew said, taking a drink out of one of the children's juice cups.

Carolyn gave him a strange look.

He laughed. "With this many kids, your own needs fall by the wayside. If I get thirsty, I'll drink just about anything. Not milk, though. Milk spoils. What were you saying about Veronica? She must have stopped off at the grocery store, or decided to work late.

40

She's generally home by now." He gave her a lopsided smile. "I don't know why I'm telling you. I keep forgetting that you're her boss."

"Veronica's been murdered," Carolyn said. "Someone . . . shot her."

It was as if a tunnel had opened up between them. The noise of the television and the children's voices disappeared. Drew sat the boy down on the floor, staring at Carolyn with a bewildered look on his face. For a long time, neither of them spoke. "I don't know that many of the details yet," she continued, rubbing her sweaty palms on her slacks. "The police found her in a room at the Motor Inn on Thompson." He started to say something, then stopped, his mouth hanging open. She didn't know what else to do, so she kept talking. It was better to fill the air with words than silence. "She mentioned checking on a probationer when I talked to her this morning. I'm so sorry, Drew. You know how much I loved her."

He stood and walked toward the back of the house, leaving Michael in the living room. Carolyn followed him, finding him in the master bedroom on the bed. She went over and stood beside him. "Please say something, Drew," she said, watching a tear roll down his cheek. "There are things . . .

things that have to be done. The children . . . plans . . . relatives . . . a funeral home." She was bombarding the poor man. She looked around, almost as if she was searching for an escape hatch she could jump through. She wasn't good at this type of thing. "I'll give you some time alone."

"Please," he said, covering his face with his arm.

Carolyn left, pulling the door closed behind her. Michael stared up at her, sensing that something was wrong. "I want my daddy," he said, reaching for the door handle. "I'm hungry."

"Come on, sweetheart," she said, taking his hand and leading him down the hallway. "We need to find Peter and Jude, okay? I promise I'll get you some food, just not right this minute."

"Mac and cheese," he said. "And Pop Tarts."

"Sure," Carolyn said, hoping Brad would get there before she lost it. Peter, the seven-year-old, was pushing toy trucks and cars over a rubber mat that had been made to resemble a city. Since he seemed to be preoccupied, she continued on to Jude's room, cracking the door and peering inside. It didn't appear as if the girl was home. Clothes were scattered everywhere, the beds were unmade, and the computer on the desk was turned off. Stacy shared the room with her older sister. Carolyn wondered why they hadn't converted their garage the way she had to give the older girl some privacy. Where in God's name would they put a live-in nanny?

"Do you know where Jude is, Michael?"

"Dunno." He shrugged. "Are you gonna be our new babysitter?"

"Not exactly," Carolyn said. Their house was smaller than the one she'd just sold, not more than twelve hundred square feet. She felt a chill and looked over her shoulder, expecting to hear Veronica's boisterous laugh and learn that it was another of her practical jokes. Her death didn't seem real, and yet at the same time, it seemed so immediate it was terrifying.

Carolyn stared at the framed photos lining the wall in the hallway. She'd lived so much of Veronica's life she felt fractured, as if a part of her had disappeared. The boy broke away and went sprinting back to the room he shared with his brother. She heard something crash into the wall and rushed to see what had happened. Michael was sitting in the middle of the room bawling.

"He threw a car at me," Peter shouted. Seeing Carolyn, he looked confused. A look of recognition appeared, and he went back to playing as if she weren't there.

When Carolyn turned around, Drew was standing in the doorway. "What am I supposed to do? I don't . . . I mean, do we have to call a funeral home now? Can't it wait until tomorrow? I have to find Jude. She doesn't have a cell phone. Veronica took it away from her. Sometimes she doesn't come home for days. I can drive by some of the places where she hangs out."

"Don't worry about a funeral home," Carolyn said, realizing there would be an autopsy. "The most pressing thing at the moment is for you to identify the body. The police want you to go to the morgue. You can call your regular babysitter if you'd like, or we can wait until Brad Preston gets here. He's bringing Linda Cartwright. She's one of our investigators. She can watch the children for you. She's got two kids about the same age as Michael and Peter."

Peter turned and stared at her, a somber expression on his face. She wondered if he'd figured out what they were talking about. She hadn't wanted to do it this way, in front of the children, but it was too late now.

"When is Mommy coming home?" Peter asked in a strained voice.

"I don't know," Drew said without thinking. "I can't do what you said, Carolyn. I don't want that to be my last memory. Besides, I need to track down Jude. Why can't you identify her?"

Carolyn sat down on one of the twin beds, pulling Michael into her lap. "I guess I could," she said, stroking the child's arm. A mother's touch, she thought. Veronica's children would never feel that again. Maybe Hank had been justified in asking her to break the news to Drew, but she was too emotionally involved. A stranger might have been better. "They say it's important. It helps you begin the grieving process."

"I want my wife back," Drew said. "I don't want to start the grieving process."

"Star Wars," Michael said, clapping. He hopped out of her lap and dug in a box, returning and handing her an action figure.

"That's Grievous," Peter told her.

"Please, can't we talk in the other room?" Carolyn handed the boy back his toy. Her stomach was churning with acid. Veronica was in the morgue and she was here, surrounding by everything she knew and loved.

"The kids want to be wherever we are," Drew said. "One room is as good as the other."

The doorbell rang and he left to answer it. Carolyn stayed in the children's room, hoping she could keep them entertained. She stretched out on the floor, removing a handful of action figures from the box and offering them to Michael. While his brother's head was turned, he snatched a truck off the mat. Peter exploded and kicked him. "You messed up everything again."

A pretty brunette in her late thirties stuck her head in the room. Linda Cartwright nodded at Carolyn, and then squatted down beside the children. "You guys wouldn't want to go to Dave and Busters with me, would you?"

"I wanna go," Michael said, throwing his arms in the air.

"Who are you?" Peter asked.

"My name is Linda," she told him. "I'm a friend of Carolyn's. And what's your name, big guy?"

"Peter," he said, sizing her up. "Can you cook?"

The kids must think they're interviewing nannies, Carolyn thought, tugging on Linda's sleeve. Veronica hadn't said anything about hiring a live-in. Since she worked at home three days a week, it made more sense to take the children somewhere else. Stacy and Peter were in elementary school and Michael was in preschool. Why would they pay a live-in when they were strapped financially?

"Peter," Linda said, "why don't you and Michael put your toys away before we leave? If you're good, I'll buy you lots of game tokens."

"Mickey needs a car seat," Peter told her, sounding wiser than his seven years. "Mom makes me ride in a booster seat. It's okay if you don't have one."

"Guess what?" Linda said, smiling. "I have two car seats, and one's a booster. My boy, Ryan, is six and Timmy just turned four. Maybe you can come over and play with them one day. I'll be right back, okay?"

Linda's cheerful demeanor disappeared once they stepped outside the room. She was strong, Carolyn thought, the type of person you'd want beside you in a crisis. Brad had made a good decision in recruiting her to help out. "They don't know their mother's dead yet."

"I gathered," Linda answered. "You know Drew better than the rest of us. I'll get the kids out of here so you two can talk. Has he notified Veronica's family yet?"

Carolyn shook her head. "There's another kid in the kitchen. Her name is Stacy." She stopped and chewed on a cuticle. "Drew asked me to go to the morgue and identify the body. He says he can't handle it."

"Can your fiancé go with you?" Linda asked, tilting her head. "You're awfully pale, Carolyn. I'm not sure you should be driving. Brad told me you've known Veronica since grade school. Is that true?"

"Yes," she said. "We went to St. Andrews together. We were cradle Catholics."

"Shouldn't you call a priest, then?"

"No," Carolyn told her. "Drew's an atheist, and Veronica was furious over the way the church handled the sex scandals. The last person she'd want in this house with her kids is a priest."

"That's too bad," Linda answered. "Faith can plug a lot of holes at a time like this, particularly when there're young children involved."

"Nothing can plug this hole," Carolyn told her, heading to the living room.

She exchanged a few words with Brad, embraced Drew, and left to go the morgue.

CHAPTER 4

Tuesday, October 12 — 8:15 P.M.

One side of Veronica's head was gone. Her blond hair was caked in blood, and her face was unreconizable. Carolyn bent over and stared at the gold wedding band on her left hand. "It's her," she told the morgue attendant, a portly Irish man with red hair and freckles. When he started to zip the bag up, she added, "I'd like a few minutes if you don't mind."

"Take all the time you want," Sean O'Malley said. "Just give a holler if you need anything."

Poor Veronica, Carolyn thought. Before Marcus had come into her life, she'd envied her. She might not have had much in the way of material possessions, but she'd had everything that mattered — a decent husband, four beautiful children, a great personality. No matter how depressed Carolyn got, Veronica always found a way to pull her out of it. She'd never let her work get to her. Last year had changed that, though. But she couldn't think of that now. She had to pay her respects, let go, find a way to reconcile herself to what had happened.

Picking up her friend's lifeless hand, she said, "I love you, honey. I promise the bastard who did this to you will pay. Don't worry about Drew and the kids. It'll be hard at first, but they'll make it." She placed the dead woman's hand on her chest, the same chest the county pathologist, Charley Young, would soon slice open during the autopsy.

Why was she talking to a corpse?

Was Veronica with God now? She'd never done anything seriously wrong, at least not as far as Carolyn was concerned. Her friend didn't see it that way. Now she wondered if Veronica had been right, and her death was some sort of divine retaliation. Veronica should have taken her suspicions to the police last year. Carolyn had talked her out of it. Was she now just as responsible?

Even with the most experienced officers, there was always that one case that tore their heart out. Veronica's had been a child mutilation. She would have eventually put it behind her if the murderer hadn't been set free. The worst part was that he'd been released because of the incompetence of the county's chief forensic officer at the time. Robert Abernathy had been charged with multiple counts of falsifying and mishandling evidence, as well as perjury. Lester McAllen, the monster who'd butchered Billy Bell, was only one of scores of defendants whose convictions were overturned because of Abernathy. When Abernathy and Lester McAllen were both murdered, Veronica suspected the boy's father had killed them. She also blamed herself for contacting Tyler Bell and telling him that the man responsible for his son's death was scheduled to be released.

Carolyn wrapped her arms around her chest. If Veronica's spirit was lingering somewhere, it certainly wouldn't be inside this dreadful place. Carolyn made the sign of the cross, zipped the bag up, and quickly left the room.

O'Malley stood, handing Carolyn a white envelope.

"Is this her death certificate?" she asked. "I'm not a relative. She was my friend, but anything official should be handled by her husband."

"Turn it over," he said. "It's got your name on it. You're Carolyn Sullivan, aren't you?"

She used her fingernail to tear open the envelope. As soon as she read it, she jerked her head up. "Where did you get this?"

"It was on my desk," O'Malley told her, taking a sip of his coffee.

Carolyn's eyes flashed with fear. "Who put it there?"

"I don't know," he said. "Must have been someone on the day shift."

"Call them," she said, the paper fluttering in her hand. "This is a death threat. I have to know where it came from."

O'Malley leaned back in his chair. "We've got three people working the day shift, Louise Reynolds, Sam Ornstein, and Cory Williams. Louise usually sits at this desk. She goes bowling on Tuesday nights. I guess I can try her cell phone. Tracking everyone down will take time." He gestured toward a row of plastic chairs. "Have a seat. Want me to get you some coffee? I just put up a fresh pot."

Carolyn ignored him, reading through the words again. The letter had obviously been typed on a computer. The font was enormous and all the words were in caps.

I KNOW YOUR SON GOES TO MIT.
I KNOW YOUR DAUGHTER GOES TO VENTURA HIGH.
I KNOW YOU NO LONGER LIVE AT THE SAME HOUSE.

I KNOW MARCUS, THE MAN YOU ARE GOING TO MARRY.
KEEP YOUR NOSE OUT OF THIS, OR I WILL KILL THEM ALL.
THEN I WILL KILL YOU.

"I need rubber gloves and an evidence envelope," Carolyn said, interrupting O'Malley while he was dialing.

"I can only do one thing at a time," he complained, opening the top drawer and slapping a box of gloves on the corner of his desk.

Carolyn set the paper down and put on the gloves, then folded the note and placed it back inside the envelope. Removing the gloves, she shoved them in her purse in case she needed them later. She was too anxious to sit down. Punching the autodial on her cell, she called Hank Sawyer and read him the letter. O'Malley was talking to someone on the phone, but he looked over at her, and she could tell he was eavesdropping.

"This person knows me, Hank," she said, opening the glass doors and stepping outside in the hallway. "It has to be someone from the agency. They even know I moved recently, and that I'm getting married."

"Your house was up for sale for six months," the detective told her. "There's no telling how many people passed through that place. You probably had things lying around. You know, stuff about the wedding, maybe something from MIT. As far as Rebecca is concerned, they could figure out she goes to Ventura High because of where the house was located."

"But we moved."

"They could have assumed you didn't transfer her because teenagers hate to change schools and leave their friends."

"Fine, fine," Carolyn said, beside herself. "This person still threatened to kill me and my family. Whoever wrote the note must have murdered Veronica. Am I right?"

"Maybe," Hank said. "It could also be a nutcase. Some guy could have walked through your house when it was up for sale. Then when he heard about a probation officer being murdered, he reasoned that someone who knew you would go to the morgue, or someone at the morgue would know you and get the note to you." He paused. "The local station broadcast the story live not long after I called you. The clerk at the front desk notified them before he called us. What a bastard, huh? Everyone wants to be on TV. I hate the damn media. All they do is cause problems for us. They're still out here at the motel with their camera crews. We haven't had a tsunami, an earthquake, or a hurricane lately, so I guess they've got to find some way to give the tragedy junkies their fix."

"I don't care about the media," Carolyn shouted. "Get someone over here, damn it! My best friend got her head blown off, for Christ's sake, and someone just threatened to kill my entire family. I demand that you take this seriously. One of the morgue attendants may have seen this person. We're trying to get in touch with all of them now."

"I'm about to clear here. I'll be there in fifteen minutes. Where's Veronica's husband?"

"At the house," Carolyn told him. "Haven't you spoken to him yet?"

"No," Hank told her. "Mary Stevens called about thirty minutes ago. A woman named Linda Cartwright answered. She said Drew went out looking for his oldest daughter. You think he had anything to do with Veronica's death?"

"Absolutely not," Carolyn said. "Drew's a great guy."

"No problems in the marriage?"

"Nothing out of the ordinary," she told him, remembering the dark circles under Veronica's eyes. "I'll talk to you when you get here."

Once she concluded her call with Hank,

Carolyn saw she had four messages from Marcus. They were both busy people, and made it a habit not to call and disturb each other at work unless it was absolutely necessary. Realizing how late it was, she dialed their home number. "I'm sorry," she said after telling him what had transpired. "I just couldn't tell anyone else. I'm at the morgue. The more I talk about it, the more upset I get."

"I understand," Marcus said. "Rebecca saw it on the news, though, and was terrified it was you." The line fell silent. "Is there anything I can do? When are you coming home?"

"I'm not sure," Carolyn said. "Don't wait up for me. Once I leave here, I'm going back to Veronica's house. We dumped the kids on a woman from work. She needs to go home to her family."

"I'll stop and pick up some food and meet you over there," he said. "Rebecca is upstairs studying."

"No," she said, her voice elevating. "Don't leave her alone!"

"Rebecca isn't a baby. She drives all over the place in her car. And we have security. Why won't you let me help you get through this?"

"Please," Carolyn pleaded, "if you want to

help me, stay at the house with Rebecca."

"You can't take on the responsibilities of Veronica's family," Marcus said. "This is a terrible tragedy, honey, but you need to think of yourself. We're getting married in two weeks."

"We can't get married now. Veronica's my maid of honor. How can I have a wedding when my maid of honor is on a slab at the morgue?"

"But, darling," he said, tension crackling in his voice, "we've been planning this for almost a year. Brooke and Ethan are flying in from the East Coast. We've already received a ton of gifts. Rebecca can be your maid of honor."

"I can't talk about this now," Carolyn said, clicking off the phone. Brooke and Ethan were Marcus's children by his first marriage. They both attended Princeton, and were only a year apart in age. He'd been estranged from them for years, so she knew how important this was to him. He didn't understand how deeply she cared for Veronica. Since they'd been seeing each other, she hadn't socialized with her outside of work. Veronica and Drew couldn't afford to eat in expensive restaurants. When she'd explained this to Marcus, he suggested inviting them to his house. She was embarrassed by Marcus's wealth. How could she flaunt her future lifestyle to people she knew were living from one paycheck to the other?

Carolyn hadn't told Marcus about the letter. Everything had happened too fast. How could she protect John when he was so far away? She couldn't ask him to drop out of school. Attending MIT had been his dream, and he'd worked hard to make it a reality. An event like a wedding would offer the killer the perfect opportunity to make good on his threats.

She went to check with O'Malley. The attendant told her he'd managed to contact everyone, and no one recalled seeing anything even remotely suspicious.

Seeing Hank and a striking black woman step off the elevator, Carolyn rushed toward them. "None of the day attendants recall anyone giving them the letter, nor did they see it on the desk. The man on duty now came to work at four. He found an envelope addressed to me underneath his clipboard. He had his clipboard with him when he took me to the back to identify Veronica's body. That's when the person must have placed the envelope on his desk."

Detective Mary Stevens was tall and shapely, with luminous brown eyes and flawless skin. She wore a red shirt and jeans that hung low on her hips. Carolyn knew she must have been at the motel where Veronica was murdered, as she always changed into a red shirt when she responded to a homicide. She called it her murder shirt. "Forensics is on their way," Mary told her, reaching into her pocket for a pair of gloves. "Can we take a look at the note?"

At fifty, Hank Sawyer stood just under six feet. At one time, he'd been heavy, but he'd gone on a fitness program a few years ago, and now took pride in his physique. He still had a thick head of hair, although the gray strands outnumbered the brown. His face had a rugged look to it. Lines shot out around his mouth and eyes. "You touched it, I presume," he said, watching as Carolyn handed Mary a plastic evidence bag. After Mary removed the letter from the envelope, Hank looked over her shoulder to read it. "Since it was hand-delivered, we might find fingerprints or other evidence that could help us identify this creep."

"What about the man who rented the motel room?" Carolyn asked. "He could have been lying about his credit card being stolen."

"Not likely," Mary said, placing the note back in the plastic bag. "He was at work. At least five people saw him. He came in at eight and worked until six this evening. He brings his lunch from home, so he never left the building. He's an underwriter at National Insurance."

"Drew used to work for National Insurance," Carolyn said, her face flushed with tension. "That was years ago, though. He works at Boeing now. Where was this man's credit card stolen from, and why didn't he report it until after the murder?"

"He claims he didn't realize it was gone until we called him," Hank said, chomping on a toothpick. "He left his wallet in a locker at the Spectrum Health Club last night. The only thing missing was his MasterCard and about thirty bucks in cash."

Mary spoke up. "The motel clerk claims he rented the room to a black male in his early twenties the night before. Jonathan Tate, the man whose card was stolen, is a Caucasian male in his forties. That rules Tate out even without the alibi. It's interesting that Veronica's husband may have worked for the same company. People in the insurance business jump around a lot, though, and since you say it was a long time ago, it's doubtful if Tate and Campbell knew each other." She shrugged. "We'll check it out, though. I'd follow a snail right now if I thought it could lead me to the killer."

"Why don't you go home, Carolyn?" Hank suggested "When the crime lab gets here, we're going to have to clear everyone out except for the stiffs."

Carolyn cut her eyes to him. "One of those *stiffs* was my best friend."

"Sorry," Hank said. "It's been a long day. Tomorrow we need you to go through all of Veronica's cases, everything in the past three or four years."

"Four years! Do you have any idea how many cases our people handle?"

"There's still a chance it could be the probationer she mentioned to you this morning," he told her. "We didn't find any signs of forced entry, but it isn't that hard to get into a motel room. The guy who rented it with a stolen credit card may have left early that morning and accidentally left the door ajar. Then this Phillip Bramson could have snuck in with the intention of fooling Veronica into believing he had a right to be there."

"Did Brad Preston send you the information in his file?" Carolyn asked, running her fingers through her hair.

"Yeah," Hank said. "Bramson hasn't shown up at work for two weeks. He also didn't pay the rent on his apartment, so his landlord locked him out four days ago. Veronica's file indicated she placed a number of phone calls to him. There was also a notation that she suspected he was using narcotics again. He could have found out she was looking for him, and arranged to meet her at the Motor Inn."

"It's possible," Carolyn said. "What happened to Veronica's gun?"

"We have it," Hank said. "It may turn out to be the murder weapon. We found it in a Dumpster at the rear of the motel."

Carolyn scratched a patch of dry skin on her arm. "Veronica hated guns. He must have overpowered her. She was always afraid of something like that. She believed we were safer without guns. Not just people in law enforcement, but private citizens as well. Veronica thought if you bought a gun and kept it in your house, instead of your defending yourself with it, someone would use it against you." She paused, thinking. "If Bramson was strung out, he would never have agreed to see Veronica. He had drug terms. If he tested positive, he was looking at a certain prison term. In reality, she could have violated him for not showing up at his job. He may have lured her to the motel to kill her."

"Why didn't he just abscond?" Mary interjected.

"Addicts don't act rationally," Hank reminded her. "He may have thought he could con Veronica into thinking he was clean. When she didn't buy it, he impulsively grabbed her gun and shot her."

"But why would Bramson threaten me and my family?" Carolyn asked. "Not many murderers would risk showing up at a county facility only hours after the crime, particularly if the victim was in law enforcement. And how did he find out so much about me?" She turned to Hank. "I doubt if Bramson took a tour of my house. It doesn't make sense. Junkies look and act like junkies. My real estate agent never brought anyone to the house without screening them."

"You must know more than you think you know," Mary told her, exchanging tense glances with Hank.

Had she already put it together? Carolyn asked herself. Mary Stevens was one of the sharpest women she'd ever known. Her father had been a high-ranking officer with the LAPD. When he was killed in the line of duty, Mary had tracked down his murderer, then relinquished a lucrative position in the private sector to become a cop. Her statement had struck too close to home. If the detective had somehow sniffed out the truth about Tyler Bell, Carolyn's future was at stake. Instead of going on her honeymoon, she could end up in the county jail.

"I have to go," Carolyn said. "I'll be on my cell if you need me." Seeing Hank about to say something, she cut him off. "Don't worry, I'm not going to throw my gun away. In case you've forgotten, I've already killed one murderer. I don't need any more notches on my belt, but I'd welcome the chance to shoot this one. Do me a favor. Find him before I do."

CHAPTER 5

Wednesday, October 13 — 6:30 A.M.

The morning sun filtered in through the white wooden shutters, casting the room in a golden hue. Carolyn was snuggled in Marcus's arms. She inhaled the masculine scent of his skin as she gazed at his handsome face. When he slept, his forty-eight years disappeared and his face took on a look of childish innocence. She loved the graceful slant of his nose, his hooded, seductive eyes, his sensuous lips. Her hand drifted between his thighs; then she felt her head throbbing and the events of the day before thrust their way to the surface.

Slipping out of bed, she squatted on the wood floor, using her feet to push herself into the corner. After she'd left the coroner's office, she had gone to check on Drew and relieve Linda Cartwright. Her eyes drifted closed, and she was standing at the front door of Veronica's house.

Carolyn knocked several times, but no one answered. Using the key Veronica had given her years ago, she let herself in, not wanting to wake the children by ringing the doorbell. Empty beer cans were scattered on top of the coffee table, alongside toys, newspapers, and various clutter. Drew was asleep on the sofa.

She checked the bedrooms and found all the children in their beds except Jude. Since Linda wasn't there, she assumed Drew had sent her home.

Carolyn tiptoed back down the narrow hallway, walking over and tapping Veronica's husband on the shoulder. When he only groaned and changed position, she said, "Drew, it's Carolyn. Where's Jude?"

"How the hell do I know?" he said, his speech slurred from the alcohol. "She's probably doing dope with one of her low-life friends. I drove around for hours trying to find her. For all I know, she's shacked up with some gangster."

Carolyn sat on the edge of a chair across from him. "I'm going to notify the police that Jude is missing. I'm worried, Drew. Veronica's murder has been on the news. She should have called or come home by now."

Drew pushed himself to a seated position. "This shit happens all the time, Carolyn," he told her. "That damn kid drives her mother and me nuts. She should be in college, but all she's interested in is partying." He rummaged among the beer cans until he found one that still had a few drops left in it. Once he slugged it down, he tossed the empty can into the pile. "You got any cigarettes?"

"I don't smoke," Carolyn said. "Didn't you stop years ago?"

"Yeah," Drew said, leaning forward over his knees. "After what happened to Veronica, I'm wondering why. We knock ourselves out to stay healthy and then some maniac comes along and . . ." He covered his face with his hands. "Christ, what am I going to do? I tried to tell the kids, but I couldn't. I keep thinking I'll wake up tomorrow and Veronica will be beside me in the bed. That isn't going to happen, is it?"

Carolyn shook her head. "You have to tell them, Drew."

"I know, I know . . . All I want to do is sleep right now. I'll find a way to tell them. I just can't do it right now."

"The police are going to ask you a lot of questions," Carolyn said. "Didn't you used to work for National Insurance?"

"I worked for National Car Rentals before I got the job at Boeing. Jesus, Carolyn, that's got to be fifteen years ago. What does this have to do with what happened to Veronica?"

"Nothing," she said, folding her hands in her lap. "Were you and Veronica having problems?"

"Of course we had problems," Drew told her. "We have a screwed-up teenager, and with both of us working, we still have to scrimp to make ends meet. It didn't help that Veronica started popping out babies ten years after we had Jude. Veronica swore she was on birth control, but I think she snookered me. Then she decided Stacy had to have a brother or sister closer to her age. I don't know where Michael came from. With this many rug rats, Veronica and I either can't find the time to have sex or we're too exhausted."

He was still using the present tense, Carolyn noticed. He should have gone to the morgue instead of her. He seemed to be dealing with his wife's death as if it were a temporary situation, something along the lines of having your car repossessed. It made you feel lousy, but you could take out a second mortgage on the house, make up the back payments, and everything would be fine.

"How did she look?" he asked. "Was it bad?"

"Yes," Carolyn said, staring at a raggedy teddy bear on the floor and thinking how sad it looked. Her mind went blank, blocking out the terrible image of Veronica's blood-splattered body.

She shrieked when she felt someone pulling on her hand, believing she was at the morgue and Veronica had reached out and grabbed her. "You startled me," she said, seeing Marcus standing over her. At six-one, he had dark hair and hazel eyes with flecks of green in them. His hooded lids gave him a seductive look. Bedroom eyes, her mother used to call them. "I must have dosed off."

"Have you been on the floor all night?"

"I woke up early. I got out of bed because I didn't want to wake you."

Marcus yawned, then stretched his back. "Jump in the shower while I make you some breakfast."

Carolyn let him help her to her feet, then wrapped her arms around his waist. "Oh, Marcus," she sobbed, her head pressed against his chest. "It was so awful. One side of her head was gone."

He rubbed the center of her back. "Just relax, okay? You're exhausted. How is Drew holding up?"

"I'm not sure," she said, clasping the lapels on his plaid cotton robe. "I don't think it's really sunk in yet. He couldn't find Jude last night. I need to call and see if she came home."

"Not until you get some food in you," Marcus insisted. "An hour won't make any difference, Carolyn. This isn't going to be over in a day. You need your strength. Are you going to be able to take a day off to get yourself together, or do you have to go to the office? We have a meeting scheduled with the caterers tonight at six."

"I have to work." Carolyn began to panic, speaking so fast her mind didn't have time to keep up with her mouth. "There's no one else to run the . . . I'll have to find someone to take over Veronica's . . . we're already slammed . . . The new people can't handle the serious cases."

"Calm down," Marcus said, tilting her chin up and kissing her. "When something like this happens, the best thing you can do is to go about your business. Although it might be better if you stayed at home and got some rest, you'd probably spend the day thinking about Veronica."

"We have to cancel the wedding. Please, I don't want what should be the happiest day of my life to take place now. We'll pick another date . . . maybe next month, or after the first of the year. Your secretary should start calling people today. They'll understand when she explains. Most of my friends know Veronica. If we don't postpone it, we'll turn our wedding into a funeral." She saw the look of disappointment on his face. "I can't go to meetings with caterers, Marcus. I'm not sure I can get through today, let alone a wedding."

"Why don't we wait a few days?" he said. "See how you feel then. We've already booked our trip. The airline tickets arrived just the other day. I don't want to bring money into the picture, but we're going to take a bath if we cancel."

"I'm not going to change my mind," Carolyn said, telling him about the threatening letter.

"Personally, I think it was a prank," he told her. "People do sick things. I've received death threats before, one allegedly from a Middle Eastern terrorist group. That's the world we live in today, honey. Intimidation and fear rule, but only if you let them."

Marcus owned a company that supplied custom software to the military. Because he transported classified codes, he employed a private security team. A man was parked in front of their house now. "I'll hire more peo-

ple to keep an eye on us. I'll even get someone to shadow John in Massachusetts. Your
peace of mind is all that matters."

"You're the most wonderful man in the
world. Please understand why we have to
cancel the wedding."

"You don't need to work, Carolyn," Marcus said, a stern look on his face. "I can't
have my wife in constant danger. There are
more worthwhile things you could do with
your time. You could volunteer somewhere,
take up golf or tennis, spend more time with
Rebecca."

"We've already discussed this dozens of
times." This was the only conflict they had in
their relationship. "There's no way I can quit
now. The police asked me to go through all
of Veronica's cases. Then I'll have to find out
who's still in prison and who's been released
on parole, get their addresses, try to find
them. Criminals move every week."

"I thought this Bramson guy was the
killer."

"We don't know that for certain," Carolyn
told him. "The clerk said the man who
rented the room was black. Bramson is
white. It could be anyone."

Marcus shrugged and headed off toward
the kitchen. Even the way he walked in-
trigued her. His long legs and torso moved

purposely forward, while his head seemed to remain motionless. It was a trick of the eye, created by his graceful but deceptively fast pace.

In many ways, they made the perfect couple. They talked fast, moved fast, and made instant decisions. They worked with efficiency and determination, and they both possessed extraordinary memories. The only time Carolyn forgot anything was when she was emotionally distraught as she was now.

She rushed to the closet to find something to wear. She stopped when she saw Veronica's maid of honor dress. Removing the plastic, she fingered the pale lavender silk. She'd give the dress to Drew to bury her in. It had come from the dressmaker's a month ago. Veronica had never got around to picking it up.

Pausing in the doorway of the bathroom, she stared out over the cavernous bedroom. Veronica and Drew's entire house was only a few feet larger. Marcus's sprawling home seemed like a disgusting display of wealth. The people who actually needed this kind of space were seldom able to afford it.

As she was brushing her teeth, the three-carat diamond ring on her finger was reflected in the mirror. When she went to work, she turned it around backward. Would she ever get used to her new lifestyle? It was distancing her from her friends and coworkers. Even Brad Preston treated her differently, and they'd once been lovers.

She jumped in the shower, relishing the feel of the hot water against her skin. After she shampooed her hair and got out, she dried it with a towel. What people failed to understand was that it was Marcus's money, not hers. She hadn't reached the point where she felt comfortable having him support her. Except for the few years when her ex-husband, Frank, had taught school, she'd been the primary breadwinner. Paying her own bills allowed her to maintain a sense of independence. She hadn't fallen in love with Marcus because he was successful. She loved him because he was a great man.

Carolyn ran a comb through her hair, put on her makeup, dressed, and grabbed her briefcase and purse. She thought of herself as a wash-and-wear girl. Her naturally curly hair made it easy to care for. All she had to do was wash it. The only thing she went to the beauty salon for was haircuts. She filed her own nails, had never had a facial, and could be ready to go just about anywhere in less than thirty minutes. The first time she and Marcus had gone on a trip together, he'd nagged her to pack three days before they were scheduled to leave. While Marcus cooled his heels, certain they were going to miss their flight, Carolyn threw her clothes into a bag and was ready to walk out the door in fifteen minutes.

Rebecca came down the winding staircase with a worried look on her face. Her straight dark hair fell to the center of her back. She had inherited her father's olive skin, hair, and hazel eyes. "I heard what happened," she said. "When they said a probation officer was murdered, I was afraid it was you. Why didn't you call us?"

"I'm sorry, honey," Carolyn said, embracing her. "I just did whatever people asked of me. I didn't have time to do anything else."

"You have to quit that hideous job," her daughter said. "You don't need the money now that you're marrying Marcus. He wants you to quit, too. How do I know what happened to Veronica won't happen to you?"

"Jude is missing, Rebecca," Carolyn said, changing the subject. "I know the two of you have never been close, but have you heard anything about her recently?"

"She's a tramp, Mom. I run into her at school now and then, but other than that, I don't have anything to do with her. Wasn't she supposed to graduate last year?"

Something wasn't right. "You saw Jude at

Ventura High?"

"Yeah," the girl said. "I haven't seen her in a while, though."

"She's not attending classes," Carolyn said. "Her father said she's just bumming around. Veronica told me the same thing. She must be hanging out at the school because of her friends."

"I'm pretty sure she's enrolled, Mom. There are a lot of kids who didn't graduate with their class. Haley Snodgrass flunked and came back. I know because she's Anne Marie's big sister. Her parents insisted that Haley get her diploma instead of a GED. Rebecca glanced at her watch. "I have to go. I need to stop for gas. I love living here, but it takes me forever to drive to school. Where's Marcus?"

"Making breakfast," Carolyn told her.

Rebecca laughed. "He can't cook. What's he making, toast? Where's Josephine? She'll have a fit if Marcus makes a mess in her kitchen."

"Today is her day off."

Carolyn followed Rebecca into the kitchen, watching as she strolled over to Marcus and stuck her hand out. He fumbled in the pocket of his robe and handed her a hundred-dollar bill. Rebecca stood on her tiptoes and kissed him on the cheek.

"Thanks, Dad," she said, waving at her mother before she darted out the back door.

"Why are you giving Rebecca money?" Carolyn asked. "Since I don't have a mortgage payment anymore, I have more than enough to take care of her needs. Besides, don't you think a hundred dollars is too much for a girl her age?"

"Gas is expensive," Marcus explained, leaning back against the counter. "Since I'm the reason she's living so far from school, I think it's only fair that I pay for her gas. By the way, how exactly do you scramble eggs? Do you shake the pan or is there some kind of special device? I looked but I couldn't find one."

Carolyn laughed, a welcome relief from the tension. The countertop was covered with pots, pans, graters, slicers, and various utensils. Only a person who'd spent his life staring at a computer wouldn't know how to do something as simple as scrambling an egg. "Cereal sounds great," she said. "I saw some strawberries in the fridge yesterday. We can put some on our cornflakes."

"Are you sure?" Marcus said, looking relieved.

"Why don't you set out the bowls? I'll get the cereal, milk, and strawberries." Carolyn was settling into a semistate of normality when she jerked her head around. "See if you can catch Rebecca. We started talking about Jude . . . I don't want her out of my sight until you get someone to protect her."

"Bear is on her already," Marcus said, referring to the six-five, three-hundred-pound Hispanic bodyguard who'd worked for him since he'd moved to Santa Rosa three years ago. Although Bear's size intimidated most people, he was a gentle, sweet man. He kept a picture of his mother on the visor, and would cry if he saw a dead dog in the roadway. He was a crackerjack marksman, though, and wouldn't hesitate to kill someone if they threatened the safety of his employer. "The agency is sending two other men," Marcus told her. "They should be here before you leave for work."

"But I didn't tell Rebecca what we were doing," Carolyn said, reaching for the portable phone on the counter. Things were getting away from her, and like Marcus had pointed out, the situation wouldn't be resolved overnight. She was worrying about Drew, Veronica's children, her job, her wedding, the threats, and at the same time, mourning the loss of her friend. When she tried to juggle too many balls, she dropped all of them.

"Bear's the best," Marcus said, walking

over and placing his arm around her. "Trust me, Rebecca won't spot him. If she does, I'll fire him. They promised to get someone to look after John by the end of the day. Since nothing may come of it, there's no reason to call and distract him. I doubt if I could pass some of the courses John's taking, and he's only a sophomore. MIT is a tough school."

Carolyn returned to the table and robotically spooned the cereal into her mouth, blinking as she realized what was clouding her mind. Going to the police with Veronica's suspicions about Tyler Bell was a moral dilemma she had already struggled with and resolved. Now everything had changed. She would have to track him down right away. If she thought there was even a remote possibility that he was involved in Veronica's death, she would handcuff him and deposit him at the police station.

Had she really withheld information? It was Veronica who'd thought Bell could have been behind the deaths of Robert Abernathy and Lester McAllen, and as far as Carolyn knew, there had been no evidence to support such a premise.

She dabbed at her mouth with her napkin, kissed Marcus good-bye, and headed to the garage. He hadn't attempted to engage her in conversation while she was eating. He knew she was thinking. When he worked at home, she showed him the same courtesy.

Carolyn would call Drew from the road. All she could do was attempt to move things forward. She had to train herself to investigate Veronica's murder the way she would any case. Crimes weren't solved the way they were on TV. Sometimes they took months, even years. If only one piece of the puzzle fell into place, it would be a good day.

CHAPTER 6

Wednesday, October 13 — 11:00 P.M.

Carolyn and Brad Preston were seated on a bench facing the fountain in the center courtyard of the government center. The sun was out and the temperature was in the mid-seventies. The smoke from wildfires of the day before was gone, moved out to sea by the ocean breezes.

Working in Veronica's partitioned office all morning had been difficult. Every time Carolyn took her eyes away from the computer screen, she was surrounded by Veronica's life. There were pictures of Drew and the kids, jokes, Post-it notes, cheap knickknacks the children had given her. She could even smell her cologne, Eternity Moment by Calvin Klein. Drew had given her a bottle for her birthday the previous month. Veronica thought the name was hysterical. She recalled how they'd laughed about it. "How can it be eternity if it's only a moment?" Veronica had said. "Are people stupid or what?"

She was glad that Brad had suggested they speak outside. On days like this, it was easy to see why real estate prices in Southern California had continued to skyrocket. While most of the country braced for winter, it was spring all year long. "I downloaded everything on Veronica's computer," she told him. "I'll upload it to the machine in my office as well as my notebook. That way, I can work on it at home."

"Good," Brad said, squinting in the midday sun. People were streaming in and out of the courthouse — attorneys carrying briefcases, defendants with downcast faces, prospective jurors, as well as senior citizens who passed time sitting in on trials.

Tall and blond, Brad Preston lived life as an adventure. In all the years Carolyn had known him, she'd never seen him despondent. At forty, he still possessed boundless energy, even though lines were beginning to form in his handsome face. He could still stay out all night drinking with his race car buddies and show up at work the next day bright-eyed and as alert as a man half his age. He'd never married because he was addicted to the thrill of the chase. According to

Brad, a person no longer wanted something after they got it. It was the fantasy that was exciting, not the reality.

"Veronica was having an affair, you know."

"That's not true," Carolyn said, shocked he would imply such a thing. "I'm her best friend, Brad. Don't you think I'd know if she was cheating on her husband? Veronica worshipped Drew." The more she thought about it, the more annoyed she became. "The poor woman died only yesterday, and people are already spreading malicious rumors. What else did you hear? That Veronica was robbing banks in her spare time?"

"I saw her," Brad said, rubbing his neck. "Remember when we had that big storm last spring, the one that caused the power failures and mud slides? I was coming back from lunch when I walked past Veronica's car in the parking lot. It was that white Ford Explorer she drove before we issued her a county clunker. I heard moaning sounds coming from inside, so I put my face to the window to see if something was wrong. There was old Veronica, bare-assed and humping away."

Carolyn's hand flew to her chest. "In broad daylight, in this parking lot, in a car for Christ's sake? It had to be someone else, Brad. Veronica would never do something like that."

"It was her all right," Brad said, a mischievous grin on his face. "I'd recognize that ass anywhere. To be honest, she didn't look half bad. I even gave thought to making a play for her. Most women aren't spontaneous enough when it comes to sex. They have to go through all these rituals. Then there are dozens of restrictions, as if sex is some kind of sport that has to be played by their rules."

Since Carolyn's engagement to Marcus, Brad had made it a habit of constantly reminding her of their past relationship. It wasn't because he was in love with her. She'd given up on that years ago. Everything was a form of competition to him. He counted it as a loss when a woman did something to forever close the door. As long as the woman was single, he knew he could always slip back in. "You're talking about me again, aren't you?" she said. "I had young children when we were seeing each other. I didn't want them to walk in and see their mother having sex on the kitchen table." She stopped and cleared her throat. "It's not the right time for this kind of discussion, Brad. Who was the man Veronica was with?"

"I don't want to be distasteful. You said it wasn't the right time to talk about sex."

"Stop it, Brad," Carolyn said, giving him a

disgusted look. "I was referring to us, not Veronica."

"She was on top and the windows were fogged up. My guess is it was another probation officer. It could have been a onetime thing, although Veronica didn't look like she was riding this pony for the first time."

"Maybe it was Drew," Carolyn suggested. "He told me last night that they had trouble finding time to have sex because of the kids."

"Anything's possible. It just didn't strike me as the kind of thing a couple who'd been married as long as they had would do. Of course, I've never been married."

Carolyn fell silent as she thought. "I'll have to confront Drew. This is too important to overlook. If Veronica was having an affair, her lover might have killed her. Maybe that was who she was meeting at the motel."

"I don't know Drew that well," Brad told her, plucking a leaf off one of the shrubs. "He seems like an all-right guy. Before you ask him if he was banging his wife in the parking lot, check around first, see if anyone suspected Veronica was seeing someone on the side."

Carolyn wondered what else she didn't know about her friend. If Veronica had died of natural causes, she would have taken her secrets to the grave. Now her life would be scrutinized not only by the police, but by everyone who knew her. "You're right. It would be cruel to mention this to Drew, especially so soon. What are we going to do about the workload in the unit?"

"I spoke to Cameron Wheeler this morning," Brad told her, referring to the head of the agency. "He agreed to transfer in three officers from field services. Veronica's death has shaken up a lot of people, Carolyn. Wheeler wants you to work in conjunction with the PD until this is resolved. He talked to the chief over there, and they're putting together a task force. Hank Sawyer will run the show. You and he are big buddies, so I'm sure he'll be glad to have you." He stood and stretched his back. "You're still going to have to pinch-hit for us. I'm trying to narrow down these transfers to officers with prior experience in investigations, but right now I'll take anyone with a heartbeat."

"That means training," Carolyn said, feeling overwhelmed again.

"Oh, by the way," he said. "On the day we had the blackout, I was curious so I counted heads to see who was missing once the lights came back on. Everyone was accounted for except Veronica and Stuart Greenly. She came in first. He came in about five minutes later."

"But Stuart is married. I went to his wedding. His wife is a former model. They've only been married about a year. Not only that, he's in his late twenties. Why would he be interested in a woman almost old enough to be his mother?"

"He's a man," Brad said. "Nothing says you have to be in love with a woman to have sex with her. If Veronica was offering it, not many guys would turn her down. Want to grab a bite in the cafeteria?"

"Not after that speech," Carolyn said, narrowing her eyes at him. "I'm glad you reminded me of why we broke up. Whether you believe it or not, there are men out there who aren't interested in having sex with anyone they can get."

Brad stomped his foot, flashing his megawatt smile. "Damn, you're cute when you're mad." He placed his arm around her neck, pulling her to him. "Don't you feel better now?" he whispered in her ear. "Put that to work for you, and you'll catch your killer. All this stuff about a person being innocent until proven guilty is for the courts, not the street. Everyone is a suspect, even me."

Out of necessity, Carolyn abandoned her rule of not eating junk food and steered the

Infiniti through the drive-through at In and Out Burgers. She inhaled her cheeseburger before she hit the next traffic light, then began picking at her fries.

She'd been trying to reach Drew all morning, but the line had been busy. He'd either taken the phone off the hook, or he was making calls to relatives. She decided to stop by the house on the way to the police station. She hoped he'd told the children by now. A second later, she changed her mind about seeing him.

Brad might be an insensitive oaf on occasion, but his advice was usually sound. She needed to fuel herself on outrage, not grief and sadness. Veronica would want her death to be avenged, and outside of her husband, no one would care as much as Carolyn. Walking into a houseful of weeping children could put her back where she was yesterday. She dialed Drew again. This time he answered.

"KADY has a broadcast van in front of my house," he said, out of breath. "I caught one of their damn reporters with his nose against the boys' bedroom window. What do these people want from me? Veronica wasn't a celebrity."

Murder sells, Carolyn thought. "Everything will blow over in a few days, Drew. You can stay with me if you want. Either that, or check into a hotel."

"I'm on the phone," he said to one of the children. "I promise I'll come to your room in a minute." He picked up where he left off with Carolyn. "I can't stay in a hotel. I don't even know how I'm going to pay for Veronica's funeral."

Carolyn wondered if they had life insurance. Even if they did, the company might not settle the claim until the coroner made an official ruling as to the cause of death. "Have you heard from Jude yet?"

"No," he said. "Crystal is bringing her things over tonight. I'll go out and try to track her down again. She wasn't supposed to move in until next week."

"Where is this woman going to stay?"

"In Stacy and Jude's room," he told her. "I'll move Stacy's twin bed into the master. As far as I'm concerned, Jude doesn't live here anymore. Veronica and I had already decided to kick her out last week."

"Do you really want to do that right now?" Carolyn asked him, shocked that he would be so heartless. "She just lost her mother. Where will she live? How will she support herself?"

"That's her problem," Drew said. "Jude is resourceful, Carolyn. She'll probably move in with one of her friends, or shack up with one of the punks she hangs out with. I can't have that kind of element around my house."

"Did Jude go back to school?"

"Shit, no," he said. "We were going to send her to college, but she blew that. Why? What did you hear?"

"Rebecca saw her at Ventura High. She was under the impression Jude was enrolled in classes, that she was trying to get the credits she needed to acquire her diploma."

"I need to get off the phone," Drew told her. "The kids need me and I have to pick up the house before Crystal gets here. Things are bad enough without her thinking she's moving into a pigsty. If I hear from Jude, I'll let you know."

"Please," Carolyn said. "Have the police talked to you yet, Drew?"

"They were over here this morning. I'm afraid I wasn't much help to them. They don't think I killed her, I hope. They wanted to know where I was yesterday morning. I took the day off to do some things around the house. Veronica was after me to put up some shelves in the boys' room, so I went to Home Depot. I spent the rest of the day puttering around in the garage."

"Did you buy anything at Home Depot?"

"No," he said. "I just wanted to figure out

how much it would cost."

Carolyn said she'd speak to him later and disconnected. She got the number for Ventura High and waited while the cell operator connected her. A woman in the principal's office confirmed that Jude was enrolled as a student. She started to call Drew back and tell him, then decided to think it over first. If Jude was going to school, why hadn't she told her parents? Something didn't fit, and when something didn't fit, it could be important.

Carolyn thought she'd made a fairly good start on a crime of this magnitude. Drew couldn't prove where he was at the time of the crime, and Jude was trying to put her life together without telling her parents, even though they'd threatened to throw her out on the street.

She turned onto Dee Drive where the police department was located, parked, and reached into the backseat to get her computer notebook. She remembered what Brad had told her as she walked toward the front of the building. Everyone is a suspect.

Carolyn couldn't imagine anyone with that many children not carrying life insurance. How much did Drew have Veronica insured for? If she'd been having an affair, he could have found out and killed her.

Drew was now a suspect with two motives, and they were the oldest in existence — jealousy and money.

Chapter 7

Carolyn strode into the homicide bay at the Ventura Police Department. She said a few words to a detective named Gabriel Martinez, and then made her way to Hank Sawyer's office. He was on the phone. He covered the receiver with his hand. "Mary's in the conference room. I'll meet you there as soon as I'm free."

Carolyn found Mary Stevens with her head down, seated at the end of the long table, partially hidden behind stacks of papers and books.

When the detective looked up and saw her, she gathered up a bunch of photographs. "They're crime scene," she said, her brows furrowed. "You might not want to look at them."

"In case you haven't heard, I've been assigned to your task force," Carolyn told her.

"If I'm going to be involved in the case, I need to see everything."

"Good," Mary said, handing her the pictures. Behind her was a large bulletin board. "I was about to put them up. I guess you might as well desensitize yourself to them. We've got them on a CD, but we'll have to make you a copy." Her eyes went to the notebook Carolyn was carrying. "I can give you mine and you can load them onto your hard drive if you've got enough memory." She stopped speaking abruptly. "I don't know where my head is today. Of course you don't want them on your computer."

Mary glanced at a clean-cut young man sitting a few chairs to her left. "Oh, this is Keith Edwards. He's going to do a lot of the grunt work for us. Keith, Carolyn is a supervisor at the probation department. She was a close friend of the victim."

Edwards appeared to be in his mid to late twenties. He had sandy blond hair and greenish eyes, and was dressed in a starched white shirt, a striped tie, and a pair of tan slacks. He had the air of a new guy trying to make an impression. He circled to the other side of the table and pumped Carolyn's hand.

"Pleased to meet you," he said with a southern drawl. "I'm sorry about your friend. This must be hard for you."

"Keith is on loan from patrol," Mary explained. "He relocated here six months ago from Atlanta. Gary Conrad is also on the team, but he's out beating the bushes for leads. Gabriel Martinez will pitch in whenever he can."

Gary was a seasoned detective. Carolyn didn't know him that well, but she'd heard Hank and Mary talk about him. Gabriel was a good man as well.

"You can set up anywhere you want." Mary moved a stack of thick books aside. "These are mug shots. We've got the motel clerk coming in later today to see if he recognizes anyone."

"Did the lab have time to process the letter I got at the morgue?"

"I'm glad you brought it up," Mary told her. "We need to get the four morgue attendants to come in and look at mug shots." She shuffled through her paperwork, and then punched numbers into her cell phone. While she was waiting for the call to go through, she said, "Just so you know, I take care of things whenever I think about them. That's how I make certain I cover all the bases. My weakness is that I'm not good at delegating. If I do it myself, I know it's done. Hank mentioned it on my last performance review, so I'm trying to improve." She turned to her right. "Keith, call the lab and see if they've had time to process the envelope and letter yet."

Carolyn took a seat at the opposite end of the table, not wanting to be disturbed while she went through the crime scene photos. After she set them down on the table, she placed her hands in her lap and leaned forward. The first picture showed Veronica on her back in a bathtub, fully clothed. A large splatter of blood was visible on the back wall, the streaks heading downward. She must have been sitting partially upright when the killer shot her. Carolyn assumed the bullet had propelled her head backward, and then her lifeless body had slid down. Because of the tub's curved sides, her neck was twisted at an awkward angle. Her legs were open as if she were about to give birth. Seeing her like this was worse than seeing her body at the morgue.

Carolyn bit down on the inside of her lip, tasting her own salty blood. Whoever had done this to her sweet friend didn't deserve to live. If she found him, she would kill him, regardless of the consequences.

Her mind drifted into the past. She was seven years old, standing in the kitchen of her old house, peering into the oven at the

96

chocolate chip cookies she and her mother were making. The doorbell rang and her mother went to answer it, returning and telling her it was Veronica.

"Close your eyes," the girl said, giggling.

When Carolyn opened them, Veronica handed her a beautiful doll, dressed in a sparkly silver evening gown with a fake fur jacket. Earlier that afternoon, they had fought over the doll, and Veronica's mother had sent Carolyn home in tears. When Carolyn had taken it from the shelf in Veronica's room, she knew it was a special doll, the kind you weren't allowed to play with. Veronica's grandmother had sewn all the clothes by hand. She pushed the doll back toward Veronica. "I'm sorry I touched it."

"It's yours now, silly," her friend told her, refusing to take it. "Granny said I could give it to my most special friend in the world. We're going to be friends forever. That means I'll always be able to see it."

Carolyn surfaced from the past and forced herself to pick up another photo. Veronica wasn't wearing panty hose, so the crotch of her white cotton underwear was exposed. One shoe was still attached to her foot, the other resting on the floor by the tub. She noticed what appeared to be a tan-colored cloth lying on her chest near her neck. She wasn't certain if the crime scene officers had placed it there as a marker or the murderer used it during the crime. She sorted through the rest of the pictures, selected ten, and laid them out on the table as if she were playing a game of solitaire.

Something looked wrong.

Carolyn opened her notebook and powered it up, then returned her attention to the images. The tub was too clean and Veronica's clothes didn't appear to have any bloodstains on them. How was that possible? Mary saw her bending over the photos and sent a magnifying glass sliding across the slick surface of the table. "Thanks," she mumbled without looking up.

She recalled Veronica wearing an emerald-green blouse, but in the photographs it appeared darker. A moment later, she realized the blouse was wet. "The killer cleaned her up, didn't he?"

"Looks that way," Mary said, holding the phone against her ear. "I'm on hold with the morgue. After he shot her, he must have soaked her in the tub to get the blood off her body and clothes. Weird, huh? He didn't wash the blood off the wall behind her head, so why worry about the rest?"

"Does that mean anything?"

Mary held up a finger when the person

came back on the line.

Carolyn picked up another photograph. Veronica's body had been turned on its side, and her blouse pulled up. It looked as if there was some kind of rash on her back. The next image showed a similar rash on her buttocks and legs.

Mary concluded her phone call and addressed Carolyn's question. "Charley thinks he scrubbed her with Comet. The motel maids use Comet to clean the bathrooms. He probably stole it off one of their carts."

"Didn't someone hear the gunshot?"

"The volume on the TV was turned up full blast," Mary said, propping her head up with her fist. "As far as other guests went, most of them had either checked out or weren't in their rooms at the time of the shooting."

Hank burst in, taking a position at the front of the table. Behind him was a large viewing screen. The room was also equipped with teleconferencing capabilities. Cameras were mounted along the ceiling, and in the center of the table was a microphone shaped like a pyramid. "I was going to wait and address everyone after Conrad came back in, but I wanted to make certain Carolyn was here. Veronica may have committed suicide."

"What?" Carolyn said, bolting to her feet at the end of the table. "If this isn't a homicide, I don't know what is."

"We obviously thought the same thing," he said, "or we wouldn't have put together a task force. Veronica's gun was found in the Dumpster behind the motel. Ballistics just confirmed it's the murder weapon."

"You can't kill yourself and then go walking around," Carolyn said, raising her voice. "Who's the idiot who thinks it's a suicide?"

Mary was tapping her fingernails on the table. "I think you better explain, Hank."

"If you guys will stop interrupting me, I will," he snapped. "Maria Lopez, the maid at the motel, called and changed her story. I had to get Gabriel to interpret because she doesn't speak English. She's here illegally and was afraid she'd be deported. She touched the gun when she bent down to see if Veronica was still alive. Instead of wiping her prints off or just waiting until we got there, she panicked and took the gun out of the room, tossing it in the Dumpster with the rest of the day's trash." Hank paused to catch his breath. "Lopez was planning to leave town when her neighbor talked her into coming forward."

"Where was the gun before she picked it up?" Carolyn asked.

"On the floor next to the tub," the detective said. "Charley Young is one of the idiots who thinks there's a possibility it was a suicide." He paused, waiting for the officers to mill over what he'd told them. "We didn't find Veronica's prints on the gun. The prints we assumed were the killer's must be the maid's. She doesn't have a driver's license, so she's never been printed. Gabriel is on his way to Lopez's house to bring her in so we can confirm those were her prints."

"If Veronica shot herself," Carolyn argued, "why weren't her prints on the gun? You just said Lopez didn't wipe it down. It was Veronica's gun, so her prints had to be on it. They weren't there because the killer cleaned the gun."

Mary spoke up. "We found a washrag in the tub with the body, Carolyn. It was the brand and color the motel used, so I didn't think it had any significance. I thought it just fell in the tub from the towel rack when the killer shot her. Veronica could have wiped her own prints off, and then wrapped the washrag around the gun when she shot herself. She may not have wanted people to know that she took her own life, especially her children."

"Bullshit," Carolyn said, refusing to accept it. This was a sensitive issue for her. Her father had committed suicide, and during a trying time in her brother's life, he had also threatened to kill himself.

Her last conversation with Veronica had occurred only hours before her death. She'd criticized her recommendation in the Patricia Baxter case. Asking an officer of Veronica's stature to rewrite a report was like slapping her in the face. But Carolyn had let too many things slide already. Her friend's work had become sloppy, and many of her reports were filed late. Preston had called her on it, as it reflected on the entire unit.

Had Carolyn been the one to push her over the edge?

Veronica had also been vague about whether or not she was going to be her maid of honor. She was shattered enough by the woman's death without thinking she might somehow be responsible. Perhaps being involved in the investigation was more than she could handle. "How did Veronica get that rash on her back and legs?" she asked. "It looks like carpet burn. And the person who rented the room was a black male using a stolen credit card. How do you explain that?"

"Let's try to deal with one thing at a time," Hank said, taking a seat and placing his hands on the table. "Forensics found traces of Comet in the tub and on Veronica's clothing. We originally thought the killer scrubbed her with the stuff to make sure he got rid of all the evidence. Charley says there's a possibility that Veronica may have been allergic to some of the ingredients in the cleanser. All she had to do was sit in the tub and she would have experienced the same reaction. If the killer scrubbed her, there'd be a rash on the front of her body as well the back." He stopped and ran his finger underneath his nose. "The Motor Inn isn't exactly the Ritz. They still use actual keys. Veronica could have rented the room in the past with the intention of killing herself, then chickened out. She could have kept the key intentionally or by accident."

"So she drives by the place yesterday," Mary said, "notices the parking lot is empty, and uses the key to enter the room. I hate to admit it, but it makes sense."

Carolyn continued to pace.

Hank looked down at the table, then raised his eyes and focused on Carolyn. The Motor Inn was built thirty years ago. A credit card or a driver's license would have opened the door. Veronica's husband had her insured for a million dollars, Carolyn. In a suicide, her family would get nothing. If she was murdered, the double indemnity clause would kick in. Leaving two mil to your husband and kids might be worth staging your own death."

"Okay," Carolyn said, linking eyes with Hank, "tell me how she got the blood out of her clothes after she allegedly killed herself."

"She filled the tub with water," Hank speculated. "Or it might have been full from an earlier bath. She could have released the plug just before she pulled the trigger. As to the blood on her clothes, the forensic guys didn't want to spray them with Luminol until they tested for other chemicals. I'm sure the lab will find blood in the fibers of the material."

Mary slipped out of the room, returning with four cans of Coke. She gave one to Keith and Hank, then walked down and handed one to Carolyn. Sitting down on the edge of the table with her back to the men, she said in a hushed voice, "I'm sure you had a rough day yesterday. Why don't you go home and get some rest?"

Carolyn pressed the cold soda can to her forehead. "I won't be able to rest until I know what really happened. I appreciate your concern, though. I feel like I'm already getting on everyone's nerves."

"Not at all," Mary told her. "Hank went to the chief and demanded that you be part of the task force. He did it because you knew Veronica, you're an excellent investigator, and also so we could look out for your safety."

"Marcus hired bodyguards for Rebecca and John," Carolyn said, setting the Coke down and wrapping her arms around her chest. "I'm not sure if we need them now. Veronica may have dropped the note off at the morgue herself, and no one noticed it until later. I couldn't figure out how a stranger would know so much about me. Suicides sometimes do things like that to make it harder to back out."

Once they returned to their seats, Carolyn told them what she'd learned about Jude, and requested they broadcast an attempt to locate her. They'd hit a dead end on Phillip Bramson. Gary Conrad had spoken to one of the men at the car wash where he'd been employed. He told him Bramson had mentioned leaving the state several weeks back. He'd sold his car, so the vehicle information they had was no longer valid.

Carolyn had intended to track down Tyler Bell, but she hadn't had time. Now that there was a possibility Veronica had committed suicide, contacting him didn't seem as urgent. If Bell had committed three murders in Ventura, two of which he'd gotten away with, she doubted he would flee the area. She would privately follow up on the things

Brad had told her regarding Stuart Greenly. There was no reason to tarnish Veronica's reputation unless the new information had some bearing on the case.

At four o'clock, Carolyn carried her computer notebook to Mary's office and printed off a list of the men and women Veronica had investigated or supervised during the past four years. She distributed them to the people in the conference room, leaving an extra set for Gary Conrad. "These are the offenders who aren't presently in custody in Ventura," she told them. "I should be able to provide you with more detailed information by tomorrow. You might want to have someone run the names through the national system and see if they're in jail in another jurisdiction. I'd like to stay longer," she added, "but I need to go back to my office and start reassigning Veronica's caseload."

Hank followed her outside in the hall. "This is a homicide until we establish definitive proof she committed suicide."

The stress of the past two days was taking its toll. Carolyn's eyes were swollen from crying, and her neck and back muscles were aching. "That may never happen," she told him. "You know what's the worst thing about this? If I hadn't had my head up my ass, I might have stopped her."

Hank scowled.

"You can't blame yourself. What about her husband? He lived with her. He told us everything was fine." He waited as a uniformed officer walked past. "I didn't mention it before, but we found a bottle of pills in her purse. She was taking an antidepressant called Lexapro." He stopped and pulled out a toothpick, shoving it between his teeth. "Something about Drew Campbell rubbed me the wrong way. It was almost as if he'd been expecting something like this to happen. He even hired a nanny the day his wife died. Did Veronica say anything about them hiring someone?"

"No," Carolyn said. "If she was taking medication, though, it might not have been safe for her to look after the children. It's understandable that Drew wouldn't want anyone to know. Some people see depression as a weakness. Maybe he felt bad that he couldn't make his wife happy."

"Have you seen the broad he hired?"

"You mean the nanny?"

"Yeah," Hank said, resting his back against the wall. "She came by to pick up a key to the house this morning while we were there. She looked about sixteen, but Drew said she was eighteen. He says she has seven brothers and sisters. Her family lives a block over, so why does she have to live in his house? It doesn't look right for a guy to move in a young girl a day after his wife's death. What do you think?"

"I agree." Carolyn wondered if something was going on between Drew and the girl. She wouldn't be surprised if he'd been having an affair, but not with a girl the same age as his daughter. From what Brad had told her, Veronica played around as well. "Should I say something to him?"

"Not now," Hank said. "Let's just sit back and keep our eye on this guy. Maybe we're wrong and Veronica was murdered. The hubby may turn out to be our killer. We have some great cards on this hand, so we might as well play them."

"You've lost me."

"Your friendship with the deceased gives you an open door. And you're a master at working people and getting them to tell you things they had no intention of saying. Did Veronica have family?"

"Her parents are dead," Carolyn told him. "Emily, her kid sister, is an attorney in San Francisco. Veronica didn't get along with her. I know her, of course. She's a control freak. Whenever she came to town, she stayed in a hotel because the kids drove her crazy."

"What about Drew?"

"He's an only child. His mother died last year. His father died from congenital heart disease when Drew was a kid."

"Have you seen Veronica's will?"

Carolyn shut her eyes and then opened them. "I know where you're going with this, Hank. I didn't see it, but I know what's in it. If something happened to Veronica and Drew, I was supposed to be appointed guardian of the children. I did the same thing with her. She probably changed it. If your suicide scenario turns out to be accurate, Veronica hated me."

"Why do you say that?"

"Think about it, Hank," Carolyn said. "If you cared about someone, would you send a letter threatening them and their family?" Reading the answer in his eyes, she said, "I didn't think so. Call me if you need me."

CHAPTER 8

When Carolyn walked into her office, she found Brad Preston sitting at her desk. "I'm trying to parcel out Veronica's cases," he said. "We got slammed again today. I'm sorry, Carolyn, but we can't let you take vacation leave right now. I even went to Wheeler to see if there was some way we could cover it. I told him it was your honeymoon, but he said you'd have to cancel it. Wheeler wants you to continue working with the task force, so that means we're short two people."

Carolyn stared at her in-box. The files were stacked so high, there was a second stack beside it. Brad started to get up. "Stay there," she told him, dropping down in a chair in front of her desk. "There may not be a task force." She explained what had transpired at the police department, that the coroner might rule that Veronica's death had been a suicide. "Do you know if Stuart Greenly is around?"

"Yeah," Brad said. "I saw him maybe five minutes ago. Are you going to talk to him?"

"Yes," Carolyn said, pushing herself to her feet.

"Wait," he said, loosening the knot on his tie. "Don't mention my name. I don't want him to walk out on us. We can't afford to lose another investigator. And don't you want to talk to him here?"

"No," she said. "If I call him into my office, it will seem too official. I thought he might be a suspect, but now I don't know what to believe. If he was having an affair with Veronica, he may know more about her state of mind than anyone else."

The majority of the probation officers had already left for the day. With the new work-at-home program, even during peak hours desks sat empty. Carolyn entered Stuart Greenly's cubical. He was talking on the phone and laughing. If he'd been Veronica's lover, her death didn't appear to have upset him. His dark hair was fashionably cut. He dressed like a college professor. Today he was wearing brown slacks and a Brooks Brothers shirt with a button-down collar. An expensive-looking sport jacket was draped over the back of his chair.

Carolyn had heard that Greenly had a large trust fund, and had taken a job as a probation officer after he'd flunked the bar exam six times. Working beneath his abilities must bolster his confidence. He occasionally came across as arrogant, but the probation officers in the unit seemed to like him. She waited until he completed his call, then cleared her throat to get his attention.

"Carolyn," he said, falling serious. "This thing with Veronica is awful. People are calling me, telling me the job is too dangerous. You two were good friends, so I —"

She cut him off. "Why don't we go somewhere private where we can talk, Stuart?"

"This is pretty damn private," he told her. "I'm probably the only one still working. Remember that on my next performance review, will you? Preston was tough, but you're downright brutal."

"Was that a personal call you were on when I came in?"

"Hey," he said, smiling, "you got me. One of my friends wanted to buy me dinner, but I passed. Only someone really dedicated would turn down a free meal, especially with the kind of money the county pays us."

"We'll talk in an interview room," Carolyn told him. "I don't think you'd even want the janitors to eavesdrop on this conversation."

"Wow," he exclaimed, "you certainly know how to get a guy's attention."

On the right side of the floor was a row of rooms. Probation officers used them to interview defendants and victims, dictate reports to the word-processing pool, or as a place to retreat when the noise level inside the unit became too distracting.

They entered the room nearest Greenly's office. Carolyn closed the door behind her. Greenly took a seat at a small table. She remained standing.

"What's going on?" Greenly asked, rubbing his chin.

"Were you having an affair with Veronica?"

"No," he said. "Why would you think such a thing? Tessa and I have a great marriage. You even came to our wedding. Besides, Veronica is . . . was . . . well, she was older. I don't want to say anything out of line here, but she was also a little whacko. Did she tell you something was going on between us? She must have been infatuated with me. Now that I think about it, she did act odd when I was around."

In most instances, Carolyn would soften her subjects with small talk, waiting for them to relax before she began interrogating them. Today, she didn't have the energy. "Don't lie to me, Stuart," she said. "We know you were sleeping with her. Would you rather be questioned by the police, or do you want to tell me the truth?"

He stood and shoved his chair back to the table. "I don't have to put up with this kind of crap," he shouted. "You're out of your mind if you think I had anything to do with Veronica's death. Why would I want to have sex with a fat cow like her? Tessa was on the cover of dozens of magazines. Even if she wasn't gorgeous, I love her and have no reason to cheat on her."

Except that you're a man, Carolyn thought, remembering what Brad had told her. "Someone saw you, Stuart. They saw you having sex with Veronica in the backseat of her Ford Explorer. It was the day the power went off in the building."

"Who saw me? Whoever it was, they were mistaken. The day of the storm, I went home to check on Tessa. We live close and she's terrified of lightning. If you don't believe me, you can ask her." He stared Carolyn straight in the eye without blinking. "Can I get back to work now? I'd like to get out of this hell-hole before midnight. Preston assigned me ten new cases today. Four of them were Veronica's. The filing deadline is the end of next week, and as far as I can tell, she hasn't even looked at them." He paused and then continued ranting, "I told Preston I'd work around the clock to get them done. I go out of my way to be helpful and this is the way I get treated. I don't need this lousy job. If you want, I'll turn in my resignation right now."

"No, please," Carolyn said, backtracking. "I apologize. I shouldn't have come down so hard on you. If you were involved with Veronica, I was hoping you could shed some light into what was going on with her. You said she was whacko. What are you referring to?"

"I'm not sure," he said, relaxing. "She seemed out of it recently. She asked me questions about things she should have known. Shit, Veronica was my training offi- cer. I never thought she would be asking me how to compute a sentence. Then one day last week, I was leaving to interview a guy at the jail, and Veronica told me to forget it, that I could make up his statement and no one would know the difference. At first, I thought she was joking, but then I realized she was serious."

God, Carolyn thought, it was worse than she thought. "Thanks, Stuart," she said, stepping aside so he could leave. "Do me a favor. If you think of anyone who might have been involved with her, please let me know."

"No problem," he said. "I shouldn't have called her a fat cow. I was annoyed, okay? I don't like to be accused of something I didn't do. The truth is, I liked Veronica. She was a nice person. Do the police have any leads as to who killed her?"

"A few," she said. "I'll keep you posted."

Once Greenly left, Carolyn closed the door and sat down at the table, staring at the white-painted wall in front of her. Veronica's mental state must have been steadily deteriorating. Carolyn had been so caught up in her new position and her upcoming wedding, she'd failed to see that her friend was in trouble.

Veronica's image materialized again, standing on her front porch with her most prized possession, the beautiful doll her grandmother had given her. She remembered the fresh scent of her shampoo, her toothy grin, the blue shorts outfit she'd been wearing. It was strange, she thought. It wasn't Veronica as an adult who was haunting her. It was the child. Maybe there was some meaning there, hidden deep in her subconscious. That day so long ago, she had touched something forbidden. Whenever she and Veronica had a fight, they'd both cry and make their parents miserable until they made up. Even as a child, Veronica had been a better person. She was always the first one to say she was sorry.

Carolyn returned to her office and called Marcus, telling him she wouldn't be home in time for dinner. He told her not to worry about it, as Rebecca had ordered in a pizza, and he was trying to catch up with some work from the office. "I love you," she told him, experiencing a rush of emotion.

"Not as much as I love you," Marcus said. "Do whatever you have to do, honey. I gave it some thought today. You're right about postponing the wedding. I had my secretary start calling people."

"What about our honeymoon? You said we were going to lose money if we canceled it. Brad told me they can't get by without me because of what happened to Veronica. He even took it to Cameron Wheeler, the head of the agency. Wheeler wants me to work on the task force investigating Veronica's death."

"I bought trip insurance," Marcus said. "I was just trying to make certain you wanted to call off the wedding. After a tragedy like this, I didn't think you should make any rash decisions. Everything will be fine. Remember to eat, and I'm not talking about candy bars. I know you're a chocolate junkie."

"You're beginning to sound like my mother," Carolyn joked. He'd already figured out most of her idiosyncrasies. When they went out to dinner, and someone mentioned having a dessert, she would push her food around on the plate until the waiter took it away, saving her appetite. "I'm a hopeless case. Mother gave up on me years ago."

"I don't give up," Marcus said. "You might as well get used to it."

When Carolyn hung up, she felt an infusion of energy and strength. Simply hearing his voice helped chase away the demons. She placed her computer notebook and a stack of case files inside her briefcase, locked up the office, and headed to her car in the parking lot.

As the chilly night air engulfed her, her thoughts returned to Veronica. She and Drew had been high school sweethearts. Like all couples, they'd had their share of problems over the years, but there was never any doubt that they loved each other. And even if Jude was difficult, Stacy, Peter, and Michael loved and depended on their mother. How could a person kill herself when she was surrounded by love? Mental illness maybe, but Veronica hadn't been that far gone. She might have been overwhelmed enough to take shortcuts in her work, yet there was no indication that she'd been paranoid or delusional.

Carolyn experienced an eerie sensation. She stared up at the windows of the jail. Ever since they'd built the complex, she'd hated it. Housing inmates in such close proximity to the people who prosecuted and punished them was a recipe for disaster. She saw the outline of the prisoners' bodies. Depending on where she parked, they could make out what kind of car she was driving, and during the day, even read the license plate.

Because she'd returned from the PD when the courts were in session, the only available parking spot was in a back corner of the lot, next to a row of tall palm trees. She heard a sound behind her, but when she turned around she didn't see anything. A strong wind had kicked in, whipping her hair into her face. What she'd heard had to be blowing leaves and other debris.

Carolyn could barely see her car it was so dark. She caught a glimpse of her red Infiniti and started walking toward it when a hard pointed object jabbed her in the back. At first she thought it was a branch that had fallen off one of the trees. A second later, she realized it was the barrel of a gun.

A deep voice said, "Don't move or turn around."

She ran a few feet, then got tangled up in

her feet and fell. What appeared to be a man's shoe came down on the right side of her face.

Carolyn's hands were free, but she couldn't move her head. All she could see was the man's shadow on the pavement, but she could tell the majority of his weight was on his left leg. If she could hit him hard enough at the back of his knee, he would topple and she might be able to escape.

As she began to raise her arm, he stomped on it. "Help!" she screamed now that he'd moved his foot off her face. "Police! Call the —"

"Shut the fuck up!"

Carolyn's purse was no longer on her arm. She had no idea how far away it had landed. She patted the ground with her hand, desperate to find her gun.

"I told you not to move, bitch!"

There was something distinctive about his voice. Did she know him? Was it an accent? It sounded muffled, as if he was speaking through a handkerchief or scarf. Then again, there was something about his voice that seemed mechanical, like an automated voice or someone talking to you over a speakerphone.

"I warned you to stay out of this. Now I have to kill you."

The noise from the gunshot was deafening.

Carolyn waited for the bullet to sear its way into her flesh. Nothing happened.

"Where'd he go?" a voice called out from a distance.

Feet slapped against the pavement. The sounds got louder, then stopped. Brad's face loomed over her. He knelt down on one knee, gasping as he tried to catch his breath. "Are you hurt?"

"I'm not sure," Carolyn said, the panic returning. What if the bullet had severed her spine? That could be why she didn't feel anything. "Did he shoot me?"

"We have to get out of here," Brad said, yanking her to her feet. "He may still be around. Stay down."

They bent over at the waist and weaved in and out between the cars until they came to Brad's black Viper. Except for the custom paint on the exterior, the car looked as if it had been driven off the showroom floor. Brad had modified it for the racetrack, however, but occasionally drove it to work. Fixing cars up and selling them was one of the ways he supplemented his income. He hit the button on the key fob and unlocked the doors, then shoved Carolyn inside. As soon as he fired up the big engine, he tossed his cell phone to her.

"Call 911. The suspect didn't return my fire, but that doesn't mean he isn't armed. Tell them to have two or three units roll code. They can find the spot if they look for your red Infiniti."

Carolyn made the call, then disconnected. "My purse. I have to go back for my purse. He can find my address, and my gun is in there."

"Only an idiot would stop to pick up your purse." Brad stomped on the accelerator and sped out of the parking lot. He raced down a side street, then took a sharp right into an alley. "Call the PD back and have someone meet us over here. If Mary Stevens or Hank is on duty, get one or both of them to respond. Whoever attacked you must be the bastard who killed Veronica."

Carolyn's face and arm were throbbing. The strange feeling she'd experienced after she'd heard the gunshot must have been numbness. Either that or raw fear. She looked around, but she hadn't been paying attention. She didn't have time to put on her seat belt, and she'd been jostled around inside Brad's speeding car. "Where are we?"

"We're in the alley behind S. Hill Road." He stopped the car and turned off the ignition. "The house numbers are on the trash cans. Shit, I can't read them. Wait, I've got it.

It looks like 954. Tell them I'm driving a black Viper with a yellow racing stripe. They can't miss it." Once she completed the second call, he asked her, "Did you get a good look at the guy?"

"Not with his shoe in my face," Carolyn told him, messaging her arm. "Promise me you won't say anything to Marcus. He was pressuring me to quit my job even before Veronica was murdered."

"Now you know why I'm single," Brad said. "Tell him he can't have you all to himself. We need you. You better make sure you know what you're getting into, Carolyn. This guy sounds selfish."

"Because he doesn't want me to get hurt?" she argued. "That's ridiculous. Marcus is one of the most generous men I've ever known."

"Hey, just remember I warned you. Rich men have a tendency to be demanding. You've been on your own for a long time. I can't picture you kissing up to any guy. Well, me maybe, but I'm not in the running."

"God, am I going to have a bruise on my face?" She reached for the visor, thinking it had a mirror, then remembered that the Viper wasn't a luxury car.

"Let me take a look at you." He turned on the interior light, then placed his finger under her chin.

They were so close, Carolyn could feel his warm breath on her face. At one time, they had loved each other. He linked eyes with her, cleared his throat, and then turned away. "You're going to feel like a train wreck tomorrow, but you'll be fine. If there's a bruise, you can cover it with makeup."

"You saved my life."

"Don't humor me," Brad told her. "As a marksman, I suck. I don't think I could have hit the guy if he'd been standing a foot away wearing a neon target. I got terrible news from the doctor the other day."

"My God, are you sick? Why didn't you tell me?"

"I didn't want anyone to know."

Carolyn put her hand on his shoulder. "Please, Brad, I'm your friend. You don't have some kind of disease, God forbid."

"I need glasses."

Carolyn knew him well enough to know he wasn't joking. "Do you realize how incredibly vain you sound? You're forty years old. Since you don't seem to realize it, youth doesn't last a lifetime. A few years down the line, and you'll need a lot more than glasses."

His eyes expanded. "Not Viagra."

Carolyn laughed. "You guys finally have

something to be embarrassed about now. Women have been trying to be something we aren't for years. We've worn push-up bras, false eyelashes, fake hair, and that was before women closed out their Christmas accounts and spent the money on plastic surgery. Why won't you need Viagra, Brad? I want to hear this one."

"I just won't," he said, a stubborn look on his face. "You've slept with me. Do you think a guy like me would ever need Viagra? I'm a machine, man. I'll never lose it. My dad's still going strong and he's almost eighty. Men in my family don't have those kinds of problems."

"Someone just tried to kill me, and you're worried about glasses and Viagra. Give me a break, Brad."

They saw the headlights of a vehicle. "Call the PD and see if that's them behind us," he said. "We're a sitting duck if it's the guy who jumped you."

Before Carolyn could punch in the numbers, Hank Sawyer pulled up alongside them in his unmarked unit, speaking to them through the open window. Even now that he'd slimmed down, he still sat in the car the way a heavy man would, spread out and slouched. After they told him what had transpired, she said, "His voice sounded strange, Hank."

"In what way?"

"At first I thought I knew him. Now I'm not sure. His voice was muffled, as if he were trying to disguise it. I thought I heard some kind of accent."

"From where?"

"I don't know," she said, feeling foolish that she couldn't remember more. "I was scared, okay? You start counting seconds when someone says they're going to kill you."

Brad leaned over in front of her. "He booked as soon as I squeezed off a round. I don't think the guy had a gun, or he would have returned my fire. He may have poked her with his finger or a stick. If he hadn't mentioned the letter, I would have pegged him as a purse snatcher."

Carolyn thought for a moment. "He didn't actually mention the letter. He said, 'I warned you to stay out of this. Now I have to kill you.' "

"That's close enough," Hank said. "It doesn't mean he's our killer, though, just the guy who sent you the letter." He tossed a large black object through the open window. "One of the patrol units found your purse under a pickup in the parking lot. When are you going to start wearing your shoulder what I'm thinking?"

"I don't know," Carolyn said. "I'm assuming it was a boyfriend. Drew said she hangs out with some unsavory characters. We're seeing more of these cases every day. You know, girls Jude's age or younger who become involved in abusive relationships. Because she refused to incriminate him makes me think that's what's going on here."

"Don't you think it's a little strange that Jude shows up like this on the same day her father decides to throw her out of the house?" Mary asked. "The doctor said a lot of her injuries weren't recent. Because of Veronica's death, Drew knew people would be looking into every aspect of his life. If we found out he beat his daughter, we might think he killed his wife."

Mary had been at home when Carolyn called her. Since she hadn't said anything, she assumed she didn't know about the incident in the parking lot. Drew hadn't been home, which made her wonder if he could have been the one who attacked her. But Stacy was with him. It was hard to believe Drew would bring his daughter along. He knew Carolyn carried a gun. If she'd been able to get to it and had started firing, Stacy could have been killed.

"First, we find the mother dead in a cheap

holster? Carrying your gun in your purse is worthless. You might as well not have one."

"I'm a supervisor now," Carolyn told him. "Unless someone goes on a shooting rampage in the office, I have no reason to protect myself."

"Oh, I see," Hank said, pissed. "Like you didn't need a gun tonight. You could have shot him, Carolyn, and saved us from having to track him down. If you don't start looking out for yourself, you'll end up at the morgue with your friend."

Carolyn put her hands over her ears. "Enough, for God's sake!"

"Lay off, Hank," Brad said. "She's exhausted and emotional. I wouldn't even have had my gun on me if I wasn't taking it home to clean it."

Hank told Carolyn to file a report with the patrol officer at the scene, then took off.

"He's upset because he doesn't want anything to happen to you," Brad said as he drove her back to the parking lot.

When he stopped alongside the patrol unit, she leaned over and kissed him on the cheek. "Thanks for being there, Brad."

"No problem."

"By the way, why were you there?"

Brad laughed. "I forgot where I parked my car. Are you going straight home when you finish here?"

"Not yet," Carolyn said. "Hank wants me to sniff out Drew, try to find out if he's involved. I'm going to swing by the house, check out this young nanny he hired, and see if there's any news regarding Jude."

Brad shook his head in frustration. "You know why you're always in trouble? Because you go looking for it. For all we know, Drew may be the one who attacked you tonight. Now you're going to show up on his doorstep. How convenient. Jesus, Carolyn, go home. You can stop by Veronica's tomorrow. I've never seen a woman push herself the way you do. Don't you ever get any enjoyment out of life?"

"Whenever I can," she said. "You risk your life all the time on the racetrack. At least I don't do it for thrills."

"If Drew kills you, don't call me. I'm going out for drinks with my friends. I'd ask you to come along, but martyrs aren't that popular." He held up his cell phone. "I'm turning it off, see? You're on your own."

Carolyn chuckled. "How could I call you if I was dead?"

"You know what I meant. I saved your scrawny neck, and you're making fun of me. If the guy had a gun, he could have shot me."

"You'll never grow up, Brad."

"Whatever," he said, burning rubber as he roared off across the parking lot.

A young patrol officer stepped up beside Carolyn. "I should cite that guy for speeding. He can't drive like that on the street, let alone a parking lot."

"Don't waste your time."

"Why? Because he's your boss?"

"Because you'll never catch him."

"I've been in a pursuit with a Viper before," he said. "They're not that fast."

Carolyn smiled. "You don't know what's under the hood of this one."

Carolyn rang the doorbell for five minutes before someone finally answered. A young girl with long blond hair that covered the right side of her face peered out at her. She looked more like a child than an eighteen-year-old. "I'm a friend of the family," Carolyn said. "You must be Crystal?"

"Drew isn't here," the girl said in a monotone. "He went to the grocery store. You'll have to come back later." She thought a moment, then added, "You should maybe call him. He told me he didn't want to see anyone right now."

"I'll wait," Carolyn said, stepping past her into the living room. Crystal was either learning impaired, or there was something else wrong with her. She didn't make eye contact, and continued standing in the door-way after Carolyn was inside. When she dropped her arms to her side, her hands disappeared inside the sleeves of her sweatshirt.

The living room looked worse than it had the night before. Beer cans were still scattered across the coffee table, toys thrown everywhere, and there was a large purple stain on the carpet. Michael came running into the room crying. He attached himself to Carolyn's leg. "My mommy went to heaven, and Daddy says Jude can't live here anymore. Daddy got mad at me 'cause I spilled my grape juice."

Carolyn scooped the four-year-old up in her arms. "It's okay, sweetie. Don't cry." She turned around to look for Crystal. The girl was walking in the direction of the kitchen when she tripped on a toy fire engine. Instead of picking it up, she righted herself and continued walking. Some nanny, she thought. She looked as if she needed someone to look after her instead of the other way around. What in God's name had Drew been thinking? "Is Jude here, Michael?"

"Yes," he said, sniffling.

Carolyn sat down on the sofa and stroked Michael's back until he climbed off her lap and went to play with a toy. The situation was tragic, but children were remarkably resilient. She saw a shadowy figure in the hallway. When she went over to see who it was, she realized it was Peter. He also looked as if he'd been crying. His chin was tucked against his chest. "Is Jude in her room?" she asked him.

Peter shrugged, refusing to answer. Carolyn continued down the hallway. She would have to talk to Drew about getting the kids into counseling right away.

Other than the room the boys shared, the doors were all shut. She opened the door to Jude's room, then realized it was the bathroom. Veronica's daughter was stepping out of the shower.

"Get the hell out of here!"

Carolyn gasped. Jude's body was covered with purplish bruises. She grabbed a towel and covered herself.

"I'll be out in a few minutes," she said. "I thought you were one of the kids. If you can't wait, use the bathroom in my dad's room."

Carolyn closed the door and locked it behind her. She reached over and pulled the towel away, trying to see how badly the girl was injured. "Who did this to you?"

"I fell, okay?" Jude told her, snatching the towel back. "Can I have some privacy, please? I don't walk into your bathroom and stare at you when you're naked. Are you a lesbian or something?"

"Please, honey, you need medical treatment. If you won't tell me who did this to you, at least let me help you."

"No one can help me," Jude said, stepping into a pair of jeans and a black long sleeved T-shirt. "I have to be out of the house by the time my father gets back. Now will you leave me alone?"

"Where are you going to live?" Carolyn asked.

"On the street, I guess. What difference does it make? My mother's dead. No one cares what I do, as long as I don't do it here."

"Stay with me," Carolyn offered. "Please, Jude, I have more than enough room. I was at the hospital when you were born. Rebecca would be thrilled if you stayed with us. We're living at my fiancé's house in Santa Rosa and her friends are all in Ventura. Whatever your problems are, I'm certain we can work things out."

Jude ran her tongue over her lips. "You got any cash on you?"

"I can't just give you money," Carolyn told her. "If you don't come with me, I'll have to notify the authorities."

"I'm an adult. I haven't broken the law.

Why don't you leave while you can? You don't know anything about me. I'm a freaking loser. If you don't believe me, ask my father."

Carolyn pulled the girl into her arms. "You're not a loser, sweetheart. I don't know why your father is doing this, but I'm not leaving until you agree to come with me."

Jude placed her hands on Carolyn's shoulders, shaking as she sobbed. "I just want to die. I can't take it anymore. He'll find me wherever I go. I was sure he was going to kill me. I didn't care. I wanted him to kill me."

"Who?" Carolyn pleaded. "You have to tell me who hurt you. Was it your boyfriend? If you give me his name, I'll have him arrested."

"I can't," the girl said. "You don't understand. He'll get out. Then he'll come after you, too." She shoved Carolyn in the chest. "Go away. I shouldn't have said anything."

Jude pushed past her, running down the hall to her room. Carolyn went to the front of the house and tried to reassure the other children. Someone was missing. She was so distraught, she couldn't remember who. "Stacy," she said, grabbing Peter by the shoulders. "Where is she?"

"She went with my dad," the boy told her. "Where's Jude going? She's not going to heaven like my mom, is she?"

"No, honey," Carolyn said, knowing she had to do something about the younger children immediately. She couldn't remove them from the home without a court order. "I'm leaving now," she told Peter. "Your father will be back really soon. Help Michael get ready for bed. I promise I'll check on you in the morning."

Carolyn left, waiting by her car until Jude came out the front door. Carrying a plastic garbage bag filled with her things, she took off down the street. Carolyn ran after her and tackled her, both of them tumbling into the damp grass. Twice in one night, she'd had to wrestle with someone. Brad had been right. She should have gone home.

Rolling Jude over onto her back, she snapped on a pair of handcuffs. This was not the way to cuff a prisoner, but she didn't want to cause Jude anymore discomfort than necessary. "I'm sorry," she said, leading her to the Infiniti and opening the passenger door. "I'll take them off as soon as you calm down."

"Bitch," Jude snarled. "You have no right to do this to me. I could sue you for false arrest. I haven't done anything wrong."

Carolyn reached over and fastened the girl's seat belt, then hit the automatic door locks in case she tried to jump out of the car. Jude stared sullenly out the window while they drove.

"You're wrong, Jude," Carolyn told her, pulling into the parking lot of Community Memorial Hospital ten minutes later. "Under section 5150 of the Welfare and Institutions Code, you can be held for seventy-two hours if I believe you're a danger to yourself or others. Right now, I'd say you're a danger to yourself."

"Fuck," the girl said, "you're going to have me locked up in a mental hospital? I thought you were my friend."

"I am," Carolyn told her. "And I promise nothing like that will happen if you cooperate. I want a doctor to look at you. As soon as they check you out, I'll take you to my house. No one has to know where you are, understand? And I guarantee you no one will hurt you. Because of his work, my fiancé has bodyguards. They're watching his house right now. You can stay in our guest room." She paused and then added, "Do we have a deal?"

Jude held her hands out in front of her. "Take these damn things off. They're hurting my wrists."

"I'm not going to do that," Carolyn said. "Not until you give me your word that you'll stay with me. If you won't do it for me, do it for your mother."

"Fine," Jude said, tears pooling in her eyes. "I'll stay with you. Now you have to give me your word. Promise you won't tell my father where I am."

"I promise," Carolyn told her, unlocking the handcuffs.

CHAPTER 9

Thursday, October 14 — 12:05 A.M.

Carolyn had dozed off in the ER waiting room. Mary Stevens tapped her on the shoulder. "I talked the doctor into letting you take Jude home, but they'd prefer to keep her for a few days and run some tests."

"She won't stay," Carolyn said, sitting up in her seat. "She'll walk and then we might not be able to find her. Did they run a drug screen?"

"She's clean, but that doesn't mean she doesn't use. Some drugs pass through the system fairly quick." Mary asked her if she wanted some coffee. When Carolyn declined, she headed to the vending machine, returning and staring at the contents of the paper cup. "This is the worst shit I've ever tasted. I'm not certain it's even coffee. It looks like a cup of mud." She tossed it into the trash can. "So much for that. Okay, the doc says Jude needs complete bed rest for at least three days. You'll have to take her to a private physician for a follow-up. The X-rays didn't show any broken bones. Her ribs are badly bruised, though, and she appears to' have taken a few blows to her kidneys and lower abdomen. There's some internal hemorrhaging, but not enough to require a transfusion. If she becomes lethargic and gets really pale, I'd suggest you call an ambulance."

Carolyn rubbed her eyes, smudging her mascara. "Did you get pictures of the bruises?"

"Yeah," Mary said, massaging her shoulder. "She put up one hell of a fight, though. There's no signs of a recent sexual assault, but the doctor found evidence of at least two abortions. The ob-gyn, Dr. Alexander, couldn't finish the exam. She's going to have one hell of a shiner tomorrow morning. Jude kicked her in the face. I think the only reason they agreed to release her is they don't want to deal with her. If they admit her, she'll be placed in the psych ward."

Veronica had mentioned Jude undergoing only one abortion. Of course, Carolyn thought, this wasn't something you discussed openly, even with your closest friends. "Did she tell you who beat her?"

"Nope," Mary said. "Are you thinking

what I'm thinking?"

"I don't know," Carolyn said. "I'm assuming it was a boyfriend. Drew said she hangs out with some unsavory characters. We're seeing more of these cases every day. You know, girls Jude's age or younger who become involved in abusive relationships. Because she refused to incriminate him makes me think that's what's going on here."

"Don't you think it's a little strange that Jude shows up like this on the same day her father decides to throw her out of the house?" Mary asked. "The doctor said a lot of her injuries weren't recent. Because of Veronica's death, Drew knew people would be looking into every aspect of his life. If we found out he beat his daughter, we might think he killed his wife."

Mary had been at home when Carolyn called her. Since she hadn't said anything, she assumed she didn't know about the incident in the parking lot. Drew hadn't been home, which made her wonder if he could have been the one who attacked her. But Stacy was with him. It was hard to believe Drew would bring his daughter along. He knew Carolyn carried a gun. If she'd been able to get to it and had started firing, Stacy could have been killed.

"First, we find the mother dead in a cheap

motel," Mary said, sitting down next to Carolyn and stretching her long legs out in front of her. "Now we've got her obnoxious, abused daughter on our hands. I know Veronica was your friend, but this family needs its own police department. This is a nightmare."

"More than you know."

"Jude had a cell phone in her purse that came up stolen. I called the owner, a girl named Sally Owens. She says it disappeared while she was at school the other day, so Jude may have found it and intended to give it back the next time she saw her. Of course, it wouldn't surprise me if she stole it. Sally's not close with Jude, but she failed to graduate last year, so she's in some of the same classes. Sally has a better excuse. She has leukemia. Right now, it's in remission."

"Did you ask her if Jude had a boyfriend?"

"Slow down, will you?" Mary said. "I'll tell you everything if you'll stop talking and listen."

"You were the one doing all the talking," Carolyn said, opening her purse and pulling out her compact to check her face. Right now, it was just red and a little swollen. She dusted it with face powder. Then she opened and shut her hand several times, trying to make the muscles loosen so the pain would

go away. She was so tired, she had trouble focusing her eyes.

"If you'll stop rubbing your eyes, you won't have a problem."

"Please, Mary," Carolyn said, fed up with people telling her what to do. "If I want to rub my eyes, I'll rub my eyes."

"Knock yourself out," Mary tossed back. "The next time you have something hanging out of your nose, I won't tell you."

"Just tell me about the boyfriend."

"Bitch," Mary shot back.

Both women glared at each other, then burst out laughing. "Okay," the detective said, "now that I've chipped away some of that doomsday dust you carry around with you, Sally claims Jude was infatuated with a guy named Reggie Stockton. Stockton graduated last year. He was dating another girl who dropped out of school. Jude used to tell everyone he was her boyfriend, which wasn't true, according to Sally. If this other girl is no longer in the picture, maybe Stockton reconsidered and started going out with Jude. Here's the kicker. Stockton is black."

Carolyn became excited. "He could be the person who rented the motel room. Jude may have been in an abusive relationship like I said. Veronica could have found out and gone after the guy. He got her gun away from her and killed her."

"Let's not jump to any conclusions," Mary said. "Just because the guy's black doesn't mean he's a murderer. We're beyond that type of thinking, aren't we?"

"You're the one who emphasized his race," Carolyn argued. "I've never been prejudiced against anyone. Track down Stockton and bring him in for a lineup. If the room clerk at the motel identifies him, we may have our killer."

The emergency room was packed. A child sitting next to them vomited, and the two women got up and continued their conversation outside. "Even if Drew isn't responsible for what happened to Jude," Carolyn said, leaning against an ambulance, "I'm not sure he's fit to care for three young kids right now. He's drinking, and he hired a young girl as a nanny who acts likes she's brain-dead."

"Have you talked to Veronica's sister yet?" Mary asked. "Under the circumstances, I'd rather see the kids with a relative than a stranger."

"I don't have any contact information on Emily. I'm sure Drew has it, though. She's an attorney in San Francisco."

"Is she married?"

"Single."

"If the sister's an attorney," Mary reasoned, "she shouldn't be hard to find. You know Veronica's maiden name, don't you?"

"Robinson. But Emily doesn't like kids. Veronica wanted me to raise the children if something happened to her and Drew."

"You can't take on the world, woman," the detective told her. "How would you work and take care of three kids? You've got Rebecca and Marcus to consider. If you're not careful, you're going to lose your man. Trust me, that guy is first-class goods. If I had someone like that on the hook, I wouldn't take any chances."

"It might be better if we separate Jude from the younger children," Carolyn said. "I'll try to get her to tell me who beat her. As soon as we know, we can file assault charges. Of course, if it's her father, we may be looking at something more serious."

"I don't know how long Jude's been away from home, but the doc doesn't think she's been eating. Are you sure about this? Now's the time to bail out. There may be more than just one problem with this kid. If you want my opinion, there's a shitload of them."

"I have to take her," Carolyn said. "Veronica was my best friend."

"What about your wedding?"

"We've already decided to postpone it. I have to look after Jude, Mary. I promised her that I'd protect her."

"One thing I learned from my mama," Mary said, "is never make promises you can't keep. This girl is trouble. If it doesn't find her, she'll go out looking for it.' "

"Sounds like Jude and I have a lot in common," Carolyn said, returning to the hospital.

By the time they pulled into the circular driveway at Marcus's home in Santa Rosa, it was one thirty in the morning. Jude hadn't said a word during the thirty-minute drive. Carolyn carried in a paper bag they'd given her at the hospital, containing two bottles of prescription medication. One was a muscle relaxant and the other a painkiller. Checking the paperwork, she saw that it was time for Jude to take the pills.

"This place is gigantic," the girl said, gawking at the size of the living room. The cathedral ceilings made it seem even larger. "What does this guy do for a living?"

"Marcus is a computer programmer," Carolyn said, leading her into the kitchen. "Once I give you your medicine, I'll show you your room. I have some pajamas you can wear. I'll bring in the things you brought from home in the morning. The doctors want you to stay in bed so your body can heal." She read the back of the bottle. "You need to eat something. You're not supposed to take these on an empty stomach."

"My stomach isn't empty," Jude told her. "I ate a ton of graham crackers at the hospital." She snatched the pills out of Carolyn's hand, popped them in her mouth, then walked over and put her head under the faucet.

"We have glasses."

Jude wiped her mouth with the back of her hand. "Don't worry," she said, "I don't drink out of toilets."

Veronica's daughter was so tough and belligerent, Carolyn wondered if she'd picked a fight with someone, maybe even another girl. She started to ask her, then decided against it. She couldn't see a female administering such a severe beating. Because of the bruises, she hadn't paid much attention to anything else, but she did recall thinking that Jude was too thin. Just because a person was slender, however, didn't mean she wasn't fit. Jude's younger sister, Stacy, seemed to be developing in the same fashion. Stacy, though, looked as if she was going to be tall like her father. Jude was the same height as Rebecca, around five-six.

She escorted Jude to the guest room on the first floor, down the hall from the room she shared with Marcus. "I'll be back in a minute with a robe and some pajamas." She tilted her head toward the adjoining bathroom. "Make yourself at home. I'll have Josephine pick up some shampoo, deodorant, and other necessities for you in the morning. If you want anything in particular, make a list."

"Who's Josephine?"

"Marcus's housekeeper," she explained. "She's a great cook. Tell her what you like and she'll make it for you."

When Carolyn returned with the nightclothes, Jude was passed out on top of the bedspread. Carolyn turned out the light and sat in a chair in the dark. The guilt and emptiness she'd been experiencing seemed more bearable now. Before she left the room, she brushed Jude's hair back and kissed her lightly on her forehead. A part of Veronica lived on in her children. By making sure they were safe, Carolyn had a chance to redeem herself for not being there when her friend needed her.

The kind of sleeper who woke at the first trace of light, Marcus had blackout drapes in the bedroom, so when Carolyn awoke, she assumed it was still early. When she realized he wasn't in the bed, she rolled over and squinted at the clock, seeing it was after nine. She saw a note on the end table. Marcus said he'd decided to let her sleep, and that he'd already called Brad Preston and told him she wouldn't be coming to work today.

God, Carolyn thought, hoping Brad had made good on his promise not to tell Marcus what happened the night before. Jumping out of bed, she shoved her arms in her terry cloth robe. Just because she didn't own a company like Marcus didn't mean the work she did wasn't important. People like herself were the backbones of society. Without them, the fires wouldn't get put out, the injured wouldn't be transported to hospitals, trash would litter the streets, and criminals would terrorize the city.

Carolyn went to the bathroom and stared in the mirror. The bruise on her face wasn't as bad as she'd thought it would be. Her arm looked bad, but she could cover it with a long-sleeve shirt. Maybe the person who'd attacked her was just a twisted prankster. If he'd wanted to, he could have really hurt her. She covered the area on her face with the gooey makeup one of the wedding planners had insisted she buy.

Had Marcus or Rebecca even noticed that Jude was in the guest room? Carolyn rushed down the hall, looking inside and finding the girl asleep under the covers. Closing the door, she was crossing the living room toward the kitchen when she collided with Josephine. "Forgive me," she said, kissing the woman on the cheek. Marcus thought it was strange that she kissed the housekeeper. She adored Josephine, but the main reason was they were both Catholic. The church called it the "kiss of peace." Particularly in countries like Italy, where Josephine was from, the old traditions were still practiced. "We have a houseguest," she told her, "a girl. She's had a rough night, so let's try not to wake her."

Josephine was a tiny woman with gorgeous olive skin. She stood five feet and couldn't weigh more than a hundred pounds. Regardless of her size, the woman could move a piano as if it were made out of plastic.

"I made Jude breakfast early this morning," Josephine said, speaking with an Italian accent. "She took her medicine and went back to bed. Saint Jude is the patron of lost causes. His real name was Judas. We didn't want our prayers going to the bad guy, so we call him Jude instead."

"I know," Carolyn said, thinking Jude might be a lost cause herself. She liked having another Catholic in the house. Marcus had been raised Presbyterian. She couldn't be married in the church because of her former marriage to Frank Polizzito, the father of her children. Marcus had hired some kind of rent-a-priest who'd agreed to perform the ceremony in the backyard. The priest at the church she attended had told her she couldn't sleep with Marcus even after they were married, because the marriage wasn't sanctioned by the church. In some areas, the church went too far. Not many men would marry a woman who refused to sleep with them.

Carolyn thought Jude appeared to be settling in pretty fast for someone who'd put up so much resistance. She poured herself a cup of coffee, then picked up the bottle of painkillers. When she realized it was empty, she raced into the guest room and shook Jude by the shoulder.

"Stop, that hurts," the girl said, rolling over and peering up at Carolyn. "I thought I was supposed to stay in bed and rest."

Carolyn held up the empty bottle. "Did you take all these pills?"

"Yeah," she said. "I hurt like a bitch."

"Get up, I have to take you to the hospital," Carolyn told her, whipping back the covers.

"Chill out, will you?" Jude shouted. "I'm

149

conscious. I'm not going to die. There were only fifteen pills. I took some during the night and a few more this morning. Do you have any idea how hard it is to kill yourself with painkillers? It would take ten bottles of Darvocette, maybe more. Before you died, you'd barf them up. I didn't take any of the muscle relaxants. I know they can stop your heart if you take too many. Now, can we stop talking about dying? It reminds me of my mother. Not all my pain is physical."

Carolyn took several deep breaths, then slowly let them out. The girl had a valid point. "Are you certain you're all right?"

Jude winced as she shifted her position. "I'm alive, aren't I? That's good enough for me if it's good enough for you."

"Let's come to an understanding," Carolyn said, placing her hands on her hips. "I'll treat you like an adult if you'll act responsibly. I have to make a few phone calls. I'll have Josephine bring in a pot of coffee. Drink it all. I don't want you to sleep until the pills wear off. It's either that, or a trip to the hospital."

"Whatever," Jude said, rolling over and covering her head with a pillow.

Carolyn called Brad from the phone in the bedroom, bringing him up to date on the situation with Jude. "Does Drew know she's with you?"

"I hope not," she said. "She made me promise not to tell him. I'm not certain if she's afraid of him, or just mad because he made her move out and gave her room to the so-called nanny."

"Jude may have witnessed the murder. Don't come to the office today. Try to put together more information for the PD on Veronica's cases. I've already assigned everything that came in yesterday. I split Veronica's work between Linda Cartwright and Stuart Greenly. Our transfers —"

"My God, Greenly!" Carolyn said, cutting him off. "I confronted him just before I left the office last night. He vehemently denied having an affair with Veronica. Now that I think about it, innocent people don't generally react the way he did."

"Elaborate."

"He threatened to turn in his resignation. He bad-mouthed Veronica, calling her a fat cow. He even said she was crazy, that she told him to fudge on his reports and just make stuff up."

"Not a very nice way to speak about a coworker who was just murdered," Brad said, "particularly since Greenly wants to be perceived as a cultured guy, with his preppy clothes and phony Boston accent. Someone told me he grew up in Malibu."

"The accent!" Carolyn said, excited. "Remember, I thought the guy who attacked me had some kind of accent. Greenly was hopping mad, Brad. Maybe he's our killer."

"Hey, run it by the task force. Veronica might have thought it was more than a roll in the hay, and tried to force him to leave his wife. It would certainly be embarrassing if he was having an affair with her and the truth got out. How would it look for him to be cheating on his beautiful young wife with a woman Veronica's age?"

"He's got a problem with his ego, anyway," Carolyn said, thinking they were onto something. "I heard he flunked the bar exam six times. Is that true?"

"I think so," Brad said. "I told you I'm not sure it was Greenly in the car with Veronica. If you want my opinion, the biggest lead you're going to find is in your guest room. When Wheeler was considering my replacement, I told him if the devil got himself arrested, Carolyn Sullivan could get him to confess. Don't tell me you can't get inside the head of one little girl. Get back on the horse and bring this baby home."

"You're underestimating Jude," Carolyn countered. "I know because I did the same thing. She hasn't been a teenager for years,

Brad. She's already had two abortions. She's a woman in every sense of the word."

"So?" he said. "What difference does that make?"

"Most of my success stories involved men. Females are far more devious. Besides, I'm emotionally involved."

"That gives you even more of a reason. Can't you do for Veronica what you've done for strangers?"

She carried the portable phone to the doorway and stared down the hall. There was something about Jude that frightened her. It took an enormous amount of willpower to protect someone who'd beaten you. "Let me go, Brad, so I can figure out how to break through to her."

Carolyn opened the French doors in the master bedroom and stepped outside to the enclosed atrium. There was a bubbling fountain in one corner, and the walls were covered with climbing roses in exquisite colors. Sitting down in a green padded lounge chair, she tried to enjoy her coffee while she formulated her strategy. Before she could get Jude to talk, she had to understand her.

Was she afraid the batterer would kill her if she reported him? That meant she'd lost confidence in the police and authority figures. Had she committed a crime and was fearful of being found out? Maybe one or both of her pregnancies had been the result of a rape? If so, had her parents blamed her and hushed it up to save face in the community?

When Carolyn had talked an offender in custody for a minor offense into confessing to murdering his wife in another state, she'd appealed to his ego. Discounting the obvious consequences, the average murderer wasn't callous enough to boast about killing someone. The offender she'd got to confess had been a sociopath, a person with no remorse and no respect for human life. She doubted if Jude had anything worth bragging about, even if she had committed a number of crimes, and she felt fairly certain that she wasn't a sociopath. If she was, everyone around her was in jeopardy.

The most likely scenario was the one she'd mentioned to Mary, that Jude was suffering from battered woman syndrome. Victims endured abuse because they knew it led to a period called the "loving reunion," where the batterer swore undying love, showered them with gifts, and promised never to hurt them again. The victim was empowered because she held the key to the batterer's freedom. Some victims craved the "loving reunion" so much, they purposely incited the batterer. It was a perplexing and vicious cycle, many times ending in death, and not always the death of the victim.

Carolyn thought of another possibility where physical abuse went unreported — prostitution. From what Drew had told her, Jude had disappeared for days at a time. She'd also known her parents were about to evict her. Could she have been selling sex for money?

Carolyn went inside and dressed in a pair of jeans and a lightweight blue sweater.

No matter what the temperature was outside, it always seemed cold inside Marcus's house. Houses this big and well insulated were always chilly.

Padding barefoot on the hardwood floors, she opened the doors to the guest room and found Jude propped up in bed, drinking coffee and watching television. Josephine had brought her an insulated coffeepot on a tray.

"Guess I'm gonna make it." Jude smirked. "Can't follow the doctor's orders and stay in bed, not when I have to pee every five minutes from all this god-awful coffee."

Carolyn stretched out beside her. A commercial for Lucky Charms was on. "What are you watching?"

"Toons. There's no such thing as grown-up

TV at our place. Since I'm homeless now, I guess I can kiss TV good-bye."

"Why didn't you tell your parents you were going to school?"

Her eyes drifted over to Carolyn, but she didn't answer.

"The school said you were doing well in your classes, that by midterm, you should be able to get your diploma. It doesn't make sense that you didn't tell your mother and father. I'm sure they would have given you their full support if they'd known what you were trying to accomplish."

"You don't know shit," Jude snapped, getting up and walking toward the bathroom.

She was wearing the same black T-shirt, but her jeans were draped over the chair, and all she had on were a pair of white cotton panties that appeared to be several sizes too large. The bruises looked even worse than they had the night before. After ten minutes had passed, Carolyn went to the bathroom door and found it locked.

She carried the tray back to the kitchen, stared at the clock until another ten minutes had passed, then returned and pounded on the bathroom door. "What are you doing in there?" she asked. "I can't let you hurt yourself, Jude. If you don't come out, I'm going have to get someone to break down the door."

The girl flung the door open, glaring at her. "I was taking a crap," she said. "Are you always this hysterical? Jesus, I should have let them put me in the nuthouse."

Carolyn knew it was time to change her tactics. Trying to befriend her wasn't going to work. "I'm going to call your father," she said. "I'm responsible if something happens to you."

Jude's defiant attitude disappeared. She locked her fingers around Carolyn's arm. "You promised me," she cried. "I'll leave, okay? I'm not going back there with my dad. I'd rather sleep in the gutter."

Pain shot up Carolyn's injured arm. Like Josephine, Jude was stronger than she looked. At least she had an excuse for the bruises now.

Jude released her, and wiggled into her jeans, then searched under the bed for her shoes. "I should have known you'd go back on your word," she told her, sitting in the chair as she put on her dirty socks and laced her worn-out tennis shoes. "Everything you said to me last night was bullshit."

Carolyn blocked the doorway. "You're injured. For all I know, you're suicidal. I can't allow you to leave. When your father gets here, we'll decide what to do. Tell him you've been going to school, and I'm sure he'll let you move back home."

Jude's eyes flashed in fury. "You think my asshole father's going to take care of me?" she shouted. "Who do you think did this to me? He's been forcing me to have sex with him since I was eight."

Carolyn's mouth fell open. She remained silent as Jude paced around the room. She'd pushed her to get a reaction, but this was an explosion.

"You want to know who killed my mother?" Jude blurted out, picking up a paperweight and hurling it against the wall. "My father killed her." Tears streamed down her face. "I was thirteen when the bastard got me pregnant the first time. You know why? Because he couldn't get it up when he wore a condom. He told my mother I was a prostitute. I was too scared to tell her the truth. Then he knocked me up again when I was fifteen. I went back to school because I wanted to surprise my mother. I thought she might love me instead of thinking I was a slut and a baby killer. The only reason I didn't graduate last year was because my dad was always making me ditch school. He couldn't have sex with me when my mom and the kids were around."

Jude flopped face first on the bed, her

shoulders shaking as she sobbed. Carolyn went over to comfort her. She placed her hand on her back, but she slapped it away, craning her neck around. "You know why he wanted me out of the house, don't you?"

Carolyn tried to maintain a calm demeanor. Inside, she felt like ripping Drew Campbell apart with her bare hands. "Because he was afraid someone would see your injuries?"

"No," she said, sitting up and crushing the pillow to her stomach. "Things like that never bothered him. He tells everyone I hang out with gangsters who use me as a punching bag. One time he told Mom I was a masochist and liked people to hurt me. He had an excuse for everything." She began rocking. "He wanted me out so he could replace me with someone else."

"You mean Crystal?"

"He wouldn't be interested in someone her age, unless he'd already had her, and could fantasize about when he fucked her as a kid." She stopped rocking and stared out over the room. "Crystal's got three younger sisters. Maybe he thought he could get to one of them. I think he hired her because she's borderline retarded, and he knew she wouldn't cause problems. You know so much, I thought you would have figured it out. Who did he move into his bedroom?"

"Stacy," Carolyn said, her eyes enormous. "Good Lord, Jude, we have to get her out of that house immediately. Why didn't you tell me this last night?"

"I didn't think you'd believe me."

Carolyn dropped down in the chair, stunned by what she'd heard. "He moved Crystal into the house so it wouldn't look suspicious for your sister to sleep in his room."

"Probably," Jude told her. "When I was there, I watched out for her. He starts slow, you know. He hugs you, kisses you, gives you presents, makes you feel special. He tells you not to tell anyone because the other kids will get jealous. By the time he starts touching you in places he shouldn't, you don't even notice. He distracts you by watching a movie with you, or he slips into your bed while you're sleeping. Gradually he works up to the real stuff. You know, fucking you. Then the presents get bigger, more expensive. Why do you think my mom and dad had money problems? You know what's pathetic? I don't even have anything to show for all those years. No iPod, no TV, no fancy stereo. My mother wouldn't even let me drive my car, and it's a rusted-out tin can. I spent all the money he gave me on dope. I had to drug

myself, or I would have ended up in a nut-house."

"I believe you," Carolyn told her, several moments passing before she continued. "But you've made very serious accusations about your father. What makes you think he killed your mother? Were you there when it happened?"

"No, but my mom was getting suspicious," Jude said, tossing the pillow aside. "I've wanted to tell her the truth for years, but she never seemed to have time for me. I even started dropping hints. My brothers and sisters make so much noise, I'm not even sure she heard me." Jude's eyes drifted downward. "When I didn't come home, it was because he'd hit me. He told me to stay away until my bruises healed. When Mom started working at home, I thought it would stop. He didn't seem as interested in me as he'd been before. Then I saw him touching Stacy."

Carolyn knew Jude was suffering, both emotionally and physically. It was gut-wrenching to talk about something this horrendous, after years of keeping it locked inside. The most urgent thing at the moment was to find some way to comfort her. "I'm going to send Josephine to the drugstore to get the prescription for more pain pills. You

161

have to promise me you'll only take them once every six hours. Will you do that for me?"

Jude nodded. "I'm sorry. I was just hurting so bad last night. I feel better today. The night my mom died, I slept on the floor at the bus station. I was afraid if I came home, he'd kill me, too."

Carolyn sat on the edge of the bed and embraced her. "I'm going to take care of you," she told her. "No one knows you're here except Mary Stevens, the police officer who came to the hospital last night. We have an armed guard watching the house. I'll tell him what your father looks like, and he'll call the police if he comes anywhere near the house."

Jude's eyes glazed over. She was retreating into her subconscious. She needed to be under the care of a physician as well as a psychiatrist. Incest was one of the most damaging of all sex offenses. What she'd been through would follow her the rest of her life. "Look at me, honey. I'm not going to let anyone hurt you. I was lying when I told you I was going to call your father. I had to find a way to get you to tell me the truth. I want you to rest now. I'm not going to leave the house, but I have to make some phone calls, and later today you're going to have to tell Detective Stevens what you told

me. Can you do that?"

Tears pooled in Jude's eyes. "What if they don't believe me?"

"They're going to believe you," Carolyn assured her. "You have to trust me. I know it must be hard for you to trust anyone. Your father's going to jail. If I get started on this right away, he could be behind bars by tonight."

"Who'll take care of Stacy and the boys?"

"Either your aunt Emily or a foster family." When Jude's face fell, she added, "It's only temporary, sweetheart. The main thing is to get them to a safe place."

"What if he gets out?"

"I'll do my best to make certain that doesn't happen," Carolyn said. "You can help me by telling the police the truth. They're going to ask you a lot of questions. It's not going to be pleasant. If I could keep you from having to go through this, I would. The more specific you are about the things that went on between you and your father, the longer his prison sentence will be."

"Dad said I'm too old now that I'm eighteen, that the things that happened when I was younger won't count because too much time has passed." She began to panic. "This isn't going to work. It's my word against his. I've been in juvenile hall. Everyone's going to think I'm lying. He'll find me and kill me if I talk to the police. You can't protect me forever. Rebecca will know I'm here. So will the man you live with." Jude climbed off the bed. "I've got to leave town. All I need is to borrow some money. Once you tell the police, he'll know I'm here. I'll take care of myself. I always have. Just keep him away from my sister."

"Stop!" Carolyn shouted. "If you run away, your father won't be punished for what he did to you. He lied to you, Jude. There's no problem with the statute of limitations, not on crimes of this nature. And what about your mother?"

"She's already dead."

"Didn't you love her?"

Jude's face shifted into hard lines. "Maybe my mother knew and didn't do anything. She loved my father more than she loved me."

"That's not true," Carolyn said. "Your mother would have made certain your father spent the rest of his life in prison. That's probably why he killed her."

"You really think so?" Jude asked, wiping her eyes with the edge of her T-shirt.

"I know so," Carolyn said. "Give me a chance. I'll give you enough money to make a new start. I'll even buy you a plane ticket to anywhere you want to go. Once you get your diploma, I'll help you get into college. Your mother had life insurance. Quite a lot, actually. If your father is convicted of killing her, you and the other children will get the money."

"Humph," Jude said, becoming acutely interested. "How much money is it?"

"Enough," Carolyn said. "All you have to do is stay and tell the truth. If you don't, your sister may go through what you have. You don't want that, do you?"

"No," Jude said, getting back in the bed and curling up in a fetal position. "Tell me what to do and I'll do it. Right now I just want to sleep."

Carolyn slipped out of the room and closed the door. She stood motionless, as terrified as Veronica's daughter. Instead of celebrating her wedding, something she'd looked forward to for over a year, she had placed herself in the path of a tornado. She forced herself to enjoy a moment of quiet before she fulfilled her promise and dived into hell.

CHAPTER 10

Thursday, October 14 — 4:45 P.M.

Carolyn sat beside Jude on a white sofa in Marcus's living room. The exterior of the house resembled a hacienda, but the furnishings were formal. Bronze sculptures stood on marble pedestals. Marcus had an extensive art collection. He'd also purchased several paintings from her brother, Neil, who painted in the style of the old masters. A Waterford crystal lamp sat on the end table, and the cherry-wood floors were partially covered with intricately patterned Persian rugs.

Hank Sawyer and Mary Stevens were seated across from them on a love seat, and Marcus was in a burgundy-colored high-backed chair. Carolyn had arranged for Rebecca to spend the night with a friend in Ventura. A doctor who was a personal friend of Marcus's had come to the house earlier to check Jude's injuries. In addition to the pain

166

medication, he'd given her a mild tranquilizer to help her deal with the sensitive questions Mary Stevens was about to ask her.

Carolyn had already written a report for protective services, as well as given her statement to Mary for the criminal complaint. Hank had written the request for an arrest warrant for Drew, then hand-carried it to a judge to sign. Kevin Thomas at the DA's office had agreed to file multiple counts of sexual abuse of a minor, as well as aggravated assault charges and rape, representing the more recent crimes.

Marcus stood, knowing it was time for the men to leave. "Would you like to see what I'm doing with the barn?" he asked Hank. "I have an office out there. If we get bored, we can watch TV." He looked over at Carolyn. "Call me when you guys are finished."

As soon as they left, Mary removed her laptop from her briefcase and placed it in the center of the coffee table, then adjusted the camera and microphone. She turned the computer around so it was facing Jude. "I want to make sure I get all the facts straight. Is this okay?"

"No," Jude said, knocking the microphone away. "I'm ashamed enough as it is. All I need is a stupid video floating around about the gross things I did with my dad. What if it ends up on the Internet? Things never go away, you know. Even when you delete something on your computer, it's still there."

"We won't use it, then," Mary said, closing the computer and pulling out a yellow pad and a pen. "There's something we need to get straight, Jude. You're filing a criminal complaint against your father. Because you're an adult, we can't prohibit the press from releasing your name. I'll do my best to see that it doesn't happen, but I can't make any promises."

Jude's jaw dropped. "You're going to tell the newspapers and TV stations? Why would you do that to me?"

"I'm not going to tell them," the detective answered. "They have access to police reports and court files in adult matters. The proceedings will be open to the public unless the judge decides differently. That means anyone can come, even strangers. You have to be prepared, Jude. It doesn't mean that everything you tell me or testify to in the courtroom will be reported. I'm sure you've read about cases like this before. Most of the sensitive details are omitted."

Jude cut her eyes to Carolyn. "Why didn't you tell me it was going to be this way? I'm not going through with this now. No wonder you had that doctor give me tranquilizers.

You're not my friend. You just want to use me like everyone else."

"That's not true." Carolyn placed a hand on her thigh. "Don't you want your father to pay for what he's done? You told me you were certain he killed your mother. And what about Stacy? We talked about these things this afternoon."

A hushed silence fell over the room. Jude stared at a spot on the wall, her arms stiff at her side. "Fine," she said. "Everyone already thinks I'm a slut and a retard. As soon as this is over, I'm going to leave town and change my name. Ventura sucks."

Mary asked her a string of rudimentary questions, such as her age, date of birth, address, and Social Security number, then placed her yellow pad in her lap. "When did your father start molesting you?"

"I'm not sure," Jude said. "Probably when I was a baby. To be honest, I can't remember when he didn't molest me."

"Why don't we start with the most recent incident and work our way back? Did your father sexually assault you on the day your mother was killed?"

"No, it was a few days before."

"It's important that you be specific, Jude. Your mother was killed on Tuesday. Was it Sunday?"

"Can you please stop talking about my mother dying?" she said, her eyes glistening with tears. "It's my fault she's dead. I threatened to tell her. That's when he beat me. If I'd kept my mouth shut, Mom would still be alive."

"You can't blame yourself, honey," Carolyn said, reaching into her pocket and handing her a tissue. "Just because your father abused you doesn't mean he killed your mother."

"Oh, he killed her."

"How can you be certain?"

"Because he took me to the same shitty motel."

Mary asked, "The Motor Inn?"

"Yeah."

"When were you at the Motor Inn with your father?"

"The day he beat me." Jude leaned forward. "I was going to starve myself to death. The problem was it isn't that easy. I lost weight, but I'm not dead, am I? It was a dumb plan. Before you'd die, you'd pass out. Then people would find out and force you to eat. I knew a girl who was anorexic. She passed out at school and they took her to the hospital and stuck a tube down her throat. She ended up in a mental hospital. Shit, I don't even know what happened to her.

She's probably still there." She paused and blew her nose. "I stopped eating after my dad told me I was fat. Up until a year or so ago, I had sort of a boy's body. You know, not much of a chest and a flat ass. For some reason, I started filling out. Maybe I was a late bloomer, or I might have been eating more because of stress. I was trying to get off dope so I could concentrate on my schoolwork. I used meth. People get fat when they stop doing meth." She paused and took a deep breath. "When Mom started working at home, it was hard for Dad to get to me. That was the first time he'd ever rented a motel room. You have to give them a credit card, and he couldn't use his or Mom would have found out. She paid the bills."

"It's important that we know what day you were at the Motor Inn," Mary repeated. "Can't you remember? Carolyn tells me you've been attending Ventura High. If it was the weekend, you wouldn't have been in school."

Jude waved a hand in front of her face. "You don't get it, do you? Days and times are just a blur for me. I wasn't eating enough to keep a bird alive. If I was in school, I wouldn't have been at a motel with my asshole father. Write down it was either Saturday or Sunday. That's the best I can do, okay?"

"How did you get to the motel?"

"In my dad's car."

"Do you know how he paid for the room?"

"No," Jude said, fidgeting in her seat.

"Your father took off work on Tuesday," Carolyn said. "Are you sure that wasn't the day you were with him?"

"Isn't that what I already said?" she answered, defensive. "I wasn't there when he killed my mother. If I had been, don't you think I would tell you?"

"Do you remember the room number?"

"God," Jude exclaimed, slapping the sofa with her palm. "Why don't you just shut up and listen? My dad took me to the motel and forced me to have sex with him. I told him if he didn't leave me alone, I was going to tell my mother. He went crazy and started hitting me. I was going to call the police, but I chickened out. I've been in juvenile hall twice, you know. Once for stealing, and another time for dope. My dad said the police wouldn't believe me."

"How did you get away from him?" Mary asked, jotting down notes on her pad.

"I snuck out of the room when he was asleep," Jude said. "I walked to the Greyhound bus station. I stayed there until I came home. Then the prick told me my mom was dead and that I couldn't live there anymore."

"Is there any way we can document the previous times your father abused you?" Mary said, tapping her pen against her teeth. "Were you treated by a doctor? Did you tell anyone, say one of your girlfriends? Did anyone see bruises or other signs of injuries on your body?"

"I haven't been to a doctor since I had my last abortion."

"When was that?"

"I think I was fifteen. If you want to know when my dad had sex with me, check the attendance records at the schools I went to. He made me pretend I was sick. That's the reason I didn't graduate last year. I got an incomplete in two of my classes."

"I'll check that out," Mary told her, asking her the name of the junior high and grade school she had attended. "Now I have to ask you specific questions about what your father did to you. Did he force you to have oral sex with him?"

"Duh?" Jude said. "Of course he did."

"How many times?"

"I didn't keep track. Fifty, a hundred."

"And you had sexual intercourse, is that true? That means penetration."

"Yeah. Do you want to know if he sucked

my toes, too?"

"Different sex acts represent different crimes," Mary explained, not responding to Jude's sarcasm. "Some carry a greater penalty than others. I know how embarrassing it is for you to talk about these things, Jude, but I have to provide this information to the district attorney so they'll know what kind of charges to file. What age do you believe you were when your father first engaged in sexual intercourse with you?"

"The day after my eleventh birthday."

"Did this occur once a month, once a week, or just every now and then?"

"Once or twice a week."

Mary asked her a few more questions, then terminated the interview. Jude excused herself and went to bed.

"I checked her record before I came over here," the detective said. "She wasn't arrested for possessing a joint, Carolyn. She was dealing. She mentioned one arrest for theft." Removing a thick file from her briefcase, she fished out Jude's juvenile record and handed it to Carolyn. "In case you don't want to take the time to add them up, there's sixteen arrests. She was even charged with assault on an officer. She threw a bottle at a cop who was trying to disperse a crowd at a rock concert. He had to have ten stitches in his head. You know what we're talking about, don't you?"

Carolyn washed her hands over her face. "She's not a credible witness. Jesus, Mary, she fits the classic profile of a victim of incest. Why would she obey the law when her father was routinely beating and raping her? Frankly, I don't know how she survived all these years."

"She also lies."

"Her whole life was a lie."

"I realize that," Mary told her. "There's several reports in her file that you should read. She assaulted a younger girl at juvenile hall, then blamed it on another inmate. Regardless of what happened to her, she has a history of violence. Are you certain you want her to stay with you? Protective Services can find a placement."

"Right," Carolyn said facetiously. "Who's going to take in an eighteen-year-old with an extensive criminal record? Veronica was my best friend. I might not be able to look after her other children, but I'm going to do everything I can for Jude."

When Hank and Marcus returned to the house, they followed Carolyn into the kitchen so she could put up a pot of coffee. The kitchen had stainless steel appliances, and a wood-burning fireplace. Everyone gathered around the center island.

"I don't understand why the DA won't file murder charges against Drew," Carolyn said, pouring water into the coffeepot. "He doesn't have an alibi, and we've established a motive."

"Kevin Thomas won't file charges he can't prove," Hank told her, tossing a toothpick into the trash can. "Jude didn't witness her father kill her mother, nor could she place him at the scene of the crime."

"She did place Drew at the scene of the crime," Carolyn said. "Tell him, Mary."

"Jude says her father took her to the Motor Inn, but she insists it wasn't on the day her mother was killed. I'll fill you in on all the rest of the details later. She's fuzzy on dates and times. You think Kevin Thomas will run with it?"

"Hard to say," Hank answered, digging into a bowl of jelly beans. "The lab hasn't finished processing all the evidence yet. It doesn't look good, though. They even dismantled the drains in the motel room. The killer must have let the water run for some time in both the tub and the sink. If there was anything in there, it's gone now. We don't have fingerprints. We don't have DNA. And we have a young black male allegedly renting the room. If the DA took a case like this to trial, it would end up in acquittal."

"Were you able to track down Reggie Stockton?"

"No," Mary answered, glancing down at the floor. "We spoke with several students at Ventura High. Stockton works at Circuit City. We reached his mother by phone. She works for an agency that provides home health care. The family is originally from New Orleans. After their home was destroyed during Katrina, they decided to relocate here. Mrs. Stockton said Reggie had a number of girlfriends, but she doesn't know of anyone named Jude. I didn't want to question Jude about Stockton yet. We got a copy of his picture from the yearbook. We're going to put together a photo lineup tomorrow and show it to the clerk from the motel. He didn't recognize anyone from the mug shots we —"

Marcus interrupted. "You can't let Drew go free. He's a murderer, for Christ's sake. Look what he did to his own daughter."

"He won't go free," Carolyn told him, pouring out four cups of coffee, then placing them on a silver tray next to the containers for sugar and creamer. "The penalties for sex crimes are stiffer than murder. Even if they do prosecute Drew for Veronica's death,

177

they'll have trouble proving premeditation. The sentence for second-degree murder is twelve years to life. With good time and work time credits, Drew could be out in seven. Each time he forced Jude to engage in a sex act constitutes a separate crime. Start stacking up the counts, and he could end up serving the rest of his life in prison. Also, the majority of sex offenses committed against children are written so they have to be served consecutively." She told Marcus and Hank what Jude had told them about her father making her feign illness on the days he wanted to have sex with her. "Are you going to check her attendance records, Mary, or do you want me to handle it?"

"You've got the girl," the detective said, spooning sugar into her cup. "I'd much rather handle the investigation. If she's telling the truth, the school records will substantiate her story and help us establish a timeline."

"The poor kid," Marcus said. "Her father should be taken out and shot."

"You mean like her mother?" Mary said, arching her eyebrows. "Although it's not a pleasant thought, Veronica may have known what was going on. If your child was sick all the time, you'd be concerned enough to take her to the doctor. Of course, we have to verify that what Jude told us is true."

"Veronica didn't know," Carolyn argued. "She abhorred child abusers. What pushed her over the edge was the Bell . . ." She clamped her mouth shut, staring at the two detectives. It was too late. Hank had already put it together.

"I remember that case," he said, setting his empty coffee cup on the counter. "Lester McAllen killed and dismembered the Bell boy. The bastard got his, though, regardless of Robert Abernathy."

"Abernathy was chief over forensics, wasn't he?" Marcus asked. "He was falsifying DNA evidence so he didn't have to go to the trouble of testing it. When they caught him, every case he'd handled went down the toilet. What did you mean when you said McAllen got his, Hank?"

"The son of a bitch was murdered," he said, shoving the bowl of jelly beans to the other side of the counter. "I hate people who keep candy sitting around. I think they do it purposely so their visitors will get fat."

"You were telling me what happened to McAllen," Marcus reminded him.

"Someone gunned him down in Camarillo only a few days after he was released from prison."

"Did you ever find out who did it?"

"Not to my knowledge," Hank said. "It happened in Camarillo, so it wasn't our jurisdiction. To be honest, I don't think anyone gave a rat's ass who killed him."

"What happened to Abernathy?"

"Same thing. He was shot on the porch of his house in Oxnard. I don't remember the time sequence, just that the Abernathy homicide took place prior to McAllen's conviction being overturned."

"Sounds like a vigilante," Marcus said. "The chances of both these men being killed without their deaths being connected is slim, wouldn't you say?" He turned to Carolyn. "Wasn't McAllen your case? I remember us talking about it."

Beads of perspiration formed on Carolyn's forehead and upper lip. If anything could muddy the waters, it was Tyler Bell. She had to find a way to shut Marcus up. "I promised Jude her father wouldn't get out of jail," she said. "What do you think, Mary?"

"You know more about bail reviews than I do," she said, giving Carolyn a puzzled look. When an offender was considered for bail, a probation officer was assigned to write a report and make a recommendation. "I don't know why you'd make a promise like that at this stage of the proceedings."

"That's the only way she would agree to

talk to you." Carolyn picked up Marcus's and Hank's coffee cups. She was so nervous, she dropped one on the way to the sink. "I don't generally drink coffee this late in the day. It makes me jittery. Why don't you sit down at the table until I clean this up?"

Carolyn went to the utility closet and returned with a broom and a dustpan. The two detectives and Marcus took seats at the table.

"So," Hank said, "what's the criterion for making bail these days, Carolyn?"

"Criminal history," she said, feeling more relaxed now that she'd shifted the conversation away from the Bell case. "I'm sure Drew doesn't have a record. His established ties in the community will fall in his favor. The court also has to consider the risk he poses to the community. If they don't file murder charges, Jude will be the only victim. The court can make certain she's not in danger by placing her in protective custody inside a detention facility. That means they won't have a valid reason for not setting bail."

"A detention facility," Marcus said. "Isn't that a jail?"

"More or less," Carolyn told him, sweeping the cup into the dustpan, then depositing it in the trash. "Even though Jude's eighteen, they might let her stay at juvenile hall."

"Wait a minute," Marcus said, scowling. "You're telling me they're going to let her father do whatever he wants while they lock Jude up like a criminal? You've got to be shitting me."

"That's just the way things are. It always seems like the victims are being punished in child abuse cases. Sometimes the mother even turns against the child if the father is sent to prison, particularly if he's the primary breadwinner. In the long run, though, the victims are better off than if no one intervened."

Marcus cracked his knuckles. "How much money can Drew get his hands on?"

"I'm not sure," Carolyn told him. "If they didn't refinance recently, he may have substantial equity in the house. All he has to come up with is ten percent of the bail amount."

"He can't sell the house overnight," Marcus said. "You said they were hard up."

"A bail bondsman will put up the money. All Drew has to do is sign a piece of paper. If he fails to appear, they can take the house and sell it."

"No one's going to lock this girl up in a detention facility," Marcus said, his face flushed in anger. "We'll go to the damn bail hearing and talk to the judge. I'll hire five guys to protect her if her father gets out. If he so much as steps a foot on this property, they'll shoot his perverted ass. Jude is staying with us, understand?"

Mary glanced at her watch. "When does Emily's flight get in?"

"Nine fifteen," Carolyn related. "Are we going to be able to get the kids out of the house and to the airport in time? Emily wants to take them back to San Francisco with her tonight. She's booked tickets for them on the eleven-thirty flight. Her secretary's coming with her to help out."

Hank and Mary had decided it was better if Carolyn wasn't present when they arrested Drew and removed the children. She refused to leave Jude, anyway.

"We've got three units on their way over there now," Hank said. "Kim Masterson of Protective Services is meeting them at the house. Two of the patrol officers are female, so that should make things move more smoothly. It's still going to be tight, Carolyn. Once they arrest Drew, the other officers will help Masterson pack up the kids' belongings."

"That's not necessary," Marcus said, his jaw set. "Carolyn and I have a cashier's check made out to the sister. She can buy them new things in San Francisco. Call your people and tell them to grab the kids and split. I've already arranged to meet Emily at the airport."

Hank stepped aside to place the call on his cell phone.

"We'll have to bring the children back when we prepare for the trial," Mary said. "I'm not sure what they saw, but I know the DA will want to talk to them. There may be other charges if Drew molested Stacy."

Marcus stood to leave, walking over and kissing Carolyn. "I'll call you from the airport. As soon as I give Emily the check, I'll head home. Why don't you try to get some sleep?"

Carolyn had never loved him more than she did at that moment. He'd done so much, he was practically carrying her. Most people would be reluctant to get involved. Marcus had jumped in without hesitation, offering his time, contacts, and financial resources.

Once he left, Mary said she needed to go back to the station to start putting together her report. Carolyn walked her to the door, then returned to the kitchen, finding Hank back at the center island tossing jelly beans in his mouth. "I thought you didn't want to eat those."

"Once I get started, it's hard to stop." He glanced down at the few remaining candies.

"They look so lonely there, I might as well finish them."

"Who do you think sent me the threatening letter? It's got to be the same person who attacked me in the parking lot."

"My guess is Drew," he said, flicking a piece of lint off his jacket. "The day of the murder, he left the house right after you. He told Linda Cartwright he was going out to look for his daughter, but he could have gone to the morgue instead. He specifically asked you to identify the body, didn't he?"

"Do you think he killed Veronica?"

"It's certainly stacking up that way. The biggest hurdle we have to overcome is the guy who rented the room. Drew could have hired someone off the street to do it. Then you've got to get past the fact that the credit card was stolen. Maybe Drew picked a black guy believing it would eliminate him as a suspect. He knew we'd assume whoever rented the room was the killer."

"My God," Carolyn exclaimed, "the man is maniacal. He knows the system because of Veronica. This wasn't an impulsive act, Hank. It was premeditated murder."

Hank rolled his neck around to release the tension. "Even if you're right, how are we going to prove it?"

"Okay," she said, excited. "Drew beat Jude

because she threatened to tell her mother. Not only that, Jude knows he's targeted Stacy as his next victim. He's beaten Jude before. This time he really hurt her. She disappears. Now he's got this ticking bomb walking around. He takes off from work the day of the murder. When people take a vacation day, they usually take it on a Monday or Friday so they can have a three-day weekend, not on a Tuesday."

"Makes sense," Hank said. "Keep talking."

"Drew said he went to Home Depot to find out what it would cost to put up some shelves in the boys' room. He claims he didn't buy anything, so there's no way to substantiate his story. He could have gone to Home Depot after work one night or during the weekend." Carolyn held up a finger. "Now, even before he knows his wife's been murdered, he hires a nanny to take care of the children. He hired this girl Crystal because he needed someone fast and she lives in the area. He also knew she wasn't that smart, and wouldn't figure out that he was molesting Stacy."

"Let's talk about the stolen credit card," Hank said. "The Spectrum Health Club doesn't provide keys to the lockers. This guy Tate used a combination lock."

"How did Drew get into his locker, then?"

"Tate says he may have forgotten to check if the locking mechanism was engaged. It was locked when he got back, which is why he didn't notice the missing credit card."

"Veronica's purse was found at the scene," Carolyn said. "Mary's report said she had almost a hundred dollars in cash, as well as her credit cards. That rules out a drug addict like Phillip Bramson, and probably anyone else Veronica ever handled on the job. The only person who wouldn't be interested in taking her money is Drew." She started to tell him about Stuart Greenly, but after what she'd learned from Jude, it didn't seem plausible that he was their killer.

The detective pushed himself to his feet. "I'll run this by Kevin Thomas tomorrow morning. I'm going to stop by the jail and see what I can squeeze out of Drew. Will you be at the arraignment?"

"No," she said, a determined look in her eyes. "But when the bail review comes in, you know what the recommendation will be."

Hank laughed. "You're going to crush this guy and he won't even know what hit him."

"That's the plan," Carolyn said, walking him to the door.

CHAPTER 11

Thursday, October 14 — 11:15 P.M.

After Marcus returned from the airport, he tiptoed into the bedroom. Not wanting to wake Carolyn, he went to the bathroom down the hall and took a shower, then slid into bed beside her.

"I can't sleep," she said, rolling over. "Make love to me."

"We've got the rest of our lives, sweetheart," he said. "Sleep is more important than sex right now. Just relax. I'm here now. Everything went fine at the airport. Emily's a little frenetic, but under the circumstances, who wouldn't be?"

"Please, I want you," Carolyn insisted. "I need to feel you inside me. I keep seeing Veronica's body at the morgue. Make me feel alive again, Marcus."

He kicked the covers off, kissing her on the mouth and then working his way down to the place between her legs. Carolyn cried out in pleasure. The feeling was so exquisite, her mind was washed clean of thought. She laced her fingers through his thick hair.

He stopped and looked up at her. "Did you hear something?"

Carolyn raised her head, seeing a shadowy figure standing at the back of the room. "It's just the wind," she lied, lying back down. She kept her gun in the top drawer of the nightstand. How had the intruder got past the security guard? Why hadn't the alarm gone off? Adrenaline pumped through her veins. She had to get her gun before he realized she'd seen him.

She adjusted the pillow under her head so it reached the edge of the mattress. Tossing her hands over her head, she moaned and bowed her body upward so the intruder couldn't see what she was doing with her hands. She slipped her right hand underneath the pillow, extending her fingers until she reached the pull on the drawer. Seizing her 9mm, she took aim over Marcus's head. "If you move, you're a dead man."

"Will you stop pointing that stupid gun at me?" Jude said, stepping into the light from the bathroom. "Man, you're good. Mom would never have been able to do what you just did. She didn't have the reflexes."

Carolyn dropped her outstretched hands. Marcus had already rolled off her, and now crawled up beside her on the bed. He covered their exposed bodies with a sheet.

Carolyn asked, "How long have you been standing there?"

"I'm not sure," the girl said. "I just wanted to talk to you. I didn't know you guys would be going at it. I'm not into watching, if that's what you think." She laughed. "Once I came in here, I kind of got stuck. I thought about sneaking out through the patio door, but I was afraid the alarm would go off."

"You could have tried knocking," Carolyn said, snatching her robe off the end of the bed and shoving her arms into it.

"The door was open. That's why I thought it was okay to come in. I had a nightmare. I dreamed my dad got out of jail and killed me."

"This is my fault, Carolyn," Marcus said. "I must have left the door open by mistake. It was late and I didn't think."

"Fine," she said, although she didn't feel fine. "Why don't you go back to your room, Jude? I'll come and talk to you in a few minutes."

"It's okay," she said, "I'm not scared anymore. You looked like you were having a good time, so I'll just go back to bed. Then you can . . . well, you know."

Jude left, closing the door behind her. Marcus laughed. Carolyn gave him a dirty look. "It's not funny," she said, walking over to the dresser. "Jesus, I could have shot her. Once she saw us, she should have left. She just stood there and watched. It's creepy. I mean, she didn't even act embarrassed."

"Lighten up, baby," Marcus said. "Jude's an adult. Between DVDs and cable TV, kids these days see people having sex all the time." He cracked up again. "The look on your face was priceless. This is one of your hang-ups, isn't it? That one of your kids would walk in while we were making love. At least it was Jude instead of Rebecca."

Carolyn threw on a pair of jeans and a tank top, the same surly expression on her face.

"Aren't you coming back to bed?" Marcus asked. "Why did you put your clothes on?" When she didn't answer, he walked over and wrapped his arms around her waist. "You're not going to let this ruin our sex life, are you? It was too dark to really see anything."

"Look," she said, spinning around to face him, "I'll get over it, just not tonight. If Jude's asleep, I'll try to get some work done. First, tell me more about Emily. Do you think she can handle Veronica's children?"

"In due time," Marcus said, shuffling back

to the bed. "I feel sorry for her. From what she said, she's built up a lucrative law practice. She doesn't plan to come back to LA right away. Veronica wanted to be cremated, and it would be too difficult for her to make the trip with the children. Surprisingly, she wasn't that shocked about Drew. She always thought there was something wrong with him."

Carolyn kissed Marcus good night and went to the guest room to speak to Jude. When she found the room empty, she decided she must be in the kitchen getting a late-night snack. When she didn't find her there, she called the guard. "Did anyone leave the house, Randy?"

"No," he said. "Hold on while I check with Sean. He's covering the back." A few moments later, he came back on the line. "Everything's secure, Mrs. Wright."

"I'm not Mrs. Wright yet," Carolyn corrected him. "Forget it, it doesn't matter. Call me anything you want. Just make sure you let me know if our houseguest tries to leave, or if anything else goes on that appears even remotely suspicious."

Carolyn went upstairs, finding Jude in Rebecca's room. She had on one of Rebecca's sweatshirts and was stretched out on her stomach on the floor, watching television

and munching on a bag of potato chips. Seeing Carolyn in the doorway, she looked up. "I feel better in here. I have a problem sleeping. It started when I was a kid . . . well, you know."

"I'm sure Rebecca won't mind," Carolyn told her, thinking it was understandable that she would feel more comfortable in another teenager's room. The drawers to her daughter's chest were open, though, and clothes were tossed on the bed, the chair, and the floor. She bent over and picked up a wet towel draped over Rebecca's desk chair. Glancing into the adjoining bathroom, she saw the tub was still filled with water, and the counter was littered with hair products and cosmetics. She felt fairly certain Rebecca hadn't left her room this way. Since they'd moved in with Marcus, she'd become a neat freak. Not only that, Josephine had come in today, and she would never leave a room in this state. So, she thought, dumping the towel in the hamper, Jude was messy. This might be the only normal trait the girl possessed.

"Are you hungry?" Carolyn asked. "You're far too thin, Jude. You need to gain some weight. Did the doctor talk to you about that this afternoon?"

"I've been eating everything in sight since

I got here. This is such a cool place, Carolyn. It's got great energy. And I love having a maid to cook and clean for me."

"Josephine is a housekeeper, Marcus's housekeeper. Rebecca takes care of her own room. Until we get married, I'm as much a guest in this house as you are, Jude."

"Whatever," the girl said, noting Carolyn's displeasure and changing the subject. "Marcus looked like he was good in bed. All most guys think about is their dicks. Him being rich makes the deal even sweeter. You got yourself a real catch."

Carolyn sat down on the edge of the bed. Her skin felt hot and clammy. "It's not appropriate for you to make comments about my sex life, Jude. And it wasn't right for you to come into our bedroom, even if the door was open. Please, don't do that again."

"No problem, boss," Jude said, smirking. "You can go back to lover boy now. I'm fine. Don't worry. I'll clean up the room."

Carolyn left, a disturbing sensation in the pit of her stomach. Jude's mood swings were maddening. One minute she was angry and belligerent, the next pathetically sobbing, making a person want to risk everything to protect her. Now she was acting as if she owned the world and everyone in it. Her behavior was typical of sexual abuse victims,

Carolyn reminded herself, particularly incest. At a very young age, Jude had been handed the key to not just her father's, but her entire family's future. All she had to do was blow the whistle and their world would have come crashing down. No matter how a person achieved it, that type of power was intoxicating. The price she'd paid was tremendous, but Jude was now resourceful, manipulative, clever, and resilient.

Carolyn would have to keep a close eye on her.

Hank stepped up to the window at the Ventura County Jail. "Hey, Cutty," he said to a young dark-haired officer. "I'm here to see one of your esteemed guests, Drew Campbell. Get someone to pull his ass out of the presidential suite and throw him in an interview room."

"I wish you wouldn't call me Cutty, Lieutenant," the officer said, stiff-jawed. "My name is Zan. Everyone's forgotten about what happened but you. Don't you think I've taken enough flake?"

"No, I don't," the detective said, serious. "Anyone dumb enough to drink a fifth of Cutty Sark in an hour, then have to be rushed to the hospital to get it pumped out of his belly, has a serious problem. You need to be in AA, my friend. I told you I'd sponsor you."

Zan threw his hands in the air. "Fine, you win. I'll call you next week. I'm not an alcoholic, though. I only drink on my days off."

"You're still an alcoholic," Hank stated, staring at his nameplate. "What kind of crazy name is Zan, by the way? Was your mother playing a computer game when you were born? Forget it. Get my man. I don't have all night here."

Once he was buzzed through the security doors, the detective removed his gun and placed it in a locker. He'd been sober for almost ten years, but he still attended AA meetings on a regular basis. Weekend drinkers like Zan never thought they had a problem. Hank hated to see a guy flush his life down the toilet.

The jail was actually a pretrial detention facility, and as a result of housing over a thousand inmates with a rated capacity of 412, the fairly new facility had the infrastructure of a thirty-year-old building. About twelve years ago, the county had erected another detention center, the Todd Road Jail, in the city of Santa Paula. Todd Road was designed to hold over 750 sentenced male inmates.

Overcrowding was a major problem, both

at the local and the state level. The city of Ventura had a population of just over a hundred thousand. The county, however, had close to eight hundred thousand. Although the PD only serviced the city, the probation, sheriff's, and DA's office had jurisdiction over the entire county.

Drew Campbell wasn't accustomed to luxury, but he was in for a rude awakening. A jail in a county like Ventura, though, couldn't compare to the conditions inside one of the Los Angeles facilities, where riots were commonplace events. And prison was twice as bad. Even hardened cons refused to tolerate child abusers. Many of them left in body bags. Unless he was acquitted, Campbell had bought himself a one-way ticket to hell.

Another officer escorted Hank through the quad on the second floor, stopping and unlocking the door to a small room. When he stepped inside, Drew Campbell peered up at him with desperate eyes. This was the part of the process the detective enjoyed the most, his first glimpse of a predator encased in the jaws of justice. He liked seeing them in their orange jumpsuits, amazed at how such a simple piece of clothing could humble the most confident of men.

Technically, he should advise the jail to

place Drew in protective custody. Discounting the nature of the charges, he was what Hank considered a pretty boy, with his shiny silver hair, pale blue eyes, clear, smooth skin, and refined features. Since the inmates didn't have jobs like they did at a prison facility, their contact with men outside their quads was limited. This made the chances of a violent assault by a group of prisoners less likely. But there were always ways to get to someone. There were the men inside the quads, the tunnel where prisoners were transported to court, and the one with the least consequences, a guard willing to look the other way. Some guards did it for money, but the majority did it because they thought the inmate deserved whatever punishment his fellow prisoners wanted to administer. Hank had no intention of bringing up the issue of protective custody, not for a man who had repeatedly raped and beaten his daughter.

"God, I'm so glad you're here," Drew said. "They took my children. This is a mistake, a horrible mistake. Veronica was murdered. I don't understand what's going on. It's like the world is coming to an end. I tried to talk to the officers who came to arrest me, as well as that woman from Social Services. No one would tell me anything."

Hank pulled out a chair and took a seat, reading Drew his rights.

"I don't mind talking to you without an attorney," he said. "I don't have anything to hide. Just get me out of this place. I'm terrified. I've never been arrested in my life. I need to take care of my kids, figure out what to do about Veronica's funeral."

"Jude told us what you've been doing to her," Hank told him. "She says you've been forcing her to have sex with you since she was eleven, that you beat her whenever she resisted. Her injuries have been documented, Drew, so don't waste my time denying it."

"I didn't do anything to Jude," Drew protested. "Don't you understand? She must be getting back at me because I made her move out of the house. You have no idea what my daughter is like. Christ, check her arrest record. She's been in and out of juvenile hall a dozen times. Shit, she was even caught dealing drugs at school. How could you possibly take her word over mine?"

Hank pulled out a toothpick, sticking it between his front teeth, then moving it to the side of his mouth. "For starters, you don't have any bruises on you."

"I swear, I've never touched that kid," Drew said, his voice shaking. "Jude would have slugged me if I did. That black thug she's been hanging out with must have beaten her up again. That's one of the reasons I insisted she move out of the house. Both Veronica and I tried to keep her from seeing him. I have three young children, Hank. The guy's a gangster. I was afraid people would start shooting out our windows and kill one of the kids. How would you like to have that kind of element around your family?"

"Do you know this boy's name?"

"Reggie." Drew rubbed his chin. "I think his last name is Stockton, but I'm not certain. He might be Jude's pimp. She's been prostituting herself for years. When she told you all these lies about me, did she tell you how many abortions she's had?"

"Yes, she did," Hank said, watching the surprise register on his face. "Your daughter believes you murdered your wife, Drew. The district attorney's office is considering filing homicide charges in addition to the sex crimes. You're in deep trouble."

His panic intensified. "Now you think I killed Veronica! I loved my wife. I would never have done anything to hurt her. Talk to Carolyn. She'll think you're out of your mind. We had a beautiful family, a good marriage. Anyone who knows us will confirm what I'm telling you."

"We don't give a shit what other people think," the detective told him. "Any man who could hide the fact that he was having sex with his daughter for eight years could hide anything. You took a day off from work on a Tuesday, the same day Veronica was murdered. You can't account for your time, outside of claiming you went shopping for shelving, which you didn't buy." He paused and leaned over the table. "Jude says you took her to the Motor Inn to have sex with her. That's where we found your wife's body. She also said she threatened to expose you, which gives you motive. So now you've got both motive and opportunity. Sounds like a pretty good case, doesn't it?"

The blood drained from Drew's face. His hands locked on the arms of his chair.

Hank stood, kicking the chair out of his way. "And that doesn't take into account the million-dollar life insurance policy you carried on your wife. Since she didn't die of natural causes, you get twice that amount. Do you know what constitutes first-degree murder, Drew?" He paced, then spun around. "Of course you do. Veronica was a probation officer. Let me tell you how this went down. You knew that one day Jude might tell her mother what you'd been doing to her, so you made provisions. You bought the life insurance last year."

"I took out the same amount of insurance on myself," he argued. "I was trying to make sure my family would have money to live on if something happened to one of us. How can you fault me for that?"

"It was my understanding that you were having financial problems," Hank countered. "How could you afford the premiums?"

"I worked overtime."

The detective brought his fist down on the table, causing Drew to jump. "I told you not to waste my time with lies. It wasn't enough that you destroyed your daughter's life, you were prepared to kill your wife to protect yourself. You're such an evil man, you even wanted to profit from the woman you murdered."

"It's not true," Drew said, his face flushing. "I don't have to listen to this. I — I want an attorney."

Hank ignored him, too fired up to stop. "You rented a room at the Motor Inn to have sex with your daughter a day or two before the murder. Whether you realize it or not, the poor girl was trying to starve herself to death. That's how miserable you made her life. Then when she realized you were priming her sister, Stacy, to be your next victim, she threatened to expose you, believing you'd become enraged enough to kill her. Do you know what kind of courage it takes to incite someone to kill you? And she almost did it, didn't she?" Hank reached over and grabbed Drew's hands, flattening them out on the table so he could look at them. "Where did you get that cut on your knuckle?"

"I — I'm a technician at Boeing," Drew stammered. "I build things with my hands."

Hank shifted his jacket on his shoulders, trying to keep from beating him senseless. The more he talked, the more convinced he was that Drew Campbell was a murderer. "Something went wrong, didn't it? Jude escaped when you fell asleep. When you weren't able to track her down, you lured Veronica to the same motel on Tuesday. By now, someone else had rented the room. They left early that morning. But you'd kept the key so you had no trouble getting in. Besides, you didn't rent the room the first time. You paid someone else to do it for you. You think that guy is going to take a murder rap for you? He's a low-level criminal who deals in stolen credit cards. He'd roll over on his own mother."

The armpits of Drew's jumpsuit were

soaked in perspiration. "I want an attorney. I refuse to answer any more questions without an attorney present."

"You'll get your damn attorney," Hank barked, whipping a handkerchief out of his pocket and wiping his face. "You don't have to answer any questions, Drew. We don't need you to answer any questions. You know why? Because we have all the answers. Your wife had no reason to fear you. That made it easy for you to get your hands on the gun you knew she carried in her purse. You called and asked Veronica to pick Jude up at the motel. We know the girl wasn't allowed to drive her car, that she sometimes disappeared for days and then called her mother to come and get her. You told Carolyn that yourself. And we know why Jude had to stay away during those times. You didn't want her mother to see the bruises from where you'd beaten her. You're one of the most sadistic son of a bitches I've ever seen. You ordered your wife to get in the bathtub before you shot her. You thought you could contain things that way. Then you looked the mother of your children in the eye and blew her brains out."

Drew's eyes flooded with tears. "Stop, please. You can't . . ."

The detective ignored him. "The next

thing you did was soak the body in a tubful of water, thinking you could get rid of any evidence that would link back to you. But you didn't get rid of all the evidence, and you weren't able to kill the person whose testimony will convict you, the daughter you tortured." He leveled a finger at him. "You're going to get the death penalty, fucker, and I'm going to be there to watch you die. Think about that because I'm going to be looking forward to it."

Drew sat in shocked silence as Hank walked over and depressed the buzzer for the jailer. When the same officer appeared, he said, "Get this asshole a phone so he can call his attorney."

Chapter 12

Marcus left for work early, leaving Carolyn in the house with Jude. Since it was Josephine's day off, she woke Jude and cooked her a cheese omelet.

"Your father's in jail," Carolyn told her, pouring herself a cup of coffee and carrying it to the kitchen table. "I can drive you to school if you feel up to it. There's no reason you can't get your diploma. You may have to miss a few days for the court proceedings, but I'm sure I can make arrangements with your teachers so you can keep up with your work."

Jude picked at her food, then set her fork down, staring out over the room. "I was doing it for my mother. She's dead. It doesn't matter anymore."

She seemed so lost, Carolyn thought. How could she not be? Her family was destroyed.

206

Peter, Michael, and Stacy were in San Francisco with an aunt who had never shown any interest in them. They must also be suffering. At a time like this, Jude and her siblings should be in familiar surroundings with people who loved them. Being the older sister herself, she knew Jude was probably worrying about the kids along with everything else. Tonight, she would make certain to call Emily so Jude could speak to them. "Getting your diploma matters even more now, honey," she told her. "If you quit, your father will have stolen that from you, along with everything else. Your mother would have wanted you to succeed. Like I told you, if your father is convicted, the life insurance money will be divided among the children. You could go to college. Even if you don't get the insurance money, Marcus and I could help with your tuition. He's a generous man, Jude, and he's deeply concerned about you. He told me you could stay here as long as you want."

"Everyone at school will know Mom was murdered," Jude said, finishing her omelet and shoving her plate aside. "Detective Stevens said people may find out what my father was doing to me. The kids look down on me already because I didn't graduate with my class. How do you think they'll treat

207

me when they find out I've been giving blow jobs to my father?"

"You can't stay in the house all day, Jude. I have to work. Going back to school will keep your mind occupied. You're a strong girl. I think you can handle it. No one's going to ridicule you about your mother's death, and if anything comes out about the situation with your father, it'll be a long time from now. Why don't you give it a try? If you don't feel comfortable, I'll come and get you."

The area around the girl's mouth turned white. She placed her hand over her mouth, rushing over and vomiting in the sink. Carolyn ran cold water on a dishrag and pressed it against her forehead. "I'm sorry, sweetheart. Since you haven't been eating, I should have given you something bland until your system gets back to normal. You didn't vomit intentionally, I hope."

"Did you see me with my fingers down my throat?"

"I have some soda water," Carolyn told her. "Let me get you some to rinse your mouth out." She removed the bottle from the refrigerator and poured it into a glass, then handed it to her.

"Thanks," Jude said, taking a swallow, then spitting it out. When she looked over at Carolyn, her eyes were damp with tears. "I miss my mother. And I miss Stacy, Peter, and Michael. They might have pestered me to death, but I loved them. Now I don't have anyone."

Carolyn embraced her. "It's okay, honey. We'll forget about school for today. Just stay home and rest. I'll call Josephine and see if she can come in. That way, you won't be here by yourself."

"No, please, I'll be fine," Jude insisted. "With all the coffee, I didn't get much sleep yesterday. Will those men still be watching the house?"

"Not today, Jude. They work for Marcus's company. They're only here when Marcus is here. That is, unless there's a reason." Carolyn remembered the threatening letter. She wasn't really concerned now. She felt fairly certain Drew had written it, hoping to either throw the police off track or to intimidate her from investigating Veronica's murder. He should know her well enough to know that wouldn't happen. "I might be wrong about the security. I'll call and check. You go back to bed. Before I leave, I'll bring you the bottle of soda water and some saltine crackers. Then if your stomach settles down later, you can try to eat some chicken soup. Josephine made some yesterday. It's in the refrigerator. All you have to do is heat it up in the microwave."

After Jude left, Carolyn pushed a speed-dial button, hearing the husky voice of Francis Menlo, the man they called Bear. "Are you at the house, or in LA with Marcus?"

"Mr. Wright instructed me to watch the house today."

"Good," she said. "Our houseguest, Jude, is going to be here by herself. If anything comes up, get in touch with me right away."

She disconnected and went to the bedroom to get dressed. Standing inside the enormous closet, she felt as lost as Veronica's daughter. The room resembled a finely appointed library. The walls and shelves were covered in cherry wood, then finished with lacquer. There were slots for shoes, special brass fixtures for ties, and a large cabinet with drawers. Her modest wardrobe looked out of place next to the rows of Marcus's suits and the stacks of perfectly folded shirts with the cardboard from the cleaner's still inside.

Carolyn selected a pair of black slacks and a pink turtleneck, and was reaching for the matching jacket when she changed her mind. She wasn't in the mood to wear her professional clothing. Returning to the bedroom, she put on a pair of jeans, a white shirt, and a burgundy vest.

Before she left the house, she took the soda and crackers to the guest room, then remembered that Jude had spent the night upstairs. She'd have to let Rebecca know before she came home today. The room had only one bed, so they'd have to sort out the sleeping arrangements later. There was another bedroom directly across from Rebecca's. Hopefully, she could talk Jude into moving in there. It wasn't right to take her daughter's room away from her, particularly since she'd just gotten settled. But then again, under the circumstances, it wouldn't hurt Rebecca to sleep in the other room for a few days.

Seeing Jude under the covers with her eyes closed, Carolyn left the soda and crackers on the end table and crept out of the room.

Carolyn called Brad Preston from the car, updating him on the events of the night before. "If you think you can get by without me until this afternoon," she said, "I'd like to go straight to the police station. Mary's going to try to track down Jude's boyfriend, a guy named Reggie Stockton. I just got off the phone with Hank. He talked to Drew last night at the jail. He claims Jude is lying, and that Stockton is a gangbanger who beat her. He also said Stockton might be her pimp.

Working at Circuit City doesn't sound like a job for a pimp. What do you think?"

"Sounds like Drew is dumber than I thought he was," Brad told her. "The least he could do is come up with a credible story. I don't know, though. Drew just doesn't seem like the kind of guy who would have sex with his daughter, let alone murder his wife."

"They never do," Carolyn reminded him.

"Try to show up over here after lunch. I know you've got a mess on your hands, but we're getting more behind every day. None of the new transfers have experience in investigations. I'm personally handling a shooting, a robbery, and a homicide."

Carolyn disconnected, turning down Dee Drive. She had to get in touch with Tyler Bell. If Veronica had tried to flush the truth out of him about the Abernathy and McAllen killings, Bell would have to be considered as a suspect, and Carolyn would be forced to bring this to the attention of the task force.

What they needed to determine was if Jude was telling the truth about her father taking her to the Motor Inn two days before the crime. Why would she lie at this juncture? Maybe she was merely confused about how things had gone down. The girl hadn't been eating properly, and she'd been physically assaulted, both conditions that could impair memory.

Parking and collecting her computer from the backseat, Carolyn entered the police department and signed in with the desk officer. She assumed the task force was still working out of the conference room, so she headed in that direction. The only one seated at the long table was Keith Edwards, the young officer they'd borrowed from patrol.

"Oh," Edwards said, standing. "I guess you're wondering where everyone went. The clerk from the motel came in on his way to work. Detectives Sawyer and Stevens are showing him a photo lineup with the black guy in it."

"I would assume if they're trying to determine if he can identify Reggie Stockton, everyone in the lineup would be black. You're from Atlanta, right?"

"Yes," he said, avoiding her eyes.

"You're not in the South anymore, Keith," Carolyn said. "It might be better if you used his name instead of referring to Stockton as the black guy."

He sat back down. "I hear you loud and clear. It won't happen again. They're in Hank's office. Detective Conrad is picking up Jude Campbell's school records. I don't have much to do right now. I guess no one trusts me. All they do is send me for coffee and food."

She set her computer down on the table and pulled out a chair. "I'm sure they trust you, Keith. Give them time and you'll have more than you can handle. Did you get word from the lab on the letter I received?"

He perked up. "They didn't find any prints other than yours, but they found a hair. They want you to come by the lab so they can get a DNA sample from you. Maybe we'll get lucky. The hair might belong to the perpetrator."

Carolyn reached up and yanked several hairs from her head, placing them on a piece of paper, then folding it into a small square. "I don't have time to go to the lab today. I'd appreciate it if you'd take this over there for me."

"Right away," Edwards said, grabbing his jacket off the back of his chair. He picked up the envelope, then stopped. "You're not my commanding officer. I'll have to wait and run it by Detectives Sawyer and Stevens."

"Just do it, Keith. I'll tell them I sent you." Carolyn looked at his face. He didn't look much older than John. Once you turned forty, she'd discovered, everyone looked like a kid. The worst was the doctors. It took a long time to become a physician.

Turning on her computer, Carolyn accessed Veronica's contacts, finding a telephone number for Tyler Bell. The situation was tragic. His eight-year-old son, Billy, had been kidnapped, sexually assaulted, then dismembered by Lester McAllen. The boy was an only child, and the wife had been so anguished she'd committed suicide. Bell had owned a successful painting company, and prior to their son's death, the couple were living the American dream. Having lost both his son and his wife, Tyler Bell had fallen on hard times. His company had gone bankrupt, and his home went into foreclosure. At his lowest moment, Veronica had called and informed him that his son's killer might go free because of Robert Abernathy. After Abernathy was murdered by an unknown assailant a few days later at his home in Oxnard, Veronica suspected Bell might be responsible. She had not, however, shared this information with the Oxnard PD.

A month or so later, Lester McAllen's conviction was overturned. He was shot and killed in Camarillo, a town not far from Ventura. Oxnard had been unable to match prints found on the fence leading to Abernathy's home as the killer had an oily substance on his hands. Veronica finally confided in Carolyn, telling her that Tyler Bell had mentioned an identical substance he used to remove paint at the end of the day. Veronica had noticed it when she'd shaken hands with him during the original investigation, and Bell had apologized, telling her he had sensitive skin.

Since McAllen and Abernathy had scores of enemies, even within the criminal justice system, and Veronica had nothing more than speculation that Bell had killed them, Carolyn had advised her to wait and see if anything else developed. McAllen had been a monster who deserved to die. Abernathy, though, had turned out to be somewhat pathetic, regardless of the havoc he'd wreaked on individuals like Tyler Bell. When the autopsy was performed, they discovered the forensic scientist had been suffering from retinitis pigmentosa, and had almost completely lost his eyesight.

Instead of resigning his position as any responsible person would have done, Abernathy had covered his disability by falsifying evidence and perjuring his testimony in the courtroom. In the cases involving DNA, Abernathy would have an assistant test the sample drawn from the defendant and then pass it off as the DNA collected from the crime scene.

The morning Veronica was murdered, she'd made a veiled reference to Tyler Bell by stating that she'd developed more sympathy for people who made mistakes. Had she been on her way to meet Bell that day? Race was now as significant as Bell was black.

Carolyn pulled her cell phone out to dial his number when Hank and Mary walked into the room. "What happened?"

Mary headed toward the section of the table she'd turned into her temporary office. Papers and files were strewn everywhere. "The clerk, Benny Gonzales, is an idiot," she blurted out, furious. "Not only that, he's a habitual marijuana user, a fact he failed to mention until today. He was probably stoned the day of the murder."

"So, he didn't recognize Stockton?"

"I guess you could say that," the detective answered. "The first person he identified was Eddie Shaker from patrol. We showed him another photo lineup with Stockton in it, and he identified a guy who's serving nine years for armed robbery at Chino. Against my better judgment, I try again. This time, he fingers Stockton. Think that's gonna fly in a courtroom?"

"Drew Campbell is our killer," Hank said, taking a seat beside Carolyn. "We got Benny to bring in the records from the motel. The place itself is part of our problem. With a guy running it whose brains are fried, you can imagine what a sorry state their records are in. The credit card receipts aren't linked to specific rooms, just the names of the guests and the dates of their stay. The owner died, so the motel has been in probate for three years. The attorney I spoke to says the new owners are going to tear it down and build a strip mall."

"Did you show the clerk Drew's picture?"

"That's the good news I was about to tell you," Mary said, twisting her shoulder-length hair into a knot at the base of her neck. "Benny says Drew looks familiar. He has no idea if he rented him a room, or if he ran into him in the grocery store. This guy is such a piss-poor witness, I doubt if Kevin Thomas will put him on the stand. The defense would destroy him, and we'd end up worse off than if we didn't use him." She doodled on her notepad, then looked up. "We could rehab Benny before Kevin talks to him. You know, sober him up, get him some decent clothes, throw some cash at him. If we coach him, he might remember renting Drew a room the day of the murder."

Carolyn turned ashen. "You didn't say that, did you?"

"No," Mary said, dead serious. "And you

didn't hear it."

Hank shot her a stern look. "I want this asshole as much as you do, Mary, but we've got to play by the rules."

Mary exploded, standing and hurling a file across the room. "Drew didn't play by the rules when he shot his wife in the head. Was he playing by the rules when he raped and beat his daughter? I'm not going to stand by and let this guy walk just because he can afford to hire a top-flight attorney. I'll take him out myself if we can't make a case against him."

Gary Conrad had come in without anyone noticing. He ducked, ending up in a paper blizzard. "Hey," he said, "are we having fun, Mary, or are you trying to tell me something? PMS, right? Are you women all on the same schedule? Jeez, my wife was on a rampage this morning, too."

Mary glared at him and stormed out. Carolyn followed her, finding her in the ladies' room, holding on to the sink and sobbing.

"I'm all right," she said. "I haven't been getting enough sleep."

Carolyn had never seen her that upset. "It happened to you, didn't it?"

Mary linked eyes with her, wiping the tears away with her fingers. "Is it that obvious?"

"Not really. I've talked to a lot of rape victims. How old were you?"

"Ten," the detective said, sucking in a deep breath. "My older brother . . . we shared the same room. At first, I didn't know it was wrong. No one talked about those kinds of things in our house. My dad was a cop and my mom taught Sunday school. When I was thirteen, Jordan was killed when his school bus crashed into a brick wall during a rainstorm. I thought it was my fault because I'd prayed so hard for him to stop hurting me." She reached over and clasped Carolyn's hand. "Promise me you won't tell Hank and the others. If the men sense even an iota of weakness . . ."

"I understand," Carolyn told her. "Take your time. I'll see you back in the conference room." She walked toward the door, then turned back around. "Can I ask you just one question? If you don't want to answer it, tell me."

Mary reached in her purse and pulled out her lipstick. "Go ahead."

"Did you tell anyone?"

"No."

"Why?"

The detective smiled. "That's two questions." She finished applying her lipstick, slipping it back into her purse. "I didn't tell because I was afraid. I was certain my parents would hate me. Jordan told me it was my fault. I was scared of the dark, so I used to climb into bed with him. After he died, of course, there was no reason to tell anyone."

"Thanks," Carolyn said. "Just so you'll know, I feel the same way you do. I couldn't live with myself if I let the person who killed Veronica get away with it. She was my best friend, although I wasn't always hers. That's the cross I have to carry. There's one more thing."

Mary undid her hair, fluffing it out with her fingers. Her beautiful face was surrounded by ebony curls. She checked her appearance in the mirror, then gave Carolyn her full attention.

"Before we both go out gunning for Drew," Carolyn told her, "let's make certain he's guilty."

"When do you have to leave today?"

"I promised Brad I'd be back by noon."

"It's almost ten," Mary told her. "Stockton should be at the Circuit City in the Esplanade Shopping Center. Want to come with me?"

"Absolutely."

CHAPTER 13

Mary Stevens was dressed in a pair of tight-fitting black pants and an orange knit blouse, which showed off her shapely figure. She was the kind of woman whose looks and presence instantly captured people's attention, and she didn't mind using them to her advantage. Several people turned and stared as the detective whisked past them, Carolyn trailing behind unnoticed.

"Stockton sells car stereos," Mary whispered in her throaty voice. "Let's play him before we pull out our badges."

She headed toward a well-built young male. "Hi," she said, her eyes drifting to his name tag to confirm it was Stockton. "My friend and I are looking to upgrade our system. Got any recommendations?"

Jude had good taste, Carolyn thought, sizing up her boyfriend. She estimated Stockton's height as slightly over six feet. He must be an athlete, as his muscles strained inside the fabric of his white shirt. His hair was neatly trimmed, and his facial features were nicely proportioned. His dark eyes were large and fringed with thick lashes.

"What kind of system do you have now?"

"I think it's a Pioneer," Mary answered. "Our car's ten years old, so all we've got is a tape deck."

Stockton became animated. "You should get a system that's Sirius-ready, with a built-in amplifier and MP3/WMA playback capabilities. If it was me, I'd buy an Alpine. It's an excellent product, and it's reasonably priced." He went over to one of the displays, pushing the PLAY button. When nothing happened, his body tensed. "How the hell do they expect us to sell this shit if the demos don't work?"

Mary exchanged glances with Carolyn before she turned back to Stockton. "You're something of a hothead, aren't you? I doubt if your manager would approve of you talking like that in front of a customer."

He thrust his chest forward, his face shifting into hard lines. "Go buy your fucking stereo somewhere else. I'm trying to earn money to go to college. What are you two, anyway? Lesbians?"

"No, Reggie," Mary said, opening her jacket where her badge was clipped on her belt. "We're cops. How does that grab you?" So he wouldn't cause a scene in the store, she took his hand and pressed it downward until he winced. "Let's go outside where we can talk."

"Am I under arrest?"

"Not yet," she said, releasing him. "Cooperate and you might not have to spend the night in the county jail. It won't look good on your college application, know what I mean?"

After they placed Stockton in the back of the unmarked police unit, Carolyn slid into the passenger seat and turned sideways so she could see his face. Mary connected with the young man's eyes in the rearview mirror. Stockton tried one of the doors and found it locked. When he realized he couldn't roll down the window, either, he slapped back in the seat.

This must be his first time in a police car, Carolyn decided. "When did you start dating Jude Campbell?"

"Shit," he said, his voice a high-pitched whine, "is that what this is about? I was never with Jude. She's psycho, man. She went around school telling everyone we were together. My girlfriend and I got into a big fight because of her. She broke up with me and skipped town. She said Jude was stalking her. Jude even passed her a note at school the other day saying she was going to kill her."

"What was your girlfriend's name?" Mary asked, craning her neck around.

"Haley Snodgrass."

"Do you know where can we contact her?"

"No," Stockton said, his face glistening with perspiration. "Haley must have really freaked out. She took off a few days ago. She didn't tell anyone where she was going. Talk to her parents."

Mary said, "Tell me more about Jude. Was she into drugs?"

"What wasn't she into?" he said. "She had sex with almost every guy at Ventura High. There were rumors that she'd had three abortions, and that she let the guys from the navy base in Port Heuneme do her for money."

Carolyn inserted herself into the conversation. "Are you aware that Jude's mother was murdered?"

"Yeah," Stockton said. "Are you the same cops who called my mom? She's scared to death of the police. I was a good student. You can check my records. I even got a partial scholarship to UC Irvine. It isn't enough, though." He kicked the back of the seat. "That's why I had to take a year off and work at this lousy job. We lost everything in the hurricane. I refuse to take my mom's money. My dad would have taken care of us, but the cops shot him."

"The New Orleans PD?" Carolyn asked.

"Who do you think? The rotten bastards were shooting people, robbing people, raping women. It was a madhouse down there. I mean, if you ever wonder what hell is like, just look at the pictures. All my dad was doing was rummaging around on the street, trying to find us some food and water. Four cops drove by and popped him for absolutely no reason."

"Are you certain it was the police?"

Stockton brushed his finger under his nose, a muscle in his eyelid twitching. "I was standing just a few feet away, along with five other people. After everything was over, two of the cops were busted, but only for looting. We never found out where the other witnesses went. For all I know, they died. There were dead bodies all over the place."

"Look," Mary said. "I'm going to let you go back to work so you don't lose your job. We may want to ask you some more questions, so don't leave town. Here's my card. If you think of anything else that might be helpful, give us a call." She removed a second card and a pen, then handed them to Stockton. "I'm sure you have a cell. Write down your number. That way, we won't have to disturb your mother if we need to get in touch with you again."

Stockton hesitated, then scribbled something on the back of Mary's card. He started to hand it back to her, but she told him to leave it on the seat. Once he did, she got out and opened the back door for him, placing her hand on his head to keep him from bumping it on the top of the police car.

Waiting until he was inside the store, she told Carolyn to get her an evidence bag from the glove box. With the tips of her fingers, she picked up the card and deposited it inside the plastic. "Well, we got his fingerprints," Mary said once she'd climbed back in the driver's seat. "What do you think?"

"The poor kid has been through hell."

"I'm not talking about Katrina," the detective said. "Do you think he's telling the truth about Jude?"

"He seemed forthright." Carolyn stared out the front window. "He didn't display any of the classic tells you see when a person is lying. Something bothered me, though. I'm not convinced everything he told us was the truth."

"No one tells the complete truth. And this guy will never trust a cop again." Mary cranked the ignition, but she left the car idling as she thought. "Did you notice how he kept his hands in his lap the whole time? He was trying not to touch anything. Stockton may look like an average, clean-cut young man, but I don't think that's the case. A person who's seen and been through the kind of things Stockton has must be emotionally scarred. And he's shrewd, just like our killer. He knew I wanted his fingerprints. The problem was he didn't know how to get out of it without giving himself away."

"But the clerk didn't ID him."

"The clerk is a pothead, remember? And he did ID Stockton eventually. The person we need to find is Haley Snodgrass. I know you have to get back to your office, so I'll track down her address and see what her parents have to say."

"Let's say Stockton did rent the room," Carolyn said, fastening her seat belt. "What motive would he have to kill Veronica?"

"If what he said about Jude being infatuated with him is true, he might have rented the motel room because he wanted to set her straight, and didn't want anyone to see them together. Then he lost his temper and beat the shit out of her. Now if we pick up the story the way Jude tells it, substituting Stockton for Drew, she could have called her mother for help somewhere before or after the beating. With his distrust of police, Stockton might go to all kinds of extremes to stay out of jail."

"I get it," Carolyn said, excited. "Veronica shows up after Jude escapes, finds Stockton in the room. She demands to know where her daughter is. They struggle. Stockton gets her gun away and shoots her. You know what that means?"

"Yeah," Mary said, looking behind her as she backed out of the parking space. "Drew may be innocent. Jude could have manufactured the sexual abuse story because she was pissed at him for throwing her out. She might also have done it to protect Stockton. It certainly wouldn't be the first time we've seen an abused female cover for the male batterer."

"His girlfriend dumped him," Carolyn continued, "and by his own admission, Jude was an easy lay. He could have taken her to the motel to have sex with her. Maybe Jude tried to turn their encounter into something it wasn't and Stockton lost it." She placed a palm on her forehead. "God, we took Drew's children away. I feel terrible. I should be comforting Drew, not persecuting him."

The detective reached over and patted her hand. "Don't feel bad, sugar. The odds are stacked that Drew is guilty. I was a victim myself, remember? Jude was telling the truth. I'd bet my life on it. It makes perfect sense for Drew to kick her out. He knew if anyone saw the bruises, they'd start asking questions and he'd end up a suspect in Veronica's murder. The nanny did it for me. He didn't even wait for his wife's funeral to start priming a new victim. What other excuse would he have to move Stacy into his bedroom?"

"Then how does Stockton fit into the picture?"

"He probably has nothing to do with it," Mary said. "All guys his age are hotheads. If a cop had killed my father, I wouldn't want the police to have my fingerprints."

"We forgot to ask Gary what he found out from Jude's school records."

"Speak for yourself," Mary said. "I talked to him while you were busy with Hank. Jude has a extensive history of absenteeism, going all the way back to the fifth grade. Gary's going to follow up and speak to the family doctor. As far as Stockton is concerned, all we've been doing is speculating. We've barely cracked the surface in this case. Right now, everyone is guilty."

"Gee," Carolyn said, smiling, "you sound like Brad Preston. He said the same exact thing to me the other day."

"Preston is a prick. A righteously handsome prick, but nonetheless, a prick."

"You went out with him, didn't you?"

"What is this?" Mary said, scrunching her face up. "Are you trying to get me to reveal all my secrets in one day? Yeah, I went out with him. I hate to admit it, but I even slept with him. I was about to get in over my head when I saw him with a girl who didn't look a day over eighteen. I broke my own rule, so I guess I deserved it."

"What's that?"

"Never date a man who's got a better ass than you."

"He's dynamite in bed, though," Carolyn said, remembering the times they'd spent together. "Marcus is better, of course."

"Sure he is," Mary said, steering the car onto the ramp for the 101 Freeway. "Brad isn't bad. He could never keep up with the brothers, though. Have you ever been with a black man?"

"No," Carolyn said. "I was a virgin when I met Frank. I haven't had that many lovers since we divorced. I had a date with Earl Miller from the sheriff's department. I liked him, but he didn't call me back."

"You know what they say," Mary said with a sly smile. "Once you go black, you never go back."

Carolyn pointed her finger at her. "Now, if I'd said that, it would be considered racist."

"No, it wouldn't," Mary argued. "Anyway, I'm just messing with you."

"When's Drew's arraignment?"

"At one this afternoon. I thought you weren't going."

"I've changed my mind," Carolyn said, glancing at her watch. "Step on it. I'll have to check in with Brad, and it's already twelve thirty."

The detective floored the Crown Victoria, zigzagging through traffic as the needle on the speedometer shot to just under a hundred. When she skidded to a stop in front of the government center, Carolyn climbed out on shaky legs, feeling as if she'd just gotten off a roller coaster. She stuck her head in the window. "I'll never ask you to step on it again, okay? Maybe you should reconsider Brad. You two are perfect for each other."

"Oh, yeah," Mary said, laughing. "Brad baby has to go to a racetrack. I can speed any time I feel like it. It's one of the perks of being a cop."

CHAPTER 14

Friday, October 15 — 12:55 P.M.

Carolyn rushed past Rachel's desk into Brad's office, harried and out of breath. She'd snagged her hose getting out of Mary's car, and since she didn't want to go to court in jeans, she was zipping up the black skirt she kept in her office. "I need to go to Drew's arraignment. I promise I'll work all night at home. His daughter is living in my house, for Christ's sake. We came up with some new information. We talked to the guy Jude was —"

"Slow down," Brad said, tossing his pen down on his desk. "I didn't understand a word you just said."

"Please, Brad, I have to go to Drew's arraignment and I have to leave right now. Judge Thornton has a fit when someone comes in late."

"If it's that important," he said, standing

and grabbing his jacket off the back of his chair, "I guess I should go with you."

Brad stopped and told Rachel where he was going, then jogged to catch up to Carolyn. "Thornton is in Division Thirty-two, right?"

"Thirty-six." Not wanting to wait for the elevator, Carolyn raced down the stairs to the first floor, crossed the lobby, and darted outside to the courtyard. People were eating their lunches on the benches surrounding the fountain, while attorneys and other individuals were making their way to court for the afternoon sessions.

Brad stepped in front of her to open the door. "I think you said something about new information. Want to tell me about it?"

She quickly filled him in on what had occurred with Reggie Stockton.

"You really think Jude made up all that stuff about Drew?"

"It's possible," Carolyn said, smoothing down her hair before they entered the courtroom.

Only a handful of people were present, but Carolyn wanted to be close enough to see Drew's facial expressions. They slid into the second row behind the prosecution table. Judge Christopher Thornton wasn't on the bench yet, but Drew's attorney was already seated at the adjacent table. She leaned over and whispered in Brad's ear, "Is that Jacob Farrow?"

"You got it."

"His fees are outrageous," Carolyn told him. "He's one of the best defense attorneys in the county." She glanced over at District Attorney Kevin Thomas. At forty-five, he was a slender, wiry man with reddish blond hair and hazel eyes. "Thomas must be pissing his pants. If anyone can get Drew off, it would be Farrow."

Two bailiffs escorted Drew Campbell to the defense table, dressed in the jail-issued orange jumpsuit, his hands cuffed and his feet shackled. Once he was seated next to his attorney, he turned around and stared straight at Carolyn. The look out of his eyes was scathing, and a corner of his lip curled in contempt.

After the bailiff called the court to order, Judge Thornton entered through the back door and climbed the stairs to the bench, his black robe swirling around him. He'd received his appointment at the age of thirty-three, and was the youngest judge in the Ventura system.

In the courtroom, Thornton looked imposing, and even top attorneys like Jacob Farrow became nervous when they had to argue a case in front of him. Carolyn had followed Thornton to his chambers one day to discuss one of her cases, having to stifle a laugh when she realized what a tiny man he was. With heels, she looked down on him, and she was only five-four. He reminded her of a twelve-year-old boy dressed in a magician's costume. Regardless of his diminutive size, he was an attractive man. His skin was fair and unblemished, and his dark eyes flashed with intelligence. He spoke fast, and she'd heard he possessed a photographic memory. One of the DAs claimed Thornton had once recited every word spoken during a two-hour hearing. He also possessed razor-sharp hearing. Now that he was on the bench, Carolyn knew that even a whisper could draw a reprimand.

"Do you have a copy of the information, Mr. Farrow?" the judge asked, his speech crisp and articulate.

"Yes, Your Honor," the gray-haired attorney said, standing. "I also have a discovery order I'd like to submit." He walked over and handed it to the clerk for dispersal.

When the judge received the copy, he set it aside. To file discovery, requesting all information and evidence the other side had on the case, was routine procedure. As the case continued, more discovery orders would be filed by both parties, along with dozens of motions and petitions.

The courtroom fell silent, except for the rustling of papers by the clerk as she prepared the file. Thornton spoke, his gaze fixed on Drew. "Mr. Campbell, How do you plead to count one, a violation of section 288.5 of the California Penal Code, continuous sexual abuse of a child?"

Swallowing hard, Drew said, "Not guilty, Your Honor."

Everything struck home for Carolyn. Now it was real. The charges were appropriate, the punishment severe — a mandatory term of up to sixteen years in prison. And this was only the beginning. Carolyn listened as the other charges were read.

"How do you plead to count two, a violation of section 261.6 of the California Penal Code, rape, where the act was accomplished by threatening to inflict extreme pain, serious bodily injury, or death?"

"Not guilty."

Carolyn knew this count represented the most recent offense, when Jude was legally an adult. The penalty was a maximum of six years in prison, and could run consecutive to the first sixteen-year term. Drew was now looking at twenty-one years.

Judge Thornton continued, "How do you

plead to a violation of section 269 of the California Penal Code, aggravated sexual assault on a child?"

"Not guilty, Your Honor." Drew pulled his collar away from his neck.

These were serious, despicable offenses, Carolyn thought, and Drew's attorney knew the road ahead of him would be long and arduous. He was probably questioning his judgment in taking on a case of this magnitude. If Drew ran out of money, Farrow couldn't simply dump him and walk away. He must hold some conviction that Drew Campbell was innocent.

Even Carolyn began perspiring. Drew wasn't a stranger off the street. How many times had she been in his home, shared meals with him, laughed with him, cried with him? The criminal justice system was like an enormous machine, with the ability to gobble up lives and spit them out in shattered pieces. The worst part was that Carolyn was responsible for setting this machine in motion.

The last count carried a sentence of sixteen years to life, making the grand total thirty-seven years to life. Certain limitations were attached to the first count, continuous sexual abuse of a child. No other count could be filed unless it represented a separate and distinct period of time, or an additional victim, many times a sibling. Hank must have gotten in touch with Kevin Thomas after she and Mary had left to speak to Reggie Stockton, advising him of Jude's documented record of absenteeism. This was the kind of evidence a prosecutor dreamed of. Section 288.5 had become law to cover crimes where there was no way to establish a date and time. All the prosecutor had to prove was that three incidences of sexual abuse had occurred.

Drew's face had turned a sickly shade of white. Carolyn saw his hands locked on the arms of his chair. He probably didn't know that his entire life was on the line. Did he look guilty? Surely he would have known that his actions might one day come to light. Of course, his motive in murdering Veronica to ensure her silence was now firmly established.

Brad leaned over and whispered, "Thirty-seven to life, and Thomas didn't even file murder charges yet. I'm glad I'm not in Drew's shoes right now."

A second later, the gavel came down and Carolyn jumped, staring straight ahead so the judge didn't think she was the culprit.

Thornton knew exactly who was responsible. "Sir," he said, glaring at Brad, "if you wish to talk, please exit this court."

Brad patted Carolyn on the knee, then slipped out the side aisle.

Judge Thornton proceeded with the arraignment, selecting a date for the preliminary hearing. At this stage in the process, the prosecution only had to establish that a crime had in fact occurred and that there was probable cause to believe that the defendant had committed it. During the trial, the burden of proof would be more specific, and the prosecution would be charged with proving Drew's guilt beyond a reasonable doubt.

Jacob Farrow had taken his seat and was conferring with Drew in hushed whispers. He rose to his feet again. "Could we address the issue of bail at this time, Your Honor?"

"I was just about to order the probation department to conduct a bail review, Mr. Farrow."

"I know that's routine procedure," Farrow continued, "but we believe there's a conflict of interest. The defendant's wife was a probation officer. As you probably know, she was recently murdered. Due to the charges filed against Mr. Campbell today, it's highly unlikely that he'll receive an unbiased recommendation from the probation department."

Judge Thornton braced his head with his

hand. "How do you propose I remedy this problem? That is, if a problem exists."

"The court should determine bail for my client, independent of any other considerations."

"I object," Kevin Thomas said. "Why should the defendant receive special consideration? The probation department is the agency charged with preparing these reports for a reason. As you know, Your Honor, they compile criminal histories, check employment records, ties to the community, weigh the risks the defendant poses to the community. Respectfully, the court isn't prepared to make this type of recommendation. The people believe the defendant should be held without bail. The victim is terrified of him."

Farrow shot out, "These charges are an outrage, Your Honor. Mr. Campbell is a decent, law-abiding citizen. The victim in this case is a rebellious teenager with a bone to pick with her father. She's been incarcerated in juvenile hall on numerous occasions, once for selling narcotics. She also has a documented history of lying to correction officers."

Thornton's brows furrowed as his voice boomed out over the courtroom. "Need I remind you, Mr. Farrow, your client is the person who must defend himself against these charges? The victim is not on trial. And if you persist in making any more disparaging remarks, I'll hold you in contempt of court." He stopped and took a breath. "A bail review will be prepared by the probation department. The hearing will be held in this courtroom on Monday at three o'clock. Until then, the defendant will be remanded to the custody of the Ventura County Jail."

CHAPTER 15

Friday, October 15 — 2:15 P.M.

Carolyn stopped off in the cafeteria, wolfing down a rubbery cheeseburger and a Snickers bar, then went straight to Brad's office and flopped down in a chair. "I should have warned you about Thornton. He might be heavy-handed on some issues, as you noticed, but he moves the calendar faster than any judge I've ever known and his decisions are always sound. After you left, Farrow argued that Thornton should decide Drew's bail today because we would be biased. Thornton shot him down and assigned us the bail review, then blasted Farrow for assaulting Jude's character."

"What kind of evidence does the PD have in Veronica's murder?"

"Not much," Carolyn said, sighing. "Basically motive and opportunity. We found a hair on the letter I received at the morgue.

The lab hasn't had time to process it yet. Let's keep our fingers crossed that it turns out to be the killer's and not mine. Mary is convinced Jude is telling the truth. The things Stockton told us rattled me, though. I have to keep reminding myself that Jude is an incest victim, or I wouldn't be able to tolerate her behavior."

Brad leaned back in his chair. "Is she a credible witness?"

"It depends on which side of the bed she gets up on," Carolyn told him. "She's highly unpredictable, and when you push her, she pushes back hard. From the way things went today, it appears Farrow's main line of defense will be to discredit her. Other than the bruises, it's basically her word against her father's. Her juvenile record certainly won't help, if they're able to get it on record. And if Farrow gets Stockton or some other kid who knows Jude to testify, which we have to assume he will, the case could go down in flames."

Brad picked up a large stack of files. "Most of this stuff should already be on your computer." He opened one and handed her the autopsy pictures. Until a person saw the aftermath of violence, homicide was only a word. "Victim is a forty-two-year-old nurse who was murdered by her twenty-year-old son, John Richard Butterfield, aka Ritchie Stick, Two Finger Banana, and Johnny B. Kool."

"What in the hell is a two-finger banana? Is the guy a rapper or something?"

"A wannabe maybe," Brad told her, taking a sip of his coffee out of a mug with a picture of a race car on it that Carolyn had given to him for Christmas several years back. "Have you had your ration of caffeine for the day, or do you want me to have Rachel get you a cup? It's your favorite. Chocolate macadamia nut."

"No, but thanks," Carolyn said, shuffling the first picutre to the bottom of the stack and examining the next one. "Give me a quick rundown."

"The defendant comes from a white middle-class family," he told her. "Oxnard PD claims he has ties to several violent street gangs, all of them black. Father works for a textile manufacturing company. The older brother is in his last year of college at UCLA. The defendant was the black sheep of the family, no pun intended. The DA who prosecuted him is Orin Aronson. The conviction was for second-degree murder. The lab counted twenty-one stab wounds. Murder weapon was a hunting knife."

"Any signs of mental illness?" Carolyn

asked, studying the bloody corpse. The worst thing about a violent death was the degradation. No matter how many times she saw it, it still made her stomach turn. The woman's clothes were in shreds. One of her breasts was exposed, along with her buttocks. From the looks of it, she had multiple stab wounds in both areas, as well as her lower abdomen. "There's something sexual about this, don't you think? Look at the areas he targeted."

"Probably," Brad said, yawning. "I worked at home until three this morning, then got up at five. I really don't care what motivated sonny boy to start carving up old Mom. All I want to do is get this thing assigned, finished, and submitted."

"You're getting old," Carolyn said, studying the next picture. "You used to be able to party all night and put in a twelve-hour day. Who do you want to handle this?"

"Hey, I've been assigning cases all week. This baby is yours. All I know is it has to go to one of the new transfers. Our regular people are so buried, they'll never see daylight. Linda Cartwright is a sport, but when I dumped ten new cases on her this morning, she threw a fit and threatened to throw in the towel."

Carolyn scratched her left wrist. When she

got nervous, she had a tendency to break out in hives. "Do I know any of the new people?"

"Doubtful," Brad told her. "They've been hiding out in supervision picking their noses. James Rowley is pretty sharp. He used to race a few years back. Then he got married and his wife made him give it up."

Carolyn smirked. "Racing cars doesn't qualify a person to handle a murder investigation. Sometimes I wonder how you got promoted."

"It's not a sentencing nightmare like Drew's case will be if he's convicted. Second-degree murder is simple. Twelve years to life. What's the big deal?" He placed the file on top of the stack and shoved it to the edge of his desk. "You can't nitpick every case that comes along, Carolyn, not if you're going to keep working with the PD. It's about time you learned to supervise, don't you think?"

Carolyn stood, walking over and picking up the stack of file folders. "It's time *you* learned the law. The victim was stabbed. A knife is a deadly weapon. That's an enhancement." She flipped open the file and scanned the pleading, jostling the stack of folders in her arms. "The DA pled it as an enhancement. The defendant also has a prior felony conviction. That falls under 1170.12. I know this one by heart. 'If a defendant has one prior felony conviction that has been pled and proved, the determinate term or minimum term for an indeterminate term shall be twice the term otherwise provided for the current felony conviction.' Try explaining that one. Your twelve to life just flew out the window."

Brad tossed his feet on top of the desk. "I don't have to explain anything," he said. "I'm an administrator now." He closed his eyes. "Get back to work. It's time for my nap."

"By the way," Carolyn said, knowing he was teasing, but unable to resist putting a dent in his testosterone-driven ego. "Mary Stevens told me she slept with you. She called you a prick."

Brad's eyes flew open. "A little prick or a big prick?"

Men, Carolyn thought, disgusted. He didn't care that she had to assign a high-profile homicide to an officer with no experience in court investigations, but he snapped to attention when she mentioned sex. "She said you couldn't compete with the brothers. Does that answer your question?"

He jerked his head back as if she'd slapped him. "Damn women," he said. "When did you get so vindictive? Can't we have some fun every now and then?"

"I canceled my wedding," she reminded him, blowing a strand of hair off her forehead. "My best friend and top investigator was murdered. Her sexually abused daughter is living in my fiancé's house, and her husband may spend the rest of his life in prison. There's not much I feel like joking about right now."

Brad sat up in his chair and picked up a pen. "You wouldn't have Mary's home number on you, would you?"

"Why? You want to try again to see if you can get a better score? You're incorrigible, Brad." Carolyn headed toward the door, then turned around and glanced back at him. "Maybe you *should* take a nap. I like you better with your mouth closed."

When Carolyn returned to her office, she found Kevin Thomas waiting for her. "I hope you don't mind," the district attorney said. "Your door was open."

"Not at all," she told him, circling behind her desk. "Have a seat. Do you want some water, coffee, soda?"

"I'm fine," Thomas said, placing his briefcase in his lap and opening it. "I need to take Jude Campbell's deposition. I'd like to schedule it for tomorrow."

Carolyn sat down in her chair. Although Drew's trial was months away, they had only three weeks until the preliminary hearing. She'd been surprised that Hank had talked Thomas into getting a warrant for Drew's arrest so fast. With any suspicion whatsoever of child abuse, however, getting a court order to remove the children was a snap. The district attorney's office generally shied away from filing prematurely on a case this complex and serious. In most instances, they would have taken more time. She assumed they'd acted fast because of the fact that Drew might also be a murderer, and they were fearful of leaving him at large in the community. Once a defendant was arraigned, the clock began ticking. They could ask for continuances, of course, yet eventually the judge got fed up and forced them to go to trial. "Do you want to do it at my fiancé's house, or in your office?"

"I realize it might be more comfortable for the victim if we deposed her at your home, but I think it's important that she gets used to speaking about the situation with her father in an official setting." He used his finger to adjust his glasses higher on his nose. "I'll make arrangements for a victim's advocate to be present, someone who can be with her throughout the criminal proceedings. I'd appreciate it if you would call Ms. Campbell now so we can set a time."

"I was just about to check on her." Carolyn had no doubts that Kevin Thomas was a competent prosecutor, but he was somewhat peculiar. She noticed how his inexpensive brown suit hung loosely on his shoulders. He certainly didn't spend hours in the gym the way Brad did. Thomas was dreadfully thin, to the point that he didn't look healthy. She hadn't seen him in a few months, but he appeared to have lost a great deal of weight. Her brother, Neil, had a slender physique, but he dressed stylishly, turning it into an asset instead of a negative. She'd always been jealous that she hadn't inherited his metabolism. Neil could eat a truckload of food every day and never gain a pound.

Kevin Thomas moved and talked in slow motion. Listening to him was sometimes exhausting, and even the judges dreaded having him plead a case before them. The attorney was also a perfectionist, which wasn't always bad when you were dealing with people's lives. His handwriting was miniscule. She'd heard that this was indicative of low self-esteem. In most instances, she didn't put much stock in handwriting analysis, at least when it came to revealing character. With Thomas, however, it seemed to fit.

While the attorney sat there like a statue, Carolyn dialed the main line at the house. It was after four, and Rebecca picked up the phone. "It's me. Can you be a sweetheart and put Jude on the phone?"

"Where are you?" the girl shouted. "I called your office, but your answering machine picked up. I left three messages on your cell phone."

"I forgot to turn it back on after I left court," Carolyn explained. "Is something wrong?"

"Big time. Jude's gone. The bitch stole half of my clothes, even my bridesmaid's dress for the wedding. Not only that, she clipped the two hundred bucks I was saving out of my nightstand, then tried to bust open Marcus's safe with a hammer. She even took my iPod. It took me a year to download all those songs."

Carolyn placed her hand at the base of her throat. "I have a family matter I have to take care of, Kevin," she said. "Do you mind stepping out for a few minutes?"

"No problem," he said. "Would you like me to close your door?"

Her mouth was already parched. She smiled stiffly. "Please," she said. "It's always something when you have a teenager." Her daughter was screaming in her ear, the young person she had taken on the responsibility to protect was missing, and the attorney was taking forever just to close his damn briefcase.

Once she was alone, Carolyn cupped her hand over the phone. The walls were thin, and she didn't want Thomas to eavesdrop on her conversation. "Calm down, Rebecca. How could Jude leave? Bear was on duty today, and I set the alarm when I left this morning. Are you certain she isn't somewhere on the property? What about the barn?"

"What about the car?" her daughter tossed back. "She took Marcus's Jeep. When I couldn't get you, I called him at work. He's on his way home. Bear wanted to report it to the police, but Marcus told him he better ask you first. He didn't remember the license plate number, anyway. He was surprised it even started. Bear said the jumper cables were gone from the garage, and that Jude must have jumped it off the Range Rover."

Carolyn's future husband was a car collector. One of the reasons he'd purchased the house in Santa Rosa was it had enough land to build a five-car garage. "I have to go," she told Rebecca. "We'll figure everything out when I get home. If Jude calls, get in touch with me immediately. Oh, and try to get her to tell you where she is."

"Where do you want me to call you? On your cell phone? I called you three times and you didn't answer."

Carolyn yanked her cell out of her purse and turned it on. In addition to the messages Rebecca had left, Marcus and Bear had tried to get in touch with her. "My phone's on now. I'm in a meeting, but I'll be there as soon as I can. Don't go anywhere. I need you there in case Jude calls."

"Duh, Mom," Rebecca said. "People who steal things don't usually call to say hello. Marcus isn't going to marry you if you keep doing stupid things. Then what will we do? We already sold our house. I can't believe you let someone like Jude stay here. Shit, you might as well bring a murderer home."

"Don't curse," her mother said out of habit.

"Why not? You'd say dirty words, too, if someone ripped off all your stuff. For all I know, she did. I didn't check your closet. How did she know the safe was in the floor in the pantry? Even I didn't know until —"

"I'm hanging up, honey." Carolyn disconnected and placed her head in her hands. Jude must have been terrified her father would be released from jail. They had to find her. Without a victim, the DA would have no choice but to withdraw the charges and release Drew. She unscrewed the cap from a bottle of water on her desk and took a long swallow, then went to tell Kevin Thomas the bad news.

CHAPTER 16

Friday, October 15 — 6:30 P.M.

Carolyn saw the black-and-white sheriff's unit when she steered the Infiniti into the circular driveway. Marcus was outside talking to the deputy. She'd called and told him not to press charges against Jude. Ventura PD had already broadcast an attempt to locate the Jeep Wrangler.

On the way home, Carolyn had stopped off at the bus depot since Jude had mentioned staying there in the past. Mary Stevens had called Reggie Stockton to see if he knew where Jude had gone, as well as the girl whose cell phone she'd had in her possession at the hospital.

Marcus had changed into a pair of jeans and a red turtleneck sweater. When he saw Carolyn, he walked over to the Infiniti, opened the door, and extended his hand to help her out.

The evening air was damp and chilly. The weather report had predicted rain. She could already smell it in the air. She stepped into his open arms, pressing her head against his chest. "I'm so sorry, Marcus. I should have let Social Services find a placement for Jude. I blame myself because I left her alone in the house. I was going to ask Josephine to come in, but Jude swore she'd be fine, that all she wanted to do was sleep." She pulled away. "Did she take anything valuable? Rebecca said she tried to get into your safe."

"With a hammer," he told her. "All she did was ding it up."

"How did she know where it was?"

"You can find anything if you look long enough," Marcus told her. "That old Wrangler isn't worth more than a few grand. Rebecca was bent out of shape, though. I promised her I'd replace everything Jude took."

"Where's Bear?"

"He went home with his tail between his legs. He's lucky I didn't fire him. The guy is supposed to protect me from terrorists and foreign agents, and he's outsmarted by an eighteen-year-old girl. Was Jude standing nearby when you punched in the alarm code?"

"I don't think so," Carolyn told him. "No,

wait. The night I brought her home from the hospital, she was right behind me. I didn't think anything of it. I mean, she was in a new place, so I just assumed she wanted to stay close. You think that's how she got the code, right?"

"Yeah," he said, placing his hands on his hips. "I should have replaced the alarm pad with a palm sensor like I have at the office. I didn't think I needed it since we had on-site security, and I don't keep classified material in the house."

"How did she get past Bear?"

"She threw some pots and pans out the back door. By the time Bear ran around to see what was going on, she'd already taken off in the Wrangler."

"Did it have much gas in it?"

"It doesn't matter," Marcus said, kicking a snail off the driveway. "She took Rebecca's money, then picked up another three hundred from the drawer in the kitchen where Josephine keeps the cash I give her for groceries."

The deputy walked over, clearing his throat to get their attention. "I think I've got what I need, Mr. Wright. We didn't list any of the items the girl took as stolen, but we'll send out notices to all the pawnshops."

"Thanks, Officer," Marcus said. "Jude's

been through a rough time. Make certain your people go easy on her if they find her. We just want to know that she's safe."

Carolyn didn't say anything, but there was a lot more at stake than Jude's safety. If the DA decided to withdraw the charges against Drew, he could sue for false arrest. Technically, the district attorney could prosecute without Jude's cooperation, but it wasn't the wisest way to proceed. If the case went forward and Drew was acquitted, he could never be prosecuted again for those specific crimes. A person could spend more time in prison for sex offenses, particularly those committed against minors, than for murder. The Butterfield case, where the son had murdered his mother, was different as the defendant had a prior felony conviction.

They stood side by side on the front porch, gazing out over Marcus's avocado orchard. "Tell you what," he said, "why don't we take Rebecca and go out for a nice dinner? We can go to that French place you like so much."

Carolyn listened to the wind rushing through the trees. Her despair at the overall situation was beginning to take hold. If she wasn't careful, she could lose Marcus. They'd only lived together a short time. He had stress of his own. His company had recently lost a number of government contracts. He needed a woman who would be there for him, not someone who brought home more problems. "I'd love to go out tonight, honey, but I have too much to do. You and Rebecca go without me."

"Are you sure? We could go out tomorrow night."

She reached up to kiss him. He cupped his hands under her hips and pressed her tight against his body. "Now that our houseguest is gone," he said, "maybe we can pick up where we left off last night."

"Oh, Marcus," Carolyn said, pulling away. "How can you forgive me for getting you involved in all this? Our beautiful wedding . . ." Her voice trailed off. "I've ruined everything."

"No, you haven't, sweetheart," he said, cradling her in his arms again. "I wouldn't love you if you weren't such a caring person. No one would want to get married with all this going on. At least you're in a position to do something."

Carolyn chewed on a cuticle, stopping when she saw blood oozing out around her nail. As a child, she'd gnawed on the loose skin around her fingernails to the point where she looked like a person with leprosy. The kids stayed away from her, fearful they would get a disease. It was funny how old habits could resurface when a person was under stress.

"Helping Jude was the right thing," Marcus told her.

"I'm not so sure about that now."

"She did what she did because she's scared. If I was in her shoes, I might have done the same thing. Her bastard father made her life a living hell. If you can't trust your parents, who can you trust?" He fell silent, his hands closing into fists at his side. "I think Veronica knew. She just chose to ignore it. How could she not know? It went on for years."

Marcus's mood kept rising and falling. He was a positive person by nature, yet even he'd been short-circuited by the events of the past few days. "If Veronica knew," Carolyn said, peering up at him, "she paid a terrible price. I saw the pictures from the crime scene."

"Once we get through this, everything's going to be great. Our wedding will be even better. We've got more time to plan, take care of all the loose ends. Now, are you going to be waiting for me tonight?"

Carolyn's eyes drifted down. "I need to talk to Drew."

"What?" Marcus said, his voice elevating.

"I don't want you anywhere near that despicable man."

"You don't understand. He's the only one who knows where Jude might have gone. He knows her friends, her hangouts."

"Leave it to the police."

"I'm going to play him, Marcus, make him think I'm on his side. The police are his enemies now. He'll never talk to them."

"Jesus Christ!" he exclaimed. "You're insane. How can you look at me and tell me you're going to intentionally manipulate a murderer?"

"Have you forgotten?" Carolyn shot back. "That's what I used to do before my promotion. And I was good at it, really good. Besides, there's a chance that Drew might be innocent. Hank probably came down on him hard, thinking he could crack him. Men won't humble themselves to the degree that a woman will. Even if they did, it probably wouldn't work. Women are softer, less confrontational. Please don't fight me on this, Marcus. It's something I have to do."

Marcus glared at her, then went inside the house and left her alone on the porch. Carolyn waited for a while before she went to reason with him.

She found him at the bar in the den, making himself a martini. She took a seat on a bar stool. "If you insist, I won't go," she told him, placing her hands on the marble counter. "Jude is desperate, Marcus. She's a young girl, alone and afraid. Forget about the case. Think of what could happen to her. She hasn't recovered from the beating. Good Lord, she was trying to starve herself to death. She threw up this morning, probably because her stomach isn't used to digesting food. She may try to leave the state. A few hundred dollars isn't going to last very long. What's she going to do when it's gone? Think about it, then tell me I should leave it to the police."

He gulped down the martini before an swering. "Go," he said, gesturing with his hand. "When this is over, you're going to turn in your resignation."

Carolyn's yanked her hands back as if he'd slapped them. "Is that an ultimatum?"

Marcus set his glass down. "Yeah, I guess it is. Try to see things from my perspective. I love you, Carolyn. I don't want to have to go to the morgue and identify your body. I may not be the richest guy in the world, but I earn enough that my wife doesn't have to risk her life for a living."

She slid off the stool. "I'm going to talk to Rebecca before I leave. We've already can- celed the wedding, so if you want out, now's the time to do it. The job I do is important. Someone has to do it, regardless of what it pays. I'm a supervisor now. I don't have to deal with criminals on a regular basis. I have no idea what you do for a living, other than it has something to do with computers. For all I know, you could be a CIA agent. Since you require bodyguards, whatever you do is obviously dangerous."

"My work is classified," Marcus told her. "You know I can't discuss it, Carolyn. I could be prosecuted for treason."

She fixed him with an icy gaze. "I've never once asked you to quit, have I?"

Before he could answer, she walked out of the room. When she reached the foot of the stairs, Marcus caught her from behind and spun her around. "I need you," he said. "And whether you realize it or not, so does Rebecca."

"Rebecca may not like what I do," Carolyn told him, "but she understands. That's all I'm asking of you, Marcus." Pulling away, she continued up the stairs.

"How in the fuck did we lose our victim?" a male voice echoed through the detective bay at the Ventura PD.

Mary jumped up and met Hank in the aisle. "Calm down," she told him, placing her hand in the center of his chest and feeling his heart pounding. "You're going to give yourself a heart attack. We broadcast the license number on the Jeep Wrangler. Someone will pick her up."

"Drew Campbell is a murderer," Hank said, gritting his teeth as he yanked his tie off. "I'm sure of it, even if we don't have enough evidence yet to convict him. I saw it in his eyes, understand? If we can't find the girl, the bastard will walk."

"I know, I know," Mary said, hating it when he got this worked up. For years, he'd carried around fifty extra pounds and abused his body with alcohol. Although he'd stopped drinking and lost the weight, his arteries might still be clogged. She'd seen it with her father. When they'd conducted the autopsy after he was killed, the medical examiner told her he probably would have suffered a major heart attack sometime in the near future.

She followed Hank into his office, waiting for him to remove his jacket and sit down before she brought him up to date on the most recent developments. "Reggie Stockton is an imposter," she said. "I got his prints when I went to speak to him this morning. His real name is Reginald Louis Marcel."

"No shit?" Hank said, giving her his full attention. "Does he have a record?"

"Wait," Mary told him, "you haven't heard the best. This guy came here from New Orleans after Katrina and enrolled in high school. His DOB makes him twenty-four years old. At the time of the hurricane, he was pending trial on a narcotics charge, as well as carrying a concealed weapon. The rest of his criminal history was lost, but according to the New Orleans PD, Marcel was one of the inmates who escaped when the jail flooded."

"Pick him up, for God's sake."

"We tried," she said, sucking in a deep breath. "He walked off his job at Circuit City right after Carolyn and I spoke to him this morning. I met a patrol unit at his mother's place while you were at dinner. Mrs. Stockton says he came home, packed some of his things, and took off." She held up a palm. "Hold on, Hank, the story gets even better. Reggie isn't really her son. She was one of the people holed up in the convention center, if you remember that nightmare. When they were moved out to other shelters, Reggie was mistakenly listed as her son. He's a good-looking guy, and he has a way with the ladies. She's a widow with no family. Get the picture?"

"She didn't know the guy was a thug?"

"Nope," Mary said, swinging her leg back and forth. "Also, Stockton claimed his father was killed by a New Orleans cop. He said he'd gone out to search for food when a couple of uniformed officers drove by and shot him for no reason. This guy's good, Hank. I took the bait, and so did Carolyn. New Orleans said there was a rumor that rogue officers were shooting random civilians, but it turned out to be unfounded."

Mary saw the corners of Hank's mouth turn down. She placed both her feet on the floor and squared her shoulders off, knowing she was about to be reprimanded.

"You had this guy, right? Why didn't you bring him in for questioning? We could have put him in a lineup. Benny might have recognized him if he saw him in person." His fist came down on top of a pile of papers. "Damn it, Mary. Not only have we lost the victim, we may have let the killer slip through our fingers. This was sloppy police work and you know it."

"I admit I screwed up," Mary told him. "But didn't you tell me a few minutes ago that you were certain Drew killed Veronica? Except for the fact that Reggie is black and went to the same school as Jude Campbell, we had nothing to substantiate an arrest. It took three attempts for Benny to pick him out of the lineup. Christ, Hank, we only showed him eighteen guys. We were nowhere near a positive ID, and at the time, everything was leaning toward Drew. Reggie comes across as a clean-cut young man. Maybe he came here and cleaned up his act. He could have got in with the wrong crowd in New Orleans while he was in high school, and saw this as a second chance. When he realized I was going to run his prints, he fled. That doesn't mean he's a killer. All it means is he doesn't want to go to jail."

"Let me tell you something," Hank said. "Guys like that don't wake up one morning and decide to walk the straight and narrow. There's no telling what kind of criminal activity this man was involved in. He was probably dealing drugs at the high school."

The phone rang and Hank hit the button for the speaker. "We've got a body, Lieutenant," Gary Conrad said, out of breath. "A man was walking his dog in an orchard near Foothill Road. The dog dug up what he thought were human remains. When patrol called me, I thought it was probably some kind of critter. I'm out here now and it's definitely human. The grave is pretty shallow. Stand by, I'm going to try to get a look at the face."

A cloak of tension fell over the room. Mary

stared at the floor, while Hank's skin tone faded from red to white.

"It appears to be a female in her late teens or early twenties. I don't want to disturb the crime scene any more than I already have, so that's about all I can tell you."

Mary asked, "Is it Jude Campbell?"

"Not sure," Conrad told her. "I asked the dispatcher to notify CSI and the coroner. I've got more patrol units rolling. We'll secure the perimeter until you get here."

Before Mary made it to her feet, Hank had grabbed his jacket off the back of the chair and raced out of his office. "We're on our way," she told Conrad, rushing to catch up.

CHAPTER 17

Friday, October 15 — 7::30 P.M.

Carolyn pulled the Infiniti into a parking space in front of the jail, turned on the dome light, and opened her briefcase. On her way home, she'd called the number for Tyler Bell. A machine had come on, but it was a voice-generated announcement, so she wasn't certain if the number was still Bell's. It was visiting hours at the jail. She could use her badge and see Drew any time she wanted, but she knew she'd draw heat if she went now when it was so busy.

She pulled out her computer and went on-line, searching for painting contractors to see if anything came up under Bell's name. Just because he'd fallen on hard times after his son's death didn't mean he wasn't working. When that failed, she entered the county's database and searched for business licenses. "Got you," she said, punching the phone number into her cell.

"You have reached Bell Industrial and Residential Painting," the recording said. "Our office hours are —"

Carolyn hung up. It was a man's voice, though. She knew what Tyler Bell looked like, but she'd never seen or spoken to him in person. If she left a message, he might panic and disappear. She would get up early tomorrow morning and drive by the address to see if she could catch him. She had to eliminate Bell as a suspect. She'd already sat on it far too long.

Carolyn stared at the clock on the dashboard. She started to review some of the cases Brad had given her, but changed her mind. Even though she might inconvenience the staff at the jail, she needed to speak to Drew now.

She walked into a sea of humanity. There had to be sixty people crowded in the waiting room. She was assaulted by the smell of stale milk, dirty diapers, alcohol, and body odor. She'd never seen so many tattoos in her life. A reed-thin girl with dirty, stringy blond hair fidgeted in her seat. Her left arm was completely covered with tattoos, as well as the upper portion of her chest. Tattoos were a good way to hide tracks, and this girl was obviously a user.

Pushing and shoving her way to the front of the line, Carolyn tossed her badge into the metal bin. "I need to see Drew Campbell," she told the bailiff, a young dark-haired man.

"Hey, Kirsh," he called out, swiveling around on his stool. "I got a PO that wants us to pull a prisoner during visiting hours."

Sergeant Bobby Kirsh's bald head filled up the window. "Come back in an hour, Carolyn. These people must think we're dispensing free crack or something. There's no way we can take care of you right now."

"Ah, come on, Bobby," Carolyn cooed, smiling to show off her dimples. She'd never possessed the kind of bold, take-your-breath-away beauty that Mary Stevens had, but she had a few years left of cute and sexy. "You know I wouldn't ask if it wasn't important."

"Yeah, sure," he said. "Everything's important." He pointed across the room at a Hispanic woman sitting spread-eagle with a grimace on her face and her hand pressed over her swollen abdomen. "That lady is gonna give birth any minute. She refuses to leave until she sees her husband. I'm not in the mood to deliver a baby. You know what kind of mess that makes? Give it up and come back later."

Carolyn fell serious. "Don't you know who Drew Campbell is, Bobby? He killed Veronica Campbell. She was one of my probation officers. She was also my best friend."

"Humph," he said, brushing his hand over his head as he glanced at the prisoner's record on the computer. "I don't see any homicide charges, just a shitload of sex crimes."

"Would I lie to you?"

"Probably," Kirsh said, nudging the bailiff. "Have someone pull Campbell and put him in a room. She won't leave until we give her what she wants. She's holding up the line." He glanced at the pregnant woman who was now panting. "And call an ambulance. No kid should take his first breath inside a jail."

When a bailiff unlocked the room where Drew had been deposited, Carolyn rushed over to embrace him. "This is so awful," she said. "I've been arguing with Hank and the DA all afternoon, trying to convince them that the charges are unfounded. How could they put you through this?"

A look of relief appeared on his face. "Thank God someone believes me. When I saw you in the courtroom today, I didn't know what to think. I'm getting paranoid, Carolyn. Where are my kids?"

"They're staying with a nice family until

this is cleared up," she lied, not wanting him to know that the children were with Emily in San Francisco. "Let's sit down, okay? Do you need anything?"

"Not really," he said. "I swear on a stack of Bibles that the things Jude told the police aren't true. You know the problems we've had with her. Veronica's death must have pushed her over the edge. Jude needs to be in a mental hospital or some kind of in-patient drug rehab."

"I agree," Carolyn told him, keeping her voice low and measured. "You hired a good lawyer, Drew. Maybe that's something he can take care of for you."

"Farrow charges a fortune," Drew said, cracking his knuckles. "As soon as they let me out of this place, I'll find the lying little brat myself. Can you imagine a kid, any kid, doing this to her father?"

"Why don't you let me help you?" Carolyn said. "The police won't tell me where Jude's staying. Since she's an adult now, they may have let her stay with friends. If you give me the name of the people she hangs out with, I'll start checking around. At least she knows me. I might be able to talk some sense into her."

"Do you have some paper?" Drew asked, swiping at his mouth with the back of his hand. "This place is turning me into an animal. The other day I ran out of toilet paper and had to wipe my ass with my pillow. My neck is killing me now since I've been sleeping without anything supporting my head."

Carolyn had brought along a small notepad and pen. She placed it on the table to let him know she was ready.

"Let me give you some background first," Drew said, adjusting his position in the chair. "Jude's closest friend used to be a girl named Haley Snodgrass. They were into the same things. You know, hanging out, partying, getting high. Sometime last year, Haley started dating a black guy named Reggie Stockton. She brought him by the house a few times and he didn't seem like such a bad egg. To be honest, I asked myself what he was doing with Haley and Jude. Then there was a big fight. Haley caught Jude making out with Reggie one night and came unglued. She used to camp out at our place all the time. Last week, Haley came over while Jude was out and picked up all her things. She claimed Jude had stolen something from her, but she wouldn't tell us what it was. Veronica and I were relieved in a way. The last thing we needed was another teenager lying around the house and eating our food."

"So you think Stockton was beating Jude?"

"Yeah," Drew said, pausing to clear his throat. "I certainly wasn't beating her. Knowing Jude, though, the injuries could have been self-inflicted. That's why Veronica and I didn't report it to the police. I'm not sure if Jude is a hypochondriac, or if she's simply a lazy kid who craves attention. Ever since she was in grade school, she's been concocting one reason or another to stay home from school. One day I caught her holding the thermometer against a lightbulb to trick me into believing she had a fever. In the beginning, we'd run her back and forth to the doctor. After a while, we ignored her. Later, I thought the stints in juvenile hall might bring her around, but for Jude it was just another adventure. Veronica called her a drama queen. Jude reminded her of her sister, Emily."

"Interesting," Carolyn said. "Was Jude anorexic?"

He laughed. "God, no. I think Haley went through a stage like that before she and Jude broke up. I used to tease Jude and tell her she had her mother's ass. Boy, did she hate that!"

"Veronica mentioned that Jude had lost a lot of weight recently. Was she dieting?"

"All the girls diet. Look at the way they're

dressing today. You have to be a rail to show your belly and wear skirts up to your ass. I personally think it's disgusting. What can I tell you? Once a kid turns eighteen, you don't have any control over her. All you can do is tell her to shape up or get out. Jude refused to shape up, so I kicked her out. We should have tried tough love on her years ago."

"Don't you think you picked the wrong time to take such a stance?"

"No," Drew said. "My wife was murdered. I'm stuck with three kids and no mother. I have to work to feed them and put clothes on their back. Crystal isn't that bright, but she knows how to take care of children. I can't rely on Jude. She'd take off and leave the kids alone."

"But why did you move Crystal into the house?" Carolyn asked. "Didn't you realize it didn't look right to move a young woman in only days after your wife was killed?"

"I don't care how it looked," he tossed back. He reflected a few moments, then added, "I guess I made a mistake there. Is that what got everyone up in arms?"

"It may have played a part," Carolyn told him, twisting sideways to stretch her back. She studied his body language. His right arm was resting on the table. His face appeared relaxed. She'd hit all the hot spots, and Drew hadn't so much as flinched. He was either a pathological liar, or a wrongly accused man whose faith in the system made him believe he would eventually prevail. When she worked in such close proximity to criminals, particularly those prone to violent offenses, a kinetic form of energy seemed to fill the air. When he spoke about his wife and daughter, Drew didn't blink, tap his feet, or fidget. His father had been born in England. He'd inherited not only his father's fair skin and refined features, but his detached demeanor. She decided to shake the tree harder. "Veronica thought you were having an affair. Are you involved with another woman, Drew?"

"Of course not," he said, taken aback. "When would I have the time for such nonsense? I have to get up at four every morning. I work in LA, for Christ's sake. Half my life is spent stuck in traffic."

"Did you ever have sex with Veronica in the backseat of her Ford Explorer in the parking lot at the government center?"

"Shit, Carolyn," Drew said, grimacing. "Are you on acid or something? These are the most ridiculous questions anyone has ever asked me. Veronica have sex in a public place? You've got to be kidding me. Since

Michael was born, she wouldn't even let me see her with her clothes off. She never lost the extra weight. I mean, it wasn't as if I didn't know."

"Are you attracted to children, Drew? Do you fantasize about having sex with them?"

Drew stood and threw his hands in the air. "Get the hell out of here," he shouted. "I thought you were my friend. Did that mealy-mouthed DA send you in here to trick me into saying something he could use against me? I should have known better than to trust you."

"Calm down, Drew," Carolyn said. "I promise no one sent me to extract information from you. I'm only trying to prepare you. These are the kinds of inflammatory questions you can expect during the trial."

"Farrow doesn't want me to testify. I can see why now."

Carolyn waited until he collected himself, then said softly, "How are you handling Veronica's death?"

"I'm not, actually. I guess all this" — he gestured with his hand — "is serving some useful purpose. I'm so terrified they're going to send me to prison, I don't have time to think about anything else. My biggest regret is that Veronica and I didn't spend more time together. I loved her, you know."

"I'm sure you did," she said, reaching over and touching his arm. "Can you give me those names and addresses now? It's getting late, and if I'm going to make a stab at finding Jude, I need to get going."

By the time Carolyn reached the locker area, she was a hundred degrees past exhaustion. She took a seat on the bench as she sorted through her thoughts. She possessed a seemingly endless capacity for work. Her father had been a brilliant, but mentally tortured, mathematician, who used to go days at a time without sleep. She recalled running into him in the middle of the night in the kitchen.

"Why are you worried about sleeping?" he'd asked. "Are you tired the next day? Are you unable to focus on your schoolwork?"

"No," Carolyn had told him, pouring herself a glass of milk and taking a seat at the table.

"There you go," her father had said. "Stop trying to make yourself into a lesser mortal. Instead, use your energy for what it is, a gift."

Sleep must have been more important than her father realized as he had killed himself. As she removed her gun and purse from the locker, she realized what was wrong with her. She wasn't physically depleted. She was conflicted. Was it because she had the ability to see things from the perspective of the person she was with? This was her secret, the underlying reason she'd established a reputation as an outstanding interrogator. When the offenders she questioned looked in her eyes, they saw a reflection of themselves staring back. But once the contact was severed, she reverted to herself. This hadn't happened with Drew. Was Veronica's husband truly innocent? If so, the killer was at large, and that was something to fear. Not only had she distracted the police with her belief that Jude's story was true, but she'd defied the killer's order that she not get involved.

One of her weaknesses was a tendency to unnecessarily complicate things. Maybe Jude was a first-class liar, Drew was a decent husband and father, Tyler Bell hadn't been involved in either Abernathy's or McAllen's death, and whoever killed Veronica had simply decided to make it open season on probation officers.

"That works," Carolyn said aloud.

Bobby Kirsh was manning the counter while he chatted with another bailiff. He used a muscular arm to move the officer aside. "Everything go okay? Your inmate didn't get out of hand, did he? I didn't get a chance to work out today. I'd be happy to straighten out his attitude for you."

"I'm sure you would, Bobby," Carolyn said, glancing up at the security camera. "I just realized my fiancé was right."

"You did, huh? In what way?"

"It's time I get out of this business."

"Only if you take me with you," the sergeant said, buzzing her through the security doors.

CHAPTER 18

Friday, October 15 — 8:30 P.M.

Hank and Mary were strangely silent as they sped over the dark residential streets. She had pulled out her red murder shirt, then tossed it back in her duffel bag. Veronica Campbell had been a member of the law enforcement family. Now it appeared the killer had moved down a generation. Having lost her father in the line of duty, Mary was trying to assimilate the horror of a young girl's death, as well as compute all the possibilities. Seeing the lights and police cars up ahead, she said, "I'm not feeling very good about this thing right now. How about you?"

Hank didn't answer, braking hard and steering the car toward the dirt road adjoining the orchard. Most of this section of Ventura had been parceled out to developers. The land was considered prime real estate since it was high enough to provide views of the ocean. Only a few remaining residents had maintained the original orchards. This grove was planted in orange trees. Mary could smell them as soon as they parked and stepped out of the car. They didn't need to display their badges, one of the benefits of working for a fairly small department like Ventura.

"Olsen," Hank barked to a uniformed officer. "Who do those cars over there belong to? If they're media, get rid of them. They can't park this close to the scene. If they refuse to move, tow them."

Mary had long legs, and had learned to keep up with Hank's quick stride. The officers stepped out of their way. She spotted Gary Conrad in a circle of light approximately twenty feet away. Reaching into her pocket, she pulled on a pair of rubber gloves. As hard as they tried to preserve evidence, they had to get to the grave. She imagined vital evidence crunching underneath their feet.

Gary was forty-five, had shaggy brown hair, a physique gone to pot, and a round face that was prematurely wrinkled from his years as a surfer. "The path you came down is where the old man walks every night," he told them. "He's the caretaker. The owners have a second home in the Virgin Islands, and won't be back for three months. I've tried to keep everyone confined to this one area. Follow me. I'll take you to the body. I asked for Charley Young. I figured that's who you'd want on this one. Am I right?" Young was the county's chief forensic pathologist.

Hank walked with his head down, his flashlight pointed at the ground. "Was Charley available?"

"Yeah, we got lucky," Gary said, turning up the collar on his jacket. Now that the sun was down, it was damp and chilly. "He's not here yet, neither is CSI. All I've got right now are six guys from patrol, along with a couple of narcs who were in the area. Since it's Friday night, most of the people who live around here must be out on the town. The media's already snooping around, though." He stopped walking several feet before the grave. Portable spotlights had been set up. "She could be the Campbell girl, Lieutenant, but I'm not certain. The features on the body are distorted."

Mary dropped down on her knees, brushing off more dirt and leaves from the corpse's face. She'd been involved in the exhumation of numerous bodies. Seeing a face staring up at you from the ground never lost its shock value, and this was obviously a young person, which made it even more tragic. The mouth was open wide, the eyes clenched shut, her face frozen in a death mask of horror. "It's not Jude Campbell," she said, rocking back on her heels. "This girl's been in the ground for longer than a few hours."

To her left, Mary noticed a steep embankment. "The killer probably parked on the service road like we did, then rolled her down that embankment. I doubt if he used a shovel. The grave is shallow and the ground is soft enough that he could have scooped it out with his hands."

The detective carefully removed more soil from the torso. She saw what looked like a breast implant, then realized it was a rotting orange. Something was protruding from the ground on the right side of the body. At first, she thought it was a plant of some kind, but then she realized it was a hand. The fingernails were painted pink and the fingers shaped into a claw. She scooted over to the left side and uncovered the other hand, finding it in the same position. "Christ, he buried her alive! She was trying to claw her way out."

"Let's hope the bastard didn't wear gloves," Hank said. "He may have cut himself on a rock."

Something blue flickered on the victim's right ring finger. "Put the spot on this, Gary," Mary said, trying to get a better look at it. She reached into her jacket pocket and removed a small brush she carried, taking it from the plastic case and using it to dust the dirt off. "My God, Hank, it's a Ventura High graduation ring from last year. That means she was a classmate of Jude's."

"I'll wait here for Charley and crime scene," he told her. "Go back to the station and check missing persons. And call Carolyn, see if she's heard anything regarding Jude yet. These cases have to be connected."

"You don't believe Drew Campbell did this, do you? Its so brutal."

"And what he did to his daughter wasn't brutal?" Hank responded, his shoulder twitching with nervous energy. "We may have been coming at this from the wrong direction. The incest threw us off. Drew could be a sadist who decided to start acting out his fantasies by killing young girls. He enjoyed beating and degrading his daughter, but he might not have had the balls to actually kill her. So he went shopping for victims among her friends. That nanny he hired . . . what was her name?"

"Crystal Truesdale."

"Maybe it wasn't the younger daughter he

was setting up for his next victim. Get her down to the station and see what she can tell you."

CHAPTER 19

Friday, October 15 — 9:15 P.M.

"Can I legally enter the house?" Carolyn asked after Mary told her about the new homicide. She'd just pulled out of the government center parking lot after leaving the jail, and was stopped at the light on Victoria. "What were the terms of the original search warrant?"

"We didn't have a warrant," the detective said. "We submitted a request for one today, but the judge hasn't signed it yet. In any case of suspected child abuse, Protective Services has the right to remove the children from the home without the benefit of a court order. We arrested Drew on probable cause. This gave them another reason to take the kids, since they couldn't very well leave them to fend for themselves. You still have a key, right? Didn't you tell me that you and Veronica always kept keys to each other's homes in case of an emergency?"

"Yes, but that's not what I'm concerned about." Carolyn made a left turn on Victoria, then pulled off on the shoulder so she could concentrate on their conversation. She'd planned on driving by Tyler Bell's painting company on the chance that the address she'd come up with was his residence. A lot of independent contractors worked out of their home. "What if I do find some kind of incriminating evidence against Drew? Won't it be inadmissible without a warrant?"

"Only if you go in there specifically to look for evidence. You're going to box up the kids' clothes and toys to send to Emily. Isn't that right, Carolyn?"

"I think you should run it by Kevin Thomas first, Mary. Too many cases have fallen apart because of illegal searches. The courts can see through these types of things."

"Fine," Mary said, perturbed. "Just remember that if Jude doesn't turn up by Monday, Thomas will have no choice but to withdraw the charges. Stressful situations cause killers to act. Killing is their release. You don't think Drew has been under extraordinary pressure since his arrest? Once he's back on the street, there's no telling what he'll do." Her voice elevated. "Jesus

Christ, woman, this girl was buried alive! Can you imagine what a terrible way that is to die?"

Carolyn felt the hairs prick on the back of her neck. "Are you certain she was buried alive?"

"Cause of death isn't official yet, of course, but that's what it looked like to me. I didn't see any gunshot wounds or ligature marks around her neck. I think he beat her to the brink of death, then buried her. The lazy bastard didn't even dig that deep of a hole. She almost clawed her way out, poor thing."

"Okay, I'll go to Veronica's house," Carolyn said, taking the car out of park and making a U-turn. "What should I look for?"

"Phone numbers, pictures, weapons, souvenirs like hair or jewelry, anything that doesn't look right. Concentrate on the garage. If he has anything, that's where he probably stashed it. Just take some paper with you and write down what you find. Try not to touch it, but don't panic if you do. You've been in the house on numerous occasions, so we'd expect to find a shitload of your prints. What I don't want is for you to contaminate any evidence that might belong to one of the victims."

"My God," Carolyn exclaimed. "You're making it sound like Drew's a serial killer."

"He could be a serial killer in his infancy."

"I'm sorry, Mary. I'm not convinced he's guilty of anything, let alone this girl you think was buried alive. I spoke to him tonight at the jail."

"So you went on a fishing expedition?"

Mary knew her well, Carolyn decided. "Drew thinks I'm in his corner now, so make sure no one says or does anything to the contrary. We can use this to our advantage, depending on how things play out." She paused to collect her thoughts, then continued, "He was remarkably relaxed and confident for someone in his position. You know, no hesitations, no searching around for the right words, no awkward pauses. Everything just flowed out of him."

"Would you classify him as cocky?"

"Not necessarily," Carolyn answered. "Why?"

"Because you might exude confidence, too, if you thought you were going to get away with multiple murders. Drew knows his daughter's accusations may not hold up in court. And you, of all people, should know that violent predators seldom look the part. Ted Bundy was sophisticated, intelligent, and charming."

"I'll let you know if I find anything."

Carolyn parked the Infiniti across the

street, not wanting to stir up the neighbors' curiosity. Even if Drew was innocent, his reputation was forever tarnished. When people were accused of crimes of this nature, the taint of scandal stuck with them for life. All the people on this block, where Drew and Veronica had lived for almost twenty years, would only remember the night he was led away in handcuffs.

The small stucco house looked so dark and forlorn, Carolyn had to force herself to go inside. The grass was already too high. She'd have to get someone to come over and mow it, or people would realize the house was vacant and vandalize it.

When she reached the porch, she fumbled for the key in her purse, then inserted it into the lock. When she stepped inside, she flipped the light switch by the door, but nothing happened. Why would the electricity be turned off? Surely, Veronica had paid the bill. Drew had never been good with money matters. It just dawned on her why the motel room where Veronica's body had been found might have been rented with a stolen credit card. Drew couldn't very well have something like that turn up on their MasterCard. Veronica would have spotted it immediately. She'd suspected Drew of seeing other women for years.

Carolyn went over to the lamp on the end table beside the sofa, thinking the overhead light fixture must have burned out. It didn't work, either. She'd seen this phenomena before, where numerous lightbulbs in a house went out at the same time. It was more common in newer homes, but it could occur anywhere. In a new home, the bulbs were generally inserted at the same time, creating a cycle of burnouts and replacements. She felt inside the lamp and couldn't find the bulb. Strange, she thought, continuing toward the hall.

Odors she associated with children lingered in the stale air: souring milk, urine, Johnson's baby shampoo. She could almost hear their laughter and feel their youthful presence, as if it had imprinted itself into the walls. Would Veronica's children ever live in this house again? Why did tragedy have to strike their young lives?

Carolyn suddenly felt a chill. Was there a window open somewhere? The police wouldn't have left without making certain the house was secure. Her pulse quickened. She thought of horror movies, where people felt a gust of cold air when a ghost walked past them. If there was anyone who had a reason to linger in a spirit form, it was Veronica.

Not paying attention to where she was walking, Carolyn tripped over a large object. Getting up and dusting herself off, she decided to go to the car for her flashlight when her eyes adjusted to the darkness and she made out the shape of a body on the floor.

She dropped to her knees, picking up a frigid hand. She felt for a pulse and didn't find one. Certain the person was dead, she stood to run out of the house, terrified the killer was hiding in the darkness.

She moved a few feet, then stopped, smelling something familiar. A second later, she realized it was the conditioner Rebecca used on her hair. It was only sold at beauty supply stores, and her daughter purchased it with her own money.

Carolyn's stomach came up in her throat. She spotted something else of Rebecca's, her brown leather ankle boots trimmed in fur. "God in heaven, help me!"

Her hands were shaking so bad, she had to dial 911 twice. As soon as the dispatcher answered, she screamed into the phone, "Send the police and an ambulance! My daughter . . . Hurry, she might still be alive."

Carolyn leaned down and opened Rebecca's mouth, breathing into it. "Baby . . . oh God . . . it's Mom." She ran her fingers up to her sternum, finding the right place to begin the compressions. How long had she been here like this? Her skin was so cold.

She continued ventilating and compressing even when she heard the sirens approaching. Thank God, she'd left the front door partially open. Even a few seconds could cost her daughter her life. She leaned down to check for a heartbeat when the paramedics came barreling through the door. She looked up, her face streaked with tears, her eyes wild with fright. "I think I heard a heartbeat. It was so weak, I can't be sure."

An overweight middle-aged paramedic pointed a flashlight on the girl's face, while a younger blond man placed a stethoscope on her chest. "Is this your daughter, ma'am? Did she OD on pills?"

Carolyn was so relieved, she couldn't think. She made the sign of the cross. "Thank you, God," she said, looking up at the ceiling.

"We need to know what she took."

"I don't know. I thought she was my daughter, but she's not. Her name is Jude Campbell. Is she going to make it?"

"The kid was mainlining," the older paramedic said, finding a needle and a spoon a few inches away on the floor. "Looks like heroin."

Carolyn moved out of the men's way. She tried the light switch in the hallway, and it worked. Jude had overdosed in the living room, so she must have wanted it dark. Carolyn went to the kitchen, turned on the light, then saw the back window was smashed out. Since Drew had taken her key away, Jude must have broken it to get into the house. Carolyn felt like an idiot. This was the first place she should have checked when Jude disappeared. She'd driven by on the way to the jail, but when she didn't see Marcus's Jeep or any lights on inside the house, she'd assumed Jude wasn't there.

Returning to the living room, she wrapped her arms around her chest, wincing when the older paramedic stabbed Jude in the chest with a huge needle filled with adrenaline.

Jude shrieked and opened her eyes, her arms flopping at her side. "Where the fuck am I?"

"Just lie still," the paramedic said, gesturing for his partner to bring in the gurney. "You just about killed yourself, little lady. How long have you been shooting heroin?"

Jude turned her head away. "I wanted to die. Why didn't you let me die? I was sure I took enough to kill me." While they started an IV, she saw Carolyn. "Bitch," she snarled,

297

saliva rolling down her chin. "Can't you leave me alone? First, you lock me in your stupid mansion. What were you going to do, keep me as a pet for you and your rich boyfriend?"

The older paramedic glanced up at Carolyn. "A real sweetheart, this one. I saw some evidence tape outside. Is this a crime scene? Where are the police?"

Hank appeared in the doorway, opening his jacket so the paramedics could see his gold detective shield clipped on his belt. "Looks like you found our victim," he told Carolyn. "What happened here?"

"This girl isn't a victim, Detective," the blond paramedic said. "She didn't have any visible tracks, but she admitted she shot herself up with heroin. I bagged the syringe and spoon." He reached into his pocket and handed them to Hank. "We'll be taking her to Community Memorial. Have your lab confirm there was nothing in there other than heroin and give them a call. They'll probably keep her for a few hours for observation, then send her home. I checked her wallet and her driver's license says she an adult."

"We'll meet you at the ER," Hank told him, a stern look on his face. "When she leaves the hospital, she's going to jail."

"You're going to officially charge her?" Carolyn asked, reminding herself of everything Jude had gone through. "If you do, Hank, she'll have even less credibility as a witness than she already has. Most of her record is juvenile. We could have gotten around that. What are you going to charge her with? Possession of heroin? A junkie witness isn't worth crap."

The detective pulled out a toothpick, twirling the small sliver of wood in his fingers. "You think I'm going to let her skip out on us again? We identified the victim we found in the orchard. Her name was Haley Snodgrass. According to her parents, she didn't come home from school Tuesday. They thought she'd run off with Stockton, so they didn't report her missing."

Jude struggled against the restraints on the gurney. "You sadistic bastards," she shouted. "Why did you bring me back? Just so you could send me to jail? I hope you both rot in hell."

CHAPTER 20

Marcus had been asleep by the time Carolyn had crawled into bed at one o'clock the night before. Although it was Saturday, she knew Tyler Bell might have a painting contract. She needed to get to his place of business early if she wanted to catch him.

She tried to slip out without him noticing, but they were tangled up together. "Come here," Marcus said, pushing her down on her back and climbing on top of her. "I'm going to start having wet dreams if we don't make love. Before I asked you to marry me, you were insatiable. Now you don't have time for me. I hope this isn't a preview of what our marriage is going to be like."

"Don't be silly." Carolyn kissed him. "I want you too, honey, but I have to take care of something important this morning. I've put it off far too long."

Marcus rolled off her, a frustrated look on his face. "Where could you possibly be going at this hour?"

She stroked his arm. "Please understand. I found Jude last night at her house. She'd overdosed on heroin. She was wearing Rebecca's boots. I thought it was Rebecca. I've never been so scared in my life. Hank insisted on booking Jude at the jail. Without her, we don't have a case against Drew."

Marcus picked up a pillow and stuffed it under his neck. "The girl needs psychiatric care. The last thing you should do with a suicidal teenager is lock her up in a jail cell. I'll pay for her damn treatment if that's the problem."

"She'd escape," Carolyn told him. "Don't worry, she's in protective custody. The jail deals with potential suicides all the time. A doctor will take a look at her, maybe prescribe some type of medication. The first thing we need to do is find out how serious a drug habit she's got. We don't want her diagnosed as mentally ill right now."

"Her perverted father made her that way," Marcus argued. "Are you going to tell me a mentally disturbed girl can't be raped and beaten?"

"It's a difficult situation," she explained, finding her robe at the foot of the bed and putting it on. "There aren't any collaborating witnesses, and Jude's credibility is seriously tainted. There's documentation that she's falsely accused other people. This type of sex crime isn't as easy to prosecute as it was in the past. Look what happened in the Michael Jackson case. And the same thing applies to all these priests that are being prosecuted for something they allegedly did years ago. Who knows how many of them are actually guilty? Once the church started settling for large sums of money, everyone lined up for a piece of the action."

"You're going to have a hard time getting anyone to stand behind you on that one," he said. "The only reason you're sympathetic is because you're Catholic."

Carolyn no longer wore the silver cross with a flower in the middle that her mother had given her for her first communion. With a cross around her neck and an Irish name, everyone assumed she was Catholic. She'd been debating the sex scandals with people ever since they had surfaced. She wished the church had handled things properly. Along with the rest of the world, she'd been horrified at the information that had come to light. "I'm just trying to explain why Hank wanted Jude in a secure environment," she said. "Kevin Thomas from the DA's office is going to take Jude's deposition this afternoon. I need to be there, Marcus. Now that this other girl has been murdered, we have no idea what we're dealing with. The coroner doesn't have an exact time of death yet, but he's estimating around five days, which would put it around the time Veronica was murdered. The Snodgrass girl was severely beaten, then buried alive. We don't know if the killer intentionally buried her alive, or mistakenly thought she was dead."

"Christ," Marcus said, kicking the covers off. "Do they think Drew is responsible? This is sick stuff. How could Veronica live with this man so many years and not realize he was insane? I mean, the woman worked with criminals."

"Drew's only been in jail a few days, and the injuries on Snodgrass are similar to the ones Jude said her father inflicted. When I spoke to Drew last night at the jail, he said Haley Snodgrass practically lived at their house. Maybe he molested or raped her, then killed her to keep her from going to the authorities. Either that, or Jude may have confided in Haley. It's unrealistic that a girl her age wouldn't tell someone, especially her best friend." The wood floor was cold beneath her feet. She felt around under the bed until she found her slippers. "We're almost

certain the cases are connected. The Snodgrass girl was dating Reggie Stockton. This
was the guy Jude was infatuated with. According to Drew, the two girls had a falling-
out over him. Stockton, by the way, has been
living under an assumed name since he left
New Orleans. He was in jail pending trial on
two felonies when Katrina hit. Stockton,
along with most of the inmates in that particular facility, managed to escape. They had
to unlock the cells or they would have all
drowned."

"Sounds like Stockton is the one who
should be in jail."

"He may turn out to be the killer," Carolyn
agreed. "But if that's the case, how do Veronica and Jude fit into the picture?"

Marcus became animated. Living with
Carolyn had turned him into an amateur detective. "Jude was stuck on him, so maybe
she went to the motel with him willingly.
Then he did or said something that caused
her to think he killed this Haley girl. So she
calls her mother after he beats her and
leaves, asking her to pick her up at the motel.
Veronica shows up and Stockton is still
around and jumps her. Jude is there when he
shoots Veronica, so she's terrified to go to the
cops for fear they'll think she participated in
the killing. She lies low for a few days, then

gets pissed when she comes home and her father boots her out of the house. That's when she lies and says her father sexually abused her. Pretty good, huh? What do you think?"

"I think you watch too much TV." Carolyn gave him another kiss, then walked over to the dresser. "Jude's school records support her story, as well as Drew hiring a nanny as an excuse to move Stacy into his bedroom. Stockton skipped town yesterday after Mary and I spoke to him. I'm sure the police consider him a suspect."

"I figured everything out for you and you didn't even listen," Marcus told her, rolling over on his side. "I'm going back to sleep."

"Will you keep your eye on Rebecca today?" she asked. "None of the present suspects may be our killer. For all we know, he's targeting teenage girls. Hank was right. The jail is probably the safest place for Jude right now."

Marcus got up, padding naked in the direction of the bathroom. "I promised to take Rebecca shopping. Jude didn't happen to tell you where she left my Wrangler and the things she stole from the house, did she?"

Carolyn had tossed on a pair of jeans and a black turtleneck sweater. She needed to shower and wash her hair, but she didn't have time. "No," she answered, spraying herself with cologne. A wave of sadness washed over her, and she gently placed the bottle back on her bureau. The fragrance smelled like honey. Veronica had given it to her when she'd started dating Marcus. "He'll want to lick you all over when he gets a whiff of this," her friend had told her. "One of us needs to get laid every now and then, and I doubt if it's going to be me."

At least Veronica hadn't lived to find out who her husband's sex partner had been, Carolyn thought, picking up her handbag and briefcase. She paused at the door, waiting for Marcus to come out of the bathroom. "Don't give up on me," she said. "I love you."

He walked over and kissed her. "I'm not going to give up on you, baby. I just love you so much, it's tough when you don't have time for me. If you can break free, maybe you can meet Rebecca and me for a quick lunch."

"I'll try my best."

Carolyn walked down the long hallway, her tennis shoes whisper quiet on the parquet flooring. The house was so big, she felt as if she lived in a hotel with only three occupants. She thought of all the homeless people, wondering how many bodies they could shelter if the house was outfitted correctly. What would Marcus think if he knew some of the strange thoughts that passed through her mind?

Her dream had finally come true. A handsome, intelligent man adored her and wanted to spend the rest of his life with her.

As she backed the Infiniti out of the garage, her eyes swept over the exquisite landscaping, the avocado orchard, and the reassuring black car parked at the end of the cobblestone driveway. Joel, the weekend guard, waved to her as she drove past him. She waved back and turned right to make her way to the freeway.

Fate had struck a cruel blow, Carolyn thought, and not just in the death of Veronica or the despicable crimes committed by Drew. A man like Marcus wouldn't wait forever. If she wasn't careful, she could end up in the same position as Veronica had been in, wondering who was having sex with her husband. Unlike Veronica, however, she and Marcus weren't married yet. All he had to do was ask her to move out and the fairy tale would be over.

The morning was overcast and cold. The weather report had predicted rain, and the scent of it was already in the air. Carolyn turned onto a residential street behind Telegraph Road, searching the numbers for the address listed for Tyler Bell's painting company at 853 Pearl Street. Seeing what appeared to be a duplex, she pulled over and parked at the curb. A white truck with BELL INDUSTRIAL AND RESIDENTIAL PAINTING on the side was parked in the driveway. Her guess had been accurate. Tyler conducted business out of his home.

Before she got out of the car, Carolyn reached into the backseat for her shoulder holster and strapped it on. Removing her 9mm from her purse, she inserted it in the pocket, then closed the front of her black nylon parka. She'd made a vow that she wouldn't take another life, but the deaths of Veronica and Haley Snodgrass had changed her position. People who worked in law enforcement had to acknowledge the risks they were taking, that they might someday have to make the ultimate sacrifice. All Carolyn had ever hoped for was that her death would be fast and as painless as possible.

Being buried alive didn't fall into that category.

The block was quiet. Tyler's neighbors were probably taking advantage of the weekend to catch up on their sleep. An elderly man stepped outside to pick up his newspaper, but otherwise, no one was around.

Carolyn walked to the door and knocked. When no one answered, she knocked harder. Finally, she heard noises inside. "It's Carolyn Sullivan with the probation department," she shouted. "I need to speak to you."

The door opened. Tyler Bell stood in front of her, dressed only in a pair of baggy gray sweatpants. His hair was cropped close to his head, and he appeared several inches taller than Marcus, which would put him around six-three. A handsome man, his chest, arms, and abdomen were ridged with muscles, and his dark coppery skin looked healthy and smooth. Could he pass for a man in his twenties? Yes, she decided, as long the person didn't look in his eyes. She introduced herself, telling him she was with the probation department.

"I just got out of bed," he said. "What do you want?"

"May I come in?" Carolyn asked, drops of rain striking her face. "Looks like the weatherman was right this time." She glanced at her lightweight jacket, then rubbed her hands together to warm them. "It's cold."

"Give me a minute," Bell told her, leaving the door open and talking as he headed toward the back section of the duplex. "Just flop wherever you want. I don't usually have company, so excuse the mess. I'll throw on a shirt, then put us up a pot of coffee. I'm working on a job, but I can't paint an exterior when it's raining."

Carolyn closed the door, taking a seat at a small round table off the kitchen. The living room was cluttered with stuff he must use in his business. When Bell returned, he was wearing a green flannel shirt.

"I heard about Veronica Campbell getting murdered," he said, rummaging around in the kitchen cabinets. "I've been watching the papers for the funeral, but I haven't seen anything. I guess the coroner's office hasn't released the body yet. She was good people. Have you caught the person who did it yet?"

"No," Carolyn said, watching as he spooned coffee into the filter. "We have a number of suspects, though. How long has it been since you saw Veronica? I know she was fond of you. I'm sorry about what happened to your son."

While the coffee was percolating, Bell took a seat across from her. His long legs practically reached into the living room. "I used to have a nice house, you know. After my wife killed herself, I let everything go. I lost the only two people I ever loved. Material things don't matter after you go through something

310

like that. Veronica had a bunch of kids, didn't she?"

"Four." Carolyn waited as he pulled out two mugs and filled them with coffee, then carried them to the table.

"I hope you like it black," he said. "I don't have any milk or sugar."

"Black is fine," she said, taking a sip. "Ah, Veronica, did you see her recently?"

"Nah. Must be a year now since I even talked to her on the phone." His brows furrowed. "I wouldn't have known about Lester McAllen getting kicked out of prison if Veronica hadn't called and told me. I heard about that coroner messing up. I didn't know it meant a man already in prison could be released because of what he'd done. I hate to admit it, but I wasn't at all sorry when he got himself killed. What was his name? Abby or something."

"Robert Abernathy."

"Yeah, that's the son of a bitch's name. How could a man do something like that? Just get up on the stand and lie. I saw another article that said he was almost blind."

"I'm not trying to defend him, Tyler, but if Abernathy had told the truth in your son's case, Lester McAllen might not have been convicted. When they reexamined the evidence after the situation with Abernathy

311

came to light, the DNA sample was found to be contaminated. Abernathy used the DNA collected from McAllen after his arrest. He perjured himself because he believed McAllen was guilty, and he knew the state didn't have enough evidence to prove it."

Bell's shoulders rolled forward, and he looked around the room, avoiding making eye contact with her. He appeared to be shaken. It was obvious she'd told him something he hadn't known. Was his behavior indicative of guilt? It was a hard call. Anything that linked back to the death of his son would trigger an emotional response.

"I doubt if it's a coincidence that Lester McAllen was also murdered," Carolyn continued. "You had a motive to kill both of these men, Tyler. I'm sure there are people who would believe whoever killed these men was fully justified. Murder is murder, though."

"I didn't kill anyone," he said, fidgeting in his seat. "Is that why you came here? To accuse me of killing these people? Sure, I wanted McAllen dead, and maybe at the time, I thought Abernathy should go to hell with him. My son's killer wasn't the only criminal who went free because of that man. Have you gone to their houses and accused them? The monsters who hurt their loved ones are probably still out there. That means they have a lot more motive than me."

"Let me put my cards on the table," Carolyn said, not wanting to add to his belief that the criminal justice system had failed. "Veronica told me last year that there was a possibility that you might have killed Abernathy as well as McAllen. She blamed herself for telling you. Like you said earlier, you might not have put two and two together if she hadn't contacted you." When he started to get angry, she held up a palm. "Just hear me out, okay? The killer left a partial print on Abernathy's gate. The lab said he had some kind of oily substance on his hands, which made the print worthless. Veronica remembered you telling her that you had sensitive skin, that you used some kind of special cleaner to remove paint stains. She also told me you were a marksman in the military. Whoever killed Abernathy and McAllen knew what he was doing. Each one died from a single shot to the head."

"The cleanser I use isn't oily," he told her. "I'm allergic to petroleum distillates, so I use Gojo. I have a bottle in the other room if you want to see it."

"Let me finish what I was trying to tell you. When Veronica came to me last year with her suspicions about you, I told her to sit on it. Neither of us was upset that McAllen was dead. That may have played a large part in our decision."

Tyler Bell's mouth tightened. "What the hell do you want from me, lady?"

"Since Veronica suspected you," Carolyn explained, "she may have confronted you and you decided to kill her."

Bell jumped to his feet, pointing toward the door. "Get out! I'm not a killer. You have no right to come into a man's home and talk this kind of trash. My son was raped, then butchered. His remains were delivered to the funeral home in pieces."

Carolyn stood, taking several steps backward. She didn't feel threatened, though, just swept inside Bell's grief and outrage. "You have every right to be angry," she told him, speaking softly. "I came to you, though, didn't I? I could have taken this to the police, but I didn't want you to have to go through that unless I felt certain you were involved. We can put all this in the past where it belongs. Meet me at my office tomorrow and I'll collect a DNA sample. Also, bring along the cleanser you use." She stopped and caught her breath. "Will you do that for me, Tyler? Will you do that for Veronica?"

Bell glared at her, picking up the coffee

mugs and placing them in the sink. "I'll think about it," he said, keeping his back to her.

"Here's my card," Carolyn said, walking over and placing it on the counter. "If you can't do it tomorrow, we can set something up for Monday or Tuesday. I'm even willing to meet you in the evening so you won't have to interrupt your work. I need to hear from you in the next few days, though, or I'll have no choice but to go to the police with what I know. Veronica and I put our necks on the line for you, Tyler. We could have been charged with withholding evidence in two homicides. With Veronica's death, it's now up to three. Keep that in mind."

He turned around, more afraid now than angry. "But you want me to give my DNA to the police. Then I'll officially be a suspect. Word gets out and I could lose what little I have left."

"I promise the police won't be involved." Carolyn hoped she could hold true to her statement. "I have a connection at the crime lab. I'll collect the samples myself and have them tested against the evidence. Everything will be done under the radar. Trust me, if the tests are negative, you'll never have to worry about this again."

CHAPTER 21

Saturday, October 16 — 9:10 A.M.

Haley Snodgrass's partially dissected corpse lay naked on the stainless steel autopsy table. Charley Young was a diminutive Korean man in his early forties; Dr. Young was both exacting and mellow, traits that weren't always compatible. His black hair was neatly trimmed, his eyes obscured behind wire-framed glasses.

The first thing that struck Hank was the small amount of flesh on the victim's body. When he'd seen her the night before, she had been covered with dirt and leaves. He knew she was small, but what he saw now looked like the body of an emaciated ten-year-old.

"This one is a heartbreaker," the pathologist said, a comment out of character for a man in his position. "She was a beautiful girl, Hank. Blond hair, blue eyes, nice features. Why would a girl like this starve herself? Anorexia is a baffling disease. I wouldn't have spent all night working this case if the circumstances had been different. I keep thinking about my daughter, wondering if she might develop this when she gets older. There's no way to predict or prevent anorexia and bulimia. All we can do right now is hospitalize these people, and a large percentage relapse as soon as they get out."

"I hear you," Hank said. "That's why my wife I and didn't have kids. There's too many things that can go wrong."

"You made a mistake there," Charley said, his speech lightly accented. "Children are one of the greatest joys in life. When things go wrong, you just find a way to deal with them. Nothing in life is certain."

"Death is certain."

"True," the pathologist said. "As to your victim, the killer didn't have to inflict much of a beating. Without intervention, this girl would have died within a matter of months. Because of the gases and other factors in decomposition, she appeared larger than was. She weighs seventy-eight pounds."

"Jesus," Hank said. "I think I weighed that much by the time I was five. How do you know the killer didn't starve her?"

Charley walked over to a long table. "We cut two pairs of heavy sweatpants off her, along with several tops. She was layering to conceal how thin she was, probably from her parents and friends. Her skin would be looser if she'd been starved by the killer. Her weight loss occured over a lengthy period of time."

Hank placed his hand over his stomach. "Talking about this is making me hungry. Why don't we go out and grab some breakfast?"

"How about I go home and get some sleep?"

"Hey," Hank said, "you called me, remember?"

"I wanted you to see something interesting," Charley said, walking back to the autopsy table. "Look at the pattern of bruising. Most of the blows landed on her torso. These are the kinds of injuries we see inflicted by men who batter their wives and girlfriends. The only injury that would be visible is the one on her right cheek. Since you think there might be a connection to the Campbell case, I had them send me the photographs taken of Jude Campbell at the hospital." He opened a file folder and pinned up the snapshots on the screen he used for X-rays. "Do you see what I'm talking about? The injuries are similar."

"So it was the same guy?"

Charley made a wavy motion with his hand. "Sometimes when things are this obvious, they're that way for a reason. Look at this injury on Jude Campbell's thigh. It was made by the heel of a shoe, as were most of the other injuries. I matched it as a size eleven, so the person the shoe belonged to was probably tall." He spun back around to the Snodgrass girl. "The blow to this victim's face was so severe, her jaw was fractured. If you look closely at the pattern of bruising, you can tell this was made by a balled-up fist. See the outline of the knuckles? The injuries on the Campbell girl were superficial."

"I'm a little lost here, Doc. I mean it doesn't seem unusual to me. Jude's bastard father must have kicked her, right?"

"Let me explain," the pathologist said. "If the Campbell girl was kicked or stomped on, there would be an indentation in the skin, maybe even hairline fractures to the rib cage. It's almost as if someone slapped her repeatedly with a shoe. The rest of her injuries fall along the same lines. They're just enough to break a few blood vessels, which caused the discoloration or bruising. The Snodgrass girl, however, suffered substantial injuries to her spleen, kidneys, and ovaries."

"What are you saying?" the detective

asked, brushing his finger under his nose.

"I'm trying to tell you is there's a possibility the Campbell girl's injuries were self-inflicted."

"Jude Campbell escaped, remember?" Hank said. "If she hadn't, she would have been his second victim." He cracked his knuckles. "Do you think the bastard intentionally buried Haley Snodgrass alive?"

"Yes," Charley told him. "The beating might have rendered her unconscious for a while, but she was gasping for air when he began covering her with dirt. She might have even been crying for help or pleading with him. Since her mouth was open, we'd expect to find dirt in her throat. But this girl inhaled it. It was in her lungs. That's what killed her. The cause of death is asphyxiation."

"So let me see if we're on the same page here," Hank said, leaning back against a counter. "Haley Snodgrass could have been his first kill. Burying her alive excited him. Maybe he intended to do the same to Jude Campbell. That could be why she received a lighter beating because he wanted to make certain she didn't die. Just killing her wasn't enough. It doesn't make sense for Jude to have inflicted those injuries on herself. She didn't want anyone to know about them, so she didn't do it for attention. Carolyn walked in on her in the bathroom and saw them. She had to handcuff her to get her to go to the hospital."

Charley removed his glasses. "Is the Campbell girl's father still your primary suspect?"

Hank looked troubled.

"For the time being. Something just doesn't add up, though. Serial killers don't usually pick their offspring as victims. The closer you get to home, the more of a chance you'll get caught. And if her father did attempt to kill Jude, for whatever reason, why didn't he finish the job? Jude came home, so he had the opportunity. It was risky, sure, but guys who do these types of things don't think about the consequences. All Drew Campbell did was tell her to move out of the house."

"That works," Charley said, putting his glasses back on. "If she's not living at home, she's less connected to him. Am I right? He didn't know she was going to talk. Perhaps he planned on finding her and doing away with her at a later date, after things cooled down."

Hank shook his head in bewilderment. "How does Veronica Campbell fit into this picture? She wasn't beaten to death or buried alive. She was shot in a bathtub at a motel."

"You may have two killers running on separate tracks," Charley concluded. "Just because the Haley girl may have been killed around the same time as Veronica Campbell doesn't mean the same person killed her. I know you don't put much stock in coincidences, Hank, but they do exist. I read in the paper not long ago about two brothers who were killed in separate car accidents on the same day, only hours apart."

"Was Haley sexually assaulted?"

"I didn't find any semen in her vagina, nor any recent trauma that would suggest she was forcefully penetrated. That doesn't mean the killer didn't have intercourse with her. This girl has been sexually active for a long time."

"How long?"

Charley covered up the body, removed his gloves, and called his assistant to store Haley Snodgrass's remains. "I'm leaving, Hank. I'm going to spend tomorrow with my family. If a new case comes in, I'm not responding, so don't ask for me."

"Whatever you say," Hank said. "But you didn't answer my question. How long do you think the victim's been sexually active?"

"Since she was a child."

"Can you be more specific? Are we talking early or late teens? I mean, in today's world, there aren't that many teenagers who aren't sexually active."

"I suspect she was under the age of ten," Charley told him, sighing deeply. "If the killer raped her, she might not have even felt it. When a prepubescent female has sexual intercourse on a regular basis, genital surgery is usually required to restore the vagina to a normal size. This is more than likely the reason she became anorexic. The only thing she could control in her life was the food she put in her mouth." He reached for the door handle, then stopped and glanced back at the detective. "Now that I've told you, I'm going to warn you. If the media get their hands on this information, I'll refuse to handle any more of your cases."

Hank felt ashamed to be a man. "Don't you see? This is the same thing the doctor said about Jude Campbell. I can't see her father molesting the Snodgrass girl when she was a kid. Shoot, we don't even know if they knew each other back then. This is bizarre."

Charley turned to leave. Fearing he might get locked inside the autopsy room, the detective rushed out the door behind him. Once he'd locked up, the pathologist took off down the corridor leading to the employee parking lot.

Hank pressed his hands against the glass, staring at the small mound underneath the white sheet. Jude had told them she was trying to kill herself by not eating, but she was nowhere near as thin as Haley Snodgrass. Both girls appeared to have been sexually assaulted as children.

Stepping outside into the rain, Hank pulled his coat over his head and jogged to his police unit. Dozens of questions flooded his mind. Child pornography and pedophilia Web sites were present on the Internet, regardless of how hard law enforcement worked at getting rid of them. As technology advanced, so did opportunities for criminals and perverts. He'd read in the news the other day about a guy who'd downloaded child pornography onto his iPod.

The worst development had to do with webcams. Young teens, the majority boys, were being enticed by pedophiles to expose themselves on the Internet. And pedophiles were working together, chatting online and suggesting different ways to move a boy along. In one instance, a man had rented an apartment for a thirteen-year-old boy who was afraid his mother would catch him. The man also set up a Web site where he could take credit cards. In one year, the boy made over a hundred grand. What a terrible world children were being brought into, Hank thought, his mood as dark as the sky above him.

Did Haley Snodgrass's father know Drew Campbell? Now they'd have to get a search warrant for the Snodgrass residence. Perhaps the two men had met online years ago. Had they swapped their daughters? Just the mere thought was so repugnant, he almost sucked a toothpick down his windpipe.

Unlocking his car and darting inside, he started the engine and turned on the windshield wipers. The mechanical swishing sound had a calming effect as his mind searched through possibilities. Jude hadn't said anything about another man being involved. Maybe it was too embarrassing, or she'd been too young to remember. Had the two girls grown to a state of rebellion where they now posed a threat to their fathers? It was more difficult to control an adult than a child, and both Haley Snodgrass and Jude Campbell were going on nineteen.

Was this a desperate attempt to clean house? Had the men wanted it to look as if there was only one person, which would keep them both in the clear? Had Veronica been murdered because she'd stumbled across the truth?

At least they'd found Jude and placed her in a secure environment. She was not only a witness. She was their greatest resource. Hank would work around the clock until he brought this demented person or persons to justice. Slamming the gearshift into reverse, he backed out of the parking space, then gunned the big engine and sped off.

CHAPTER 22

Carolyn had met Marcus and Rebecca for lunch in the food court at the mall, then driven to the Ventura PD to meet Mary Stevens. The two women picked up Jude at the jail to escort her to a three o'clock meeting at the DA's office.

"I didn't sleep all night," Jude complained, a sour expression on her face. "The jailer was an ugly dyke. She went to the bathroom with me and watched me pee. I was afraid what she'd do to me if I went to sleep."

Mary met her eyes through the rearview mirror. "You're with me now, so shut up and put up. Wanda isn't a lesbian. She's been married for thirty years and has four grandchildren. You got plenty of sleep yesterday when you shot yourself full of heroin. You almost put yourself to sleep permanently."

"I wanted to die," Jude said, lacing her fingers through the wire mesh screen. "You people are completely clueless. What am I going to do at the DA's office? I've already told you everything. It really did me good. Now I'm a prisoner."

Carolyn turned sideways to talk to her. "Detective Sawyer said he would drop the charges against you if you cooperate. What you'll be doing this afternoon is giving the prosecutor your deposition. Mary and I will be there, as well as a victims' rights advocate. You'll have to take an oath that what you say is the truth."

"Then will it be over?"

If she only knew, Carolyn thought, exchanging glances with Mary. "The next step will be the preliminary hearing. A preliminary hearing is similar to a minitrial, but there won't be any jurors.

"You'll testify, and your father's attorney will be allowed to cross-examine you, as well as call other witnesses to support his case and refute your accusations. Then the judge will decide if there's sufficient evidence to hold the case over for trial."

"When this is over, will my father get out?"

"We're hoping he'll be held without bail, particularly since your friend, Haley Snodgrass, was murdered. Your father hasn't been charged with that crime." Carolyn watched

Jude's reaction, but her face remained the same, no emotional response whatsoever. "The DA, Kevin Thomas, may ask you some questions about Haley today. He's also going to ask you about your relationship with Reggie Stockton. When was the last time you saw him?"

"I don't remember," Jude said. "Why will they be asking me about Reggie? He was Haley's boyfriend, not mine."

"You liked him, though, right? We were told that you and Haley stopped being friends over Reggie. Is that true?"

"We got high on pot one night and made out. Haley went ballistic when she found out. I didn't have sex with him or anything. Reggie is a cool guy. Haley thought he was in love with her. That was a laugh. Reggie had all kinds of gorgeous girlfriends. He was popular and smart. Haley and I were considered losers. We both flunked a couple of classes. That's why neither of us got to graduate."

"Haley's father said she had an ulcer," Mary said. "That's why she missed so much school."

"That's bullshit," Jude shot out. "Haley was anorexic. Her mother tried to put her in a hospital, but her father wouldn't allow it. The last time I saw her at school, I knew she was sick again because her cheeks were caved in, and she wore all these heavy clothes, even when it was hot."

Carolyn asked, "Did you ever patch up your friendship?"

"Not really," Jude said, staring out the window. "All she talked about was Reggie. Then she'd get pissed off at me and everything would start up again. Anyway, I knew she was going to die. There was a girl in my junior high who died from anorexia. Haley was an idiot. Her father spoiled her rotten. I don't know why I stayed friends with her for so long."

"I think there's been a misunderstanding," Carolyn said. "Haley didn't die from anorexia. She was murdered, Jude. Whoever killed her buried her in an orange grove. The police found her body last night."

Jude blinked several times. "I thought I heard you say something about Haley last night. Why would someone kill her? All they had to do was wait a while and she would have dropped dead." She chuckled. "Maybe she dug her own grave and jumped in. I think she became anorexic because she wanted to make people feel sorry for her. She thought she could get Reggie back that way."

How could a layman understand Jude's

psychological makeup? Carolyn asked herself. They'd just informed her that a girl who was once her closest friend had been murdered, and she'd responded with insults and laughter. Her callous demeanor must be her coping mechanism. Acting tough was a front to cover all the years she'd been victimized. Of course, some of it wasn't an act. A child in an ongoing abusive relationship had to toughen up in order to survive. Jude was clearly a survivor.

Mary insisted on cuffing Jude when they reached the government center parking lot. Carolyn took her arm and led her to the entrance, then steered her toward the elevator, hitting the button for the third floor where the district attorney's office was located. The receptionist buzzed them through the security doors, and they made their way to the conference room.

Kevin Thomas stood. "Ladies, please have a seat. I'd prefer that Ms. Campbell sits directly across from me."

Jude's eyes went to the court reporter, who was unpacking her machine and setting up. "What's she doing here?"

"Mrs. Hubert will be recording your statement," Thomas explained, sitting down in his chair at the end of the table. "She uses a form of shorthand, which is imputed into that machine. When we're finished, she'll transcribe it, and a copy will be sent to your father's attorney, Jacob Farrow."

"She's going to write down every word I say?"

"Yes." Thomas glanced at his watch, then turned to Mary. "Is Detective Sawyer coming, or should we proceed without him?"

Mary pulled out her cell phone and called Hank. It wasn't like him to be late. She said a few words, then disconnected. "He's in the building. He'll be here any minute."

"My name is Kevin Thomas. Is it all right for me to call you Jude?"

"I guess," she answered. "Can I call you Kevin?"

"Don't call me by my first name in the courtroom, but any other time will be fine." He glanced up as Hank entered the room, selecting a seat next to Carolyn on the opposite side of the table from Jude. "The victims' rights advocate wasn't able to make it today. That's one of the reasons I wanted Ms. Sullivan to be present. I understand you've been staying with her."

"Duh," Jude said. "In case you don't know, I'm a prisoner now. That dickhead that just walked in charged me with breaking and entering and possession of an illegal substance. It was my own damn house. Is that legal?"

Thomas made a pyramid with his fingers. "We'll discuss that situation later. It has no bearing on the present matter."

After Jude was sworn in, the prosecutor asked her name and other pertinent information, then moved to the incidents of abuse committed by her father. He thumbed through a stack of papers. "You informed Detective Stevens that your father made you feign illness on the days he molested you. Is that correct?"

"Yeah."

"Can you answer yes or no, instead of using slang?"

"Maybe," Jude said, taunting him. "Will you promise me the police will drop the charges against me if I tell you what you want to hear?"

Thomas didn't move, but his face flushed. Everyone but Jude knew he was angry. "In this statement, Ms. Campbell, you should be speaking of your own accord and with no promises of any kind from myself or my agency."

"So now I'm Ms. Campbell again," Jude said, turning to Carolyn. "I can't talk to this guy. He's a prude who acts like he's got a rod shoved up his ass."

"Excuse me," Thomas said, pushing himself to his feet and leaving the room.

Carolyn got up and followed him, finding him gulping water from the fountain. "She needs therapy, Kevin. You've handled sexual abuse victims before. You know the profile."

"I can't prosecute a case with a hostile victim."

"Hank told you about the body they found last night, didn't he? Haley Snodgrass was Jude's friend. She may be acting out because she's distraught. Even before she learned about her friend's death, she tried to OD on heroin."

"Perhaps she'd react better to a female. I'll have the case reassigned."

"Jude may disappear again," Carolyn told him. "For Christ's sake, Kevin, can't you go back in there and try again? The crimes are what made her this way. As long as you react, she'll keep at you. Ignore her and you'll get your deposition. We need to get her on record now. Whoever killed Haley Snodgrass may come after Jude, or he could be out there shopping for a new victim. We're beyond sexual assault. This was an attempted murder. The killer wanted to bury Jude alive. That's why her injuries weren't that serious." Carolyn ran her fingers through her hair, beside herself. "Are you going to stick your tail between your legs and run off because a girl called you a prick?

Jesus, be a man and do your job."

Without a word, Thomas walked back into the room.

Thirty minutes of questioning went fairly smoothly. Carolyn wasn't certain what happened, but Jude began to unravel. "What will happen to my dad when this is over?"

"That depends on whether or not we get a conviction," Thomas told her. "If we file homicide charges, he could face the death penalty. As it stands now, he'll spend most of his life in prison. May we continue?"

"But what if the jury doesn't believe me? Then they'll let him go, right?"

"Yes," the district attorney said, turning a piece of paper over. "Do you remember what occurred on July ninth, three years ago? You missed school that day. It appears to have been on a Wednesday."

"I went to the beach." Jude hadn't been paying attention. She was nervously twisting the edge of her T-shirt into a knot.

"You told Detective Stevens that you recalled the events of that day, that your father made you bend over the bed and penetrated you. When you cried and pleaded for him to stop, he beat you."

"Yeah, that's what he did." She squinted and tilted her head. "I don't think I said he made me bend over the bed, did I? He just made me take my clothes off and lie there while he did it to me."

Thomas's pen began shaking in his hand. "According to your earlier statement, making you bend over the bed when your father wanted sex was an established behavior."

"Shit," Jude said, throwing her hands in the air. "My dad's a jackass, okay? What kind of father would kick his kid out of the house the day after her mother was killed? That was mean. He deserved to get his butt kicked. That doesn't mean I want them to lock him up forever or kill him. Hell, my mom's already dead and my sister and brothers have been pawned off to my aunt Emily. She hates kids."

"When you say your father deserved to be punished," Carolyn said, "you mean for all the years of abuse you suffered?"

Jude sniffed. "Not really," she said. "I ditched school because I wanted to fool around with my friends." Everyone in the room sat there in stunned silence. "School bores me. Why learn all this stupid stuff when I'm never going to use it? Then I started hanging out with a bunch of surfer dudes who smoked pot all the time. Mom and Dad tried to turn things around, but I was already too far gone. Howie getting me knocked up didn't help. I got pregnant again a few years later. I'd slept with so many guys by then, I didn't know who the father was. What can I say? I'm a slut and a loser. I'll probably never amount to anything just like my dad kept telling me." Her eyes pooled with tears. "I enrolled in school this year hoping I could get my diploma. I was going to surprise them, make them proud of me. No matter what I did, they would never have been proud of me. Mom felt like a baby killer because she arranged for me to have the abortions."

Kevin Thomas looked as if the top of his head were about to blow off. "Are you saying that you lied about your father sexually abusing you?"

"Ah, yeah," Jude said, brushing the tears away with her fingers. "Didn't you read my arrest record? I'm a world-class liar. I bet I could pass a polygraph test. Sucking dick and lying are the only things I'm good at."

"What about the injuries you claimed your father inflicted?" Thomas said, his face so stiff his lips were barely moving. "Are you denying that he beat you as well?"

"I got into a fight with a wino," Jude said. "Hey, what can I tell you? Miss Probation Officer over here tackled me on my front lawn. Then she cuffed me and threatened to lock me up in a mental hospital. I would have told her anything to get her off my back."

Carolyn leaped to her feet. "She's not telling the truth, Kevin. She's terrified her father will be acquitted and kill her. You've come this far, Jude. Don't back out now. I know you're frightened. We'll protect you."

"You mean like you protected me last night? Slamming my ass in the jail? No, thanks. I'd rather take my chances on the street." Jude smiled. "You guys didn't see the wino. I messed him up really bad. I know how to take care of myself."

Hank shook his head. "Incredible," he said. "I should take you to the morgue and let you see your friend Haley. Don't you realize what you're doing?"

"I'm telling the truth," Jude said, thrusting her chin forward. "I swore to tell the truth so I'm telling it. You people just don't want to hear it. You want your big sex case, so all of you can get on TV and become famous. Let my dad out of jail, okay?" She made a square with her finger. "He's a straight shooter. Dad would jump out a window before he'd have sex with a kid. I don't think he even had sex with my mom." She stopped speaking and stared at Hank and Mary. "Do I have to go back to jail now? You said you'd drop the charges if I cooperated and told the truth. I held up my part of the bargain."

Mary, Hank, Carolyn, and the district attorney huddled in the back of the room. Jude struck up a conversation with the court reporter, asking her what school she went to, and how long it took to become certified. "Maybe I could do that," she said. "I used to play computer games all the time. I've got really fast fingers."

"Hold her until I can prepare a statement for her signature," Thomas said. "I'll withdraw the charges tomorrow."

Hank grabbed his sleeve. "Forget the deposition for now. Give her some time to accept what happened to her friend. You can't release Campbell back in the community. There's a possibility that he's involved in a pedophilia ring. I'm certain all these crimes are related, especially the Snodgrass girl's murder. Charley said she'd been sexually active since she was a child, the same thing the doctor said about Jude. I'm preparing a request for a search warrant for the Snodgrass residence. Can't you hold off until we put this together?"

"Unless you bring me a credible witness," Thomas said flatly, "the state has no case against Drew Campbell." He shot Hank a black gaze. "Don't ever make an under-the-table deal again, Sawyer, or I'll have you thrown off the force."

"Whoa," Mary said, after the district attorney had stormed out of the room. "Where do we go from here, guys? I knew Jude was a problem, but I didn't think she was going to drop a bomb like this on us. I've never seen Kevin Thomas move so fast." A sly smile appeared on her face. "What did Jude call him? A prude with a rod stuck up his ass. She sized him up right away, wouldn't you say?"

"I'm not going to drop the charges and let her just walk away," Hank said, not interested in small talk. "The girl's in danger. Maybe she thought if she denied the stuff about her father, he'd leave her alone. I don't think that's going to happen. Drew may be working with Snodgrass's father. For all we know, there are more men involved. We've got to get the search warrants pushed through so we can seize their computers."

"I'll take Jude home with me again," Carolyn said, deciding there was no other option. "Tell her it's a provisional release, Hank, that she has to stay with me or go back to jail. And if she runs away again or uses narcotics, you'll press charges on both counts. Impress on her that she could go to prison. She got a taste of the jail last night and didn't like it. She wouldn't last a week at a state prison facility."

"She's a girl," the detective said. "A white middle-class girl, not some hard-core gang chick. No judge is going to send her to the joint. A stint in jail maybe. That's on the possession charge. She was right when she questioned the validity of the breaking and entering. It was her house."

"Charge her with auto theft, then?" Carolyn suggested. "She stole Marcus's Jeep Wrangler."

"By the way," Mary said, "patrol found it parked in the shopping center a few blocks away from Veronica's house. I had them tow it to your place in Santa Rosa. I thought you guys didn't want to press charges."

"We don't. We're just going to hold a prison sentence over her head. It doesn't have to be true. We need some way to control her until we figure out what's going on."

"Oh, I see," Mary said, scowling. "She lies. We lie. Then somehow, everything turns out perfect. I'm not so sure about that, Carolyn."

"I might consider cutting her loose and putting a tail on her," Hank said. "That way, we might actually learn something."

"I think she's involved with Reggie Stockton," Mary said, keeping her eye on Jude. "Who knows? Maybe she killed off the competition. She didn't seem upset when we told her that Haley Snodgrass had been murdered."

"Snodgrass weighed seventy pounds," Hank told them. "I doubt if a girl like Jude would consider a skeleton competition. The best plan is to kick her loose and follow her. I'll put Gary Conrad on her. She's never met him and he doesn't look like a cop." He walked a few steps away and called Conrad. "He'll be here in five minutes. He'll pick her up as soon as she leaves the courthouse."

Carolyn felt betrayed and conflicted. She was too busy to spend time with Rebecca, but she felt compelled to take care of Jude. Hank had made his decision, though, and arguing with him would be futile. He was a good friend, and a great detective, but a real hardhead once he set his mind on something. All she could do was pray that something terrible didn't happen to Jude. "Did she have any money when they booked her last night?"

"A few bucks," Mary said. "She probably pawned your daughter's stuff to buy the dope. Patrol said there was nothing of value in the Jeep."

"She has to have money for food."

Hank was fed up. "She made a big speech about how she could take care of herself. Let's see if she can prove it."

Carolyn waited until the two detectives had left, then walked over and handed Jude her card. "I'm still your friend," she said. "Whether you believe it or not, I care about you. If you get in trouble, call me. And please, Jude, be careful."

Kevin Thomas returned, placing several pieces of paper down on the table in front of Jude. "Once you read through this, sign it and Mrs. Hubert will notarize it. You have your ID with you, I hope."

Jude pulled her driver's license out of her pocket and handed it to the court reporter. She flipped through to the last page of the document, then scribbled her name.

"Don't you want to read it?" Thomas asked.

"No," she said, a flirtatious smile on her face. "I trust you, Kevin. I bet you can suck dick even better than I can."

Once the statement was notarized, he dropped a copy on the table and hightailed it out of the office.

Jude's arrogant attitude shifted to one of despair. When she spoke, the bewildered young girl finally surfaced. "Does this mean I can leave?"

"Yes," Carolyn said, placing a hand on her shoulder. "I can drop you off somewhere if you want."

"Thanks, but I'll be fine. I'm sorry I said all those ugly things to you. I'm sure Rebecca hates me for taking her iPod and all. I was jealous of her. That's why it was hard for me to stay with you. She has everything and I have nothing. I don't even have a mother now, and I'm sure my dad will never speak to me again." Tears spilled from her eyes. "I should have told my mom how much I loved her. All I did was cause her trouble. Will you catch the man who killed her?"

"We'll do our best," Carolyn said, not wanting to tell her that the investigation had been impeded by her fabrications. Her clothes were dirty and disheveled, her hair matted, and her skin tone looked slightly yellow. When she stood, she seemed to have trouble maintaining her balance. Veronica would be horrified to see her daughter in this condition. But Veronica was dead, and if Jude had told the truth today, Drew had been put through hell for no reason.

Carolyn didn't understand why Hank thought Drew was involved in a pedophilia ring involving Haley Snodgrass's father. It was true that the cases had connecting elements, yet none that would lead to such a radical speculation. Rebecca was friends with Haley's younger sister, Anne Marie.

She'd even spent the night at their home on numerous occasions. The poor people had lost their daughter. The cops had already made a tragic error with Drew. Now that Carolyn had had time to digest things, it didn't make sense that Jude would clear her father if she was fearful he might kill her. Carolyn cringed at the thought of invading the Snodgrass's privacy so soon after their daughter's death. Sometimes law enforcement did more harm than good.

All Carolyn wanted to do was go home to Rebecca and Marcus.

As soon as she left, Jude walked over and stood next to Mrs. Hubert. "I just wanted to see how you fold that machine up. When I get my act together, I'm going to check into that school you told me about."

"It gets boring sometimes," the court reporter told her. "But the money's fairly good, and as long as you don't work for the courts, you can set your own hours."

While the woman was fiddling with her machine, Jude snatched her cell phone and wallet out of her purse, shoving them in the waistband of her jeans and pulling down her T-shirt to cover them.

When Mrs. Hubert looked up, the room was empty. She stepped out into the corridor, thinking it was strange that Jude hadn't said good-bye, but the elevator doors had already closed.

CHAPTER 23

Sunday, October 17 — 9:30 A.M.

Carolyn was in the kitchen making breakfast, dressed in her pink terry cloth bathrobe. The aroma of freshly brewed coffee and homemade blueberry muffins had made its way to the second floor.

Rebecca waddled into the room, wearing sweats and oversized slippers with cat faces on them. She gave her mother a kiss and yawned. When she saw the clock, she said, "I didn't know it was so early. Just save my breakfast and I'll heat it up in the microwave later."

"I need to talk to you," her mother said, removing the muffins from the oven.

"What about?"

She wanted to question her about Haley Snodgrass and her parents. She was surprised Anne Marie hadn't called and told her about her sister's death, but the whole family was probably in shock. "Go back to bed, honey. It can wait."

Marcus came in with the Sunday paper, playfully swatting Carolyn with it, then nuzzling her ear. "The weather's lousy today. There's nothing better than sex on a rainy afternoon."

Carolyn was disappointed she hadn't heard from Tyler Bell yet. She was fairly certain he'd had nothing to do with Abernathy's and McAllen's death, but it would be nice to have the proof, particularly now that Drew had been tentatively cleared. It was for the best, though, she decided, eager to enjoy the day with her family and give her mind a rest from the events of the past week.

Carolyn and Marcus split the paper between them, and leisurely flipped through the pages as they ate. Several times he looked up and smiled. He was a quiet, dignified man. They could be comfortable together in silence, just enjoying each other's presence without the need to talk. The night before passed through her mind, the tender way he had made love to her. He knew just where and how to touch her, as if someone had drawn him a map to all the pleasure points on her body. He was a quiet lover, unusual for a man. She loved the way he looked, the sound of his voice, the way his skin smelled, the texture of his hair. She placed her fist under her chin and stared at him. When you truly loved someone, just gazing at their face could turn despair into happiness.

Marcus's life hadn't been without problems, which gave him a depth beyond the average person. His twin brother had been a prominent Manhattan psychiatrist. He'd suffered a traumatic experience as a young child that had scarred him for life. Their baby sister, Iris, had died when her stroller plunged down a cliff into the Hudson River. Their father had blamed Marcus's brother, who was only eight at the time, and their mother had been so swallowed up with grief that she'd abandoned her family. The father had compounded the situation by leaving Marcus the majority of his estate. His brother had turned his pain into rage, and directed it toward women. Even today, they still weren't certain how many women he'd murdered. They seldom spoke of it. Marcus believed nothing could be gained by dwelling on the past, especially when there was nothing that could be done to change it.

His brother had been killed, shot by one of the women who survived his attempt to take her life. Carolyn glanced out the window. He had died here at Marcus's home. On a clear day, she could see the exact spot where the police had found his body.

After his brother's death, Carolyn had suggested Marcus sell the house. He'd refused, claiming it didn't bother him. Every now and then, though, she would see him standing there alone, in the spot where his brother had died. Even though the two men had been estranged for years, losing an identical twin must have been traumatic.

She'd waited a year before accepting Marcus's marriage proposal. Since Marcus and his brother possessed the same genetic makeup, she had to dispel all thoughts that he might develop a propensity for violence. But Carolyn didn't believe people were born killers. In most instances, it was their life experiences. In others, it was some type of mental illness.

Being raised in a staunch Catholic environment, Carolyn was taught that evil could take residence inside a human body if a person was weak or didn't call on the protection of God. Now that she was an adult, her beliefs had expanded beyond church dogma. She was still devout, but in her own unique way. Yesterday, she had stopped at a church and prayed before driving home. She did this on a regular basis, and it seemed to provide her solace. She tried to take communion at least once a month, but like Marcus, she was an intensely private person and preferred to commune with God in an empty church.

She cleared the table and placed the dishes in the dishwasher, then washed the pans and put them away. "Take all of it," she said, seeing him reach across the table for the sections of the paper she'd been reading. "I need to go upstairs and spend some time with Rebecca."

"Did you read the article about Haley Snodgrass?" Marcus asked her. "Since she went to Ventura High, Rebecca probably knew her."

"Anne Marie is her younger sister," Carolyn informed him, returning to her seat at the table. "She and Rebecca are friends, so I want to see what she can tell me about the family. She didn't say anything when she came down earlier. I don't think she knows Haley was murdered yet."

"Oh," he said, setting the paper down. "I assumed it was all right to cancel the man I had keeping tabs on John. It was costing a bundle, and I've got a cash flow problem. I've waited almost a year to get paid on one job. The government is the worst. They never pay on time."

"Why not?"

"They're the government," Marcus said, shrugging. "As to the surveillance, I still want to keep someone on Rebecca. The fact that a young girl was murdered is a good enough reason for me. Do you agree?"

"For now," Carolyn told him. "After the PD executes the search warrant on the Snodgrass house, we may know more. Jude is the one I'm worried about. At least Hank assigned someone to tail her."

"She was certainly convincing."

"Jude's a good actress," Carolyn commented. "None of us are sure what was true and what she fabricated. For the time being, we have no choice but to believe the accusations she made against Drew were false. I think the coroner is ready to release Veronica's body, so at least he'll be out in time to plan his wife's funeral."

Marcus scratched the side of his face. "What about the younger kids?"

"I assume they'll be returned to Drew. No one saw any evidence they'd been abused." Carolyn spread her hands over her face. "I feel awful. I should have felt Jude out more before I went to the police. I was just so certain what she said was true. Looking back, it was like she was reading from a script. When the DA tried to nail down specifics, she fell apart."

"It's not your fault," Marcus told her, reaching across the table to stroke her hand. "You were trying to protect Stacy. I was wrong to come down on you last night. That's one of the things I love about you, your dedication to your job."

"Does that mean I don't have to resign?"

He tossed his head back and laughed. "Who are you kidding? You weren't going to quit because of me. You're too strong of a woman to let someone tell you what to do."

Carolyn's spirits lifted. "You really mean it?"

He shoved the front page of the paper to her. The lead story was Haley Snodgrass's murder. "All I can do is read about this stuff. You have the ability to actually do something about it. I can't ask you to give that up. You're good at your job. You make a difference."

Carolyn smiled. "Thanks," she said. "I might surprise you, though, and quit one of these days. I'm tired, Marcus, and I doubt if Drew or Kevin Thomas believes I'm good at my job right now."

He got up and walked over to her, pulling her to her feet, then cradling her against his body. "You're the most noble and courageous women I've ever known," he told her. "The only person you need to worry about is me, and I adore you. We've got to set a date for the wedding."

"I don't know what I'd do without you," Carolyn told him, reaching inside his robe so she could feel the warmth of his skin.

"Go talk to Rebecca," he said. "Then we'll go upstairs and take a shower together."

"Where's my breakfast?" Rebecca was sprawled out on her bed, flipping through the pages of a fashion magazine.

"We don't have room service," Carolyn told her. "All you have to do is go downstairs and heat it up."

"John called me last night. He said some weird guy had been following him. Why didn't you tell me about Anne Marie's sister? Even John knew about it."

"Well," her mother said, perching on the edge of her bed, "you wanted to go back to sleep, remember? The man John saw was someone Marcus hired to protect him. I talked to your brother last night, too. Since things have changed, Marcus is going to call off the security. Have you spoken to Anne Marie?"

"I tried to call her just now, but her line was busy. She's not even answering her cell phone."

"What are her parents like?"

"I don't know," Rebecca told her. "Like all parents, I guess. Her mother acts like a zombie. Anne Marie said she had a nervous breakdown a few years back. She takes a lot of pills."

Interesting, Carolyn thought. "What about her father?"

"Nice. Before I got my license, he used to drive us everywhere. He doesn't really act like an adult. A lot of older people are like that. I guess they're trying to hang on to their youth or something."

"What exactly do you mean?"

Rebecca tossed the magazine aside. "You know, he tries to act like he's a teenager. He buys his clothes at the Gap. Whenever we say we like a certain song or group, he says he likes it, too. A lot of times when we go to the movies, he goes with us. It sort of pisses Anne Marie off. We went to Magic Mountain one time, and he rode all the rides with us." She smiled, a look of excitement on her face. "I met a guy last night."

"Where?"

"At Johnny Rockets in the mall," she said. "He's really handsome, and he has an awesome body. He said he used to play football, but then he hurt his knee."

"Where does he go to school?"

"Thousand Oaks," Rebecca told her.

"He's a senior."

"I don't want you dating an older boy. You know how I feel about that, honey. Older boys want —"

"Sex," her daughter answered. "I just met the guy and you're already scared I'm going to have sex with him. I don't do that, Mom. I don't want to get pregnant and I don't want to take birth control pills. They make your face break out. My friend Lilly gained ten pounds when she went on the pill. I'm not ready for some guy to slobber all over me, anyway. All my friends who've had sex say it's not worth it. Girls are different from guys. Lilly's boyfriend creamed his pants before they even did anything. That's gross. I'd rather masturbate."

They'd had this discussion before, and since the situation with Jude, Carolyn wasn't sure if her daughter meant the things she said, or was merely trying to appease her. "Good attitude," she told her, standing to leave. "Keep me posted on this new guy you met. I want to know what's going on with you, especially since a girl from your school was murdered."

"I'll tell you every detail," she said. "You want to go with me if he asks me out on a date? That'd be way cool, Mom. Then you could make sure the guy wasn't an axe murderer. You could even show him your gun."

"You're being sarcastic."

"No, I'm not," Rebecca lied.

Carolyn's daughter had always been something of a brat. In the past year, she'd become less demanding and more thoughtful. Carolyn worried the new lifestyle Marcus was providing would spoil her, and she was determined to stop it at the onset.

Marcus's first marriage had ended poorly. He'd claimed responsibility, telling her he'd failed to spend enough time at home while he was building his business. He'd lost more than his wife, though. He'd also lost his children. She assumed this was the reason he doted on Rebecca. She needed to have a serious talk with him. Giving a child everything she wanted was not the way to prepare her for life in the real world.

"Can't you please heat up my breakfast and bring it to me? This is such a big house, Mom, and I was up really late last night."

"Then go to bed earlier," Carolyn told her. "I love you, but I'm your mother, not your servant."

CHAPTER 24

Monday, October 18 — 11:15 A.M.

Carolyn spent the morning assigning cases, as well as conferencing recommendations with probation officers whose reports were ready to be filed. She had submerged herself so completely in solving Veronica's murder and dealing with Jude that she felt as if she'd lost half her brain. Laws that she could quote verbatim from memory, she now had to look up. Part of it was her inability to disconnect. Hank had e-mailed her the autopsy reports on Haley Snodgrass.

After finishing her meeting with Linda Cartwright, she caught Hank on his cell phone. "Did you get the search warrant for the Snodgrass residence?"

"Not yet," Hank told her. "Right now, we're at Veronica's. The warrant came through about an hour ago."

Carolyn was confused. "But I thought

Kevin Thomas was withdrawing the charges this morning. That would make the warrant invalid."

"Judge Thornton's morning calendar was booked. The case is scheduled for two. Until the charges are officially withdrawn, the search warrant is valid. If we come up with new evidence, we might convince Thomas to prosecute. Hold on," he said, talking to one of the crime scene officers. "Get all the shoes to the lab immediately. See if any of them match the injury that was on Jude Campbell's cheek."

"Sorry about that," he said, coming back on the line. "This case isn't dead yet, Carolyn. The threatening note that was left for you at the morgue was typed on the computer in Jude's room. Someone had deleted it, even from the recycle bin. Ricky Walters, our computer expert, managed to extract a copy from the backup files."

Carolyn might not be able to remember all the complex sentencing laws, but she recalled every word that Jude had spoken. "She said something about that, remember? When Mary wanted to tape the original interview, Jude mentioned that stuff on your computer never went away, even if you deleted it."

"Finding the letter doesn't tell us who

wrote it," Hank said. "This is the only computer in the house. My bet is Drew stashed his after Veronica was murdered. There's a DSL connection in the bedroom, but no computer. I'm certain he has computers available to him at his work. Fat chance on us getting a warrant for Boeing."

"Veronica had a laptop," Carolyn told him. "The county started providing them to the officers who worked in court services when they launched the work-at-home program. I've already been through it, and I didn't see anything unusual. What about Jude?"

"I was afraid you were going to ask me that," Hank said. "Gary Conrad lost her. She stole the court reporter's wallet and cell phone. She must have snuck out the back of the building. I thought they kept all the doors except the front locked on weekends, but they don't. Too many people come in to get caught up on their work."

"Great," Carolyn said facetiously, angry that she hadn't insisted on taking Jude home with her. "So now we don't know where she is again."

"This girl is shrewd. No wonder she got bored in school. Her IQ is probably off the charts. I've seen criminals twenty years older who aren't as clever. Believe me, you don't want this chick under your roof. Blink twice, and you won't have a damn roof."

"But didn't Mrs. Hubert cancel her credit cards?"

"Yes, but not until Sunday afternoon. By then, Jude had got a cash advance of a thousand bucks on her American Express card, and purchased six first-class six airline tickets, all to different cities. We've alerted security at LAX, as well as the ticketing agents at the various airlines. Don't hold your breath. We may never see this girl again. With a first-class ticket, she can change the city and date of departure, the destination, even have the ticket placed in someone else's name. She must have bought them over the Internet."

"Which cities did she buy tickets for?"

"I'm busy right now, Carolyn, but I guess you have a good reason for asking. New York, Las Vegas, San Francisco, London, Dallas, New Orleans. Anyway, I think that's right. She doesn't have a passport, so I doubt if she can use the one for London. She'll fly to one city, then exchange the ticket for somewhere else."

"Reggie Stockton's from New Orleans. I knew she was involved with Stockton. He's your mastermind, don't you see? He sweet-talked that poor widow into letting people believe he was her son. At twenty-four, he enrolled in high school. That's where Jude must have got the heroin. Hasn't anyone picked him up yet?"

"Nope," Hank said. "I'm here working myself to death, and that asshole is probably in a first-class seat sipping champagne. Life's a bitch, ain't it?"

Carolyn disconnected, checked in with Brad, then headed to the PD where Mary and Gary Conrad were working on the Snodgrass murder.

When she walked into the conference room, Mary was typing on her computer and didn't notice. It was hard to see the surface of the table for the abundance of evidence, arrest reports, and file folders. To keep things separate, they had brought in plastic bins and written Campbell on some and Snodgrass on others in black Magic Marker. Keith Edwards cleared his throat to get Mary's attention.

"Welcome to the madhouse," Mary quipped. "I'm glad you're here, Carolyn. We can use all the help we can get." She wasn't wearing any makeup, her hair was slicked back in a knot, and she had dark circles under her eyes. "When we catch Jude Campbell, I want five minutes alone with her. She's got us chasing our tail. I don't know which end is up anymore."

Carolyn paced around the room, too anxious to sit down. "Stockton may be our murderer."

Mary pushed her chair back from the table. "Hit me with it, just make it brief. We're racing the clock here to keep Drew in custody since our star witness turned into Sybil yesterday."

"Okay," Carolyn began, trying to form her thoughts into a cohesive narrative. "Stockton was in custody in New Orleans for two felonies. If the truth came out, he could be extradited to Louisiana and sentenced to prison. Do you have any idea how bad the prisons are in Louisiana?" She paused for effect, then continued, "He was living his dream here. Going to high school, making out with the young girls. We know he and Haley Snodgrass were an item. She could have stumbled across the truth about his past, and tried to blackmail him after he ditched her. A young black male rented the room at the Motor Inn. Even if it took him a dozen tries, the clerk did eventually identify Stockton."

"But Veronica was found at the Motor Inn, not Haley Snodgrass."

"I know," Carolyn said. "Just hear me out."

"We don't have time for nonsense," Mary said without thinking. "Drew wears a size eleven shoe. Forensics is running all his shoes through the computer, trying to see if they can get a match on one of the heels against the bruises that were on Jude's body."

"What I'm telling you isn't nonsense," Carolyn shot back. "I know you're running on empty, Mary, but you don't have to insult me."

"I apologize. Keep talking."

"Haley Snodgrass follows Stockton to the motel room he rented with the intention of having sex with Jude. Snodgrass goes nuts with jealousy and threatens to tell the police about Stockton's past. Stockton beats her and mistakenly believes she's dead. Sometime during the beating, Jude runs out of the room and calls her mother. Stockton catches her and drags her back, unaware she's called Veronica. He roughs her up, but not nearly as bad as he did Haley. Veronica shows up, Stockton grabs her gun, and the rest is history."

"Why didn't he kill Jude?" Mary asked, tapping her fingernails on the table. "Do you think she'd stand by and watch him shoot her mother? She might be cold, but no one could be that callous."

"We know she took a beating," Carolyn continued. "Maybe Jude was unconscious when Stockton shot Veronica. Now he has a gun, so he could make Jude do whatever he wants. They flee the room, leaving Veronica dead in the bathtub. Stockton forces Jude to help him bury Haley. The grave was extremely shallow, and Haley weighed only seventy pounds. Jude could easily carry seventy pounds. Stockton holds the gun to her head while she digs the grave. Now he tells her that the police will believe she's the killer, that they'll find evidence on the body and in the motel room. Everyone knew Jude and Haley were fighting over Stockton. And Jude had an extensive juvenile record, so she has to believe what Stockton is threatening could come true. To throw everyone off, she made up the abuse story about her father. Stockton isn't in custody, so the threat is still there. That's why Jude ran away from my house, and why she tried to overdose on heroin."

Mary took a sip of her coffee. "Why didn't she tell us the truth yesterday?"

"Because she didn't believe we could protect her, outside of locking her up," Carolyn reasoned. "Stockton could even have told her he had connections inside the jail. Once she hit the street, I believe, he snatched her. Then they used the stolen credit cards to get cash and buy the airline tickets."

"There's only one problem with your

premise," Mary said. "According to Charley Young, Haley Snodgrass had been sexually active since the age of ten or younger. That's similar to what the doctor said about Jude. If they'd said these girls had started having sex at sixteen, I wouldn't be shocked. But ten! Think about it, Carolyn. What are the odds of two girls who know each other having a history of sexual activity that young? I believe Hank is right, and Drew as well as Haley's father was involved in some kind of pedophilia ring. Jude buying a ticket to New Orleans may mean nothing. She probably heard it was a party town." She paused and held her pencil in the air. "She may have run off with Reggie, but that doesn't mean he's our killer."

Carolyn flopped down in a chair. She hated to admit it, but Mary was right. She related what Rebecca had told her about Mr. Snodgrass, about how he acted like a kid and always wanted to hang out with his daughter and her friends.

"There you go," Mary told her. "He fits the profile for a pedophile perfectly. Keep your fingers crossed that we can get a search warrant for Snodgrass's house before he destroys all the evidence."

"Look at all the unanswered questions," Carolyn said, becoming animated again.

"Who killed Veronica and why? Was Drew sexually abusing Jude, or is it possible that she fell prey to Mr. Snodgrass years ago? Are there two killers? Are they working together?"

"What do you think we're doing here, for God's sake?" Mary said. "Start digging through the evidence. Hank has been shuttling stuff in from Drew and Veronica's house all morning. You knew these people better than anyone else, so you focus on them while we work Snodgrass. Gary Conrad is handling Snodgrass as well, but he'll be working out of his office. He claims he can't think when there's too many people around. I'm under the opinion he can't think because of all the pot he smoked in his surfer days. Now get to work. If Drew's a killer and a pedophile, he's going to go free in a matter of hours."

Hank called from the forensic lab just before one o'clock. Mary placed the call on the speaker located in the center of the conference table. "I'm with Jack Myers," he said. "He's got a match on the heel of one of Drew's shoes, but he's not certain it will hold up. The bruise on Jude's cheek was already beginning to heal when the pictures were taken at the hospital, so the image isn't that clear. He can state definitively, though, that the markings match a size eleven shoe. What did you guys come up with?"

"I've found something, Hank," Carolyn told him, clutching a small piece of paper in her hand. "Drew didn't recall purchasing anything at Home Depot the day of Veronica's murder. In reality, he did. He bought a home improvement magazine. I found it in a brown paper sack, along with the receipt."

"Not the kind of thing a man would buy who was about to murder his wife," Hank answered, his voice tinged with disappointment. "Did it have a time stamp on it?"

"Eleven forty in the morning."

"That falls within an hour of the time of death. The idiot forgot about something that could clear him. Did he pay with a credit card?"

"He did," Carolyn told him. "I recognize his signature."

"Who pays for a damn magazine with a credit card? Maybe this was his ace in the hole."

"I doubt it, Hank. Veronica gave him a cash allowance. It wasn't much, just enough for a week's worth of lunches. Everything else went on the credit card. She liked to keep track of their spending habits."

"We can prove that the threatening letter

was written on the computer in his home," Mary commented. "Between that and the shoe, do we have enough to take to Thomas?"

"It's over," Hank said. "The computer was in Jude's room. It was obvious she used it because her homework was stored on it. Thomas will say Jude wrote the letter. Drew wearing a size eleven shoe and the heel imprint being close to the bruises on his daughter's body won't do much for us, either. Jude may have inflicted those injuries on herself. Charley said it didn't appear that she was kicked or stomped because there was no indentation on any of the injuries. I'm sorry, but I can't picture a killer slapping someone with a shoe."

"I bet they'd accept that argument in San Francisco," Mary said, laughing.

"Knock it off, Stevens," Hank barked. "The chief hears you making gay jokes and you'll be back in patrol by next week."

"We lost, Hank," she told him. "I'd rather laugh than cry."

"Shit, maybe the guy deserves to walk," the detective said. "Pack up everything we removed from the house and have Keith get it back here as fast as he can. Thomas will piss his pants if he finds out we executed the search warrant. If he comes looking for me, tell him I called in sick today. As soon as they put the house back together, CSI is going to clear. There was no search, understand? Are we all in agreement?"

Once they all answered yes, Mary disconnected. Everyone just sat there, trying to catch their breath. Carolyn picked through another box of items removed from Veronica's house. She found a photo album that smelled like Veronica's cologne, and opened it. The first picture was the two of them together. The sun was shining and they were making silly faces. They'd taken the kids to the zoo that day. "I miss you," she said, rubbing her finger over the image.

Keith stood in front of her. "I need to take that."

Carolyn picked up the box and turned around to hand it to him. When he tried to take it from her, she couldn't let go. It was as if Veronica's life had been reduced to a few plastic containers. All Carolyn had left of their friendship was memories. Soon even those would grow dim.

"I'm sorry," Keith said, gently prying her fingers off the box.

Carolyn covered her mouth and rushed out of the room. When she reached the end of the corridor, she turned her face to the wall and sobbed. She wasn't good at her job, as she'd boasted to Marcus. She wasn't good at anything. Even after Veronica's death, she had failed her precious friend. She should have let Jude leave that first night instead of interfering. And instead of supporting Drew, she had become his persecutor. Veronica's children had been ripped from their home and shoved into the hands of a woman who didn't want them. How could Carolyn make anything right when everything had gone so terribly wrong?

CHAPTER 25

Carolyn returned to her office and went through the remaining cases, managing to concentrate long enough to assign at least half of them. The rest she placed in her briefcase to work on at home.

She called the jail and asked for Bobby Kirsh. When he came on the line, she said, "It's me again, Bobby. Is Drew Campbell ready yet?"

"You've called here three times about this inmate," he said. "I can't decide if you plan to shoot the sucker when he walks out of here, or if something else is going on. He's not a bad-looking guy. It wouldn't be the first time, you know. Few years back, one of the female DAs fell for an armed robber. Weren't you supposed to get married?"

"I had to call three times because the officer on duty never called me back. Drew

Campbell is a friend. His arrest was a mistake. That's why the DA withdrew the charges. Please, just tell me when he's ready to be picked up."

"We just finished his paperwork."

"Don't let him leave until I get there." Carolyn grabbed her purse and briefcase and rushed out.

When Drew stepped through the security doors at the jail, he looked five years older and ten pounds lighter. He was wearing the same clothes he'd had on the day Veronica was murdered. She recognized the grape juice stain on the front of his T-shirt. When he saw her, a look of surprise registered on his face. Carolyn set her things on the floor and hugged him. "I'm so sorry you had to go through this, Drew," she said. "I came to give you a ride home. If you want, we can stop somewhere and get something to eat."

He ran his hands through his silver hair. "When can I see my children?"

"I called Emily this afternoon," she said, picking up her things and walking with him toward the door. "As soon as you get settled again, she'll bring them home. Have you talked to them?"

"Inmates aren't allowed to make long-distance calls." Drew tilted his head up to look at the stars. "I'll never take all this for granted again. If only I had Veronica back . . ."

Carolyn took him by the elbow. For such a large man, he seemed so fragile. "I'm parked back here. It's still early. We can call the kids from my cell phone if you want."

Drew choked up, swiping at his teary eyes with the back of his hand. "I need some time to get myself together first. Where's Jude? My attorney seemed to think she was staying with you."

"She was for a while," Carolyn told him. "I don't know where she is right now, Drew. At least she finally told us the truth. I don't think she realized there would be such serious consequences. To be honest, I'm probably the one who started this whole thing. When I saw the bruises on her body, I pressured her to tell me who was responsible. I guess she was so angry that you asked her to move out, she decided to get back at you." She told him about the receipt she'd found from Home Depot, lying and telling him she'd found it when she'd gone to the house to pick up some of the children's clothes. He didn't need to know that Jude had overdosed on heroin. At least, not tonight. She was sick of lies and deception, but sometimes the truth was too painful.

"I don't think you should go to the house,

Drew," Carolyn said, unlocking the Infiniti. "You're welcome to stay with me for a few days. Marcus and I postponed the wedding. I decided it wouldn't have been right without Veronica."

"Thanks, but I'd like to sleep in my own bed. I need to plan the funeral tomorrow. I'm going to buy a family plot. You know, enough spots for all of us. If the kids don't want them later on, I guess they can sell them. I know Veronica would want it that way."

Once they were on the road, Carolyn pulled out her cell phone. "Do you want to call the children now?"

"I'll wait until tomorrow. I'm too emotional tonight. Veronica and I tried so hard with Jude. She was the most adorable little girl. You remember. She loved people. Most kids that age are shy around strangers, but not Jude. She talked a mile a minute, hugged everyone, constantly asked questions. What's that, Daddy? How does the TV work, Daddy? How far away is the moon? Where are we going? When are you coming home?"

"She took after her mother," Carolyn said, fond memories passing through her mind. "Veronica could say more in five minutes than most people could in an hour. The only problem was figuring out what in the world she was talking about. When we used to share an office, I had trouble getting any work done."

Drew smiled, but a moment later, the smile disappeared. "Things started going wrong when Jude was in the third grade. She started stealing, lying, refusing to do the things we asked her, getting in trouble at school. I mean, you expect that kind of behavior from a teenager. Did Veronica ever tell you about the time Jude slapped her? The little snot was still in elementary school and she was already hitting her mother. We sent her to a child psychologist for a few weeks. What a waste of money that was. The doctor said she sat there for the whole hour without saying a single word."

"That was around the time I was going through the divorce from Frank," Carolyn said. "I recall Veronica thinking Jude's behavior problems were the result of being an only child. She thought if she had a brother or sister, things might change."

"That was a mistake," Drew answered. "I told her we'd waited too long. Jude was eight when Stacy was born. She was used to being the center of attention, and didn't like being upstaged by the baby. About a week after we brought Stacy home from the hospital, Jude tried to pull her out of the crib. She yanked on her leg so hard, it came out of the joint and we had to rush her to the hospital. Veronica swore it was an accident. I knew Jude was trying to hurt Stacy so I lit into her with my belt. Veronica and I had a huge fight that night. I didn't hurt the kid or anything, but let me tell you, Jude never forgot it. She kept embellishing that story until she had me trying to strangle her."

Although Drew didn't realize it, Carolyn was parked in front of his house. He needed to talk, and she had gained some insight into why Jude might have concocted the story about him abusing her. In the formative stages of a child's development, a single incident could have a major impact. Not because it was genuinely traumatic, but as it could be used to garner attention, something Jude apparently craved.

"I'll never know why she turned out the way she did," Drew continued, the muscles in his face rigid. "You have no idea how much it hurts to have a daughter say such vile things about you."

Carolyn let some time pass before she resumed speaking. "I assume you've heard about Haley Snodgrass."

"Awful," he said, grimacing. "How are Don and Angela handling it? We've all been friends for years. Jude and Haley were like sisters. I thought things were turning around for a few years. Haley was a good influence on Jude, or at least it seemed that way. I was brokenhearted when they ended their friendship over that boy. They reminded me of you and Veronica. They practically grew up together."

"Did Jude spend a lot of time at Haley's house?"

"When she was younger," Drew said, rubbing the side of his face. "During the past year or two, we couldn't get Haley to go home. Jude didn't like staying over there for some reason. Don was silly, and I guess he annoyed the girls when they got older. He's like an overgrown kid. Happy go lucky, you know."

Carolyn pulled into the driveway and parked. "The house is probably a mess, Drew. When Protective Services came that night, they were rushing to make it to the airport to meet Emily's plane. I can send Marcus's housekeeper over to help you put things back in order. I'd also like to go to the funeral home with you. Veronica was my best friend. You can buy the plots, but I'd like to pay for her casket."

He gave her a curious look. "You're acting like you did something wrong, Carolyn. I'm not mad at you. I know you believed the things Jude told you. You had no choice but to notify the authorities. If it had been Veronica, she would have done the same thing."

"Thanks," she said. "I needed to hear that."

"No problem." He leaned over and pecked her on the cheek. "The only thing I'm angry about is that the police haven't caught the person who murdered her. Do they have any leads as to who did it?"

"The case should come together now —" Carolyn caught herself just in time. She was about to say that his elimination as a suspect would narrow down the suspects. "Because I knew Veronica so well, the agency gave me permission to work on the task force. We've been working around the clock, Drew. I know we're going to nail this killer. I just can't tell you when."

An awkward silence ensued. "So, I'll call you in the morning, if that's all right," she said. "I'll bring my lunch to work. Why don't you see if you can set up an appointment at the funeral home around noon?"

"Okay," Drew said, opening the car door and stepping out.

Carolyn watched as he made his way up the sidewalk to the dark house. She chastised herself for not buying some lightbulbs, maybe picking up some groceries. Just before she drove off, he came back and tapped on the window.

"I don't have a key. The night the police arrested me, I left my keys in the house."

"Here," she said, removing hers from the key ring. "I probably shouldn't have a key to your house anymore."

"You're still family," Drew said, palming the key. "I'll give this back to you when I see you tomorrow. It meant a lot to me to see a familiar face when I got out of that hellhole."

Carolyn walked into the bedroom wrapped in a towel. Marcus had already turned out the lights. He came over and tugged on the edge of the towel, his eyes feasting on her body as it slid to the floor at her feet. "How could anyone as beautiful as you be self-conscious? There are women half your age who'd kill to look as good as you."

"They don't have to kill," she told him. "All they need is a good plastic surgeon. Besides, I might not look so good if you could actually see me. When are we going to take down the blackout drapes? I never know what time it is."

"I'd wake up at dawn every day without them. Why are we talking about drapes? Drew's not a child molester. That should give you some relief." He collected her in his arms, a lusty look in his eyes. "The less time I spend with you, the more I want you."

Carolyn craned her neck around to make certain the door was closed. Jude sneaking in and watching them while they were having sex had rattled her. The strange part was it hadn't seemed to bother Marcus. She suspected he'd even found it somewhat erotic.

"Don't worry," he said, as if he could read her thoughts. "The door's locked, Jude's gone, and Rebecca would never come in without knocking."

Marcus was a sensual and considerate lover. Carolyn managed to relax and enjoy herself. Connecting at such an intimate level with a person who truly loved her made her feel like herself again. Marcus had been right. When everything went wrong, doing normal things was sometimes the best medicine.

They were both asleep when the bedside phone rang. Marcus grumbled, his body curled around Carolyn's. "Let the answering machine pick up."

Carolyn saw Ventura PD on the caller ID. Her hand shook as she reached for the phone, knowing Hank or Mary would never call her this late unless something had happened. "What's wrong?"

"I called Drew at the house but he didn't answer," Mary said, her speech rapid fire. "Jude was hit by a car. She's in bad shape, Carolyn. Her left forearm was severed."

"Mother of God, no!" Carolyn exclaimed, clutching the phone with both hands. "What hospital did they take her to?"

"VCMC," the detective told her, referring to the Ventura County Medical Center. "They were going to chopper her to UCLA but it didn't make sense. VCMC has an excellent trauma unit, and they were only a few blocks away. A nurse named Amy Fitzgerald stopped to help, or Jude would have bled to death. As soon as she called the paramedics, she applied a tourniquet, then ran across the street to Ralph's for a bag of ice to pack the arm in. Her father is an orthopedic surgeon. He's one of the best in LA. I'm in the ER now. They're doing tests to make certain Jude doesn't have any internal injuries. On the surface, outside of the blood she's lost, all they could see were a few cuts and bruises. If everything checks out, they're going to try to reattach her arm."

Carolyn placed her hand over her heart. "Was Jude driving or was she a passenger?"

"Fitzgerald was traveling southbound on Dos Caminos when she saw a dark-colored passenger car slam into the side of a parked truck. The driver left the scene, but his vehicle must have sustained damage. From the skid marks, he had to be going at least forty, maybe fifty miles per hour. It looks like Jude stepped out from behind a flatbed truck. The car swerved to miss her and spun out, crashing into the front section of the truck. The truck belongs to a landscaping company. They had shrubs in the bed, which were held in place by galvanized steel guy wires. The wires are what severed her arm." Mary paused and caught her breath. "Do you know where Drew is, Carolyn? I called the jail and they said they released him."

Carolyn was franticly juggling the phone with one hand while she yanked open her drawers and pulled on a pair of sweatpants. "I picked Drew up and drove him home. He probably got drunk and passed out. I'll go to his house and see if I can rouse him." She tossed on a sweater, then rushed to the closet for her shoes and purse.

Marcus insisted on going with her. They left a note for Rebecca on the kitchen counter. On the way out, he stopped and advised the night security guard to patrol the perimeter of the house every hour. Soon, they were speeding toward Veronica's house in his Range Rover.

Carolyn dialed Drew's number several

times, then gave up. Turning on the dome light, she toggled through her directory and placed another call. "Father Michaels," she said when a groggy voice answered. "I'm sorry to wake you. This is Carolyn Sullivan. I need to ask a favor of you. A young girl has been gravely injured. She was baptized a Catholic, but her mother fell away from the church."

"Where is her mother now?"

"She was murdered."

"Oh, my," the priest said. "Is the poor child conscious?"

"I doubt it," Carolyn said. "Please administer the anointing of the sick, Father. She's at the Ventura Medical Center. Her name is Jude Campbell."

"Of course," the priest said. "I'll go right away."

"Thanks, Father," Carolyn told him, disconnecting.

"Is that the last rites?" Marcus asked.

"They don't call it that anymore. Last rites sounds too ominous, and a person doesn't have to be dying. If Jude is conscious, she could receive what's called the viaticum, where she would receive the Eucharist, as well as the sacrament of reconciliation. She was repentant at the DA's office the other day. She admitted she lied about her father, and exhibited remorse for the things she'd done during her life. If she does die, God forbid, she'll be leaving this world in a better state than she would have before."

"You really believe all this stuff? It sounds like a bunch of hocus-pocus to me."

Carolyn stared hard at him. "Yes, I do believe in the sacraments. They're based on the teachings of Christ. I respect your beliefs. Please accept mine."

"Don't get mad," Marcus told her, seeing the annoyed look on her face. "I didn't mean anything. I ask questions so I can learn, that's all. I just think it's odd that you believe a girl who's been victimized all her life would be in danger of going to hell."

"I don't know what I believe anymore," Carolyn said. "Have you forgotten that Jude recanted the accusations against Drew? For all we know, she could have killed Veronica and Haley."

"That's asinine."

"Please, Marcus, concentrate on the road. I'm too upset to talk right now."

As soon as he pulled in the driveway at Drew's house, she bailed out of the Range Rover and ran toward the door. She rang the doorbell, then pounded on it with her fists. If only she hadn't given Drew her key. "Jude broke out a window in the kitchen to get in the night she overdosed," she told Marcus when he stepped up beside her. "Maybe we can get in that way."

They opened the side gate and walked through the grass to reach the back of the house. The police had nailed boards over the window.

"I'll go get a crowbar," he said. "I think I can get us in."

"No," Carolyn said, taking hold of his arm. "Take me to the hospital. Then you can come back if we still can't get Drew on the phone."

Mary was in the waiting room at the ER when Carolyn and Marcus rushed in. "Your priest is with her now," she told them. "No luck on Drew, huh?"

Carolyn explained that Marcus was going back to the house. "No one got a better description than a dark-colored car? Didn't anyone other than the nurse witness the accident?"

"I wish," the detective told her, cupping her hand over her chin. "We also have to consider that it might not have been an accident, especially since we can't find Drew."

"You think he intentionally ran into her?" Marcus asked. "Why? To get back at her? But isn't Drew's car white? How long ago did this happen?"

"Let's see," Mary said, glancing at her watch. "It's eleven, so we're coming up on two hours now. Amy Fitzgerald was reporting for her shift that began at nine, so the accident occurred at eight forty-five. When did you drop Drew off at the house, Carolyn?"

"Around seven." Carolyn wondered how they could stand around and speculate when Jude was fighting for her life. Something seemed to be physically pulling on her. She took several steps and then stopped. Did she really want to see Jude in that condition? She had to be drenched in blood. Although Carolyn had seen photographs of dismembered people, they'd all been strangers. Her head was swimming. She pushed past the detective. "I need to be with her. She needs —"

"Wait," Mary called out. "Amy said they're getting Jude ready for surgery. She's unconscious, so I don't see what good it will do to go in there." When Carolyn turned around, she continued, "The traffic officer handling this thinks Jude threw her left arm out when she saw the car coming toward her. The rest of her body was positioned to the rear of the pickup, which explains the lack of injuries."

"I'm going back to Drew's," Marcus said, turning and walking briskly out the exit doors.

Carolyn headed to the reception desk. They said the only way she could see Jude was if she was the next of kin. She lied and told them she was Jude's mother.

Other than one with an elderly woman, the beds were empty. She walked toward a large glass-enclosed examination room where a group of nurses and doctors were assembled, almost knocking down Father Michaels. In his late sixties, the priest had baptized both John and Rebecca, as well as officiated at Carolyn's wedding to their father.

The nurses and doctors were shouting orders as they worked over Jude's mangled body. She couldn't get close enough to see anything other than a portion of her face. Her hair was caked with blood, and her eyes tightly closed. She had a tube down her throat and IVs in both arms.

Father Michaels had already finished the anointing. He whispered to Carolyn to keep him apprised of Jude's condition, and said he would say a special Mass for her.

After he left, Carolyn tried her best not to cry, but the tears came anyway. First, poor Veronica and now her daughter. It was almost as if an evil entity was trying to wipe out an entire family.

A young petite nurse with short blond hair

and a turned-up nose rushed past her. The nurse started to enter the room where Jude was when she saw Carolyn and stopped. "You must be Jude's mother," she said. "I'm Amy Fitzgerald. I was the person who reported the accident. I know how terrible this must be for you, but Dr. Martin does amazing soft tissue work. I know because he's my father." Another nurse gestured to her from inside the room. "We're taking her upstairs now."

Carolyn looked around, expecting to see the kind of container they used to transport organs. "Where's . . . her . . . arm?"

"It's already in the operating room. I'm sure the doctor will speak to you if you hurry. Go upstairs to the seventh-floor surgical unit. I'll call now and tell him you're on the way."

Carolyn followed the arrows to the elevator, punched the UP button, and stepped inside. This was Hank's fault. He was the one who'd insisted they release Jude, when they were clearly aware of the dangers involved. No wonder he hadn't shown up at the hospital, she decided, stepping out when the doors opened.

She jogged down the hall until she saw the double doors for the surgical unit. There was a sign on the tiled floor that said she couldn't pass beyond a red line. She saw the waiting room a few feet away, but her feet felt glued to the floor. Jude was already suicidal. How could she cope if she lost her arm?

An attractive man who appeared to be in his mid-fifties, dressed in green surgical garb, burst through the doors. "Are you Mrs. Campbell?"

When Carolyn nodded, he spoke abruptly, his eyes flitting here and there. She understood. He had an urgent job to do, and he wanted to get under way as soon as possible. When you had the skills to save lives, being polite wasn't important. She wanted to tell him she wasn't Jude's mother, but now wasn't the time.

"Dr. Samuels will be assisting as well as Dr. Goldstein, an excellent vascular surgeon. Your daughter's age, coupled with the fact that she didn't incur any other major injuries, gives us a better chance of success." Dr. Martin pulled his mask over his face, spun around, and rushed back through the double doors.

Carolyn went to the waiting room, then changed her mind and headed to the hospital's chapel to pray.

CHAPTER 26

Tuesday, October 19 — 1:45 A.M.

Once Marcus pried the boards off the window at Drew's house, he shone his spotlight on the frame to see if there were any remaining glass fragments. The window opened into the breakfast nook area of the kitchen, so it was large enough for him to crawl through. Satisfied he wouldn't get cut, he entered the residence. "Drew, it's Marcus," he shouted. "We've been trying to reach you."

Hearing no response, he flipped on the light switch and made his way into the living room. Just like Carolyn had thought, Drew was passed out on the sofa and the coffee table was littered with empty beer cans. Marcus tried the overhead light in the living room, but nothing happened.

He shook Drew by the shoulder. He didn't respond. He was lying on his side facing the back of the sofa. "Come on, man," Marcus said. "Wake the hell up. Jude's been in an accident. You need to go to the hospital."

The idiot had drunk himself into a stupor. Marcus didn't have much tolerance for boozers. He might have done the same thing, though, if he'd just been released from jail. Strangely, he didn't smell alcohol. Generally when a guy was this tanked, you could smell him twenty feet away. Rolling Drew onto his back, he aimed the flashlight at his face.

"Holy shit!" he exclaimed, jumping back several feet.

Drew had what appeared to be a gunshot wound in the center of his forehead. Marcus placed his finger on his neck to check for a pulse. When he felt nothing, he knew he was dead. The way his skin felt, he must have been dead for hours.

Marcus moved away from the body and stood perfectly still, afraid to touch anything now that it was a crime scene. He started to call Carolyn, but then realized that would be foolish. Using his cell phone, he called 911 instead. "You should notify Hank Sawyer and Mary Stevens," he told the male dispatcher. "Detective Stevens was in the ER at the medical center, but I don't know her cell phone number."

"We'll take care of it, sir," the man said. "Just sit tight until the officers get there. Do you think the assailant might still be in the house?"

"I don't know," Marcus whispered, his voice shaking. He was a computer programmer. He had a license to carry a gun, but he didn't have it on him. The only time he'd seen a dead body was on TV or in the movies. "I haven't looked around. Should I? The only thing I have to use as a weapon is a crowbar."

"Listen to me," the dispatcher said. "Where are you in the house?"

"The living room."

"How did you come in?"

"Through a window in the kitchen."

"So the window was open when you arrived?"

"No," Marcus said. "I pried the boards off. The dead man's daughter's been seriously injured. When we couldn't get him on the phone, we thought he was asleep. You're not going to charge me with a crime, I hope. I told Detective Stevens what I was going to do, and she said it was all right."

"Remain calm," the dispatcher advised. "Quietly leave the house the same way you entered. The assailant is probably gone, but it might make you feel better to wait outside.

Don't hang up. I'll stay on the phone with you until the officers arrive."

"Okay," Marcus said, tracing his steps back to the kitchen and climbing out the open window. "I'm out. I'm going to lock myself in my car. It's a green Range Rover. At night it looks black. I'm parked in the driveway."

He heard sirens in the distance, and then they stopped. When he told the dispatcher, he informed him that the officers responding had turned the sirens off just in case the suspect was still in the area.

A short time later, two black-and-whites skidded to a stop in front of the house, and two officers climbed out of each car with their guns drawn. Marcus got out of the Range Rover and raced over to them. "I'm Marcus Wright, the man who called. Man, am I glad to see you guys!"

"Is that your car?" a large officer with sergeant stripes asked, gesturing toward the Range Rover. Marcus told him it was and he instructed him to drive to the corner and wait. "Someone will talk to you as soon we secure the area. Detective Sawyer says he knows you. He's en route."

Four hours had passed. It was a few minutes past six. The sun was up, and the house Veronica and Drew Campbell had lived in was once again swarming with police personnel. After Marcus had given his statement to Hank, he'd left to pick up Rebecca and bring her to the hospital so Carolyn wouldn't worry about her.

"They reattached Jude's arm," Mary told Hank. "They won't know if it's going to work for several days. The biggest problem is infection. Carolyn said they put her in a drug-induced coma to give her body a chance to heal."

"Poor kid," he said. "Now both of her parents are dead. Who's going to take care of her?"

"There's three other children in San Francisco," Mary reminded him. "I guess the sister will have to bone up on her parenting skills. Carolyn told me Veronica had made provisions in her will for her to raise her children if something happened to both her and Drew. Were you aware of this?"

"That was years ago," Hank said. "Back when Carolyn was married to Frank. Veronica probably changed her will. I think their friendship was strained because of Carolyn's promotion."

"People don't update their wills, Hank, especially people who don't have a lot of money."

"Yeah, but you can't force another person

to raise your children. Carolyn would ruin her life if she took on that kind of responsibility. Those kids should be with a relative. Drew was insured for the same amount as Veronica. That's four mil. Don't kid yourself. Emily's a personal injury attorney. Those people are sharks when it comes to money. She'll jump on it, buy herself a big house, and hire a dozen nannies."

One of the crime scene investigators walked past. "I almost didn't recognize you, Mary. You're not wearing your red murder shirt today."

"No shit," she said, turning back to her conversation with Hank. "What in the name of God are we dealing with?"

Hank stopped a patrol officer, hitting him up for a cigarette and a book of matches, then stepping outside so he could fire up. "Don't say a word," he told Mary, blowing out the match and taking a long drag. "I know what we *do* have. Mountains of work ahead of us. This cigarette is probably the closest I'll get to enjoying myself until this monster of a case is put to bed."

"You quit smoking ten years ago," Mary said, shaking her head. "Are you going to dive back into the bottle again, too? Then you can destroy both your liver and your lungs. Why did you lose all that weight and start working out if you were going to revert to your old habits?"

Hank started coughing. He reluctantly dropped the cigarette on the sidewalk and stubbed it out with his heel. "You caused that to happen by harping on me. I guess you don't want to make sergeant." He saw a local news van parked across the street, along with several reporters standing behind the police tape.

Mary's eyes brightened. "I'd love to make sergeant."

"Check back in about five years. Maybe by then you'll learn to keep your mouth shut. Let's go see what Charley and the forensic guys have for us. It's turning into a zoo out here. Standing around bemoaning our plight isn't going to accomplish anything."

"You're the one wasting time smoking and complaining."

Hank turned around and snapped at her. "I can't think with you running your mouth all the time."

"How can either of us think when we haven't had more than a few hours of sleep since Veronica was murdered? We've got to get the captain to assign us more people, Hank. There's too much to do and not enough people to do it."

"As if I don't know that," he said. "Give

me some space. You're beginning to get on my nerves."

Darryl Bates, one of the forensic techs, met the detectives in the living room. "I went over the Explorer, Lieutenant. I couldn't find anything that would indicate it had been involved in an injury accident. No blood, tissue, or damage to the vehicle of any kind. No sign it's been washed recently. The interior stinks of spoiled milk, so I doubt if Campbell has driven it since he got out of jail."

"Good work," Hank told him. "Tow it to the lab and rip it apart. If there's a drop of blood anywhere in that car, I want to know about it."

When Bates walked off, Mary said, "What are the odds that Drew ran over Jude, then a few hours later, someone came in and shot him?"

Hank glared at her, but didn't bother to reprimand her again. She would have ignored him, anyway. She was the most relentless person he'd ever worked with, one of the reasons she was such a good detective. She'd ride a case to the ground. Dr. Martha Ferguson, the forensic pathologist he'd been seeing for the past year, had a similar personality. "You know who you remind me of?" he asked her. "Martha."

"I consider that a compliment," Mary said.

"I still can't believe you two got together. When you first met her, you couldn't stand her. You called her an obsessive bitch, remember?"

Hank gave her a sly smile. "That's before I saw her without clothes. The only time she isn't telling me what to do is when we're in bed. That's why we have sex so much."

Mary laughed, punching him in the arm. "No wonder you're so full of yourself lately. I didn't think you had it in you, Hank."

The detective cut his eyes to her. "I may not be young like you, but I'm not dead."

Charley Young was peeling off his gloves. "I estimate the victim's been dead since nine or ten last night. He must have been asleep when the killer gained entrance into the residence. Whoever it was rolled him over, shot him at close range, then turned him back to his original position. The cushions on the sofa muffled the gunshot, which is why none of the neighbors heard anything. My bet is this is the person who killed the wife. The bullet wound is in the same exact position."

"Why didn't he shoot him in the back of the head if he was asleep?" Mary asked. "Why wake him up and turn him over? He put himself at risk of getting into a struggle. Drew was a big man."

"He wanted to look him in the eye," Hank

told her. "The Snodgrass girl was buried alive. The killer gets turned on by this stuff. It makes him feel powerful to kill someone. He wants to drag it out as long as possible. Did forensics find anything in or around the body?"

"No," Charley said. "All they found was a smattering of talcum powder on the victim's shirt. The killer must have worn gloves. If we do find anything, it will probably be something that will only show up under a microscope. This guy is a professional. How did he get into the house, by the way? Carolyn's fiancé said he's the one who removed the boards from the window, so he didn't come in that way."

"There's no signs of forced entry anywhere," Mary told him. "He either had a key, or he had one of those devices that can be programmed to open any garage door. You said he was a professional. Do you mean an assassin?"

"Not necessarily," the pathologist said. "Just someone who's proficient in the use of firearms and controlled enough to make certain he doesn't leave any evidence. You didn't find much at the scene of his wife's murder, did you?"

Mary gestured for Hank to step aside. "We were all over this place yesterday. Most of the evidence that's going to turn up will link back to cops. Kevin Thomas will be furious when he finds out we executed that search warrant when we knew the case against Drew was dead. We'll be lucky if we manage to keep our jobs."

"You're not telling me anything I don't know," Hank said, pulling out a toothpick. "Why do you think I'm in such a piss-poor mood? The only way to cover ourselves is to screen anything related to our people before we book it into evidence. Keep in mind that we need a suspect in custody, which we don't have at the moment, nor does it appear that we're going to have one in the very near future. We also have to be able to prove that this person is guilty. Right now, we don't have any of those things, so why waste our time sweating a wimp like Kevin Thomas?" He paused, massaging his forehead. "No man is ever going to marry you. You're too much of a headache."

Mary placed her hands on her hips. "Thanks," she said. "Maybe I have no desire to get married because most men are idiots. The search we conducted yesterday was a disaster, Hank. We were in such a race against the clock, there's no telling how many people traipsed in and out of this place. It'll take us until Christmas to process all the evidence that doesn't belong to Drew or the killer."

"Write everything up and hand-carry it to Lou Redfield at the DA's office. With these new crimes, we should be able to get a warrant to search Don Snodgrass's residence. I also want him brought in for questioning. He's the only suspect we have right now. We've got three homicides. This so-called accident with Jude could be an attempted murder. No matter how far you stretch it, everything seems to lead back to that girl."

"What about Reggie Stockton?" Mary asked. "Carolyn believes he's our man. She put together a plausible premise as to how it all fits together. The only problem was both Haley and Jude being sexually active at a young age, which supported your belief that we were dealing with a pedophilia ring. Now that Drew has been killed and Jude seriously injured, there's a chance that both of you may be right."

"How's that?" Hank asked, stepping aside to allow the men from the coroner's office to carry the body out. "Damn, they've got the news chopper hovering over the house. What were you saying? You'll have to speak louder."

"Let's say Drew gets out and goes looking for Jude," Mary shouted.

"I still can't hear you. Close the door."

Mary did what he said, but she knew it was wasted energy. Forensics was starting to transfer evidence from the house to their vans. For the moment, though, it did reduce the noise level. "Carolyn claimed Drew didn't act upset about the way things went down when she picked him up last night. Maybe he wasn't upset because Jude was telling the truth. We need to take a look at Carolyn's phone records, as well as the jail's, see if Drew could have called Jude and threatened to get back at her when he got out. She fell apart after Thomas admitted that her father might be acquitted. Jude's a smart girl, Hank. She knew her criminal record would detract from her credibility, along with her drug use and promiscuity. When we told her she was free to go, her demeanor changed. She was probably terrified."

"I knew you were going to blame me," Hank said, frowning. "How did I know she was going to sneak out the back entrance, or that she'd lift the court reporter's wallet? I figured even if Gary Conrad lost her, without any money she couldn't get far. The whole point was that she might lead us to Stockton."

"Let's say you're right and Don Snodgrass

and Drew were both pedophiles," Mary went on. "They started molesting their daughters as children and somehow got together." She snatched a coffee cup out of the hands of one of the forensic officers. "Thanks, Gretchen. I need this more than you. I'll buy you lunch as soon as I find time to eat." She took a swallow, moistening her scratchy throat. "It must be eighty degrees in here, Hank. Did the Santa Anas blow in again?"

"Body heat," Hank said. "We have fifteen people crammed in this place, along with a truckload of equipment. At least we got the corpse out. He was beginning to get ripe."

Mary removed a red scarf from her back pocket and tied it around her head to use as a sweatband. "What if either Jude or both the girls started threatening to expose their fathers? There's a good chance the men swapped them or forced them to have sex with each other, then made their own child pornography. This might be the reason they were inseparable. No one else knew their horrible secret. At the same time, a history like that could have caused them to be fiercely competitive."

"Makes sense," Hank said. "But where does Stockton fit in?"

"Stockton is the avenger."

"Excuse me," the detective tossed out. "This isn't a comic strip."

"Shut up and listen," Mary said. "Both girls dated Stockton, probably slept with him, did drugs with him, maybe even at the same time. In case you don't know, the greatest male fantasy is a threesome."

Hank looked down at his shoes. He wondered if Martha had a girlfriend who might be persuaded. He was getting excited just thinking about it. He had to remind himself he was at a murder scene.

"Uh-huh," Mary said, jutting one hip out. "Now you know why I'm not married. Can you get your mind back on police work?"

"I thought I saw something strange on the floor."

"Sure you did." She waited until she had his complete attention. "Stockton's a handsome, fit guy from New Orleans, a city that's known to have more criminals than citizens."

"That's before Katrina," Hank said. "Half of them either died, escaped, or set up business somewhere else on federal money."

"I asked you to listen."

He smiled. "No, you didn't. You told me to shut up. You can't talk like that to a superior officer. Keep it up and you'll be back in uniform."

"You can't afford to lose me. I have the best handle on this case. Can I continue please? Say Jude and Haley tell Stockton their sordid stories. Stockton brags about how he escaped from jail, and maybe even describes some of the crimes he's committed. These three had something in common. They all had things to hide. So either one or both of the girls ask Stockton to kill their fathers. Things go haywire somewhere along the way, and Haley and Veronica end up dead. Jude, coached by Stockton, tells us just enough to get her father thrown in jail."

"Can't kill a guy if he's in jail."

Mary scrunched up her face. "Drew didn't stay in jail, did he? Stockton used Drew to take the heat off. Then when Jude retracts her accusations, knowing this will result in her father's release, Stockton is poised to move in for the kill. Jude could have sweetened the pot with the cash and airline tickets. Stockton knew the jig was up once we got his fingerprints. He knew if he didn't disappear, he'd end up in prison."

Hank held up a palm. "Slow down a minute. If Stockton shot Drew, who ran over Jude?"

"Drew," Mary told him. "Don't you see? Jude may have found a spare key to the house the night she overdosed. She hands the key to Stockton, then goes to one of her regular hangouts to wait for him to do the deed. Instead, her father shows up. Maybe it was a legitimate accident. She could have tried to get away from him and he chased her down with the car. Or maybe she was hiding behind the truck, then came out when she thought it was safe only to see her father barreling straight at her. As soon as he hit her, Drew took off. At the same time, Stockton is lying in wait for him here at the house. He uses the key to enter, and when Drew falls asleep, he shoots him."

"There's only one major problem," Hank said. "Forensics says there's nothing on Drew's car that would indicate it was involved in an accident. The Explorer is white, Mary. The nurse said the car was dark. Some of the other stuff is good, though. We'll run with it as far as it can take us. You've left out Snodgrass. What part does he play?"

"Well," Mary said, "Snodgrass could have been the one who ran over Jude instead of Drew. Maybe he was afraid she would implicate him, and we'd find out he killed his daughter. He may also have been worried that Drew would spill his guts one day. If Snodgrass killed his own daughter, he could kill anyone."

"What color cars does he own?"

"A white Mercedes and a blue Jag."

"Sounds like the guy's got some bucks."

"Snodgrass is a CPA. He owns an accounting firm."

Hank wasn't buying Stockton's role in the murders. The truth was in there somewhere, though, hidden among the thousands of loose ends. Brainstorming at the crime scene sometimes produced results. They were only a few feet away from the bloodstained sofa where Drew Campbell had spent his last moments. When you studied a homicide from behind a desk, you were removed from the stark reality, even in a series of crimes this brutal. "Why didn't Snodgrass shoot Jude, then?"

"If he hit her with his car, he assumed she was dead. He doesn't want to establish a pattern, so this worked out perfectly for him." Mary paused and placed her hand on her head. "Now that you mention it, there is a pattern. Veronica was shot. Haley was beaten. Drew was shot. Jude was hit by a car. Maybe every other victim gets shot. That's an easy death compared to what Haley and Jude have gone through. I hope to God she can keep that arm."

"There's two killers," Hank said adamantly. "Drew and Don Snodgrass. Stockton is nothing more than a low-level thug, just some guy who took advantage of a disaster to escape from jail. Get cooking on the search warrant. As soon as you've got it, call me and we'll pick up Snodgrass. I want to execute the warrant while he's at the station." He turned to walk away, then thought of something else. "What happened to the other car?"

"What car?"

"Jude had a car," he said. "She said her parents wouldn't let her drive it until she got a job to pay for the insurance. I think she said it was an older model Taurus. Don't you remember? She mentioned it that first night in Santa Rosa."

"I forgot, Hank," Mary told him, a chastised look on her face. "It wasn't here when she overdosed. The only car listed in the report was the Explorer. We towed Veronica's county vehicle from the motel."

Hank had been the first one at the scene that night. They'd both dropped the ball on this one. "Either Jude has the car, or the person who ran over her has it. Pull the license number off DMV and broadcast it immediately. Make certain the dispatcher cautions that the driver may be armed and dangerous. Use Stockton's description, and send it out nationally. We know Jude isn't driving it, and it's highly unlikely a CPA knows how to hot-wire a car. If we don't make an arrest soon, there won't be anyone to arrest. At the rate we're going, all our suspects will be dead."

"I'm on it," Mary said, elbowing her way through the throng of officers.

Rebecca was sitting next to Carolyn in the waiting room at the hospital, thumbing through a *People* magazine. Marcus had fallen asleep on the sofa across from them. She tossed the magazine on the table and stared at Marcus. "Why do guys sleep with their mouths open? It makes them look like old men."

"I don't know," Carolyn mumbled under her breath. Still in shock over the tragic events related to Jude, she felt completely devastated by Drew's death. She should never have let him go inside that dark house alone. She should have stayed with him, insisted he come back to Marcus's place. She wished she could talk to her mother. Marie Sullivan was a retired chemistry professor, and possessed the type of rational mind that had always helped Carolyn put things in perspective. Just when her mother had convinced everyone she was on her death bed, she'd sold her condo and taken off on a trip around the world.

She considered calling her brother, Neil, but she knew he might only intensify her hysteria. He was definitely not the type to deal with a severed limb. Until Marcus came along, Neil and Carolyn had either talked on the phone or seen each other every day. Moving in with Marcus had seemed like the perfect time to cut the cord. Her brother's lively personality made him a delightful person to be around when things were good. When problems developed, he could be more irritating than supportive.

She looked lovingly at Marcus, remembering how disturbed he'd been after he'd found Drew's body. Right now, there was nothing she could do but cope.

She'd insisted Marcus bring Rebecca to the hospital to make certain she was safe. Since Jude had slipped out of the house without their knowledge, she didn't trust his bodyguards. Would the killer come after her now, thinking Drew had told her something when she picked him up at the jail? Not only was she at the end of her emotional rope, but she was legitimately frightened. Whoever had written her the letter and assaulted her that night in the parking lot had threatened to go after her children. "Can you call one of your friends and have them pick up your work from your teachers?" she asked Rebecca. "I don't want you to go to school tomorrow."

"But why, Mom?" Rebecca protested. "There's nothing I can do. There's nothing you can do, either. The doctor said Jude's going to be in a coma. You can call and check on her from the house or your office. It seems silly to make us all sit here. I've worked so hard to keep my grades up."

"I want you with me," her mother told her. "I need you. These people were my friends. *Our* friends, Rebecca, not just mine. Sometimes you have to make sacrifices in life. You can do your schoolwork here."

"Fine, I'll call Anne Marie."

Carolyn locked her fingers around her wrist. "Call someone else."

"You're hurting me," Rebecca told her, jerking her arm away. "Why can't I call Anne Marie? Her sister was killed. Shouldn't I be there for her? I mean, you're making such a big deal about Jude."

"I can't tell you everything that's going on right now, but you may have to talk to the police about the things you told me about Mr. Snodgrass."

"What things?"

"There's a killer out there," Carolyn said in a firm voice. "We don't know who he is, or what he's going to do next. Haley Snodgrass was sexually abused, more than likely by her father."

Rebecca tossed her hands in the air in frustration. "You're going crazy, Mom. You must be sleep-deprived or something. In my health class, we learned that going without sleep for a long time can make you delusional. Anne Marie's father is a sweet man. He'd never do perverted things to his kids." A sad look passed into her eyes. "I wish my father cared as much for me as Donny does for Anne Marie. He takes her to amusement parks all the time, gives her money, and lets her buy anything she wants. When Haley got her driver's license, he bought her a BMW convertible. It was used, but not many kids get a BMW for their first car."

"Do you call him Donny?"

"Yeah," she said. "I'm not being disrespectful or anything. He tells all Anne Marie's friends to call him Donny."

Everything was gelling in Carolyn's mind. "He didn't buy Anne Marie a BMW, did he? You told me she has to borrow her mother's Cadillac when she wants to go somewhere. That's why she can't come to see you at Marcus's house, because the gas is too expensive."

Rebecca shrugged. "Maybe Donny doesn't have a lot of money right now.

How do I know?"

"Has Anne Marie ever talked to you about her father?"

"He embarrasses her. He tells stupid jokes and tries to act like he's a teenager."

"Do you know what a pedophile is?"

"A creep who likes to have sex with kids. Good God, Mom, Donny isn't a pedophile. You think everyone is a criminal. Take a pill and chill."

"I need to check on Jude," Carolyn said, pushing herself to her feet. "Don't call anyone. Marcus will pick up your schoolwork." Afraid Rebecca would call her friend and tip her off about her father, she stuck her hand out. "Give me your cell phone."

"Here," the girl said, removing the phone from her back pocket and throwing it at her. "You don't even trust me now. I hate you. You jump through hoops for someone else's kid when you never have time for me. Between that and your job, I might as well not have a mother. You're just like Dad. He doesn't give a shit about me. It's been over a year since he even called me. Jude isn't your daughter. She's not even related to us."

Carolyn exploded. "When Jude wakes up, I'm the one who'll have to tell her whether she still has an arm. Then I'll have tell a girl whose mother was just murdered that the same thing happened to her father. Don't you have any compassion, Rebecca? Are you that self-centered?" She paced around the small room, determined not to say anything else until she calmed down. "I'm sorry I haven't been able to spend more time with you lately. Haven't I always been there when you needed me? Most of the time, you're with your friends or locked in your room. There's no law that says a mother-daughter relationship runs in only one direction."

"What's going on?" Marcus asked, bolting upright in his chair. "Why on earth are you screaming at each other?"

"It's my fault," Carolyn told him, picking the phone up and handing it back to Rebecca. "I trust you, honey. I was wrong to take your phone away. The police suspect Anne Marie's father may have killed her sister. That's why I can't let you speak to her right now."

"That's ridiculous," her daughter said, glaring up at her.

Carolyn walked over and sat back down beside her. "I'm going to tell you something, but you can never, ever repeat it. If you do, you'll start something that will come back to haunt you. The person this is about isn't here to defend herself. She died a horrible death. She doesn't deserve to be disrespected by people who earn their living off someone else's pain and misfortune."

Rebecca flicked the ends of her fingernails. "You're talking about Haley, right?"

Carolyn sucked in a deep breath, then blurted out, "The coroner who performed the autopsy said she'd been sexually active since she was approximately ten."

"That can't be true. Anyway, how could he tell?"

"Because when a prepubescent girl engages in sexual intercourse on a regular basis, it leaves scars. It can also cause permanent damage to the vagina. I'd rather you not hear things like this, but you didn't give me any option."

Rebecca stared at her in stunned silence.

"Maybe Donny, as you call him, didn't buy Anne Marie a BMW because she didn't do the things for him her sister did. I failed at protecting Jude, but maybe I can help prevent this from happening to someone else. This is the world I live in, sweetheart, and girls like Haley are why I work so hard at my job. I generally only learn about these crimes after they happen, but every now and then I get a chance to prevent them. My job is to make certain the men and women who hurt innocent people are punished. When it comes to pedophiles, there's no cure. A pedophile could be in prison for thirty years and still be compelled to molest children the day he was released."

Rebecca wiped a tear from her eye, then threw her arms around her mother's neck. "I'm sorry I said those hateful things to you. I didn't mean them. I'm proud to have a mother like you." She pulled back and glanced over at Marcus, kicking out and touching the toe of his shoe. "You did good, Mom. You got me a new father, someone who actually cares about me."

Marcus stood and came over, pulling Rebecca to her feet and embracing her. "I'm going to make certain you have a good life. I made a lot of mistakes with my own children. I won't make them with you."

Carolyn draped her arms around both of them. "You guys go on home," she said. "I'll stick around here for a while, then call and have you pick me up. Unless something goes wrong, we'll have dinner together. Marcus, can you arrange for someone to watch out for Rebecca while she's at school tomorrow?"

"Certainly."

"You mean I'm going to have my own bodyguard?" Rebecca said, excited. "That will be totally cool. Everyone will think I'm a celebrity."

Marcus smiled. "You've had a bodyguard for a long time, even before your mother asked me."

"Really? Why didn't you tell me? I never saw anyone."

"You're not supposed to see him," Marcus told her. "That's why they call it shadowing someone. I told you I wasn't going to make any mistakes this time around. My family is my most important asset."

CHAPTER 27

Carolyn stared at Jude through the glass in intensive care. Her left arm was heavily bandaged, her eyes tightly closed, and her bodily functions were being taken care of by machines. Dr. Samuels, a man in his late forties with thinning brown hair and dark-framed glasses, stepped up beside her. He spoke with a New York accent. "The reattachment went remarkably well. Barring infection, I think your daughter will be able to keep her arm."

"Where's Dr. Martin?"

"He's not available," Samuels told her. "He still has privileges here, but his primary practice is in LA now. We were lucky he was in town visiting his daughter. I'm an orthopedic surgeon as well, but Greg Martin has far more experience when it comes to this particular procedure."

419

"When will she wake up?"

"We'll start tapering off the drugs in forty-eight hours unless a problem develops. She's still going to need narcotics for pain control, but she should be conscious and able to speak with you."

Carolyn felt like a talking head. The rest of her body was numb. "Will she be able to use her arm?"

"To what extent, we'll have to wait and see. Before we start physical therapy, however, the wounds need time to heal."

Carolyn decided her ruse had to end. "I'm not Jude's mother, Doctor. Her mother is dead. She was murdered a week ago. Last night, her father was shot and killed as well. My name is Carolyn Sullivan."

Dr. Samuels blinked several times, but otherwise didn't react. "What relationship do you have to the patient? Are you her legal guardian?"

"Technically, Jude doesn't need a guardian since she's eighteen. I'm a close friend of the family."

"But, Ms. Sullivan," he said, somewhat agitated, "this patient isn't able to make decisions for herself right now. Surely, she has relatives."

"She has an aunt in San Francisco," Carolyn said, unsteady on her feet. "I may be her legal guardian, though. Her mother and father made provisions in their wills for me to take care of their children should something happen to them. I haven't verified this yet. Everything happened so fast."

"Are you all right?" Dr. Samuels asked. "I can have the nurse bring you some water. How long has it been since you've eaten?"

"I'm . . ." Everything went black as Carolyn crumpled to the floor at the doctor's feet.

"Where am I?"

"You're fine," a redheaded nurse told Carolyn. "You're in the emergency room. You fainted. Dr. Samuels ordered you a dinner tray. It should be here any minute. He said we couldn't let you go home until you ate."

"But I was supposed to have dinner with my family," Carolyn protested. "What time is it? I have to call my fiancé." She tried to sit up when she realized she was attached to an IV. "What are you giving me?"

"Just fluids." The nurse handed her a juice box with a straw in it. "The doctor suspected you might be dehydrated. Have you been drinking?"

"I don't know," Carolyn said, lacing her fingers through the bars on the bed.

"Then you're probably dehydrated. Just

relax, sweetie. Your fiancé and your daughter are on their way." She checked the IV. "This is almost finished."

Carolyn closed her eyes and fell back to sleep. She dreamed she was in a morgue. Veronica was there, as well as Drew. Jude's severed arm was resting on a gurney by itself. She screamed, but no one came.

"Wake up, honey," Marcus said. "You must have been having a bad dream. Rebecca's waiting outside with Anne Marie. Her mother called and asked if she could stay with us for a few hours. The police picked up her father, and they're searching their house. I didn't know what to do, so I said okay." He hit the button on the bed to elevate her to a sitting position, then positioned a table in front of her with a tray of food on it. "All you have to do is eat some of this, and we can get you out of this place."

"How's Jude?"

"I spoke to her nurse in intensive care," Marcus said, cutting a piece of chicken and stabbing it with a fork. "She's doing fine, Carolyn, no sign of infection. Come on, open your mouth. This looks tasty. Don't worry, we'll go out for a nice meal later."

Carolyn let him feed her. The chicken tasted like rubber soaked in mushroom soup. He gave her some orange juice to wash it down. "This is disgusting. They can't hold me here against my will."

Marcus dropped the fork, his brows furrowing. "Why do you want to cause a scene over such a minor thing? Don't we have enough problems to deal with right now? Jesus, I have a deadline to meet at work. If I don't start paying attention to my business, I could lose everything." He paced beside the bed. "I seriously underbid the competition, or I wouldn't have these contracts. That means I'm operating on a tight budget. We can't predict how long it will take to write or repair a complex program. My people need me, you need me, Rebecca needs me, other people's children need me."

Carolyn picked up the fork and shoveled the remaining pieces of the chicken into her mouth, then pushed the table away. Her problems were overpowering him. She felt sorry for him, but making money was business, and even if his company collapsed, Marcus had enough wealth to last a lifetime. She dealt with life-and-death situations. Preventing another murder took precedence over anything else, even her health, her fiancé, and her daughter. "Call the nurse to get this needle out of my arm, or I'll do it myself. I need to be there when they interrogate Don Snodgrass. I'm sorry I got you involved with my problems, Marcus. If you want Rebecca and me to move out, all you have to do is tell me."

"Why would I want you to move out?" he said, frustrated. "I want to spend the rest of my life with you."

"Wasn't your preoccupation with your business what ended your first marriage?"

He jerked his head back as if she had struck him. "I shouldn't have said anything, okay? I just didn't see a reason to make such a big deal about eating a . . ." His eyes expanded. Carolyn was reaching for the IV needle.

"I'll get the nurse," Marcus said, hurrying out of the room.

At just over five-six, Don Snodgrass was a small man, with a pudgy face and small brown eyes. His hair was thinning on top and he wore a baseball cap to cover the bald spot. Dressed in jeans and a sweatshirt with a beagle dog on the front, he sat anxiously in the observation room at the police department. Hank and Mary watched him through the one-way glass.

"The guy's pathetic," Mary said. "It's hard to imagine him killing a mouse, let alone his own daughter. Maybe we made a mistake on this one, Hank."

"What kind of man would be caught dead in a puppy dog shirt?" he argued. "He's a classic pedophile. They dress and act like kids so they can lure their prey."

"I don't know," Mary said. "He may be a pedophile, but I'm not certain he's a murderer. Let me go in first. Where's Carolyn? She was supposed to be here. Since Rebecca is a friend of his surviving daughter, she might get him to talk without an attorney. The wife obviously trusts her. She called Marcus and asked him to take Anne Marie so she wouldn't be there when we executed the search warrant. Try to call Carolyn again. God, when is that woman going to start answering her cell phone?"

Mary composed herself, then entered the room and sat down at the table across from Don Snodgrass. "I can't tell you how sorry I am for your loss, Don," she said, trying to mimic Carolyn's nonconfrontational technique. Before she became a supervisor, the probation officer had gone so far as dressing in suggestive clothing and flirting with offenders to get them to drop their guard. Even within police circles, Carolyn was renowned as an interrogator.

"Call me Mr. Snodgrass," he said, removing his baseball cap and slapping it down on the table. "If you're sorry for my loss, why are you harassing me and my family? My wife is on the verge of a breakdown. Do you have any idea what it's like to lose a child, Detective? Instead of wasting your time with me, why don't you catch the maniac who murdered Haley?"

"We're doing everything we can," Mary told him. "We just want to ask you a few questions."

"My attorney is on her way down here. If you want to talk to someone, you can talk to her. I have nothing to say to you."

Once a suspect refused to waive his rights, they couldn't question him about the crime. Since she had no desire to make small talk, Mary got up and left.

Hank poked his head in the door a short time later. "Mr. Snodgrass," he said, "a woman named Carolyn Sullivan is asking to see you. She claims to know your daughter, Anne Marie. She also said to tell you that Jude Campbell has been staying with her." He acted as if he'd forgotten something. "Oh, your attorney, Beth Levy, called and said she got tied up in court. What do you want me to do about Ms. Sullivan?"

Snodgrass's beady eyes roamed around the room. He'd already been sitting there for over an hour, and perspiration was popping out on his forehead. "I'll see her," he said, evidently mistaking Carolyn for an ally.

Marcus had brought a change of clothes to the hospital, but Carolyn's makeup had long disappeared. She walked straight up to Snodgrass and clasped his hand, one palm over another. "I'm Carolyn Sullivan," she said. "You know that, though. Forgive me, I should have introduced myself a long time ago. I met your wife once at a school function. Anne Marie is a lovely girl. How is Angela holding up?"

"Not good," Snodgrass said, his face muscles relaxing. "This foolishness with the police isn't helping. What are they trying to accomplish? Drew and Veronica were close friends of ours. I heard on the news that he was killed. And Jude . . . she was like a second daughter to me. It's all so awful."

"I know," Carolyn said, taking a seat beside him, then turning her chair so she was facing him. "I just left the hospital. I'm embarrassed to say I collapsed." She didn't have trouble mustering up a few tears. "I'm sorry," she added, reaching into her pocket for a tissue. "Are you aware Jude's arm was severed? If a nurse hadn't witnessed the accident and stopped, she would have bled to death."

Snodgrass froze. He looked as if he'd been encased in glass.

"The good news is she didn't suffer a brain injury. We're hoping she can identify the driver when she wakes up. At least the nurse got the vehicle description. The police think it may not have been an accident, that someone could have intentionally hit her."

When he spoke, he seemed preoccupied. "I thought she was killed. I guess I was so shocked when I heard about Drew, I blocked everything else out."

Interesting, Carolyn thought, putting on her most compassionate expression. The driver of the hit-and-run vehicle might have made the same assumption. "Maybe it struck too close to home. You know, because Jude and Haley were such good friends."

"The girls had a falling-out last year. Angie and I felt it was for the best. Haley was the more stable of the two. That is, until she developed an eating disorder. We thought it was just a phase she was going through. From what I . . ." He stopped speaking, staring at the one-way glass. "It's really hard for me to talk about this. Out of curiosity, how did you know I was here? Anne Marie mentioned that you were a probation officer. That's not the same as a police officer, is it?"

"No," Carolyn told him, sensing he was getting suspicious. She wanted to see what else she could get out of him, but she didn't want to burn herself. If it came out she was working with the task force, his attorney could claim she'd violated his rights. "Angela called and spoke to my fiancé while I was at the hospital looking after Jude. She asked if Annie Marie could stay with us while the police searched your home."

"What are they looking for?"

Carolyn stood to leave. She couldn't lie to a direct question without stepping out of bounds. "I'm sure the police will release you, Donny. I hear you hired Beth Levy. She's a former DA, so you're in good hands. I doubt if you'll need an attorney. How could anyone believe you had anything to do with these dreadful crimes? The police are just doing their job. You know, trying to eliminate every possibility."

Carolyn had intentionally called him "Donny" to see how he reacted. If he was a pedophile, using a name he associated with his victims should trigger memories. He looked into her eyes, but he didn't speak. There was something different about Snodgrass, something that hadn't been there when she'd entered the room. Suddenly it came to her — resolve. He'd made some kind of decision, one he was determined to follow through on. Whether it was finding his daughter's killer, destroying evidence, or leaving the country, she couldn't say. Whatever it was, though, it was major.

Carolyn returned to the observation room where Hank and Mary were waiting. "As soon as Beth Levy gets here," she said, "the game's over. She'll demand that you charge Snodgrass or release him. Did they find anything incriminating at his house?"

"Gary Conrad seized three computers," Hank said, having just got off the phone. "One belonged to Haley, and the other to Anne Marie. We assume the father used the computer in the spare bedroom they'd converted into a home office. We can't get into the damn thing. It's got all kinds of passwords."

"That shouldn't be a problem for our guys," Mary told him. "They live for this kind of stuff. I sent Ricky Walters out there. He can get into anything."

"I've already talked to Ricky," Hank said. "Snodgrass's computer has bios passwords, whatever that means, as well as Windows passwords. Ricky said if they don't get lucky, they'll have to reinstall Windows and they might lose some of the data. Even if we get into the damn thing, he says people who set bios passwords generally encrypt their files."

Carolyn asked, "Did you check out his cars?"

"There was nothing to indicate they'd been involved in an accident."

"Any child pornography in the house?"

"Shit, no," Hank said, spitting a toothpick into the trash can. "I hate technology. No one keeps real pictures lying around these days. They scan it all into their computers. Remember that child porn ring the feds cracked last year? They never got into their computers. The assholes had it set up so the data was wiped automatically if you entered the wrong password more than three times."

"Maybe there's something on the girls' machines," Mary suggested. "At least we might be able to find out what was going on in Haley's life before she was killed." Her face brightened. "I've got an idea. Marcus is a programmer. He's got to be top shelf if he has contracts with the military. Right, Carolyn? If Ricky or one of the other guys can't get into Snodgrass's computers, do you think he'd be willing to help us?"

"Why wait?" Carolyn said, pulling out her cell. "Now that Snodgrass knows we suspect him, he could skip out on us. I'll call Marcus now. He was on his way to Snodgrass's house to drop off Anne Marie."

"Wait," Mary said. "The warrant gives us

permission to remove the computers from the premises. You don't want Marcus trying to get into the computers at the house. Snodgrass is a CPA. He probably has confidential information on his clients stored in that machine. We can't give a civilian access. It could invalidate the warrant. Then if we find anything, we can't use it."

"You're right," Carolyn said. "I wasn't thinking. I'll have Marcus come here instead." She started to make the call, then stopped. "You'll still be giving him access to Snodgrass's computers."

Hank turned to Mary. "Are you in or out?"

"How are you going to handle it?"

"I'll have Ricky take the computers to Marcus's office instead of bringing them here. They can work on them together."

Mary was a by-the-books cop. They'd already been bending the rules, and she was afraid it could backfire on them. She was willing to place her career on the line to catch a killer, but she was concerned they might compromise the case and not be able to convict him. All Ventura needed right now was another Robert Abernathy. "Can we trust Ricky?"

"Yeah," Hank told her. "I caught him gambling on the Internet one time when he was supposed to be working. I didn't report him, so he owes me."

"I'm in," Mary said. "Call Marcus, Carolyn. We also need the address to his office. You take care of Snodgrass, Hank, and tell Ricky to meet me there with the computers. Stall as long as you can. If we find anything, I'll call you."

Marcus took Anne Marie home, then dropped Rebecca at a friend's house before he headed to Los Angeles. Carolyn wanted to stay at the PD and work.

"Snodgrass hired a pit bull," Hank told her, taking a seat at the long table in the conference room. "I wanted to hold him until we found out what was inside his computer, but Beth Levy pitched a fit. I had to cut him loose, or I think she would have plucked my eyes out."

"Beth's a good attorney," Carolyn said. "I wish she hadn't left the DA's office and gone into private practice."

"I assigned Gabriel Martinez to tail Snodgrass for now. Tomorrow, I'll borrow some people from narcotics."

When none of the members of the task force were present, they had to collect everything they'd found at the various crime scenes and lock it up in the evidence room, then take it out the next morning. Carolyn looked through the boxes, seeing several new ones labeled DREW CAMPBELL, but she didn't see any marked SNODGRASS. "Where's the stuff from Snodgrass's house?"

Hank sighed. "All we got were the computers. The search warrant was restricted to anything that was related to child pornography. I don't know what to think. The guy's an oddball, but he may not be involved in anything illegal. He evidently didn't know his daughter was buried alive. When I told him, he used up a whole box of Kleenex bawling."

"He probably *is* devastated," Carolyn answered. "Pedophiles love their victims. They don't think they're doing anything wrong. Since Haley was his daughter, he would be even more emotionally involved. If he's guilty, I doubt if he wanted to kill her. He was either terrified of going to prison or someone forced his hand."

"You mean Drew, right?"

"Maybe," she said, using her cell to call the hospital to check on Jude. When she disconnected, she told him, "They say she's doing well. Barring any complications, she should be conscious sometime tomorrow. Let's hope she can give us some answers. She's been through a terrible ordeal, so I'm not sure we're going to get much out of her right away."

"Will she be able to use her arm?"

"The doctors aren't sure what her limitations will be," Carolyn explained. "The wound has to heal before they can start physical therapy. She could still lose it if something goes wrong."

Thinking Jude might lose her arm now that the doctors had reattached it made Carolyn feel like screaming. To occupy her mind, she rifled through the boxes marked JUDE CAMPBELL. There was a stack of school books, several spiral notebooks, as well as a large canvas backpack. It wasn't the type school kids carried, more like something hikers used when they went on overnight treks. She glanced in another box and saw a blanket, gloves, and several heavy sweaters, assuming another officer had removed them when he went through the backpack. It was sad, she thought. Jude must have lived out of this bag during the times when she stayed away from home. She wondered why she hadn't taken it the night Drew threw her out of the house. Instead, she'd put her things in a plastic garbage bag. The girl was probably shaken up over the confrontation they'd had in the bathroom, and merely wanted to get out of the house as soon as possible.

"Gary Conrad went through those things already," Hank told her. "You're wasting your time. If you want, I can drive you home. Marcus may be tied up all night."

Carolyn ignored him. She turned the backpack on its side, brushing out what looked like pieces of gum wrappers and a sprinkling of white powder. She put some on her tongue to make certain it wasn't cocaine or speed.

"It's aspirin," Hank told her. "We had it tested."

"There's something in here. These things have so many compartments." Carolyn unzipped all the pockets and shoved her hands inside, feeling around with her fingers. Deciding what she felt was a piece of cardboard that served as the bottom of the pack, she tossed it down on the table. A flap fell open, revealing another compartment. She unzipped it and pulled out a small book with a sunflower on the cover. It looked as if some of the pages had been ripped out. She jerked her head up. "My God, Hank, this is Jude's diary. No one said anything about finding a diary."

"Gary's an idiot," Hank said, frowning. "What does it say?"

"I'll have to read it." The book was about to fall apart. Carolyn carefully opened it and was instantly riveted. Jude's handwriting was small and cramped. The pages weren't dated, so there was no way to tell when they were written. She wrote about how much she loved Reggie, how she would die for him, and her fear that her father would find out she was dating a guy who was black. She mentioned that she was afraid for her sister, that she'd seen her father touching her, and vowed to do whatever it took to keep him away from her. Toward the end, all she wrote about was her weight. She went days without food, drinking only coffee and water. Then she allotted herself one orange per day, which she cut into three pieces. It was obvious that Jude was unraveling, as her handwriting became sloppier and the entries dwindled down to a few fragmented sentences. "Breasts almost gone. Felt dizzy today. Can't pass out, or they'll put me in a hospital and tube-feed me. Won't be long now. He's been giving me that look all week."

Carolyn stood and handed the book to Hank. "Everything Jude told us about Drew was true. She was trying to starve herself so her body would look like it did before she went through puberty. I wish we had the missing pages."

"Jude is skinny," Hank said. "But the

Snodgrass girl didn't even weigh eighty pounds. Charley said she was anorexic. Don't tell me they were both anorexic?"

"A shrink might classify this as anorexia since Jude fits the profile," Carolyn explained. "She was starving herself for a purpose, though, to keep Drew from going after Stacy."

"Does she say anything about Haley and her father? I still think these two men were involved in some type of pedophilia ring. I was going over the FBI's Crime Classification Manual this morning. They call more than one pedophile working together a Cottage Collector. They use pornography as a means to communicate with other pedophiles."

"I just can't see either Don or Drew whipping out pornographic pictures of their daughters one day over the barbecue," Carolyn told him. "Don knew Veronica was a probation officer. Approaching Drew would have been far too risky."

"Okay," Hank said. "What if Drew was the one who started it? They could have met each other in a chat room, then realized they knew each other. Shit happens, you know."

Carolyn was more interested in the diary. "From what I can tell, Jude wrote some of these pages in the days leading up to

Veronica's murder."

"Are you okay?"

"No," she said, fighting back tears. "I need to go outside and get some air."

Hank came over and put his arm around her. "Drew's dead, Carolyn. He can't hurt Jude or anyone else. Isn't that some consolation?"

"Not really," Carolyn said, rushing out of the conference room.

CHAPTER 28

Marcus's office was located in an office building in Century City. He waited in the parking lot until Mary and the police department's computer expert arrived, then took them up in a private elevator that could only be operated with a key. His offices encompassed the entire floor.

The name of his company was not on the door. All the sign said was PRIVATE. Ricky Walters was carrying Don Snodgrass's computer. A hyperactive man in his late twenties, he had dark, unruly hair, and a tall, wiry frame. Mary followed the men into a small reception room. The only furniture was four industrial-type chairs.

"This is basically for show," Marcus explained. "We don't allow visitors."

"Why all the cloak-and-dagger?" Ricky asked, looking around the small room.

440

"What exactly do you do? I thought you were a computer programmer."

"I am," Marcus said. "My work is classified. I'm sorry, but you'll have to wait out here." He started to take the computer, but Mary stopped him.

"This computer is evidence in a homicide. I can't let it out of my sight. Surely you understand our position. What if I'm asked to testify as to who had access to it? Snodgrass's attorney could claim we planted any information we might find. Why should I take a chance like that when I'm not certain you can help us?"

"Oh, I can help you," Marcus said, a confident expression on his face. "I just can't allow you inside my lab."

"We're police officers, for God's sake," Mary said, raising her voice. "Are you telling me we drove all the way down here for nothing? Why didn't you tell me this before?"

"You solicited me, remember?" Marcus shot back. "If you'll calm down and let me take the machine, I can solve your problem within minutes." When Mary just glared at him, he added, "Okay, fine, but I need time to set up."

He walked over to an intercom, depressing the button to talk. "It's me, Jim. Stash any classified material we have lying around, and turn off all the monitors except for the ter-aflop. You and the rest of the guys go grab a coffee at Starbucks. Leave out the back door."

"What's going on, boss?"

"I've been asked to take care of a problem that doesn't involve you and the others. I'll call you as soon as I'm finished."

"Sure thing," the voice said. "I'm all for Starbucks."

"Can they bring me a double espresso?" Ricky asked.

"Are you crazy?" Mary said, placing a hand on one hip. "You're already jumping out of your skin. Just being around you makes me nervous." Once Marcus turned around, she added, "I really appreciate this. I'm sorry I got carried away. We're desperate to solve these murders. What we need might be inside this stupid box."

Ricky Walters's eyes were enormous. "You have a teraflop? You must make more money than God to afford a teraflop. Shit, I'd love to work for you. I could go to the car and get my notebook. My resume is on it."

"What's a teraflop?" Mary asked, having heard the word but not entirely certain what it meant.

"A supercomputer," Ricky said. "A ter-aflop means a trillion floating point operations per second. A baby like that's worth a minimum of twenty million. IBM made one called the Blue Gene/L that does 280.6 teraflops. They don't have to do nuclear testing anymore. A computer like this can simulate it."

"I don't own the teraflop," Marcus said. "It belongs to one of my clients."

"Who made it?"

Marcus's apprehension disappeared. Ricky's excitement was contagious. "Hewlett Packard. It's got a Linux operating system, and Intel's Itanium 2 processor. Before I opened my own consulting firm, I worked for Intel. I was one of the people who designed Itanium 2. When it started acting up, I spent six months on-site trying to fix it. Finally, they agreed to ship the thing to me, so my entire team could work on it." He used the intercom again, and no one answered. "What we're interested in at the moment is TOTS, teraflops off the shelf. You can put together a cluster that works at teraflop speeds for under a million."

Marcus placed his palm on a pad and the door swung open. Behind it was a steel wall with a code pad. He turned his back so Mary and Ricky couldn't see, and punched in the numbers. Once the steel door clanked open, he spun around and faced them. "You've never been in this room, understand? This room doesn't exist. The only reason I agreed to let you in is we're moving to a smaller location next week once we get rid of the monster."

Even though the lab was enormous, the rows of computer terminals made it seem cramped. There were eight workstations. All the monitors were blank except one. Marcus took Snodgrass's Dell computer and disappeared behind a row of glass to connect it to the Hewlett Packard teraflop. Then he dropped down in one of the chairs, booted up the Dell, and went to the bios setup utility. "I was hoping he hadn't set an administrator password, but he did." He typed a string of code on the adjacent computer, then leaned back in his chair as data flashed on the screen so fast it was nothing more than a blur. "It's running every possible eight-character letter and number combination." Before he could say anything else, the password appeared. "He used upper- and lowercase, which made it slightly more difficult. My guess is SwTaNgEl means sweet angel." He smiled at Mary. "I try to figure out personalized license plates when I'm stuck in traffic."

"So you're in?"

"Not yet," Ricky told her. "Now he's got to

crack the Windows password. I tried to find a password recovery disk in Snodgrass's desk, but he must have it locked in a safe somewhere. We can reinstall Windows, but like I told you before, it's risky."

As soon as the teraflop cranked out the Windows password, which turned out to be a random combination of letters and numbers, the main screen opened. "What precisely are we looking for now?" Marcus asked.

"Child pornography, or any type of pictures that appear even slightly erotic."

Marcus searched through the gallery section, finding photographs of naked little girls among the normal shots of dogs, families, birthday parties, Christmas, and other holidays. The girls were taking baths, playing in a rubber swimming pool, getting dressed, or chasing each other through the sprinklers. None of the poses looked even slightly suggestive, let alone erotic. "Is this what you were looking for?"

"Not exactly," Mary said, disappointment heavy in her voice. "The two girls resemble each other, so they're probably his daughters. I guess it's normal to snap these kinds of photos when kids are that young. That doesn't mean Snodgrass didn't get turned on by them, though. We need something more recent."

Marcus checked the photo imaging program used by Snodgrass's Canon digital camera. The two girls were older, and most of the shots looked like the others he'd found in the gallery. "Whoa," he said, "is this the kind of thing you're talking about?"

Mary nudged him out of his seat. Haley appeared to be around eleven or twelve. She was wearing a bikini bathing suit bottom with no top and smiling for the camera. She must have been about to enter puberty, as her nipples were slightly swollen. "This is *exactly* what we're looking for," Mary said, peering up at Marcus.

The room fell silent as Mary went through the rest of the pictures, hoping to find more similar shots. She came to one with a teenage girl lying on her stomach in a bed, nude except for a pair of white cotton panties. Her head was turned to the side, and her eyes were closed as if she was sleeping. She knew it was Haley as she recognized her profile. "What does this picture tell you?"

Ricky spoke up. "That her perverted father was sneaking into her room and taking pictures of her while she was sleeping."

"It's more than that," Mary said, zooming in on the image. "Just because her eyes are closed doesn't mean she's asleep. Look closely at her face. Wait," she said, wanting to get a closer look at the area around her eyes and cheek. "See that right there? I'm almost certain those are tears, and look at her expression. If she was asleep, she was having one hell of a nightmare." She rotated the image, seeing an object protruding from underneath the girl's hips. "I'm fairly certain that's a pillow. It's pink like the sheets. She was posed, don't you see? He must have put a pillow under her to lift up her hips so they would stand out more. He could have also wanted her on her stomach because she was older and had developed breasts by then. I think Snodgrass snapped this either before or after he had sex with her."

"Jesus," Marcus said, shaking his head. "I'm not sure I want to see this, Mary. Why don't you take the computer back to the police station now that you have all the passwords? In fact, I can remove them. That way, you won't have to mess with them."

"You can't do that," Mary said sharply. "The prosecutor might want to use the passwords to show Snodgrass had something to hide. See the exposed skin on her neck? The rest of her body is tan. Why aren't there any tan lines on her back?"

Marcus said, "A lot of teenage girls undo

their bathing suit tops when they're lying on their stomach. I recall my daughter doing it. I used to get on to her. She'd forget, sit up, and expose herself."

"Haley's not wearing bikini underwear. You can tell because the fabric is bunched up at the bottom. You can see her crack. Did your daughter pull her bathing suit down that low?"

"No, but today, you can see girls exposed like that just about everywhere."

"The lowrider pants are a fairly new fashion trend," Mary continued. "Look at the date. This picture was taken five years ago. Haley was thirteen then. The point I was trying to make is her whole body is tan. She's been sunbathing nude. Her parents don't have a pool. They may have another house or cabin somewhere, though, a place Snodgrass could have taken her where he could watch her run around naked. Can you tell when he created that password?"

"Which one?"

"Sweet angel, if that's what it means."

"Doubtful," Marcus said. "Once a bios password is changed, it's changed. You've got to understand, this is about a seven-hundred-dollar machine. Do you think sweet angel means something sinister? It sounds pretty innocent to me."

Mary stood, giving him back his seat. "If he created it after his daughter was murdered, it might be touching, almost like a prayer or remembrance. Before, well, this could refer to an incestuous relationship. Pedophiles think that way. They believe the sweet young child they're having sex with was sent to them to fulfill their special needs. They don't believe they're harming anyone. Many times they convince themselves the victim actually seduced them."

"I'll check the sites he visited on the Internet," Marcus told her, opening the dropdown box on the browser. Most of the sites appeared harmless. The majority of them were bank and credit card sites. Some were for news and entertainment. Others were commercial sites such as Amazon and eBay, along with a variety of online stores, most of them selling clothes for women. Marcus then searched through the document files. "None of the files appear to be encrypted," he told them. "Didn't you say he was an accountant? I don't see any client lists or spreadsheets. He must keep anything related to his business on his office machine. That, in itself, is unusual, since so many people work both at home and at an office." He opened Microsoft Outlook, and read through some of the e-mails. "This is mostly

Chatty Kathy stuff."

"What are you talking about?" Mary said, never having heard that expression before.

"Girl talk," Marcus told her. "I hate to burst your bubble, but I don't think this is the father's computer. It looks like it belongs to the wife. Even all the purchase receipts are for the kind of things a woman would buy. I mean, every guy likes gadgets of one kind or the other. Whoever uses this machine bought a stand for a blow-dryer, wooden hangers, nightgowns at Victoria's Secret, pillow shams, four Sassybax bras, which reduces invisible bra line, whatever that means."

"Enough," Mary said, giving Ricky a look that would drop an elephant. "I told you to bring the computer that was in the spare bedroom. What did you do, mix them up and bring me one of the girls' machines?"

"Of course not," Ricky said, defensive. "The girls' computers weren't password protected. They also weren't Dells. What's the problem? The guy still took those racy pictures of his daughter."

Mary took several deep breaths to keep from exploding. Every time they seemed to be making progress, they hit a brick wall. "I'm sorry I snapped at you, Ricky. If a mother takes a picture of her daughter scantily dressed, it's hard to classify it as child pornography. Female pedophiles aren't common, and those that exist generally work in concert with a male. It's doubtful if the Snodgrasses are that type of people, although it's not completely implausible. Husband and wife teams usually sell child pornography as their main source of income, or they're involved in child prostitution rings."

Marcus spun his chair around. "Didn't Hank think this was a pedophilia ring at one time?"

"Yes," Mary said. "Now that Drew is dead, and from what Jude has told Carolyn about Stockton, we've been focusing primarily on Snodgrass. Even if the father did take the pictures, the fact that the computer was used primarily by the mother won't help us get a warrant to arrest her husband."

Marcus tore off a piece of paper with the passwords on it, and handed it to Mary. "If you have any more problems, give me a call. I have a great program for cracking codes I can give you, but on an ordinary machine it would take forever to run."

Marcus disconnected the Dell and handed it to Ricky, then looked over at Mary. "If you don't mind, I've got a lot of highly paid employees sitting around drinking coffee. We think we resolved the problem with the teraflop, but we need to keep testing it before we ship it out and move back into our regular space."

He escorted them through the maze of doors.

"Thanks again," Mary said, pumping his hand. "When are you and Carolyn getting married?"

"Whenever you catch the killer," Marcus said, a downcast look on his face.

The detective's cell phone rang. "Holy Jesus," she said once she concluded the call. "That was Hank. We finally caught a break. The Santa Barbara PD arrested Reggie Stockton. They found him sleeping on the beach. He should be at the station by the time we get back."

"I left Carolyn there," Marcus said. "I was going to take off now and pick her up. If you don't think she'll be ready to leave, I can stay and try to get some work done. The people I work for don't like to wait, and I haven't been minding the store lately."

Mary nudged Ricky through the doorway. "Go to the car," she told him, waiting until he shuffled off down the corridor before turning back to Marcus. "I think he wants you to hire him so he can play with your fancy toys. He's good at what he does, so just so you'll know, you can't have him."

Marcus laughed. "I have all the employees I need right now."

"Oh, regarding Carolyn," Mary added, "she'll want to be present when we interrogate Stockton. She believes he may be our killer."

Reggie Stockton was seated at the table in an interview room. Mary and Hank were seated directly across from him, and Carolyn was standing in the corner.

Stockton didn't look like the same person Carolyn and Mary had met at Circuit City. His white T-shirt was torn and filthy. He hadn't shaved and had a scruffy beard, which made him look older and unsavory. He kept scratching different parts of his body. He'd tested clean for narcotics, but his demeanor was typical of a drug addict.

Stockton had waived his right to have an attorney present, so Hank dived in. "Gee, Reggie, my partner was worried something had happened to you. One of your girlfriends was murdered, and the other almost died in a hit-and-run accident." He brushed a piece of lint off his black slacks. "You're not having very good luck when it comes to the ladies."

"Look, man," Reggie said, speaking in a

thick New Orleans accent, "I don't know what the hell you're talking about. I graduated from high school last year. I was working at Circuit City and saving money to go to college. I didn't have the time or the money for girlfriends. Ask my mama. She'll tell you."

"Your mama, huh?" Hank said, narrowing his eyes. "Are you talking about that nice lady you conned into letting people think she was your mother? We know all about you. Your real name is Reginald Marcel. You were in jail in New Orleans when Katrina hit. After you escaped, you hid out at the convention center. That's where you met Mrs. Stockton. How old are you, Reggie?"

"Shit, you know everything. Why ask me things you already know?" He glared at Mary, throwing his arm toward her. "I knew she was gonna figure it out. Bitch tricked me into leaving my fingerprints in her car. That's why I took off. I'd rather live on the street than go back to New Orleans. That place is a pit, man. Hell's got to be better. The cops there are worse than the criminals. They busted me for a crime my brother committed. I haven't even seen the fucker since I was twelve, and I gotta do his time because we got the same last name."

"You've never been involved with narcotics?" Mary asked. "You're lying, Reggie. You're coming down right now. Bet you'd do just about anything to get out of here so you can score. You don't have tracks, but you're twitching and itching like a junkie. That means you smoke or snort the stuff. What are you on? Crystal meth, crack, cocaine?" She grimaced. "Wipe your damn nose. You've got snot dripping down the front of your shirt. There's probably a hole in there the size of a golf ball."

He started to use the edge of his shirt when Carolyn handed Mary some tissues. The detective tossed them at him, then crossed her arms over her chest. "Right now, I don't care what you did in New Orleans, understand? Haley Snodgrass was beaten and buried alive. Last night, Drew Campbell was shot and killed while he was sleeping. Around the same time, Jude was almost killed by a hit-and-run driver. Her arm was severed. He left her there to bleed to death."

Mary stood and began pacing. "You thought Jude was dead, didn't you? You thought you could lie low in Santa Barbara because you'd killed the only person left to incriminate you. You made another mistake, Reggie, just like you made with Haley Snodgrass."

A look of shock appeared on his face. "I

didn't do these things. I swear to God. I've been in Santa Barbara since Monday. I took the train. The engine blew in my car last month. I didn't want to take my mom's, uh, Ruby's car 'cause she's been so good to me." He rummaged around in his jeans and pulled out a small piece of paper, then pushed it across the table. "See, I've got the proof."

Mary picked it up, then handed it to Hank. It was a receipt for an Amtrak train ticket, departing at six on Monday evening. "You could have found this in a trash can, Reggie." She decided it was time to lie, hoping he might crack. "We know you're guilty. The clerk at the Motor Inn identified you as the person who rented the room where Veronica Campbell's body was found. You thought you'd covered yourself by using a stolen credit card. Your fingerprints and DNA were all over that room."

Reggie shook his head. "I must be one murdering son of a bitch. You got me killing everyone. I've never even heard of this motel, and I certainly didn't steal anyone's credit card. Why would I risk serving time in the joint in Louisiana just to rent a lousy motel room? Did Jude tell you I did these things? I'm sorry she got hurt and everything, but shit, every other word that comes

456

out of that bitch's mouth is a lie." He poked his head with his finger. "She's psycho, got it? I grabbed her tits one time at a party when I was stoned. After that, Jude told everyone we were tight. Her friend, Haley, was just as crazy. They weren't ugly or anything, they were just trash. Before they started stalking me, they hung out with gangsters and dealers. They even turned fucking tricks. A guy would have to be a fool to stick his dick in something like that. Look at me, man. I can get any bitch I want."

Hank tilted his head toward Mary and Carolyn. "What do you *bitches* think? Would you want to jump in the sack with this asshole? He stinks of piss and body odor."

Reggie raised both his palms in the air. "Hey, you got me cold on the New Orleans rap. I'm innocent, but no one gives a shit. No matter what you think, I'm not a drug addict. I knew you were gonna come after me, so I hooked up with some friends from UC Santa Barbara. They invited me to a party, and I smoked some weed. I'm itching because I've got sand crabs from sleeping on the beach. I also have a cold. Go ahead, ship me back to New Orleans. Just don't try to hang a bunch of killings on me." He looked each of them in the eye. "I don't kill people. I was trying to get a step up in life, you know.

I dropped out of school in the eighth grade to help take care of my grandma. She raised me from the time I was five. She was the only family I ever knew. I don't even know if she's still alive." He placed his hands over his face, then looked up at them with tear-filled eyes. "I've called everywhere and no one knows what happened to her. She was too old to drive, so she gave the car back to the bank. If I hadn't got busted for my brother's crimes, I would have gotten her out of that house before the hurricane hit."

"You're good, Reggie," Mary said, returning to her chair. "You should have been an actor. We've already heard your sob stories. You told us your father was killed by a cop, remember? Now you say you never knew him."

"Wait," he said, a muscle in his face twitching. "I did see an old guy gunned down by some cops."

"But he wasn't your father, right?"

Reggie hung his head. "I want an attorney."

Hank pushed himself to his feet and headed to the door, Carolyn and Mary following behind him. Once they were outside in the hallway, he said, "Book the bastard on the warrant out of New Orleans. Right now, we don't have enough to arrest him on murder charges. Get that idiot motel clerk sobered up and bring him in for a lineup. Make certain Stockton is clean shaven and wearing decent clothes, or the guy might not recognize him."

Mary had spoken to both the New Orleans PD and the DA's office before the interview. "New Orleans won't extradite, Hank. They say all the evidence was destroyed in the hurricane."

"The warrant's still active in the system, isn't it?"

"Yeah," she said, "but I'm not certain for how long. Now that New Orleans has made it clear they're not going to extradite him, we can't hold him."

"They're all screwed up down in New Orleans," Hank said. "If anyone calls us on it, tell them you tried to get through to them, but you couldn't. Collect a DNA sample from Stockton right away and shoot it to the lab. Did Jude's black Taurus ever turn up?"

"Not yet."

"Check the Amtrak train station," Carolyn suggested. "He may have left it in their parking lot."

"But the ticket was for Monday evening," Mary told her. "If Stockton was in Santa Barbara, he couldn't have committed the crimes against Drew and Jude. And if he was involved in the situation with Jude, he would have had the cash she stole and the airline tickets."

"Jude isn't as smart as Stockton," Carolyn went on. "He knew it was too risky to try to board a plane. He didn't have time to come up with a fake ID, and he had to know we'd alerted airport security. He may well have hopped the six o'clock train to Santa Barbara Monday, with the express purpose of establishing an alibi. Then he could have called Jude to come and get him. After he killed Drew and thought he'd killed Jude, he drove her car back to Santa Barbara, washed it down, and ditched it. Either that, or he sold it to a chop shop and they dismantled it."

"I don't know, Carolyn," Mary said, stepping back to let an officer pass. "I mean, it won't hurt to check it out. The Amtrak lot is considered private property, so that might be why we haven't found the car. I can't picture Stockton doing this kind of planning. To be honest, I'm not sure he had anything to do with the murders. We're a long way from eliminating Don Snodgrass. If Stockton is our guy, he mistakenly thought both Haley and Jude were dead when they were still alive. What kind of murderer does that? Someone that's never committed a crime, maybe, like Snodgrass. Either that, or someone who's emotionally distraught."

"Whoever killed Drew and Veronica weren't that emotionally distraught, or they would have left more evidence," Carolyn argued. "One of the reasons we can't solve these cases is lack of evidence, isn't that right?"

"We've had too many crimes in too short of a time frame," Hank interjected. "We've been working from preliminary forensic reports. We may have a shitload of evidence once everything is processed."

Mary spoke up. "Since he got out of high school, Stockton's been working forty hours a week at Circuit City. I believe the guy was sincerely trying to better himself, and he got tangled up in something over his head."

"Where's his cell phone?" Carolyn asked. "And what happened to the stuff he took from his house, his clothes and other possessions? You said he cashed his final check from Circuit City Friday afternoon. Why was he sleeping on the beach if he had cash? Can't you see? It doesn't add up."

"He spent his money on drugs?" Hank said, pulling out a toothpick.

"How did Reggie find a chop shop?" Mary asked. "These kinds of operations aren't listed in the Yellow Pages."

"Wait until the public defender talks to him," Carolyn said, refusing to back down. "When do you think he's going to claim he smoked dope with his so-called friends?"

Hank said, "Who cares? The jury's not going to believe a bunch of potheads."

"You weren't listening," Carolyn told him. "He said they were students at UC Santa Barbara. Just because a few college students smoked a little weed won't discredit them as witnesses. Stockton probably bought them off with the cash or the airline tickets. If he is our killer, we're going to have a hell of a time convicting him. The motel clerk picking him out of a lineup isn't going to cut it. You know why? Ask Mary, she'll tell you."

"Because he's black," Mary said, shuffling her feet around. "Benny may be a lowlife, but he's white. White people have trouble telling one black person from another."

"Morons used to say that years ago," Hank said. "Stockton's attorney can't play the race card on something as flimsy as that."

"I disagree," Carolyn told him. "Look at all the black men who have been cleared recently by DNA. Some of these men have been rotting away in prisons for decades. In almost every instance, it turned out to be a case of mistaken identity. Any lawyer who didn't incorporate this into his defense would be incompetent."

Hank squared his shoulders off. "Find the damn car."

CHAPTER 29

Wednesday, October 19 — 10:00 A.M.

Because of the developments with Jude and Drew, Brad Preston had taken over the unit, instructing Carolyn to devote her time to the girl and the task force.

Carolyn had called and left a message on Tyler Bell's answering machine. He'd never followed through on her request to submit a DNA sample; however, she didn't see him as a viable suspect in the present crimes. Later, she would try again. If Bell continued to refuse to cooperate, she would relay Veronica's suspicions to the police agencies who had investigated the deaths of Robert Abernathy and Lester McAllen.

When she arrived at the hospital, Dr. Samuels was walking out of Jude's room. "She's awake," he told her. "You can speak to her now. She's emotional, so I'm sure she'll be glad to see you. The good news is she should be able to keep the arm. Most patients are depressed until they see how the reattached limb is going to look and function. I've asked for a psychologist named Shelly Elderwood to come by and talk to her. Later, if she's still despondent, I'll make a referral for a psychiatrist who can prescribe medication. She can't take anything along those lines now, not with the drugs we're giving her for pain."

"Did you tell her about her father?"

"No," Samuels said. "Since you were close to the family, I felt it was better if you told her. Have you notified her aunt?"

"Yes," Carolyn said. "She may not be able to fly down to see Jude right away. She has a law practice, and she's in the middle of a trial. She's also taking care of Jude's three younger siblings. Before this happened, Emily wasn't close to any of the children."

As the doctor walked off, she entered the room. Jude's face was contorted in pain, and it was obvious she'd been crying. "Hi, honey," Carolyn said, smiling weakly. "Your doctor said you were doing great."

"What are you smiling about? Where's my dad? They let him out of jail, didn't they?"

"Why don't you rest now, Jude? I'm sure you're in a lot of pain."

Carolyn hadn't anticipated Jude wanting

to see Drew, not after reading her diary. She pulled up a chair and sat down, placing her palms on her knees. How much bad news could one person deliver? She'd told Drew that his wife had been murdered. Now Drew had met the same fate. At the jail, the inmates used to call her the angel of death because almost all the people she interviewed received a lengthy prison sentence.

"It's more than the pain," Jude said. "I feel like I'm in a damn horror movie. I keep waiting for it to end, but it only gets worse. How would you feel if someone chopped off your arm and sewed it back on?"

"The doctors surgically reattached your arm, not the person who struck you with a car. Maybe you misunderstood the —"

"I didn't misunderstand anything."

"About your father, I'd rather talk to you when you're feeling better."

Jude cut her eyes to Carolyn. "He's dead, isn't he?"

How did she know? "Yes, I'm sorry."

A strained silence ensued. "I know who killed him. It was that fucker Reggie Stockton. He killed my mother, too."

"It's hard to believe anything you say now, Jude. You told everyone your father killed your mother. Have you forgotten?"

"Reggie told me that I had to say those

things or he'd kill me. Look what happened to me when I told the truth. Who do you think did this to me? It sure wasn't my father."

Carolyn felt uncomfortable. Hank and Mary should be present. She hadn't expected Jude to be alert enough to provide her with any significant information. "Please, Jude, just rest now. We can talk about everything later."

"I'm either going to talk or scream."

"Fine," Carolyn said. "It might be better if you start at the beginning."

"Reggie decided he wanted to be with me instead of Haley. I thought he was a great guy until he started hitting me. Then things got even worse. He made me have sex with his friends." She began crying again. "It's my fault that my mother's dead. I loved her. I went back to school so I could make her happy. Now I don't have anyone. God, even my dad is dead."

"I'm sorry, Jude," Carolyn said. "You have me, honey. And you have your brothers and Stacy. Emily will be here as soon as she can. Everyone is praying for you. I was going to get you some flowers, but they don't allow flowers in intensive care."

"I don't want fucking flowers," Jude hissed between clenched teeth. "I want Reggie to rot in hell for what he did." She shrieked, her body buckling upward. "Call the nurse. Tell them they have to give me something stronger. Whatever they're giving me isn't working."

Carolyn used the call button on the bed.

"She's on a morphine drip," the nurse said over the speaker. "Tell her to push the button whenever she's in pain."

"Why didn't the witch tell me that before?" Jude said, using her good hand to dig inside the covers until she found the dispenser for the morphine. A few minutes later, the creases in her forehead went away and her body relaxed back onto the mattress. "What were we talking about? Oh, yeah, Reggie. He made me meet him on a side street in back of the school. He didn't want anyone to know he was seeing me because of my reputation. He usually took me to his house while his mother was at work. Then one day, he took me to the Motor Inn. He said it was a special treat. His house didn't have air-conditioning and it was really hot that day. I was feeling sick. Reggie told me I was fat, so I'd stopped eating. He also liked really young girls. You know, girls around the age of my sister, Stacy. He said if I didn't do everything he told me, he'd rape my sister. I saw him talking to her one day when she was walking home from school."

"So you had sex with Reggie in the motel that day?"

"Yeah," Jude said. "Then I threatened to go to the police. Reggie was using another name, you know. He was a criminal when he lived in New Orleans. He knew my mom was a probation officer, that if she found out about his past, he'd go to prison."

"Why didn't you just tell your mother?" Carolyn asked. "He'd beaten you before, so you had to know threatening him was dangerous. He could have killed you."

"So what?" Jude said, pushing the pump on the morphine again. "I may be only eighteen, but I've seen and done more than most people do in a lifetime. Nothing was ever going to change for me. This" — she stared at her bandaged arm — "this is the kind of thing that happens to people like me."

"You're too young to give up on life, Jude," Carolyn told her. "It's a miracle that the doctors saved your arm. Once you're well, you'll have enough money to go back to school, even graduate from college. You can stay with me, or you can get your own apartment."

"Really?"

"Yes," Carolyn told her. "Can you tell me what happened that day in the motel room?"

469

"Before I said those things to Reggie," Jude went on, "I called Mom and told her I was in trouble. I knew she wouldn't come right away because I called her all the time. I knew Mom carried a gun, so I wasn't worried about Reggie hurting her. All I wanted to do was protect my sister. I knew if my mother got there, she would either shoot his ass or make certain he spent the rest of his life in prison." She paused and caught her breath. "Mom was tough, you know. She didn't take shit from anyone, even my dad."

"What happened when your mother got there?"

"I never saw her . . . God, everything is my fault. I was an idiot. I shouldn't have called her. I wasn't thinking straight."

"Veronica didn't come to the motel. Is that what you're saying?"

"Why would you ask me that?" Jude said, angry. "You found her dead in the motel, didn't you? Shit, you think I'm making this up. I should have known you wouldn't believe me. Go home and leave me alone."

"Please, Jude," Carolyn said. "I'm only trying to make sense of what you're telling me. You have to stop being so hostile. You're alienating everyone who can help you."

The girl fell silent for a while, then continued. "I must have passed out, because when

I woke up I was on the ground beside the road. I didn't have my purse or anything, so I walked to a store and asked to use their phone. I called my mom four or five times, but she didn't answer. Someone at the bus depot told me a woman had been murdered at the Motor Inn. I knew it was Mom."

Having your arm severed was a life-changing event, Carolyn thought, handing Jude a box of tissues. She believed she was telling the truth this time, but it was hard to separate what she'd told her before from what she was hearing now. "So you were at the motel the day your mother was killed? You said you weren't there that day, that it was a day or two before."

Jude arched an eyebrow. "I also said I was having sex with my father. We know that wasn't true. Not only was I scared of Reggie, I thought people would think I killed my mother."

"What about Haley Snodgrass?"

"I don't know. Reggie must have killed her. He bragged to both of us about all the crimes he'd done in New Orleans. He thought it was funny that he'd conned this old lady into saying he was her son."

"I read your diary," Carolyn told her. "That is, what was left of it. Someone tore a number of pages out of it."

"So? What's the problem?"

"From what I read, it was your father who was abusing you, not Reggie. You said you loved Reggie, that you would die for him. Why would you write things like that if he was beating you and forcing you to have sex with his friends?"

"I hated my dad. I wrote those things because I knew you guys would find my diary and put him in jail. I thought I *was* in love with Reggie in the beginning. That was before I found out he was an older guy who'd escaped from jail. He was a dope dealer. He wanted to get into high school so he could deal to the kids. He said he'd killed people before, that he liked killing people. He also said he'd raped little girls."

"I don't understand," Carolyn said, tilting her head to one side. "Why did you hate your father if he wasn't abusing you?"

"Because he was a racist pig," Jude said. "He hated blacks, Hispanics, Jews, you name it. And he was always putting me down. He's the one who made my mother hate me. He thought anyone who wasn't white was a gangster. As soon as I heard about my mother, I came home to help out with the kids. My father threw me out, telling me he was going to hire a live-in babysitter and give her my room. How do you think that made me feel?"

Jude had expressed regret, then a short time later placed herself back into the role of a victim. Drew might not have known, but Jude was partially responsible for Veronica's death. By calling and asking her to come and get her, she'd caused her mother to unknowingly enter into a confrontation with a killer. No wonder Stockton had been able to get Veronica's gun away from her. Carolyn wondered if people did have some kind of premonition about their death. Veronica had always insisted that carrying or owning a gun placed a person in greater jeopardy. If she hadn't had the gun, Stockton might not have killed her. "What about the abortions?"

"I liked having sex," Jude said. "It made me feel good, okay? It made guys like me. I was never popular, even in grade school. I hung out with an older crowd. Older guys want sex."

"But you were so young."

"I had real tits by the time I was twelve," she explained. "The stupid kids at school made fun of me. That's when I started hanging out with older kids. When I was thirteen, I went all the way. I was popular with the boys for a few years. Then regular girls started putting out in junior high. By the time I got to high school, even the ugly dorks didn't want to be seen with me. I had to suck guys off just to get a ride."

Carolyn gasped. How could a girl from a middle class family with decent values sink to such a level? "Haley had a car. Couldn't you get rides from her?"

The morphine had finally caught up to her. Jude's eyes closed and her head rolled to one side. Carolyn sat there for fifteen minutes in case she woke up, then slipped out of the room to go to the police station.

At four o'clock that afternoon, Hank, Mary, Gary Conrad, and Gabriel Martinez were seated around the conference table, as well as Lou Redfield from the district attorney's office.

In his early fifties, Redfield stood five-ten, and was a distinguished-looking man with salt-and-pepper hair and intelligent hazel eyes. Compared to Kevin Thomas, he was a lightning bolt. "I know you people believe you can bypass Kevin by presenting the case to me. Kevin reports to the same boss I do, so you're not accomplishing anything. I'm not trying to be negative, I just want you to know where we stand."

Hank was slouched in a chair across from him. "So what do you think?"

"You have no physical evidence whatsoever," Redfield said, placing his palms on the table. "You don't have the gun used to kill Drew Campbell. You don't have the car used in the hit-and-run accident."

"Attempted murder," Mary pointed out, poking her head out from behind Gabriel Martinez.

"Whatever," Redfield said, making a jerky motion with his hand. "Your witness from the motel failed to identify Stockton in the lineup today. I realize the DNA test hasn't been completed yet, so we can keep our fingers crossed there. According to forensics, though, there wasn't much evidence left at any of the crime scenes. Sure, I can file murder charges against Stockton, but what good is it if I can't convict him? We only charge people with crimes we can prove."

"We have one of the key victims," Carolyn said. "Jude's story fits the facts of the case. Once her condition stabilizes, she can provide us with more specific details."

"Let me ask you something," the district attorney said. "Why are you trying so hard to link these four cases together? I concede that the probation officer and her husband were more than likely killed by the same suspect, especially since they were both shot in the forehead. But even there, the murder weapons weren't the same."

"Veronica Campbell was shot with her own gun," Mary said, circling around to the other side of the table and taking a seat next to Hank. "The killer left it at the scene, so he must have got his hands on another gun. The streets are flooded with guns —"

"May I finish?" Redfield said, a sharp tone to his voice. "The Snodgrass girl's death doesn't fit, and neither does the hit-and-run accident." He stopped speaking and looked hard at Mary. "The crime isn't attempted murder, Detective. The girl stepped out from behind a truck and was struck by a vehicle."

"You can't let Reggie Stockton walk out of that jail," Carolyn shouted, leaping to her feet. "He's a cold-blooded murderer."

The district attorney looked at Hank. "I thought he was being held on a felony warrant out of New Orleans."

"They aren't going to extradite," Mary told him. "His public defender found out, and demanded we release him immediately. The jail is processing his paperwork as we speak."

Lou Redfield sighed. "Then they'll have to release him. Your so-called star witness, Jude Campbell, has established a reputation as a liar and heroin addict. She recanted her story about her father abusing her. Pretty callous, if you ask me. The last days of this man's life were spent in a jail cell under the worst accusations a child could make. If you think you can hang a case on Jude Campbell's testimony, you're out of your mind. You can call every prosecutor we have, and you'll get the same answer."

"What about Don Snodgrass?" Mary asked. "You saw the pictures we found on his computer. His attorney says his wife was the primary user on that machine. She could be covering for him. Most women don't even know how to set up a bios password."

"I don't agree," Redfield said. "I'm not familiar with all the details in the Snodgrass matter. With the instances of identity theft, people have become paranoid. As to the photos, there were two teenage girls in that residence who probably had access to the digital camera. One of their friends may have taken the shots in question. I have three daughters. Not long ago, we came across a picture of one of them on the toilet. I certainly didn't take it, and neither did my wife. One of our girls finally owned up to it. She said it was supposed to be funny." He stood and picked up his briefcase. "I'm sorry, but I have to be in court in thirty minutes."

They all exchanged tense glances after Redfield left. "Jude isn't lying about Stockton," Carolyn said, furious. "I'm not sure if Drew abused her or she wrote the diary like she said to get back at him. Drew isn't our problem anymore. I'm convinced Stockton killed both Veronica and Drew, as well as tried to run over Jude. He probably killed the Haley girl as well. How can the DA's office snub their noses at us like that? We're not talking about a burglar or a car thief. Stockton might come after Jude to finish the job. Veronica and Drew were my friends." She slammed her fist down on the table. "I refuse to let this vile man walk out of the jail without suffering the consequences of his actions. Remember the night I was jumped in the parking lot? I was certain the man had an accent. I didn't put it together from the interview with Stockton at Circuit City. Maybe he trained himself to speak without an accent in order to blend in. When we interviewed him this morning, he was nervous and I heard it. I'm certain now that Reggie Stockton was the person who attacked me. I certainly don't have a problem with credibility. I want to press charges against him."

"Great idea," Hank said, tugging on his earlobe. "Preston was with you that night, right? He exchanged gunfire with the assailant. That means we can file under assault with a deadly weapon." His eyes roamed to the other detective. "We may be able to make this fly, people."

"Brad wasn't with me when it happened," Carolyn explained, pacing. "That section of the parking lot is dark, so neither of us got a good look at the guy. Besides, the bastard had his shoe in my face. He didn't return Brad's gunfire, so we can't say for certain he was armed. He did poke me in the back with a hard object, which I believed was a firearm. You can still file under 245."

"The DA's office is going to see right through this," Mary argued. "All of a sudden you know who attacked you, Carolyn, and it just happens to be Reggie Stockton, a man they declined to prosecute. Even if you described Stockton down to a mole on his dick, they wouldn't believe you. Wait until the DNA tests come back tomorrow. If we can connect Stockton to the crimes by means of forensic evidence, Redfield will have to reconsider."

Carolyn couldn't believe Mary was arguing against her rather than supporting her. "Stockton will be gone by tomorrow. He'll disappear into the woodwork and we'll never find him. He's got Jude's Taurus stashed somewhere. All he has to do is steal a clean license plate."

Hank shook his head. "You're not making

sense, Carolyn. The guy was sleeping on the beach in Santa Barbara. Why would he do that if he had available wheels? If nothing else, he could have slept in the car. It gets cold up there at night." Before she could answer, he turned to Gary Conrad. "Go park outside the jail so you can tail Stockton when he's released. Maybe we'll get lucky and he'll lead us to the Taurus."

Conrad stood and shoved his chair back to the table. "Where's Keith? I thought he was supposed to be our grunt guy."

"Keith's mother died," Mary told him. "He had to fly home to Atlanta for the funeral."

"Why do I always get the shitty jobs?" Conrad continued. "If Stockton's on foot, I'll have to follow him on foot or he'll make me."

"Maybe you're a shitty detective," Hank told him. "Some exercise will do you good. That gut of yours gets bigger every day. Quit whining and take care of it. I'll have someone spot you as soon as I can. Lose this one and you'll be back on patrol."

After Conrad shuffled out of the room, mumbling profanities under his breath, Hank linked eyes with Carolyn. "Go home, spend some time with Marcus and Rebecca, get a decent night's sleep. Tomorrow morning, we'll go to the hospital and see what else Jude can tell us. Snodgrass is still a suspect. Don't bite my head off, Carolyn, but I wouldn't be surprised if Jude sings a different song the next time we talk to her. Personally, I think the girl is a mental case." He paused, then thought of something else. "By the way, how were you going to handle the situation with her diary? It's booked into evidence now. We can't make it disappear. Jesus, it's in her own handwriting. She didn't say a damn thing about Stockton, other than the fact that she was madly in love with him. That alone would destroy the case. The defense will depict her as a liar, a loony, and a jilted lover."

"Are you going to send someone to the hospital to protect Jude?" Carolyn asked, packing up her computer notebook. "Stockton doesn't know she's talked to us. He's killed everyone else who might incriminate him."

"I don't have the manpower," Hank said. "We're stretched to the max. I don't think he'd risk going to the hospital. The guy's got his walking papers. My guess is he'll put as much distance between himself and Ventura as possible."

"I can't go home, Hank," Carolyn said. "I have to pick out caskets for Veronica and

Drew. After that, I need to go back to the hospital to be with Jude. No matter what she's said or done in the past, she's a human being. The doctors don't even know yet to what extent she'll be able to use her arm. Right now, I'm the only person who seems to care about her."

"I thought Veronica wanted to be cremated," Mary said. "Isn't that what Emily told you?"

"Drew intended to buy a family plot. I was supposed to go to the funeral home with him the morning after he was killed. Veronica never mentioned anything to me about wanting to be cremated. Emily may have told us that because having someone cremated doesn't require a lot of effort."

Mary walked her to her car in the parking lot. "This has been a terrible burden for you, Carolyn. Why isn't Emily handling these things?"

"She's in trial on a big case."

"Christ, she's a personal injury attorney," Mary argued. "She can get a postponement for a death in the family."

"She's already saddled with the three kids," Carolyn said, opening the door to the Infiniti. In reality, she was disgusted with Emily. She understood why she and Veronica had never been close. "I want to make arrangements to bury Veronica and Drew. I didn't just let Veronica down, Mary. I let Drew down as well. I should never have let him go inside that house alone. I sent him to his death, just like I did Veronica. I'm the last person to see either of them alive."

CHAPTER 30

Marcus met Carolyn at the Morton Chase Funeral Home. She picked out two caskets, both of them outrageously expensive. Her state of exhaustion had intensified to the point where her thoughts were no longer completely rational.

"No one really knows what happens when you die," Carolyn said, grabbing hold of Marcus's lapels. "Your coffin might be like your home. Drew and Veronica lived in such a plain house. I want them to be buried in something beautiful. I don't want the roof to leak, or bugs to get inside."

"Bodies decay," he said, slapping his credit card down on the mortician's desk.

"No," she protested. "I'm going to pay for it. I don't want you to spend your money. Please, Marcus, I wouldn't have picked out such expensive coffins if I knew you were

484

going to pay for them."

"It's okay, baby," he said, patting her on the back. "Let's finish the rest of the arrangements so we can go home."

Carolyn decided to have a joint service. Veronica's body was ready to be released, but Drew's had to undergo an autopsy. Sometimes the morgue ran out of room, and insisted the next of kin take possession of the body as soon as they were finished with it. She'd called Charley after she'd left the police department and he'd agreed to keep Veronica until they completed the autopsy on Drew.

She had to decide on flowers, select the cemetery plots, arrange to have a priest officiate at the services. Veronica had lived the majority of her life as a Catholic, and Carolyn wanted her to have a Catholic funeral. Drew didn't believe in God, but under the circumstances, she thought Father Michaels would agree to officiate at the service.

Rebecca had packed some of her things and decided to stay with Carolyn's brother, Neil, who had a large home in the foothills of Ventura. Neil had been giving his niece art lessons for several years, and he lived close to her school.

When they reached the Infiniti, Marcus kissed her lightly on the lips. "I'll see you at the house. Josephine made lasagna. That should give you some energy." He smiled, moving a hair off her forehead. "I'm going to put you to bed like a baby tonight. If you give me any trouble, I might have to spank you."

"I have to check on Jude first," Carolyn told him. Seeing the annoyed look on his face, she added, "I'm not going to stay, Marcus. I just want her to know I care about her. The doctor makes rounds at seven, so if I hurry I might be able to catch him."

"Do whatever you have to do," Marcus said, turning to walk off, then stopping. "You're losing it, Carolyn. I'm not sure you're even fit to drive. Leave your car here. If you insist on going to the hospital, let me take you. Forget about the lasagna. We'll stop and get something to eat on the way home, then swing by and pick up the Infiniti. When people are under this kind of stress, they have to eat regular meals, and they have to sleep. Isn't that what the doctor told you when you fainted the other day?"

Carolyn smiled, but only the corners of her lips turned up. "At least I don't have to worry about fitting into my wedding dress."

"No," Marcus said, leading her by the elbow. "The damn thing is going to fall off."

When they got to the hospital, Marcus went to the waiting room while Carolyn headed to the nurse's station. "Please, if you see a young black man anywhere near Jude Campbell's room, call 911." She gave them a full description of Reggie Stockton, and told them that he'd just been released from jail. The charge nurse, April Cooksey, said she'd tell the other nurses and place a note in Jude's chart.

"Is Dr. Samuels here?"

"He just left," Cooksey said, a black woman in her fifties. "Jude had a rough day today. He changed her pain medication to Delaudin. It seems to be helping. Dr. Samuels said her arm is healing nicely."

Delaudin was a powerful narcotic, generally used to treat cancer patients. It was also similar to heroin. Carolyn started to say something about Jude's drug problem, but stopped herself. With what she'd gone through, she deserved whatever comfort she could get.

Carolyn quietly entered her room. Jude appeared to be sleeping, so she just sat there in a chair, lost in her thoughts. If Drew had abused Jude, as her diary clearly implied, why had he been the first person she'd asked for? And she'd turned herself into an object of contempt when she'd changed her story that day at the DA's office. How could she have wanted the person who killed her mother to go free?

Reggie Stockton was the murderer.

The more she thought about it, the more fantasies she developed about killing him. She stared out over the dimly lit room as she began to formulate a plan. Gary Conrad was tailing him. Hopefully, he hadn't lost him. She could call Gary on his cell phone, find out where Stockton was, and tell him Hank had called off the surveillance. Then she could corner Stockton somewhere and shoot him.

Carolyn wanted Stockton dead, but she didn't want to go to prison. It wouldn't be fair to Marcus or Rebecca, let alone her son, John, who would be coming home from MIT for Thanksgiving next month. All these happy events she'd planned to celebrate with her new husband and family no longer seemed important. She felt trapped in a dark, bottomless pit, where grotesque images kept clicking off inside her head like a slide show. Veronica's round, pretty face was now a hideous death mask. She saw Haley Snodgrass's hands shaped into claws, and could almost hear her pitiful cries as her killer covered her with dirt. She imagined Jude's bloody, severed arm, and remembered Drew's gratitude that she had picked him up from jail.

The police had found no signs of forced entry at the house. Jude probably had a garage door opener inside her Taurus, or Stockton had stolen Drew's key the night Jude overdosed. Carolyn had given her key to Drew, so his key must have been somewhere inside the house. According to Hank and Mary, it wasn't there after his murder.

Stockton had found opportunities to kill everywhere he went. He'd even used Veronica's gun. How many lives had this despicable man destroyed?

Someone had to stop him.

Carolyn needed a clean gun, but she couldn't walk into a gun store and buy one. Many cops had "throw down" pieces, guns they carried on the off chance that they shot an unarmed person. They'd place the weapon in the person's hands, so his fingerprints would be found, thereby substantiating the use of deadly force. Generally the police officers strapped their "throw down" gun to their leg, or some other inconspicuous place on their body.

Her plan had too many holes in it. Everyone knew how she felt about Stockton, including Lou Redfield. Besides, she wasn't a cop, so she doubted if Gary Conrad would abandon his assignment without first checking with Hank.

Carolyn had always believed in the system. She had despised people like the former forensic scientist, Robert Abernathy, who had made a mockery of it. She didn't mind stepping outside the rules on occasion, but killing someone didn't fall into that category. What she had to do was figure out a way to trick Stockton into confessing and then recording it. The problem was she didn't know how she could manage it without violating his rights, which would make the confession inadmissible.

She wanted Stockton to be processed through the proper channels, but the proper channels had washed their hands of him. There appeared no other way to stop him except to kill him.

"Hi," Jude said in a soft voice. "How long have you been here?"

"Not long," Carolyn said, taking up a position beside the bed. "How's the pain, honey? I heard the doctor put you on some new medicine."

"Better," she said. "It still hurts really bad, though. The doctor said he couldn't give me anything stronger without putting me back in a coma. Is Reggie going to prison?"

Carolyn couldn't force herself to tell her.

"They didn't believe you, did they?" she said, seeing the answer in Carolyn's eyes. "I was afraid that might happen."

"Jude, what happened to your Taurus? Does Reggie have it? Is that the car he hit you with?"

"Yeah," she said, the drugs causing her to slur her words. "The bastard stole it from my house when my dad was in jail. I wanted it back when I took off so I'd have a way to get around. I called Reggie and he promised to bring it to my house. He never showed up. That's when I overdosed. I used the money I stole from Rebecca to buy the heroin. I felt bad about what I'd done to my father. I was also sad about my mother."

"But why would you call Reggie?" Carolyn said, her voice harsher than she intended. "He beat you, used you. You also told me you were certain he killed your mother."

"I wanted my car back," Jude told her. "I don't make rational decisions, okay? I've been living in a fantasy world my whole life. I can talk myself into something, then talk myself out of it in an hour. I thought I was in love with Reggie, so maybe I was in that kind of mood. I get weird when I'm alone. Leave me alone too long, and I'll open the door to

Hannibal Lector. That's the way it was for me with sex, too."

Was she saying she was a pathological liar? Carolyn wondered. "But you had two brothers and a sister. I would think it would be the other way around, that you'd want some privacy."

"I'm almost eleven years older than Stacy. Since Mom and Dad both worked, they left me with this crazy old lady. All she did was read the Bible to me. Mom had to take me to a shrink because I kept having nightmares about the devil. That's why she decided to have another kid. Dad didn't want any more. I know because I heard them fighting all the time about it."

Carolyn recalled what Drew had told her about Jude dislocating Stacy's leg when she'd been an infant. Although she probably would have been as upset as Veronica and Drew, children did foolish things. "I'm going to ask you something, Jude," she said, her tone firm. "You must swear on your life that you're telling me the truth. This isn't a game, just something to entertain you while you're convalescing. If you're lying now, there could be terrible consequences."

Jude smiled. "What are you going to do, cut off my other arm?"

Carolyn knew she had to be firm with her.

"The drug they're giving you for pain is extremely strong. Are you alert enough to answer my questions, or should I come back some other time?"

"They're giving me Delaudin. I know it's like heroin. They even sell it on the street. It doesn't really make you feel good like heroin, or maybe it's because I hurt so much. Anyway, I have a high tolerance for narcotics. Ask me anything you want. I like you, Carolyn. You're the only person who's come to visit me. You didn't even hold it against me that I stole Marcus's Jeep and the money from Rebecca's room."

Carolyn sucked in a deep breath, then slowly let it out. "Is everything you told me about Reggie the truth?"

"I swear," Jude said, locking eyes with her. "I swear on Peter, Michael, and Stacy's life. They were the only ones who ever really loved me."

"Why would Reggie kill your father?"

"Because if the police didn't believe my dad did it," the girl told her, "they might figure out he killed my mom. He said Louisiana prisons weren't the same as California prisons, that they even had chain gangs, whatever that means."

"Tell me precisely what happened the night you were hit by the car, from the time you left the district attorney's office."

Jude stared up at the ceiling. "I didn't have any money or anywhere to stay, so I clipped that court reporter's wallet when she wasn't looking. I got lost inside the building. When I found a door that would open, I saw the entrance to the jail. I didn't know the jail was back there. I freaked, thinking I was going to run into my dad."

"Then what did you do?"

"I got a cash advance on the American Express card."

"How? Don't you need a PIN?"

"I'm not a thief," Jude told her. "But things like that aren't hard to figure out. I had the lady's driver's license, so I tried her birthday and it worked. Then I decided to buy the airline tickets. I used the computer at the library. I couldn't make up my mind where to go, so I bought tickets to different places. They were first class, so I knew I could trade them in for other tickets, or maybe sell them." Jude stopped and asked Carolyn for a drink of water. She stared at her bandaged arm. "I'm going to look like Frankenstein, aren't I?"

"You'll be fine," Carolyn told her. "You'll have a scar but you can cover it up with long-sleeve shirts. Try to stay focused on what you did that evening."

"I took a nap at the library," she said. "After they closed, I went to see if I could buy some dope and get high. I was hanging around on Dos Caminos where I'd scored in the past when I saw Reggie coming up the street in my Taurus. I jumped out and waved my arms to get him to stop. He saw me 'cause I looked right at him. The last thing I remember is the headlights."

"And this is the God's honest truth?"

"Yes," she said. "How many times are you going to ask me?"

"If someone killed Reggie, how would you feel?"

"Good," Jude said without a moment's hesitation. "I'd like to kill the fucker myself, but I don't think that's going to happen. Are you going to kill him? Is that why you're asking me all these questions?"

"Of course not," Carolyn lied, staring at a spot over her head. "I don't believe people should take the law into their own hands. I just wanted to see how you'd react. I believed you when you told me your father abused you. How can I be sure you're not lying about Reggie?"

"I'm not the same person I was then," Jude said, her slender fingers curling around the bed railing. "I'd do anything to change things. I deserved to have my arm cut off for saying my dad did those horrible things to me. I loved my mom and dad. I just wish they'd loved me."

Such a sad story, Carolyn thought, leaning over and stroking her cheek. She felt something wet, and realized Jude was crying. It didn't matter that she was eighteen and legally an adult. Even ten years from now, she would still be a child without a parent. Carolyn waited until she fell asleep, then headed to the waiting room to find Marcus.

"Where have you been?" Mary Stevens said when Carolyn answered her cell phone.

"Marcus and I are having dinner at the Chart House," she told her. "I turned my phone off at the hospital. I just turned it back on. What's going on?"

"We found Jude's car. It was parked in the driveway of an unoccupied house on the west side of town. Forensics said it's definitely been in an accident. Stockton must have cleaned it, but they found blood on the right side of the front wheel. We also found a fingerprint that came back to Stockton on the passenger door panel."

Carolyn placed her palm on her forehead, then stood and walked out of the restaurant without saying so much as a word to Marcus. She felt as if she'd just been granted a reprieve on a death sentence. "Did you talk to Redfield?"

"Yes," the detective said. "You're not going to like what he said, Carolyn."

"Tell me."

"He still refused to file murder charges against Stockton. He even took it to the top. He said all we've established is that the car was used in the hit-and-run. Since Stockton and Jude know each other, it doesn't prove anything that his print was found in the car. If it had been found on the steering wheel, we would have a better case."

Carolyn was so enraged, she began hyperventilating. Marcus stepped up beside her, but she stared right through him and turned away. "These people are insane!" she shouted. "Stockton's already on the street. You can't tail him forever. He may commit another murder. He might even come after me or a member of my family."

"Redfield said to wait until forensics finishes processing the car to see if we can come up with more evidence that links back to Stockton. If you want to blame someone, blame Sean Exley. Since he's been running the DA's office, we've encountered these kinds of problems on a regular basis. Exley has political aspirations. He won't file on any case he can't win. Redfield told you that, didn't he? The county has the highest conviction rate in the state. Exley wants to use that as a platform to become mayor."

"Tell Redfield that I demand my rights as a citizen," Carolyn said, her voice shaking. "I want Stockton arrested and charged with assault with a deadly weapon." She was walking around in a circle, flailing her arms around. Since she was only a few feet from the front door to the restaurant, people were staring at her and whispering. "I'll swear under oath that it was Stockton who attacked me. I'll even swear I saw his face."

"That's a no go," Mary told her. "I mentioned it to Redfield. He agreed to do it until he read the police report. He threatened to charge you with falsifying information if you did something like that. Try to see it from their perspective. The county is still paying off settlements because of Abernathy."

"Let me go," Carolyn said, her voice trailing off in despair. "I'm going to drown myself."

"Don't say stupid things like that," Mary shot back. "You're a big girl. On my side of the tracks, we run into problems like this all the time. You're just used to getting these guys after they've been convicted. Welcome to the wonderful world of police work. Now go back and eat your damn dinner. That handsome man you're engaged to is going to find someone else if you don't start paying him some attention."

Marcus held up her purse. "You left this under the table."

"I'm sorry," Carolyn said, disconnecting and explaining what had happened. "What about our dinner?"

In his other hand was a takeout bag. "We can finish eating at the house. If we don't get out of here, they're going to sic the dog-catcher on us. You're scaring the customers away."

Carolyn lay awake beside Marcus until she was certain he was asleep, then snuck out to call Emily. In protest against cell phones and being forced to listen to other people's con-versations like she'd done to the customers of the Chart House, Marcus had installed an old-fashioned telephone booth in the hall-way. This was one of the things she liked best about the house. No matter how close you were to the people you lived with, everyone occasionally wanted to have a private con-versation. She opened it and stepped inside, pulling the folding door closed behind her. It was after eleven, but she didn't care.

A groggy voice came on the line. "Emily Robinson."

Carolyn identified herself and filled her in on the situation with Jude, as well as the funeral plans she was arranging. "You need to be here, Emily."

"As soon as you set a date for the funeral, I'll book a flight. I thought Veronica wanted to be cremated. You spent more time with her in recent years than I did, so maybe she just said that to save money. I don't think the kids should come. They need to put this behind them."

"I didn't mean just for the funeral," Carolyn told her. "You need to be here for Jude. You're her aunt. I'm just a friend of the family. She needs to see the kids as well. Surely the judge will grant you a postponement if you explain the situation."

Emily's voice rose to a shrill level. "Jesus Christ, I can't do everything. My apartment looks like a frigging nursery school. I can't even walk there's so much junk in here. I'm trying to settle up with the insurance company. Once I get the money, I'll buy a house outside the city. All three of the kids are sick with the flu. As soon as I mop up one barf, another one throws up. The nanny I hired quit yesterday. Now that I'm in trial, I need my assistant to run the office, not be stuck here babysitting. I had to get the older kids enrolled in school and in therapy. It's been a nightmare. I can't stop everything and fly to LA to sit with Jude. I hardly know the girl. Just do whatever you can. No one's expecting you to turn into Mother Teresa."

Hank had certainly pegged Emily right, Carolyn thought. He'd said she would go after the money, buy a big house, and hire nannies. "Go back to sleep, Emily," she said. "I'm sorry I called."

"Don't lay a guilt trip on me," the woman shouted. "I'm trying to cope with the fact that my sister was murdered. To be perfectly honest, I'm afraid to come to LA. Think about it. Both my sister and her husband have been killed. Someone maimed my niece. How do I know they won't come after me? And wouldn't I be irresponsible if I brought three young children into this nightmare? I haven't even told them their father is dead, let alone what happened to their sister's arm. Cut me some slack or I'm going to put them up for adoption."

Carolyn had her head pressed against the glass as she listened to Emily rant. When the dial tone came on, she realized the woman had hung up on her.

She went back to bed and tried to sleep. After thrashing around for an hour, she got up and put on her robe, padding barefoot on the wood floors to the kitchen.

She opened the Sub-Zero refrigerator and felt a blast of cold air. There were bowls full of fresh fruit, and all kinds of vegetables. She slammed the door closed. Who wanted to eat vegetables? What she needed was chocolate. Marcus didn't allow it in the house because he considered it junk food. He said if it was there, even he might be tempted to eat it. He was a health nut, and took pride in his appearance. Sometimes she thought the roles had been reversed. While women were serving as CEOs of major corporations and working under enormous stress, with barely enough time to take care of the kind of things that were absolutely necessary, such as showering, shaving their legs, or every now and then getting their hair cut, men were buying expensive clothes, obsessing about their weight and what they ate, having manicures, and getting their hair dyed. She missed the good old boys. There was something warm and cuddly about a guy with a beer belly. So what if they guzzled booze and smoked a pack of cigarettes a day? A good old boy would bring her boxes of chocolate.

Carolyn started to see if Rebecca had any candy bars stashed in her room, then remembered buying some a few weeks back and hiding them somewhere in the kitchen. She rifled through all the drawers and came up empty-handed. She always got hungry at night, so she'd probably already eaten them. Marcus thought she didn't eat enough. He had no idea how much she could shove into her mouth during the hours he was asleep.

She stood there for a while just staring into space. Ah, she remembered, she wasn't the only one in the house with a sweet tooth. Josephine was addicted to chocolate as well, and she'd once seen her put a sackful of Hershey's bars in the pantry where Marcus's floor safe was located.

She went to the pantry and moved around the bottles and cans. When she touched something hard and cold, she knew instantly it was a gun. Next to it was a box of ammo.

Carolyn examined her find. In her hands was a Smith & Wesson Model 64 38+P revolver. She preferred a 9mm with a magazine, but right now she was in a semidelusional state of euphoria. This was a sign, she told herself. How could it not be? Now she had to figure out if it was Marcus's gun, or if it had been left there by one of his bodyguards. When everyone was at work, Josephine would invite the guards in and make them lunch. Placing the gun and the box of ammo in one of the kitchen drawers, she headed to Marcus's study on the other side of the house.

First, she remembered, she had to find the key to unlock the door. With Marcus, she sometimes felt she was living inside a vault. Creeping into the bedroom, she entered his closet and found his key ring in a silver bowl where he kept his change and wallet.

Returning to the study, she inserted several keys into the cylinder before she found the right one. Now that she was in, she went to his desk and dropped down in his chair. He used an Apple computer, and had once palled around with Steve Jobs, the founder. His monitor was enormous and took up most of the surface of the desk.

She paused, her eyes sweeping over the rich cherry paneling and the rows of books on the shelves, the majority related to computer programming or some type of technology. Even his brown leather chair gave off his distinctive scent. It wasn't his cologne, hair products, or deodorant. It was just the odor of a healthy, masculine man. Whenever she smelled it, it never failed to remind her of their lovemaking. Carolyn had only been in this room on a couple of occasions. It was a shame, really, she thought wistfully.

Marcus had a number of handguns and rifles that he kept in a cabinet in the den. He catalogued everything he owned. If the gun was his, he would have the documentation.

What file folders there were seemed to hold only a few papers. She knew Marcus relied on a paperless system for his banking. She didn't have the password to his computer, so she hoped she could find the records for his gun collection somewhere in his desk. She lucked out, seeing a tab marked GUNS in Marcus's familiar, bold scrawl.

She carried the file back to the kitchen, finding the serial number on the Smith & Wesson and checking it against the list. Her fingers trembled when she saw it wasn't there. To make certain, she went through the list again, and even rechecked the serial number on the revolver.

Everything up to that moment had seemed surreal. Now it was so real, it was terrifying. Maybe by morning, she would come to her senses, or the right opportunity wouldn't present itself. Regardless, she had started something that could forever change her life.

Carolyn had taken the first steps toward committing a murder.

CHAPTER 31

Thursday, October 20 — 5:00 A.M.

Carolyn dosed off for a few hours, then awoke and managed to slip out of bed without waking Marcus. She carried her notebook upstairs to Rebecca's room where she'd hidden the Smith & Wesson.

Taking a seat at her daughter's desk, she powered up the computer and clicked on the NCIC icon. The National Crime Information Center was an enormous database maintained by the FBI. After she typed in her password, she went to the firearms section and entered the serial number of the revolver. The gun wasn't stolen, nor had it been used in the commission of a crime. That alone made it unusual. In most instances, unregistered guns could be traced back to an untold number of crimes. Criminals had rap sheets. Guns were like criminals with a longer life span.

Next, she checked the California DOJ Firearms Division, and the Bureau of Forensic Science. Then she entered the serial numbers at Smith & Wesson to see where the gun had gone when it left the factory.

What Carolyn had found in a kitchen cabinet was referred to as a *ghost gun.* Even Smith & Wesson didn't know it existed, and they'd made it. Her chances of finding a gun like this were astronomical, particularly with today's technology. Of course, people had private collections containing firearms that had been purchased before gun registration was required. The manufacturer still had a record, however. The gun she was holding in her hand was similar to a baby being born without fingerprints.

The gun appeared new, but Carolyn knew it had been fired because a round was missing. Guns didn't just magically appear, so it had to belong to someone. As long as no one could track it, she was prepared to use it.

The police knew Jude had stolen things from Marcus's house. Since the girl was in intensive care, hooked up to all kinds of monitors, there was no way she could be held responsible.

Carolyn's attention was caught by the white porcelain cross on the wall over Rebecca's bed. She remembered giving it to her for her first communion. Dropping to her knees, she pleaded with God to forgive her if she managed to succeed in her plan. She'd already killed one murderer, so if she was going to hell, she might as well take Stockton with her.

She dialed Gary Conrad's cell phone from Rebecca's private line. She knew she was taking a chance by doing so, but there was no way to pull this off without a degree of risk. "I just thought I'd check and see what was going on with Stockton."

"Shit," he said, yawning. "I'm sitting here watching the bastard sleep on the grass at Barranca Vista Park. Hank was supposed to send someone to relieve me, but everyone was tied up. The guys from narcotics we borrowed are handling the surveillance on Snodgrass."

"Did Stockton call or meet anyone?"

"No," Conrad said. "He may have come here thinking he could score drugs. No one showed up, so he just curled up on the ground and went to sleep. Patrol is so busy they can't even relieve me long enough to go to the john and grab a cup of coffee. A girl was raped last night over by the marina. They also had a three-person fatal accident involving a semitruck, as well as an armed robbery at the Rite Aid on Main Street. All this and it's not even the weekend yet. Must be a full moon or something."

"I'll talk to Hank and make certain he sends someone to relieve you," Carolyn said. "I'm gong to jump in the shower now, Gary, then make breakfast for my husband. I'll see you later at the PD."

As soon as she hung up, Carolyn went to Rebecca's closet and dug out a pair of black pants and a black sweatshirt from the pile of clothes on the floor. She stepped into a worn-out pair of tennis shoes that were two sizes too large. Fearing they might fall off, or she would trip like she'd done the night Stockton attacked her in the parking lot, she removed the shoes, put on two pairs of thick socks, and slipped them back on.

She glanced in the mirror on her way out. Without makeup, she looked younger, at least from a distance. Finding a rubber band, she tied her hair back at the base of her neck, then pulled the hood on the sweatshirt over her head. The effect wasn't what she wanted. Swaddled all in black, her fair skin made her face stand out. Pushing the hood back, she rushed downstairs.

She scribbled a note to Marcus on the bulletin board they kept in the kitchen, telling him that she'd left early to get caught up on her work. He didn't go to his office in Los

Angeles until midmorning in order to avoid rush-hour traffic. Now that the kinks had been worked out on secure teleconferencing, he could almost run his company from the study she'd raided the night before.

When Carolyn passed through the door leading to the garage, she knew she would have to take one of Marcus's cars. The red Infiniti attracted too much attention. She darted back inside the house, opened the door to the hall closet, and snatched the key for the Range Rover from the rack.

Returning to the kitchen, she wrote at the bottom of the note that the Infiniti had failed to start, so she'd decided to take the Rover.

A short time later, she was speeding toward Ventura, the Smith & Wesson tucked into the waistband of Rebecca's jeans. Except for the one missing round, the gun had been loaded when she'd found it. She poured out a handful of bullets, steered the car with one hand as she spun the cylinder and inserted the missing round, then placed the rest of them in her pocket.

If she took down Stockton and Gary or another officer came after her, she would surrender and suffer the consequences. It was shift change at the PD, so she probably had a window of time before Gary was relieved. She knew she could outrun the detective, as he was overweight and his lungs were shot from smoking. In addition to cigarettes, he'd admitted to regularly smoking marijuana, in his surfing days.

Gary had been called on the carpet for fudging on his scores at the pistol range. Carolyn wasn't a marksman, but she could hit a target, and Stockton was a large man. As long as he remained in a stationary position, she felt fairly confident she could take him.

Gary wasn't a bad cop, just lazy. She could tell by his voice that he'd been asleep when she'd called. She had to get to Barranca Vista before someone relieved him or Stockton woke up.

The location was perfect. It was early enough that the park should be empty. The temperature had dropped to the mid-forties the night before, which was considered frigid for California. Barranca Vista wasn't that large, and there were mature trees to keep her from being seen until she found the right moment to kill Reggie Stockton.

Mary was swatting at flies over a maggot-infested body when she connected with something solid. "What the hell?" she said, turning around and seeing Keith Edwards standing behind her chair in the conference room. "Don't ever, and I repeat ever, sneak up on me. You're lucky I didn't have my gun out or I might have shot you."

"I came straight here from the airport," the young officer told her, draping his suit bag over a chair. "You looked like you were having a bad dream, so I thought I should wake you."

"Thanks," Mary said, stiff and aching. "I'm sorry I snapped at you. Jesus, what time is it?" She looked up at the clock on the wall, and saw it was a few minutes past six. "I guess I fell asleep last night waiting for forensics to call me back. Only a small portion of the evidence collected from the various crime scenes has been processed. I'm hoping we'll get lucky and find something to identify our killer. How was the funeral?"

"Sad," Keith said with a long face. "Mom had been sick for years. I feel bad that I wasn't with her in the end. A least my two brothers were there. Has anything new happened?"

"More than you can imagine," Mary said, standing and stretching her back. "I'm going to the restroom to freshen up. Make us a fresh pot of coffee. I'll bring you up to speed when I get back."

When she looked at herself in the mirror, Mary thought she was looking at a stranger.

She knew things were bad when she didn't recognize her own face. Mascara was smeared under her eyes, and her lips were dry and cracking. She couldn't remember the last time she'd put on lipstick. The air had been damp the night before, and her hair had frizzed out into an enormous Afro. She didn't wear hair extensions like many of her black friends did today. It was getting to the point where more white women had curly hair than black women. Like her mama had always told her, everyone wants what they can't have.

After she splashed water on her face, she pulled a toothbrush and toothpaste out of her purse, along with her makeup case. She carried a sling-type bag that was large enough to hold a change of clothing. Unfortunately, she hadn't planned on spending the night at the police station. She grabbed a handful of her hair and fashioned it into a knot at the base of her neck, then smoothed on some gel to keep the rest of it under control. Black hair could be a problem, particularly if you neglected it. She took her shirt off and put on deodorant, applied some face cream and lipstick, then went back to the conference room.

When she walked in, Keith handed her a cup of coffee. She sucked some of it down, wondering what cops would do without caffeine. "Okay," she said, after she'd brought him up to date. "This is what I want you to do today. Go to the evidence room and sign out Jude Campbell's diary. We need to talk to some of her classmates to see if anyone can substantiate her story about Stockton. None of the entries in the diary are dated, and random pages appear to have been torn out. Don't let anyone read any of the sensitive parts."

"I'm sorry," Keith said. "What exactly do you mean?"

So damn green, Mary thought, wondering what she'd been like as a rookie. It wasn't a fair comparison, though, because her father had been a cop. "Like the sections where she refers to her father abusing her." She counted to five to make certain he understood her correctly. "The diary is about to fall apart. I'd suggest you make photocopies of the pages, then block out the sections I just mentioned. If you get to the school early, you can catch the kids before they go to their first period classes."

"How will I know which ones are Jude's friends?"

Mary shook her head. This guy might not cut it, even in patrol. Two stupid questions in a row was one too many. "You might try asking, Keith."

"Can I tell them what happened to her? You know, about her arm and all?"

"Most of them will know since it's been on the news, but just tell them she was involved in an accident. Try to talk to as many students as you can. Ask them what they know about Reggie Stockton."

"Didn't someone already do that?"

"Good question," Mary said, feeling like she was teaching elememtary school. "Gary canvassed the school after Veronica's murder, but we didn't have the diary then, and we weren't aware Haley Snodgrass had been murdered. I want you to report back to me every thirty minutes. We'd like to get a warrant to arrest Stockton as soon as possible. We're going to pull out all the stops today, so I don't want you to so much as take a piss without asking me. If I can spring someone else to help you, I will. Otherwise, you're on your own."

Keith headed to the evidence room, and Mary had picked up her phone to call forensics when she noticed another call coming through. "Speak," she said, thinking it was Hank.

Gary Conrad was hopping mad. "What am I, the Invisible Man? I've been out here since yesterday watching this asshole. It'd be nice if I could take a crap and get something to eat. I don't mind watering a few trees, but I'm not going to squat in the bushes."

Mary had intended to get someone to relieve him before she'd fallen asleep. "I'll get Keith out there right away, Gary. He just went down to the evidence room. I was going to send him to Ventura High to see what else he could find out about Jude, Haley, and Stockton."

"Send him over here, for Christ's sake. He can keep tabs on Stockton. I didn't get much information when I canvassed the school, but I can give it another shot. You realize Stockton graduated last year. People forget you when you're not around. As for Jude, I think she only had one friend, the girl we dug up, Haley Snodgrass."

"There was another girl," Mary told him, shuffling through her notes and pulling out a list of names. "Her name is Chloe Williams. I talked to her on the phone, and then I never got back to her because everything was leaning in Drew's direction. Yank her out of class and bring her to the station. Scratch that. She's a minor. We can't talk to her without her parents being present. Whatever you have to do, just get her down here. We're desperate, Gary. We located the Taurus last night. The lab found Jude's blood on it, as well as Stockton's fingerprints."

"Why can't I arrest the bastard? Then the jail can play babysitter."

Not this again, Mary thought. "Because you can't," she snapped. "Please, Gary, I'm sorry we let you sit there that long without relief. Keith will be there in ten minutes."

Gary Conrad tossed his cell phone on the seat of his unmarked patrol car. Stockton hadn't moved in hours. He couldn't have scored drugs without him seeing him. The guy hadn't even taken a leak since he'd gotten out of jail. Knowing Hank didn't think that highly of him as a detective, one of the reasons he kept giving him such lousy assignments, he began to wonder if Stockton was all right. The guy could have croaked. Maybe he'd managed to get his hands on some bad drugs. Inside the jail, a junkie dying for a fix was open for just about anything, from a gang rape to rat poison.

He played back everything that had happened since he'd started tailing the suspect. Instead of following him on foot, he'd used the car. He was certain Stockton didn't make him because he'd never once turned around. He'd lost sight of him once when he'd got stuck in traffic, but only for a few minutes. Stockton had seemed to know where he was going. He hadn't hung out on the corner waiting for a ride or tried to beg money.

Stockton had been wearing a red and blue nylon parka. When he got to Barranca Vista Park, he'd lain down on the grass and covered his head with the parka, probably so the sun wouldn't wake him the next morning.

Opening the car door, Gary removed his jacket and tossed it in the backseat. So Stockton wouldn't know he was a cop, he pulled one side of his shirt out of his slacks. Then he grabbed his half-empty paper cup of Diet Coke and poured it down the front of his clothes. He'd check to make certain the guy was breathing, then make a quick pit stop. The public restroom was only a few feet from where the subject was sleeping. If Stockton ran, he wouldn't get far.

Just as the detective stepped onto the grass, the sprinklers came on. Stockton rolled over, then sat up, looking around in a daze. Gary's jaw dropped when he saw his face. He raced back to the car, his heart pumping like a jackrabbit.

He pounded the steering wheel with his fists. A short time later, he picked his phone off the seat and hit the autodial to call Mary. He started talking as soon as she answered. "It isn't Stockton. I don't know what the hell happened. I never took my eyes off the guy. I must have followed the wrong man from the jail."

"I'm not hearing this, Gary," Mary said. "This is a sick joke, isn't it? You're mad because we didn't get someone out there to relieve you."

"No, man, I wouldn't lie about something this serious," Gary told her, seeing his detective shield flying out the window. "I only saw Stockton's driver's license photo. I wasn't there when you and Hank interrogated him. The jail released three black guys at the same time. I was certain this one was Stockton."

"You stupid, worthless prick," Mary shouted, hurling the phone across the room.

Carolyn exited the 101 Freeway at Johnson, then turned left at Ralston. Barranca Vista Park was hard to see because of a hilly embankment. She saw a few joggers in the area, but it was too early in the morning for schoolchildren or mothers with toddlers.

She looked for Gary's car, but didn't see it. She made several passes at the park to make certain. Stockton wasn't sleeping on the grass, which made her wonder if the detective had already left his post when she'd spoken to him. Stockton was sleeping on the concrete in front of the men's restroom, curled up in a ball with his parka thrown over his head.

On the drive over, Carolyn had questioned her judgment, not about ending Stockton's life, but precisely how she was going to do it without getting caught. Since she'd expected Gary to be somewhere nearby, her plan had been to use the trees as cover and attempt to land a kill shot from there. The distance was greater than she had anticipated. She needed a rifle.

Her instincts had been right about Gary Conrad. He was probably having breakfast somewhere, guzzling coffee and chatting up a waitress. And here the murderer was, not a care in the world, able to get up and walk off whenever he wanted. She felt a hard knot in the bottom of her stomach. How could anyone be so negligent? But in this case, the system had failed. A murderer was free to kill again because the DA of Ventura County, Sean Exley, didn't want a dent in his conviction record.

Carolyn took several deep breaths, asking herself if she was prepared to go through with it. She loved Marcus, her children, her mother, her brother. If something went wrong, she would wreak havoc on all their lives. John was doing great at MIT, well on his way to reaching his dream of becoming a physicist. Rebecca had finally found a father figure in Marcus.

Thoughts of her family were replaced by the faces of Stockton's victims, Veronica, Drew, Haley, and Jude. Jude had said Stockton had bragged about killing other people in New Orleans, as well as raping young girls. When people thought of pedophiles, they generally conjured up images of dirty old men. A pedophile could be any age, any race, any religion, any face.

Carolyn opened the glove compartment to put away the box of ammo, finding one of Marcus's baseball caps. She glanced at the Nike emblem on the front, then slapped it on her head. Stopping and slamming the gearshift into park, she left the engine running and got out.

Everything was set up perfectly.

Her hands began shaking violently as soon as she pulled the gun out of the waistband of her jeans. What if she failed to land a shot at this distance? She couldn't chase Stockton through a residential area. She refused to chance hitting an innocent bystander. And she didn't want to go through this to merely injure him.

Carolyn wanted this bastard dead!

Making a decision, she held the Smith &

Wesson flush at her side, the barrel pointing at the ground. She assumed a running position and sprinted as fast as her feet would carry her, diagonally cutting across the park and heading straight for the dark mound on the ground near the men's restroom.

As Carolyn ran, her body began to consume the adrenaline just as she'd planned. Her hands felt steady now, even though she no longer had to worry about hitting her target. When she killed Stockton, she would be standing directly over him.

CHAPTER 32

Hank barreled down the hall at the police department like a man on fire, his jacket flapping and his arms pumping. Mary was blocking the door to the conference room with her body. "Get out of my way," he shouted, saliva dripping down one corner of his mouth.

"Stop, Hank," Mary said, holding her hands out in front of her. "It wasn't Gary's fault."

"My ass, it wasn't his fault. Whose fault was it? The Easter Bunny's?" He tried to shove her out of the way, but she wouldn't budge.

"Just listen, okay?" Mary said. "Gary didn't follow the wrong guy. We're the ones who messed up. Stockton is still in custody at the jail. New Orleans never got around to releasing the hold on him. We should have

523

checked before we sent Gary over there. Stockton's public defender, Richard Ford, said they'd already faxed the release papers and Stockton would be released within the hour."

Hank began to calm down. "You're not making this up, are you?"

"Of course not," she said. "It's not our job to try to repair this situation, is it?" She didn't wait for him to answer. "I didn't think so. I notified the jail and they promised to call us as soon as the paperwork comes through from New Orleans. It may not come through for a week unless someone keeps after them."

"Stockton will call his attorney."

Mary smiled. "Ford left today on a two-week vacation. I doubt if he's going to call Stockton from Europe."

"Does Carolyn know about this?"

"No," Mary said, a concerned look on her face. "No one knows where she is, Hank. Marcus said she left early this morning to go to her office. I called Preston and he said no one at probation has seen her."

"Have you called the hospital?"

"They haven't seen her, either."

Hank ran his fingers through his hair. "Well, at least we know Stockton didn't kill her. Carolyn turns her cell phone off sometimes. She's probably holed up somewhere trying to get caught up on her work. Just because no one's seen her doesn't mean she's not at the hospital. You can't use a cell phone in that place."

"There's some new developments on the case," Mary said, opening the door to the conference room.

Gary was seated at the table with a hangdog look on his face. "Did she tell you it wasn't my fault?"

"Yeah," Hank said. "Get out of here. Grab a few hours of sleep and come back."

"I sent Keith over to the school to talk to some of the kids again," Mary continued after Gary left. "I had him take Jude's diary with him to see if anyone could help fill in some of the blanks. A girl named Chloe, who knew Jude, but was closer to Haley Snodgrass, said the diary didn't belong to Jude. It wasn't her handwriting."

Hank looked disinterested. "Is this really important?"

"Absolutely," Mary said, taking a seat at the table. "Chloe swears the diary actually belonged to Haley Snodgrass. She remembers seeing Haley with it on numerous occasions. Keith only showed her copies of the pages, and she correctly described the book's cover, green with a yellow flower on front."

"From what I recall, there were only a few pages and all the girl wrote about was how much she loved Reggie Stockton. We know both girls dated the guy, so why is this a such a big revelation?"

Mary gave him a stern look. "Front and back, there were twenty-three pages. The writer implied that her father was abusing her, and mentioned how worried she was about her younger sister. Did you even read this book?"

Hank pulled his collar away from his neck. "Carolyn told me what it said."

"That's been one of our problems in this investigation, the right hand doesn't know what the left hand is doing." Mary's lips compressed. "Everything from this point on has to be backed up with irrefutable evidence, or we'll never get an arrest warrant out of the DA's office."

"You sound like you're the one running this task force," Hank said, his voice booming out over the conference room. "If we had irrefutable evidence, we wouldn't be having this conversation."

Mary ignored him. She knew he considered her a threat. All intelligent, assertive women were threats to the male ego, and more so if the woman happened to be

African American. In the past, she wouldn't have had a job that didn't involve sweeping floors and cleaning out toilets. People thought they weren't prejudiced, but they were. Harvard had a great test called the IAT, or Implied Association Test, where white and black faces were flashed on the screen, and people had to associate them with words such as *bad* or *good.* The test was administered over a short period of time, so the person taking it was forced to answer spontaneously. An overall majority associated the black face with the word *bad,* even if they themselves were black.

"Keith got some of Jude and Haley's school papers so we could compare their handwriting." Mary slid over two pieces of paper. "I haven't had a handwriting analysis done yet, but you can see it. These are copies, so I've written the girls' names on the respective pages." She placed another piece of paper on the table. "This is a page from the diary we found at Jude's house. It's obvious that the handwriting is Haley's instead of Jude's. That means it was Haley who was being abused by her father instead of Jude."

"Good God," Hank said, realizing the implications. "This could support our case against Snodgrass."

Mary stopped and rubbed her eyes. "I

haven't been able to put everything together, but I'm working on it. Except for the accident, I don't think any of the things Jude told us involved her or Drew. According to Chloe, whose parents should be bringing her down within the hour so we can get a formal statement, Jude became insanely jealous of Haley because of her relationship with Reggie Stockton. Jude was in love with Stockton. Stockton was already in love with Haley. The last day Haley was seen at school was the day we had all the wildfires, the same day Veronica was killed. I also went over the forensic report on Haley's clothing. The lab found minute particles of ash in the fibers of her sweatshirt."

"It would be nice if we had the missing pages."

"Don't hold your breath," Mary told him. "I believe Jude ripped them out because Haley wrote things about her. What Jude did, essentially, if I'm right, is steal Haley Snodgrass's life. She knew this would make us see her in a sympathetic light."

"But why blame Drew?"

"Who else was she going to blame?"

"How does Stockton fit into all this?"

"Okay," Mary said, taking a swig of her cold coffee. "Remember when I said Stockton might have been the avenger? You laughed at me, but I may have been right."

Hank grumbled something, then smiled. "You're always right. That's why I get so annoyed with you. Just put this case together for me, and I'll help you make sergeant."

"I'm going to hold you to that," she told him before picking up where she'd left off. "Everything could have started when Haley dropped hints that she'd been sexually abused as a child. Maybe she didn't tell Stockton the abuser was her father. Once she disappeared, Jude could have gone to Stockton and told him it was Drew, that Drew had been forcing both her and Haley to have sex with him on a regular basis since they were children. From what Drew told Carolyn, Haley practically lived at their house until Jude started making a play for Stockton."

"What about Veronica's murder?"

"We can figure out how Veronica's murder comes in later." Mary arched her back. "Right now, let's stay focused on Jude. Once she tells Stockton what's been happening to her and Haley, she gets his full attention, precisely what she'd been craving. Haley is found dead, so Jude's lie is now cemented in fact. Stockton decides to avenge her death by killing Drew. He's committed violent crimes in the past and doesn't have a lot to lose. He feels certain either we or some other police agency will eventually arrest him and send him back to New Orleans to serve out a prison sentence. He's probably also terrified that he's going to be blamed for Haley's death."

"But I thought Jude showed the same signs of abuse that Haley did."

"That was a misunderstanding," Mary said, her eyes drifting downward. "I'm the one responsible for letting it get out of hand. I remembered what the doctor who examined Jude the first time at the ER last night actually told me. She said Jude had been sexually active from an early age, and that she saw evidence of more than one abortion. I guess my mind was so flooded with other details, I set the age somewhere around ten. The doctor never mentioned a specific age with Jude, although Charley did with the Snodgrass girl. According to what Jude told Carolyn the other day, she started having sex with boys when she was young to make them like her, not because her father abused her."

"Carolyn should have called in by now," Hank said, glancing up at the clock. "It's almost ten."

"You're right," Mary said, her brows furrowing. "Something's wrong. Call the guys who've been tailing Snodgrass. Make certain they haven't lost him. He may think Haley talked to Jude, and Jude told Carolyn. I'll start working the phones. She wouldn't stay out of touch this long. She's too involved in the case. Since she thinks Stockton was released last night, she might be trying to find him. Unlike Gary, Carolyn has seen Stockton in person."

Carolyn stood on the beach at the water's edge, the wind whipping her hair back from her face. She stared out at the sea, watching the churning whitecaps. The sun had been out that morning at Barranca Vista Park. A storm must be moving in because dark clouds were looming on the horizon. She walked out into the surf up to her waist. For a long time, she just stood there as the frigid water swirled around her body, unable to think beyond the moment.

She finally reached into the waistband of her jeans, pulled the Smith & Wesson out, and threw it as far as she could. When the sky opened up and started spitting forth moisture, she turned and waded back to the shore. She'd left her purse and shoes in the sand. She got her phone out and turned it on.

She had six messages. She ignored them

and called Marcus at his office. When a machine picked up on his private line, she dialed the number that rang in his study at the house.

"I need you," she said when she heard his voice.

"Thank God you called," Marcus said. "Where are you? Everyone's been trying to find you. I just got off the phone with Mary. She and Hank were afraid something happened to you."

Carolyn began weeping. "Please, Marcus, come and get me."

"Where are you? Why are you crying? Jesus, if someone hurt you, I'll kill them."

"I'm on the beach next to the pier and the Holiday Inn."

"You mean where we went on our first date? It's hard to hear you with the wind. Can you hear me?"

"Yes."

"Do you want me to send the police or an ambulance? Have you been in an accident? Tell me if you're hurt."

"I'm not hurt," Carolyn said, her voice shaking. "I need you, Marcus. I need you to hold me and tell me you love me."

"I'm on my way," he said. "Stay on the phone with me. Don't hang up."

"I don't deserve a wonderful man like you.

I'm not the person you think I am. Right now, I'm not even sure if I'm sane."

Marcus was already backing Carolyn's Infiniti out of the garage. He'd checked it that morning, and nothing appeared to be wrong. Not paying attention, he turned too sharply and scraped the side of the Wrangler. He didn't stop until he reached the end of the long driveway where Bear was parked in his black Chrysler. Muting the phone so Carolyn didn't hear him, he told the burly bodyguard to follow him.

He was terrified Carolyn had been kidnapped. The work he did for the military wasn't known to anyone outside his direct contacts, but even in the most sensitive areas, information was occasionally leaked. A foreign entity, or for that matter any person who believed he possessed classified information of substantial value, could be holding Carolyn hostage.

"Please baby," Marcus said, "just answer yes or no. Is someone holding you captive?" There was no response. "No matter how scared you may be, you must find a way to tell me so I can take the appropriate action. I'll do anything they say to get you back, but I won't be able to help you if you let me walk into an ambush. I'm going to ask you the same question again. Are you being held hostage?"

"No."

"Why didn't you answer the first time?"

"You forgot about what happened in the parking lot of the Chart House restaurant. That's where I —"

"Are you talking about when you shot the arms dealer?"

"I killed him a few feet away from where you parked the car last night. How could you think I'd ever knowingly lead you into an ambush? If someone kidnapped me, I wouldn't call you even if they tortured me."

"Is that what upset you?" Marcus asked, darting in and out through traffic. "You killed that man in self-defense. If you hadn't shot him, he would have blown your head off. He and the rest of those men were smuggling plutonium to North Korea."

Compared to a kidnapping, a meltdown was a minor glitch. To say Marcus was relieved was an understatement. "No one could go through what you have without coming apart at the seams, Carolyn. The only thing wrong with you is stress and sleep deprivation. I'll call Dr. Wyman. He can prescribe some tranquilizers so you can rest. By tomorrow, you'll feel like a new person."

Marcus was on the 101 Freeway now, only a few miles from his destination. He traveled through one of those odd spots where the road was completely dry, when behind him and directly in front of him, the rain was coming down in transparent sheets. He saw a bolt of lightning zigzag its way across the sky, not something you saw that often in this section of California.

He checked his rearview mirror to make certain Bear was still behind him. Was Carolyn trying to get across some type of message? In addition to bringing up the night she'd driven into an ambush, she'd mentioned torture, and not calling him if she were ever kidnapped, which in itself was alarming.

Marcus had heard on the news that a young girl had been raped last night near the marina, which wasn't very far from where Carolyn had asked him to meet her. Since he'd talked to Brad, Hank, and Mary this morning, he was certain they would have said something if Rebecca had been the victim. It seemed impossible that another tragedy could happen after the events of the past two weeks. "Talk to me, Carolyn. I'm almost there, but I'm worried about you. You aren't thinking of hurting yourself, are you?"

"No."

Bear was a top-notch driver and had managed to stay up with Marcus. They were both exceeding the speed limit, which was dangerous on the rain-slick roads. He let up on the accelerator when he exited the freeway. Instead of entering the public parking structure, he left the car with the valet at the Holiday Inn.

Bear pulled up behind him. Marcus rushed over and hit the MUTE button again on the phone, advising the bodyguard to follow him from a distance. Marcus had a license to carry a gun, but he'd locked the gun in the safe the day before. He started to ask Bear for his gun, then decided against it. Veronica's death had made him wonder if carrying a gun might be more of a risk than a benefit.

He walked toward the water, but he couldn't see Carolyn. With the rain and low cloud cover, it was hard to see anything. "Where are you?" He caught sight of what looked like a person on the ground, and began running toward her, his feet sinking in the deep sand. "Is that you? Are you sitting down? Stand up so I can see you."

Carolyn stood and waved to him. He relaxed when he saw she was alone. The moment he reached her, she threw herself into his arms.

"Everything's going to be fine, honey," Marcus said, brushing her wet hair off her face so he could look in her eyes. "I love you. You're going to be my wife. We're going to have a beautiful life together, understand? Let's get you out of this rain and into some dry clothes."

The mere thought of something happening to Carolyn because of his work was so terrifying, Marcus decided it might be time for him to change occupations. He could always sell his business and do consulting for companies that wouldn't place himself or anyone he loved at risk. He should have realized a long time ago that a person who needed bodyguards was in the wrong profession. When he had been single, it hadn't mattered.

Carolyn had her head pressed against his chest. Sweeping her up in his arms, Marcus trudged back across the sand. Bear started walking toward him, but he shook his head as a signal that he didn't need him.

CHAPTER 33

Thursday, October 20 — 11:45 A.M.

Hank and Mary were speeding to the Snodgrass residence. "Are you certain Carolyn is all right?" he asked. "Did you talk to her?"

"Marcus said she was sleeping. He refused to wake her, but he reassured me she was fine, just suffering from acute exhaustion. I told him to keep her away from the hospital and Jude. Gabriel should be there by now. It'll be interesting to hear how Jude tries to lie her way out of this one." Mary heard something on the police radio. "Someone reported a DOA in Barranca Vista Park."

"Wasn't that where Gary was staked out all night?"

Mary didn't answer, busy calling Gary Conrad at home. A handwriting expert had confirmed that the diary was written by Haley Snodgrass. When they'd interviewed Chloe Williams at the station that morning, she had also told them about seeing Mr. Snodgrass's bronze Lexus circling the school on numerous occasions. On the days Chloe saw him, Haley would say she was sick and leave school early. That's why Haley hadn't graduated with her class. Chloe assumed she was secretly meeting Reggie Stockton, even though Haley refused to talk about him. When the lab had matched an unidentified print found inside Jude's black Taurus to Snodgrass, Lou Redfield had given them the green light to arrest him.

Gary Conrad answered the phone in a groggy voice. "I didn't shoot anyone, if that's what you're thinking. If it's the same guy I followed from the jail, he probably just croaked. He looked like he was on his last legs."

Mary disconnected when Hank pulled up and parked in front of the Snodgrass house. Something looked amiss. The front door was standing open, and a teenage girl with long blond hair was sitting on the front steps of the house sobbing hysterically. Hank and Mary bailed out and raced toward her.

"My dad . . ." Anne Marie told him, gasping for breath. "I found him in the bedroom." She placed a hand around her neck, her fingers trembling. "He, he . . . Oh, God . . . I want my mother."

Mary saw something clutched in her hand. "Calm down, sweetie," she said, sitting down on the porch beside her while Hank drew his gun and entered the residence. "Can you tell me what happened?"

"I — I called my mother because the kids at school said my dad was a child molester. I wanted her to come and get me, but she had to take Kylie to the doctor. I ditched class and walked home. My dad . . . no one was here." The girl stopped speaking, staring out into space.

"Everything will be okay, honey," Mary said. "Did your father hurt you?"

The girl looked at her with eyes filled with horror. "I found him in the bedroom. He was . . . hanging from a rope. I tried to get him down. I — I couldn't reach him. I think he's dead."

Mary placed a comforting hand on her thigh as she called the station and requested an ambulance, along with additional units. Angela Snodgrass pulled into the driveway, opened the door to her Cadillac, and rushed toward them, leaving her nine-year-old daughter in the backseat. Before the girl's mother reached the porch, Mary pried the piece of paper out of Anne Marie's hands, then darted inside the residence.

Hank was in the master bedroom. Don

Snodgrass was hanging from a thick rope attached to one of the exposed beams in the high ceiling. Suicides by hanging were not always successful, but Snodgrass had made certain he would never see the inside of a jail.

An aluminum ladder rested on its side in the corner, evidently from where Snodgrass had kicked it when he'd hanged himself. In shock, Anne Marie must not have seen the ladder when she'd discovered her father.

"Did you check to make sure he's dead?" Mary asked, although she knew it was a moot question. Snodgrass's protruding tongue was black, a clear indication of death.

"I hate ladders," Hank told her. "The sucker is dead. If he was alive when we got here, he's certainly not alive now. Kind of nice when a menace like this does our job for us. At least we don't have to worry about getting a conviction."

"Shut up, for Christ's sake," Mary snapped at him. "There's a girl out there who'll carry this image to her grave. You want her to walk in here and hear you talking about her father that way? The wife showed up, as well as the younger sister. I wasn't even aware there was a younger sister. Preserve the crime scene while I go out and talk to them." She handed him the piece of paper she'd taken from

Annie Marie. "This time, try reading it. There's writing on the back as well."

The handwritten suicide note was also a confession. In letters so small they were difficult to read, Snodgrass admitted killing Haley and Veronica, although he swore Haley's death was an accident. He said Haley considered Veronica like a second mother and must have called her to come to the Motor Inn without his knowledge, thinking her position as a probation officer would assure his arrest.

The most shocking part of the letter was Snodgrass's admission that he'd been molesting his youngest daughter, Kylie, since Haley's death. The previous evening, his wife had walked in and caught him in the child's bed. He realized his "sickness" as he referred to it would never go away, and had decided to end his life so he would never harm another child.

Mary found Angela Snodgrass and her two daughters huddled together on the porch, all of them crying. "It might be better if your daughters waited in the car," she said. "We need to ask you some questions, and our forensic people will need access to the house."

"Is he . . ."

"Yes," Mary told her, her face etched with

sympathy. It was always sad to see a family in ruins. She recalled the situation with her brother, and was glad he had been killed in the car accident before she'd had to tell her parents that he'd been sexually abusing her. When her father had been killed on duty, she'd been certain she would never get over it. Even something as terrible as this family had gone through could be overcome in time. Not forgotten, but accepted as one of the uncharted events that sometimes occurred during the course of a human lifetime. Her mother had always told her that if a problem didn't kill you, it would make you stronger. She looked at the tortured faces of Anne Marie, Kylie, and Angela Snodgrass, hoping her mother's homegrown wisdom would one day come true for them.

Marcus crawled into bed with Carolyn and touched her shoulder to wake her. He hadn't needed to call Dr. Wyman. As soon as they'd reached the house, Carolyn had gone to the bedroom, stripped off her wet clothes, and promptly passed out. "I have good news," he said, kissing her on the forehead when she opened her eyes. "Your problems might be over."

"What do you mean?"

"Snodgrass confessed. Then the bastard

hung himself." He explained what Mary had told him about the diary. Carolyn bolted upright in the bed, trying to push him aside so she could reach the phone. "No, you don't," he told her. "There's nothing to do right now. The police sent a detective to the hospital to speak to Jude. From start to finish, it looks like everything that kid told you was a lie. I was taken in by her, too, so don't feel bad."

"Who murdered Drew, then?" Carolyn said. "Snodgrass didn't admit to killing him, did he?"

"Mary didn't say anything about Drew," Marcus told her, the look of relief disappearing from his face. "Please, before you dive back into this thing, tell me what happened this morning. I was terrified you'd been kidnapped, or that you were going to hurt yourself. I overheard you tell Mary you were going to drown yourself, so I didn't know what to think."

"I'm a Catholic, Marcus," Carolyn tossed out, scooting over to the other side of the bed to get out. "We believe it's a sin to take a life, even your own. I wasn't serious when I said that to Mary. Trust me, you're way off track on this one."

He followed her around as she got dressed. "You've been acting strange, baby. I know it's probably stress, but still, I was worried about you even before I got that frantic call from you."

Carolyn headed to the bathroom to comb her hair and try to make herself look presentable. Marcus leaned against the door. "I found a Smith & Wesson in the kitchen cabinet," she said, linking eyes with him in the mirror. "Was it yours?"

"No," Marcus told her. "It was probably Josephine's. She got scared when she came to work for me and found out I had bodyguards."

"It's a ghost gun."

"What the hell docs that mean?" After Carolyn explained, Marcus rubbed his chin. "Josephine probably got it from one of her relatives back East. I think they're in the Mafia."

"I guess you'll have to buy her a new gun," she said. "I threw the Smith and Wesson into the ocean this morning. That's what I was doing at the beach."

"Why would you do something like that? See what I mean, Carolyn? Don't get mad, but you've been doing some strange things lately. You have your own gun. Why take Josephine's?"

"I needed a clean gun," Carolyn explained. "I went to Barranca Vista Park this morning to kill Reggie Stockton." She stared at her image in the mirror as she relived those awful moments.

Carolyn was running across the damp grass, the gun flush at her side. Before she reached the restroom area where Stockton was curled up with his parka over his head, she felt as if an invisible wall dropped down and stopped her. What in God's name was she doing? She wasn't a vigilante. It went against everything she believed in.

Almost every murderer had some type of justification for what he had done. And killing Stockton wasn't the same as the man she had shot in self-defense. She remembered the guilt she carried to this day, and how she had prayed for God to forgive her. Her clothes were soaked with perspiration. If she killed Stockton, she would be the same as him. She would never be able to love again, feel joy again. Even if she got away with it, it would haunt her the rest of her life.

Placing the gun back in the waistband of her jeans, Carolyn walked over and pulled the parka off Stockton's head, wanting him to know how close she had come to ending his life. When she realized the man wasn't Stockton, she gasped in horror.

Racing back to the Range Rover, she felt so shamed and weak that she had to lean against the car to keep from passing out. She'd been only seconds away from killing an innocent man. The thought that she had gotten this far was terrifying.

Carolyn heard Marcus's voice and turned around, pushing aside the images from that morning. "Stockton wasn't even there, Marcus. Gary Conrad must have followed the wrong guy from the jail. I decided I couldn't do it even before I found out the man wasn't Stockton."

Marcus was beside himself. "My God, how could you even consider doing something like that? You could have ended up in prison. What about me? What about Rebecca and John? You've let Jude and her crazy stories drive you insane." He stopped and leveled his finger at her. "That girl's dangerous, Carolyn. Mary instructed me to keep you away from her. The police are in charge now. You should never have been assigned to their task force. You were too emotionally involved."

"The DA refused to prosecute, Marcus," Carolyn said, leaning against the bathroom counter. "Stockton was going to walk. You're wrong about Jude. I admit that I believed her, particularly after she suffered such a devastating injury. Even if ninety percent of what she told me was a fabrication, the other ten percent is more than likely true. I'm certain Stockton killed Drew. Jude told him he'd been abusing both her and Haley since they were children. She convinced him that Drew killed Haley. He must have genuinely cared about the girl."

"You mean Jude set her father up to be murdered?"

"Maybe not intentionally," Carolyn said, going into the closet to get dressed. Marcus stood in the doorway. "All Jude wanted was attention, Marcus. She didn't think about the ramifications. I'm not making excuses for her, but the girl has serious psychological problems. Not only does she have to recover from the accident, but if things happened the way I suspect they did, none of this will compare to what Jude may be facing if the DA decides to prosecute her for murder."

Marcus looked bewildered. "This morning you were ready to kill for her. Now you want to see her go to prison for murder."

"I wasn't ready to kill for Jude," Carolyn protested. "I was going to kill a murderer who'd been released to kill again." She stood on her tiptoes and kissed him, cupping the side of his face with her hand. "I'll check in with you later. Don't worry, I'm feeling fine now. The sleep did me a world of good. I didn't kill anyone, and you're right. We're about to put an end to this nightmare. Then, if you still want me, we can set a date for our wedding."

"Of course I want you," Marcus said. "But you have to promise you'll never think about killing anyone again."

"I promise," Carolyn said, probing deep into his eyes. "But are you sure you want to spend the rest of your life with me?"

Marcus engulfed her in his arms. "You're hell on wheels, but you're the most fascinating woman I've ever known. How could I not want you? You're one of a kind, and I'm just a high-paid computer geek." He reached down and squeezed her buttocks. "When you're not running around chasing criminals, stealing guns, or plotting to kill someone, you're a pretty good lover. Of course, there's always room for improvement."

"Same goes for you, guy," she said, extracting herself. "Oh, I'm taking the Infiniti. There's nothing wrong with it. I thought it might attract too much attention since I was planning on taking out Stockton. That's why I took your Range Rover."

Marcus shook his head.

"The police would have come after me, then?"

"Don't worry, baby," Carolyn said, laughing. "I would have posted your bail."

"You're a real sweetheart," Marcus called

out as she took off down the hallway. "If I decide to kill someone, I'll make sure to take your car."

CHAPTER 34

Thursday, October 20 — 4:15 P.M.

When they were almost ready to clear Snodgrass's residence, Mary went outside to the car and used the police radio to speak to the officer who had responded to Barranca Vista Park. "Go to scramble," she said, when an officer she recognized as Larry Felton answered, using his call sign of 2B3. "Tell me about the DOA, Larry. Is it a homicide?"

"Nah," Felton said. "The guy is a black male in his twenties. Right now, we're not certain what killed him, but he appears to have died from natural causes. He doesn't have any external injuries. The paramedics think he died from an asthma attack or choked on a piece of food. His face was blue when they got here."

"Are there any signs of strangulation?"

"No," Felton told her. "We can't find any ID. The reporting party was a jogger. He stopped to use the restroom when he found him. He said the guy camped out in the park all the time, so he assumed he was homeless. He hasn't seen him for a few days. He thinks someone in the neighborhood may have thought he was dangerous and called the police. I'll have the dispatcher check and see if anyone arrested a vagrant fitting his description recently."

Before she returned to the Snodgrass house, Mary received a call from Carolyn. "Do we have any idea where Stockton is?"

"He's still in jail on the New Orleans case," the detective told her. "What happened to you this morning? Marcus made it sound like you were sick."

"I just needed a few hours of sleep. Did you tell him to keep me away from Jude, or that I'd been kicked off the task force?"

The line went silent. "Jude's been manipulating you, Carolyn. Isn't it obvious now that Snodgrass confessed? Jesus, his wife caught him in bed with the eight-year-old. She took the girl to the doctor to make certain he hadn't had intercourse with her. She's all right, thank God, but Anne Marie came home from school early and found her father. When we got there, she was hysterical. I really feel for them. Can you imagine what the wife has gone through? She hasn't begun to recover from her daughter's death. To know the man you're married to has been having sex with your child for years, then learning he murdered her to protect himself, must be earth-shattering."

"Where's Anne Marie? I'll have Rebecca call her. They've become close since all this happened. I'm sure she could use a friend right now."

"They're staying with the wife's mother. Hold on. I'll give you the number."

After Mary gave her the information, Carolyn said, "Who did you send to the hospital to talk to Jude?"

"Gabriel Martinez. He tried to get her to tell him the truth, but she clammed up and slept all afternoon. Gabriel is on his way to the Snodgrass house. Hank and I were planning on going to the hospital and trying our hand with Jude. The only missing link right now is Drew. It's doubtful Snodgrass killed him. The bastard confessed to killing his daughter, as well as Veronica. I can't think of a reason for him to kill Drew, unless Drew suspected he was involved in Veronica's murder. Did Drew say anything along those lines when you picked him up from the jail?"

"Nothing, and that's not something he would keep to himself. After sitting in jail, he would have been signing his own death warrant if he went after Snodgrass. Regardless of the fact that Jude cleared him, he could have ended up taking the fall for both murders. Do you agree?"

"Makes sense," Mary said. "We know Jude used the information in Haley's diary to concoct the accusations about Drew. That's why everything sounded so credible. Redfield is considering filing charges against her, but he doesn't know what to file yet. I wasn't trying to exclude you, Carolyn. Hank and I just need to be present to advise Jude of her rights. You want to meet us at the hospital and see if you can get her to cough up the truth? If anyone can do it, you can, especially now that we found out who wrote the diary."

"I'll meet you there in thirty minutes."

Carolyn entered Jude's room with Hank and Mary. She'd asked that they give her a few minutes alone before they advised Jude of her rights. Hank shook his head.

Jude was awake, a tray of food sitting on a table beside her. "Why are they here? Some dickhead cop showed up today, asking me all kinds of questions. I've been waiting for you all day. Why haven't you come to see me?"

Carolyn knew there was only one way to play it, and it wasn't going to be pretty. She turned to Mary. "Advise her of her rights. I have a daughter of my own to take care of. I have no desire to spend time with someone who's done nothing but lie to me." She began walking toward the door.

"Please," Jude cried. "Don't leave me. You're all I have."

Carolyn slowly turned around. "If you don't come clean with me this instant, I'm never going to come and see you again. Do you understand me? The police know you stole the diary from Haley. They know you used the personal things she wrote in it to make false accusations against your father. You told Reggie your father had been abusing both Haley and you since you were children. Isn't that right, Jude?"

Tears glistened in her eyes. "I told you I made up the stuff in the diary because I was mad at my dad. God, what's wrong with you people? I was in a terrible accident. My arm was cut off. I could have died. I didn't kill anyone. Why did you advise me of my rights?"

"Come on," Carolyn said. "You watch TV. You know what a plea agreement is, or what they call cutting a deal. Just to make sure, I'll explain it to you. Reggie's going to be charged with first-degree murder. That's a crime that carries the death penalty. He's going to spill his guts. We call that rolling over on someone. Who do you think the district attorney is going to believe?"

"Reggie's a criminal. Why would they believe him over me?"

"The truth has a distinctive ring to it, Jude, something you've failed to realize. The DA will offer Reggie second-degree murder if he hands you over. That's only twelve years to life. If you were Reggie, what would you prefer? Twelve years or death?"

Jude screamed, "I didn't kill anyone!"

"Do you really think a jury will believe Reggie killed your father because he didn't want to be sent back to New Orleans? The hurricane destroyed all the evidence, so that would never have happened. Reggie is a clever young man, Jude. Even if he didn't know that New Orleans couldn't prosecute him, all he had to do was go underground like he did after he escaped from jail. Why take a chance and commit a murder? Reggie didn't even *like* you, Jude. He was in love with Haley. We've talked to your friends. You were stalking Reggie. You ended a lifelong friendship with a girl who desperately needed you. Her father would have been in custody by now if you'd told us the truth. More importantly, your own father might still be alive. Don Snodgrass confessed to murdering your mother." Carolyn paused to catch her breath, then continued, "Why did Haley call Veronica, huh? You knew all along what Haley was going through. That's why she stayed at your house so much, to get away from her father. You told her your mother could help her, didn't you?"

Mary handed her a tissue, and Jude blew her nose. "Was that wrong, too? She made me promise not to tell anyone. She was scared of Donny. He beat her up really bad when he found out she was seeing Reggie. I tried to get her to talk to my mother. I told her she would make sure he went to jail."

"Then you decided to steal the one thing Haley had left, her boyfriend. Why, Jude?"

"Because I wanted someone to love me, too." The first glimpse of the innocent child Jude had once been appeared. Swaddled in white bandages and bedding, she looked almost like an infant.

"Your mother and father loved you," Carolyn said, her voice softening. "I spoke to your dad the night Reggie killed him. He was concerned about you. He wasn't bitter about the allegations you brought against him. All he wanted was for you to be safe and happy."

"When I told Reggie those things," Jude said, her good hand clutching the sheet, "I didn't think he would kill anyone." She turned around and glared at Mary. "You're recording this, aren't you?" Facing Carolyn again, she added, "I guess it doesn't matter anymore. This is hard for me, you know, telling the truth."

"Why is that?" Carolyn asked, wondering if a pathological liar could actually provide an answer to such a question.

"Because I've always had secrets, things I couldn't tell anyone. After a while, you disappear into the stories you make up, so you can't tell one from the other. It's a lot easier that way, especially when you know people will look down on you or hate you if you tell the truth. How did I know Haley called my mother from the motel?"

Carolyn felt her heart pounding. Everything suddenly slammed together. Jude looked so pathetic, she had to resist the urge to rush over and comfort her. "Did you ever have sex with Mr. Snodgrass?"

A strange look appeared in the girl's eyes. "It was Haley's diary, but the story was about both of us. We wrote it together. She kept it at my house, so her parents wouldn't find it. Her father started messing around with us when Haley was nine and I was ten."

"Jesus," Mary exclaimed, glancing over at Hank.

"He gave us money," Jude continued,

"bought us all kinds of neat things, took us to Disneyland. At first, it wasn't that bad. He would just cuddle with us when I spent the night, usually while Haley and I were watching TV or a movie. Then he started putting his hands inside our pajamas. My mom and dad were always working. They didn't hug or kiss me very often. I liked having Donny touch me. I didn't like it later on, though."

"What happened that changed things?"

"I got pregnant."

The room took on the atmosphere of a movie theater during a scene so tense that no one even reached for their popcorn. It was as if there was a spotlight focused on Carolyn and Jude. When either of them spoke, their voices echoed off the tiled floors. Hank and Mary were standing motionless, completely riveted, and at the same time, not sure if this wasn't just another of Jude's elaborate fabrications.

"And it was Don Snodgrass who impregnated you?"

"Yes," Jude said, pressing her head down on the pillow. "I didn't start having sex with other guys until later. Haley made me promise not to tell my mom. Her father kept telling her that if she got him in trouble, they'd lose their house and have to live like poor people. He said her mom, Angela, wouldn't believe it, that she'd hate her for ruining their lives. Angela didn't work. I don't think she ever worked. All she did was take care of the kids and spend money."

"Did Mr. Snodgrass impregnate you the second time?"

"No, I was having sex with all kinds of guys by then. I don't know who got me pregnant that time. Haley couldn't date or anything because her father wouldn't let her, but I could do whatever I wanted. She was jealous of me. When she started seeing Reggie, I would say she was spending the night with me so her father didn't find out. Haley didn't have a bad reputation like I did, and she was prettier than me. She got really skinny. I think she could wear a size zero or something. I tried to diet, thinking Reggie would like me more. I lost weight, but I was still a cow compared to Haley."

They were losing some of their focus. Carolyn knew she had to bring Jude back around. She wasn't interested in discussing diets and reputations when Stockton's release could come through any moment. "When did you tell Reggie that your father was the one abusing you and Haley?"

"Not until she disappeared," Jude said. "I didn't know Haley's father killed her. My dad used to whip me with a belt. That didn't mean he would kill me. I thought they sent her away to a boarding school or one of those hospitals where they treat anorexia. Reggie was really upset. He kept asking me if I'd heard from her, or if I knew what had happened. That's when I decided to tell him."

"Why name your father?"

"I don't know, really. Maybe because I was scared if I told Reggie it was Haley's dad, he would go to the police and Haley would never speak to me again. I didn't know then that Reggie was an escaped prisoner. He told me that later."

"But Haley had already disappeared?"

"I thought she would come back."

"I thought you and Haley weren't getting along."

"We weren't," Jude said. "We'd been in big fights before and always made up. I didn't know she was already dead." She asked for a drink of water. Mary poured it into a special cup with a straw and lid. After she handed it to her, she returned to her position beside Hank.

"Who beat you, Jude?" Carolyn asked. "Was it Reggie?"

"No," she said sheepishly. "I just hit myself with one of my dad's old shoes. I wanted Reggie to believe my dad beat me up. It was kind of like special effects, and I'd seen Haley before after her father hit her, so I knew how it looked. Reggie felt a lot more sorry for me when he saw the bruises." She finished the water and placed it back on the nightstand. "Do I have to keep talking? You know everything now. I'm a bad person. So what else is new? I've been in trouble since I was born. Reggie killed my dad because of me. There, you wanted to know the truth. Now you know it. Send me to jail. I don't care. I could never make it on my own, anyway."

"Is there any way you can prove the things you've told us today?"

Jude was quiet for a while, thinking. "Why would I want to help you prove something that would send me to jail?"

Mary stepped forward. "If you cooperate and agree to testify against Reggie, the DA may charge you with a less serious crime. I can't make any promises, you understand, but there's always the chance that they might even decide not to prosecute you."

"Humm," she said. "What kind of proof do you need?"

"You've heard about DNA, right?" Mary continued. "Do you have anything with Don Snodgrass's semen on it, or some other type of body fluid, such as saliva or blood? How long has it been since you last had sex with him?"

"Over five years."

"So that's not going to help us," Mary said, disappointed. "If you hadn't had an abortion, we could have confirmed Snodgrass was the father of your child."

"I didn't abort his baby," Jude said, dropping a bombshell. "My mom wouldn't let me have an abortion the first time I got pregnant. She made me give the baby up for adoption. I wore big shirts and things, so no one at school knew I was pregnant, outside of Haley. I went into labor when I was six months. I was afraid the baby would die, but they told me he was all right. He just needed to be in an incubator. I only had two abortions. I got pregnant three times."

Everyone crowded around Jude's hospital bed. "Where's the kid?" Hank said, beginning to believe her. "Did you use an adoption agency? What hospital did you give birth in?"

"It's almost time for my shot," the girl said, wincing in pain. "We didn't use an adoption agency. My mom handled it through this lady attorney that used to be a DA. All I know was her name was Beth. No, wait, I think her last name was either Levin or Levy. It sounded like the jeans. That's why I remember it."

Hank told Mary, "Get Beth Levy's ass on the phone. If she gives you any flack, tell her I'm going to book her as an accessory to murder. And call Charley. Find out if they've established a time of death on Don Snodgrass yet."

"Why?" Carolyn asked, concerned now that Jude was writhing in pain. She walked over and pushed the call button for the nurse, then leaned over and whispered in her ear, "I'm proud of you, honey."

Mary was calling the station to get Beth Levy's number. "Because the wife may have been the first one to find Snodgrass," she said, pulling out a pen and scribbling the attorney's number on the back of her hand. "That means she would have had access to the note he left. Since her husband committed suicide, she can't collect on his life insurance. The last thing she would want would be an illegitimate child floating around, someone who could make a claim on his estate."

"Did Haley's father know you had his baby?"

"Yeah," Jude whimpered. "That's the last time I had sex with the bastard. I didn't tell my mom, though. No one else knew but Haley and the attorney lady."

A flurry of activity broke out in the room. Hank called Redfield at home to get permission to charge Stockton with Drew's murder. An older nurse with frizzy gray hair and the face of a drill instructor came in to give Jude her injection of Delaudin. When she heard the two detectives talking on their cell phones, she shouted, "No cell phones inside the hospital. Don't you read the signs? If you don't leave this minute, I'll call security."

Hank and Mary made a hasty retreat, continuing their conversations as they walked out. "Please," Jude pleaded, looking over at Carolyn, "don't make my mom leave, Maggie. I haven't seen her all day."

"She's your guardian, honey," the woman told her, inserting the narcotic into the IV. "Your mother is dead."

"But she loves me," Jude said, reaching through the bars on the bed railing.

Carolyn clasped her hand, experiencing a rush of maternal emotions. Tears spilled from her eyes. In the end, love had saved the day.

EPILOGUE

Monday, October 31 — 6:30 P.M.

The air was crisp and fresh. Children were out trick-or-treating, and the rehabilitation wing of the hospital where Jude had been transferred was decorated for Halloween.

Jude still used a sling to support her arm. The reattachment had been a success. All the therapists had to do now was build up the atrophied muscles. The nerves and blood vessels were functioning perfectly. In time, Dr. Samuels believed, she would regain close to normal use of her left arm and hand.

Because of the extraordinary circumstances, the DA decided not to press charges against Jude in the death of her father. The lab had matched Stockton's DNA to a hair found on the sofa where Drew was shot. Two days ago, Stockton had cut a deal, agreeing to plead guilty to second-degree murder.

Angela Snodgrass had confessed to finding

her husband after he had hanged himself, and disposing of the last page of his suicide note, which referred to the abuse he'd committed against Jude. Angela hadn't known about the pregnancy, however, until Beth Levy had told her the day after her husband's funeral. Her intent was to call the police and report her husband's death when she got home from the doctor's office.

While searching through the documents stored on the Dell computer removed from the study at the Snodgrass house, Ricky Walters had come across a slew of letters and old e-mails that Angela had written to Drew Campbell. From the way it appeared, they'd been having an affair off and on for almost ten years. This was presumably the reason Angela had set up so many passwords on her computer.

Carolyn had revisited Tyler Bell, and he'd finally agreed to come in for a DNA test. The results had established his innocence in the deaths of Lester McAllen and Robert Abernathy. The killer remained at large.

One of the remaining mysteries in Veronica's and Haley Snodgrass's death would probably never be resolved. No one had any idea why the clerk at the Motor Inn had claimed a black male had rented the room. They assumed Don Snodgrass had stolen the credit card, as he was a member of the Spectrum Health Club and had been there the day prior to the murder. Either the clerk had simply been mistaken, was racially prejudiced, or Snodgrass had paid someone off the street to rent the room for him. Benny, the clerk, admitted that he seldom checked guests' IDs if they handed him a valid credit card.

The police had gone through all the calls made to Veronica on the day she was killed, both at her office number and her cell phone, and found nothing that would trace back to Haley Snodgrass or the Motor Inn. The day before she was arrested, Veronica had taken Jude's cell phone away, something they hadn't been aware of. She'd also put in a cancelation order with Verizon, so the number hadn't shown up as active when the police had checked, although the company didn't discontinue the service until midnight on the day of the murder.

When Carolyn had taken Jude to the hospital after seeing the bruises on her body, she'd had a cell phone in her possession that belonged to a girl named Sally Owens. As it turned out, Haley had used her own cell to call Jude's cell from the motel room. Veronica must have mistaken it for her own phone and answered it. It was also possible that

Haley had left a message on the voice mail and Veronica had retrieved it, believing the two girls were together.

Carolyn saw Jude walking down the corridor when she stepped off the elevator. She was dressed in a black cape and a pointed witch's hat. Now that she was eating properly and no longer using narcotics, except for an occasional pain pill, she had the glow of a healthy young woman. Her hair was shiny and soft, her skin clear, and her eyes bright and alert. Revealing her secrets after so many years, as well as owning up to her mistakes, had caused Jude to undergo a remarkable transformation.

"One of the nurses gave this costume to me," she said, laughing. "I wanted to be an angel, but she said it was either a witch or a devil. Do they know me or what? They had a party in the pediatrics ward, and I helped out with the kids. Where's Rebecca?"

"Rebecca said she'll stop by tomorrow," Carolyn told her. "Something came up and she couldn't come tonight." In addition to spending time with Anne Marie, Rebecca had started visiting Jude on a regular basis. Carolyn was pleased that the two girls had developed a friendship. Rebecca was only sixteen. Jude would soon celebrate her nineteenth birthday, but the three-year age span no longer made a difference. Mary had been shocked that Carolyn would encourage such a relationship. She'd stopped by the hospital the week before, though, and marveled at how much Jude had changed.

Jude leaned in close to Carolyn, whispering, "That guy over there keeps staring at me. I've never seen him before. Have you? He's handsome. How old do you think he is?"

Carolyn had eagerly anticipated what was about to unfold. A lot of effort had gone into making it happen, and only after it had been approved by Jude's new psychiatrist. Dr. Reynolds believed Jude had attention deficit disorder, commonly referred to as ADD. He felt this was one of the reasons she'd been so unruly as a child, and performed poorly at school. Now that she was on medication, the doctor felt she might be able to attend college one day.

Veronica had changed her will not long after Carolyn received her promotion, appointing Emily as legal guardian of the three minor children, as well as the executor of the couple's estate. The one penalty Jude had received, outside of a devastating injury and a childhood of abuse, was being denied all rights to her parents' four-million-dollar life insurance policy. Jude inherited the proceeds from the sale of their home, but Emily supervised all expenditures. She had agreed to pay the rent on a small apartment on the provision that Jude enter a three-month residential drug treatment program when she was released from the hospital.

"I want you to meet a new friend of mine," Carolyn told her, her eyes flashing with excitement. "Julian, this is Jude Campbell."

Tall and slender, Julian Harris had sandy brown hair, rust-colored eyes, and fair skin. He was dressed in a checked shirt and black corduroy slacks, and looked younger than his thirty-three years. "Can you say hello to the pretty lady, Zachary?"

A dark-haired little boy poked his head out from behind his father's long legs. He was wearing a Mr. Incredible costume. "Want to see my muscles?" He grunted and flexed. "Now you gotta give me candy."

"I do, huh?" Jude said, dropping to her knees in front of him. "How much candy did you get when you went trick-or-treating tonight?"

"This much," he said, making a big circle with his arms. "Daddy won't let me eat it till tomorrow. He says it'll make me hyper. What's wrong with your arm? Did you broke it?"

"That's a long story, Zack," Jude said,

reaching over and ruffling his hair. "I have a bag of candy in my room. If you want, I can give some to your daddy for later."

"Yeah," Zachary said, jumping around with his cape flapping.

They made their way to Jude's room, and Carolyn closed the door behind them while she handed a small sack of candy to the boy's father.

"Well," Julian said, an awkward expression on his face, "I guess we should be taking off. I need to get this fellow in bed, and that's not always an easy task. It was good to meet you, Jude. Maybe we'll see you again."

Once he left, Jude took off her costume, perching on the edge of her bed. "Cute kid, huh?"

"Adorable," Carolyn told her, smiling. "He's your son, Jude."

Her mouth fell open. "No way. Are you serious?"

"We tracked him down through Beth Levy."

"Where's his mother?" Jude stopped, cupping her hand over her mouth. "I mean, the lady who adopted him. God, I can't believe this is happening."

"She died last year of cancer. Julian is a high school history teacher. He lives in Santa Barbara. His mother lives with him and helps take care of Zachary. This is just a preliminary step, Jude, so don't get your hopes up too high. But if everything goes well with your treatment, Zachary's father might let you visit him on a limited basis. You won't have any custody rights, and he doesn't want the boy to know you're his biological mother. He might change his mind later, though. A lot of that will depend on you. How do you feel?"

"This is the most amazing thing that's ever happened to me," Jude told her, on fire with excitement. She danced around the room. Her arm slipped out of the sling, but she didn't notice. "He's so cute. I bet he's smart. His father's a schoolteacher, so he'll make sure he gets a good education. I'm so happy, I think I wet my pants. Oh, my God, isn't he the most precious kid in the whole wide world?"

"He will be to you," Carolyn said, basking in the joy of the moment.

ACKNOWLEDGMENTS

I would like to thank my dear friend and editor, Michaela Hamilton, for her always sound advice and her unique ability to help me improve on my original vision. *Revenge of Innocents* is the ninth novel Michaela has edited for me. Needless to say, we've been through many life experiences together — divorces, deaths, births, sicknesses, best sellers, mergers, disappointments, success. Michaela and I are both strong women, although you couldn't tell by looking at us. I'm a little redhead; she's a little blonde. Which of us is the devil and which is the angel seems to change from day to day. No matter what the future has in store for us, I'm confident we'll both survive.

I want to thank my loving and supportive family: my husband, Dan, my sons, Gerald Hoyt and Forrest Blake; my daughters, Chessly, Amy, Nancy, and Chrissy, as well as my adorable grandchildren, Rachel, Jimmy,

Remy, Christian, Taylor, Elle, and Justin. For the women who stand beside my sons, Barbara and Jeannie, and my sons-in-law, Jim and Mike.

Above all, I thank God for listening to my prayers and restoring my health. When I take off on my daily run, my soul sings with gratitude. I remember when hardly a day went by without pain, and the awful days when I had to struggle just to sit upright. That was before I found out I had a heart condition. Even in this, a small miracle occurred. One of my arteries was completely blocked, yet my heart formed its own natural bypass.

My beloved father-in-law, Hyman Rosenberg, used to say, "Your health is your wealth." I now realize the simple but profound truth in his statement. Although he passed away many years ago, I feel Hyman's presence beside me, whispering words of encouragement.

Last, but not least, I must mention my two precious dogs, Chico and Gracie, who sit so quietly while I'm working and keep me company when I'm thinking.